Praise for Emma Garcia and *Never Google Heartbreak*

'Her cracking pace and rapier wit, together with her robust and honest prose will be bound to win Emma Garcia a sackful of fans. Perfect for lovers of *Bridesmaids* and Caitlin Moran.'

Red Online

'Hopelessly funny, this book is a classic with a modern twist'

Company

'This feisty and honest story of a crazy-in-love woman is hugely funny – perfect easy reading.' *Closer*

'So funny and so true. Reading *Never Google Heartbreak* made me nod in recognition and cringe at remembered embarrassments but most of all it left me smiling like a natter with a really good friend.' Chrissie Manby

'A genuinely likeable and very funny heroine . . . A fun read with a great leading lady.' *Heat*

'Cringe-packed LOLZ.' *ASOS*

'Have you ever read a book where you've fallen in love with it after a few pages? . . . I really adored everything about *Never Google Heartbreak* . . . It made me laugh and cackle like a loon, made my heart swell full of love when the romantic bits kicked in . . . I can't recommend this highly entertaining book enough – it's clever, witty and downright hilarious.'

iheart-chicklit.blogspot.co.uk

'The perfect mix of cringe and LOLs' *Graziadaily.co.uk*

Also by Emma Garcia

Never Google Heartbreak

About the Author

Emma Garcia is the author of *Never Google Heartbreak*. She attended Liverpool University and Roehampton University. She has worked as a sales assistant, a waitress, a security guard, a sandwich designer, a chamber maid, a teacher, a product manager, and has written and illustrated three children's books.

She has had three 'OMG Baby!' moments and now lives in York.

You can follow Emma on Twitter @EmzaGarcia.

OMG Baby!

Emma Garcia

HODDER

First published in Great Britain in 2014 by Hodder & Stoughton
An Hachette UK company

1

Copyright © Emma Garcia 2014

A CIP catalogue record for this title is
available from the British Library.

ISBN 978 1 444 74151 3
eBOOK ISBN 978 1 444 74152 0

Typeset in Plantin Light by Palimpsest Book Production Limited,
Falkirk, Stirlingshire

Printed and bound by Clays Ltd, St Ives plc

Hodder & Stoughton policy is to use papers that are natural,
renewable and recyclable products and made from wood grown in sustainable
forests. The logging and manufacturing processes are expected to conform to
the environmental regulations of the country of origin.

Hodder & Stoughton Ltd
338 Euston Road
London NW1 3BH

www.hodder.co.uk

For my babies

Prologue

Google search: *Am I pregnant?*

Classic symptoms of pregnancy

Missed period. This is the earliest and most reliable sign if you have a regular monthly cycle.

Feeling tired. You may feel unusually tired in the first few weeks of pregnancy.

Feeling sick. You may start feeling sick, and even vomit, between about the second and eighth week of pregnancy.

Changes in your breasts. You may notice your breasts getting larger, feeling tender or tingling in the early weeks of pregnancy.

Mood swings and stress. You may feel rapid changes in mood in the early stages of pregnancy, and even start to cry sometimes without knowing why.

Changing tastes in food. You may find you go off certain things, like tea, coffee or fatty food. Some women also feel cravings for types of food they don't usually like.

'I am not pregnant,' I say this and duck behind the laptop screen and scroll down the list again. For a start, my period is reliably random, but I know it will be coming any day because my boobs hurt. I'm not sick – just had a double-shot coffee. I love fatty food . . . 'God, what a relief,' I sigh aloud, and then burst into tears. Now, where can I get a rollmop herring in this airport?

I wipe my eyes and shut down the search. 'No symptoms,' I whisper, then do a double fist pump and begin to pack away the computer. Just then a knowing voice starts up in my head, sounding something like an angel from a film.

'*YOU! Yes you, Vivienne Summers, are with child,*' it booms, '*and you know you are.*'

I sit bolt upright. Let's just remain calm and think back over the last two months. It is true that for most of July I had a lot of sex with a guy named Max. It's also true that I didn't actually personally put a condom on him, but I think I definitely *saw* one, on the floor. The fact is, at the time I was a broken-hearted husk of a person and didn't care what happened to me so long as I stopped feeling bad, and although I didn't know it at the time, I was distracted by falling in love with Max. I threw myself into the hands of Fate. Irresponsible, careless, I know. But, God, it was good.

Anyhoo . . .

Now I'm about to board a flight to Spain. I'm on the way to see Max again and I can't deal with a pregnancy situation. I'm not saying I wouldn't like to have a lovely little baby one day, one of those good, fat, smiley ones, and sooner rather than later, what with the 'fertility cliff at thirty-five' thing looming, but I'm only thirty-two. I don't have a secure job, or any job. I have none of the trappings of adulthood: don't own a home, have no concrete relationship, and am not at all sensible. I can barely meet the needs of my foster cat. I'm not even that healthy: I only eat fruit when there's nothing else, and I drink too much. Recently I've been drinking a lot. If I'm pregnant, I could have pickled the baby. It could be a misshapen thing with teeth and hair in the wrong places. I imagine doctors telling me it can't survive and me stoically arguing and feeding the twisted ball with a teat pipette and dressing it up with a jaunty little hat with something like 'Cool guy' written on, and people on the street saying, 'Oh, a baby!', then recoiling from the pram, hands clutching at their throats, gasping, 'What's *wrong* with that baby?'

Oh my God. I get up and jerkily walk around the airport in a panic. I march into the duty-free shop and try some eyeshadow testers to distract myself. I contemplate getting one of those big bricks of cigarettes, even though I don't smoke, just to have them, just to rebel.

'*Not those!*' the angel voice hisses.

I examine my tummy. OK, so it's bloated, but that'll be water retention. A lot of people get it – ankles like balloons, some of them. I stand frozen by a mountain of Marlboro Reds.

Look, the thing to remember is, I'll be back in

London next week, because I am to be best woman at my friend Lucy's wedding, and I'm hoping I'll be able to ensnare Max and drag him home with me. If there is anything to deal with (which there isn't), I'll deal with it then. Good. Sorted.

'*Get chocolate now*,' says the voice, and I feel a powerful lust for Toblerone.

I

Up the Duff without a Paddle

Google search: *Nausea*

Common causes of nausea and vomiting

- pregnancy
- motion sickness
- food poisoning
- gastroenteritis
- alcohol or drug abuse

A quick search while our plane taxis into Girona. Very reassuring. We experienced a lot of turbulence on the flight and I ate a family-sized Toblerone. Anyone would be nauseous after that.

'*That and being pregnant—*'

'Nerves,' I interrupt the voice aloud, and the woman jammed up next to me turns and smiles. 'I'm meeting someone,' I tell her. 'Max Kelly. I love him. You probably know about my public search for him using Facebook? I was on the radio? The "Où est Max?" T-shirts that were sold in Topshop? That was me,' I say, making my voice higher at the end of each question. Her eyebrows raise to say, 'Oh,' while her eyes say, 'You are unsavoury.' I turn away from her and gaze out of the window, my thoughts free-wheeling. The airport is flanked with green. I'd pictured brown desert. I'm about to see him again. The horizon trembles in the heat. My heart clatters in my ears. He's here. I think of us: laughing until we cry, telling stories, holding hands, his face the last time I saw him. I never want him to look at me that way again, and he won't, because this time I won't betray him by turning up to his art exhibition with another man. This time I'll make him happy instead and bring him back to London.

The small airport smells of coffee and pastries. There's a lot of jostling for position at the baggage reclaim, followed by the embarrassment of having to pick up Nana's 1980s suitcases, and a snaking back on itself queue at passport control. I spot a woman checking out my new cool man sandals, which are a lot like Jesus might have worn. I see she wants them. She's pointing them out to her friend. Hold on – why are they laughing? And then my heart throbs painfully because I'm through, out into a tangle of people, searching all the faces for Max. He's just a guy, just a guy, he's just a guy, I repeat to myself with each slap of my sandals.

Then I see him and I have to try and control the burning rush of blood. I have to contain an outburst of joy. He's taller; he seems huge. His dark brown hair is all long and messy and sun-kissed; he's grown a beard. His skin is a dirty nut-brown, his big feet in blue flip-flops. He wears jeans, unevenly cut off around the knee, showing hairy legs, and a faded orange T-shirt, slightly tight across the shoulders. He smiles, a flash of white teeth. Suddenly my whole body goes weak. I'm gawky, shy, awkward and almost pretend I've forgotten something and run off to the left. I don't know how to be, so I just stand there as he begins to walk over. I look at my feet, to the side, then back at him. I don't know what to do with my face or my hands; I swing my hands against my legs. And now he's standing in front of me.

'Hello,' he says casually.

I feel my bottom lip tremble.

'I'm here,' is all I can say.

'You are. That's good.'

I can't say more for the ball of emotion in my throat. He reaches out to stroke my arm.

'Glad you could come,' he says softly.

I swallow and nod and study his chest, thinking of grabbing him by the back of the neck and saying, 'I love you,' repeatedly into his hair, but chickening out.

He pulls me in and squeezes and a huge sob escapes me. 'Hey . . . don't cry!' he half laughs. 'What, do I look that bad?'

'The beard's a bit of a shock, that's all,' I manage to pull myself together.

He laughs good-naturedly and takes a step back to look me over.

'You look good. I like your sandals, very practical,' he says.

'Thanks.'

So we stand looking at each other, and he's even hotter than my memory allowed. His eyes are beautiful – full of affection and amusement. I'm not good when faced with beauty so I give him a punch on the shoulder.

'That's for disappearing.'

He presses his lips together, nodding, shoves both hands in his pockets, and bends his face near to mine. I smell tobacco and mint on his breath. I look at his mouth, and when he kisses me, the beard feels soft and not at all how I thought a beard would feel. The kiss is long and slow, and I have to break off because of my weak knees.

'I did miss you actually,' I tell him.

'I really missed you,' he says.

'Buy me a drink?'

'Sure.'

We don't move. We're just looking at each other and grinning like goons. The arrivals hall is almost empty.

Max looks back over to my forlorn trolley. 'That all yours?'

'My capsule wardrobe. I hope you haven't come on the bike.'

'Borrowed a van.'

He puts an arm around my shoulders and we stroll out into the afternoon sunshine, each pulling a faux-leather suitcase.

In the far corner of the car park is a battered Citroën van. Inside, it's completely covered with a fine white powder. Max wipes my seat a bit with his hand. I put on the seat belt, releasing more clouds of white dust, as he battles with the engine. It coughs and dies a few times before it catches and we eventually trundle away. I watch his bare foot pumping the accelerator at a junction to keep the straining engine going. Something metal is banging and rolling about in the back.

'Well, this is nice,' I shout above the din.

'Ha! Only the best for you, my darlin'!' He winds down the window and shouts, 'She's here! She flew to Spain to have sex! With me!'

'How do you know I'm going to have sex with you?'

'Well, are you or aren't you?' He brakes abruptly and gives me a flash of his pirate smile and, God, I can't wait.

'Where the hell did you get this van?'

'Ah, it belongs to a mate of mine. He's a sculptor. I think all this stuff is plaster dust. His tools are in the back.'

'Not cocaine, then?'

'Actually, it is! I decided to pick you up in a fucking coke van! I'm Scarface!' he shouts, and we laugh. 'Hey, Viv, you're here!' He grins as he accelerates onto a dual carriageway. Then he turns and winks. I feel it like a strike on the chest.

On the long straight road he drives with one hand on the wheel and the other on my leg. The touch of his fingers on my bare skin is driving me crazy. I wonder if we could pull over and do it in the back of the van, plaster dust or no.

I make myself look away. The pure bright sunshine washes the roadside sprawl of boatyards, pottery shops and fruit warehouses. Fields roll away to the left, laden vines like thrusting hands. We're driving through a bowl of green, serrated mountains piled on all sides like jagged dog's teeth and the huge wide, billowing blue sky stretching over us. The kind of sky that makes your insides fly out and shout, 'Yahoo!'

'So, we're heading up the coast. Do you see those mountains there?' He nods towards the horizon, shards of rock trailing wisps of cloud. 'I live on the other side of them, in Cadaqués. That town there is Roses.' He points to the variegated flank of a mountain sloping to the coast, studded with white houses like stars.

'You've been here the whole time?'

'This area around and about.'

'Where I could never find you?'

'But I couldn't shake you off.' He takes a half-smoked roll-up from the ashtray and lights it, smiling sideways at me.

'Meanwhile, back in London, I was publicly dissecting my own heart.'

'I never knew that,' he says, narrowing his eyes against the cigarette smoke and winding down the window.

I'm no mechanic, but I'd say we're about to lose

our exhaust pipe, going by the terrible thudding and scraping of metal. Max seems oblivious and I have to shout to be heard.

'It's all very civilised. I kind of pictured you living with goatherds in the mountains.'

'No goatherds here. That's Greece you're thinking of.'

'I thought you'd be herding something.'

'Why?'

'Because you were incommunicado. There is a phone signal here, you know. I have signal.'

'Ah, but I threw my phone in the river before I left.'

'Oh, nice one.' I imagine his phone resting in the murky-green bed of the Thames, next to a severed head.

'Stupid. Regretted it straight away,' he says.

'Well, it was working for ages. I left a million messages.'

'Technology is a wonder.'

I swallow down a wave of nausea. We're climbing on a very winding road. Travel sickness is a curse. I've never had it before. 'So why did you even bother to log on?'

He sighs, resting an elbow on the windowsill.

'Well, there I was walking down by the sea one day and it struck me: you were on my mind all the time.' He taps the side of his head with his fingertips. 'It was like you were haunting me. I couldn't get you out of my head. I kept imagining what you'd think of things and what you'd say, and I thought, fuck it. Just get in touch with the witch, confirm what an evil piece of work she is, and cut her from your heart once and for all.' He shouts this above the exhaust. He grins.

'Nice.'

'Then I turned to walk back into the town to the internet café and – no word of a lie – there's a woman walking along with a T-shirt on her, and as she turned the corner, a shaft of sunlight hit the T-shirt and I saw across it was written, "Où est Max?" Well, it was a sign. I ran up to her like a wild man and asked her where she got the T-shirt.'

'You never told me that on the phone.'

'And she said she'd only tell me after I'd made mad, passionate love to her, which I did –' he sneaks a glance across at me '– for hours. She was insatiable.'

I wrinkle my nose.

'And when she had to stop, on account of hunger, thirst and a nasty cramp in her hip, we shared a spliff and she told me the whole story about a funny-looking woman searching for her lost love named Max and how romantic it all was, with the Facebook and everything.'

'Is any part of that true?'

'No.' He throws back his head and laughs loudly. 'I went to the internet café and googled you.'

We don't seem to have climbed for long, but the ground falls away at the side of the road now, a steep drop into dark stands of trees. A scent of rosemary and thyme fills the van. The engine whines as Max changes down a gear.

'Nana got married. I wish you could have seen it.'

'Yeah . . . Is she OK, the old girl?'

'She's on a bloody gap year. Travelling round the world for a whole year with Reg. Europe at the moment. Sends silly postcards.'

'Brilliant.' He smiles. 'And what did you do with Dave?'

I think of Dave being shut in his cage at the cattery, the seething hatred in his eyes as I handed over his fish-shaped 'Top Cat' bowl.

'The cat you abandoned? In a cattery. You owe me about three hundred pounds and a silk kimono. Shredding is one of his great talents.'

'Three hundred quid? How long is he in for?'

'A week.'

He flinches as if he's been hit in the face. 'A week? One week?'

'It's a very luxurious cattery, with heated beanbags and caviar extract.'

'Caviar!'

'Extract.'

'And then what?'

'Then I suppose I'll pick him up – or we will.'

'You're only staying a week.' He frowns and bites the side of his thumb.

I hang on to the leather strap above the passenger door as we make a turn and suddenly the road snakes left, with a sheer drop to one side. My stomach heaves and I concentrate on looking ahead.

'I thought you'd stay longer.'

'I would, but Lucy's getting married.'

'She's getting married?'

'You're invited. You could escort me.'

'No way. Not after the last wedding debacle. You're a liability.'

'Actually you'll have to. She's gone mad. She's making me do a terrible dance routine involving a pole and lesbian frotting.'

He smirks. 'What'll you be wearing?'

'A tutu.'

He shakes his head and smiles. 'Well, that's funny right there,' he says.

2

One in the Oven is Worth
Two in the Bush

Ways to say you're having a baby:

up the duff
up the stick
knocked up
one in the oven
bun in the oven
expecting
with child
preggers
experiencing birth-control failure

We descend into Cadaqués and it isn't the rocky herds-man's outpost in the wilderness I'd imagined, rather it's a stunning, arty fishing village. As the road snakes lower, I look back through the trees at the town; it clings to the land between the obscene roll of two mountains, a white jostle of buildings like washed-up paper. I see why Max chose to stay here; the narrow streets of the old quarter are packed with little galleries and studios. So what I need to do is make him fall deeply in love with me again, make him so in love that he's willing to return to the scruffy arse end of London and live in a bedsit with me. I'm a resourceful girl, but I have to say it's looking like a challenge. We park the van and climb some steps to a tall white-washed building. I hope it's not much further: I'm hot and tired, and one of my sandals is beginning to rub on my heel.

'Here we are.' Max unlocks a heavy door. He grabs the bags and steps into the darkness, while I hesitate. He clatters about inside, battling with the shutters of two huge windows. Rectangles of sunlight spill over the stone floor. 'Come in,' he says over his shoulder.

I follow him into the cool room. White breezeblock walls with various canvases and half-finished paintings propped against them. A shelf made from old crates crowded with jars and paint and brushes. Piles of papers and books and a huge ironwork bed with bricks for legs. There's a bentwood chair and a chipped anglepoise lamp balanced beside an overflowing ashtray. The kitchen alcove is a cupboard, with an ancient fridge and an encrusted stovetop. To one side of the space a faded green fabric panel is slung behind a giant old hook, sectioning off a small sink, a toilet and a showerhead hanging over a sloping little drain. The place has a tomblike smell of old wet stone.

Max runs a hand through his hair. 'Er, welcome . . . Make yourself at home . . . Sit anywhere,' he says, waving his hand around as if there's a three-piece suite and assorted armchairs.

I put my handbag on the bed.

'Well, I love what you've done with the place.'

'I was going for minimalist.'

'You've achieved it.'

'Would you like a large drink?'

'This is where you've been living.' I sit on the bed.

He doesn't answer. It seems as if he hasn't heard. He's just watching me intently. I'm left grinning, grappling for another line.

'It's very neat, though, in here . . . Not like you, really.'

He walks towards me and kneels between my knees, but he isn't smiling. He strokes my cheek, holds my chin. I move my eyes side to side jokily. His eyes seem almost black under the dark frown of his brow.

'Vivienne,' he says.

'Hello!'

'Don't fuck with me. It can't be like before.'

I open my mouth to speak but think better of it and try to touch his face, but he jerks his chin away and grabs my hand.

'I want you, but only if you want me. If you have doubts, just get on the next plane home – no hard feelings. I don't want pity or to be friends.'

'I won't hurt you again. I just want to love you.' His mouth is close to mine. I listen to our breath. Feel our lips brush. 'As soon as possible.'

Then he kisses me and I move my hand up into his hair, feeling something like panic, an almost painful heart-thumping crashing in my ears; my arms go weak.

'Lie down,' he says quietly.

I flop back on the bed without taking my eyes off his face. He's kneeling between my legs. I see a tiny movement in his neck as he swallows. Then he takes off my pants. His face serious and his eyes dark. He pulls off his T-shirt and unbuckles his jeans with one hand. I feel the other everywhere: on my breasts, my belly and then between my legs, stroking and inside me. I see him for a moment kneeling over me, the bulk of him, his wide shoulders filling the window. Outside, I hear a shout, but all is quiet in the room except for our breathing and the rustle of the sheets as we move. I try to wrap my legs around him.

I feel the weight of him. I look sideways at his tanned arm and feel his breath tickling my ear.

'Vivienne,' he sighs. His fingers move on me. 'I've been dying for you,' he whispers as he pushes into me, and I feel my body pulling him in.

Afterwards I'm lying half on him, my head resting on his armpit, thinking, if I died now, it would be OK. I've lived a good life. I've known passion, bitten into some lovely things, tried to be nice to most people most of the time . . . Then I want to throw up. My mouth feels dangerously watery. I look towards the unscreened toilet and imagine suddenly having to puke there, naked. That can't happen.

'Would you like a vodka?' Max asks lazily.

I tilt my head back to look at him. 'Something fizzy.'

'I could go and get something.'

He shifts his body and slightly presses against my chest, making my boobs hurt. I turn onto my side.

'Will I go?' he asks.

'We'll both go, in a minute,' I tell him, curling into the recovery position, too weak to leave the bed.

He puts his arm around me, stroking my bicep with his rough fingertips over and over.

'You're so beautiful, Viv,' he says. 'I have wanked so many times thinking of you.'

'God, that's really sweet.' I bat his hand away; he moves it onto my bottom.

We lie there in silence. His eyes begin to close. I take deep breaths against the nausea. It comes in waves, insistent.

Oh shit, I'm pregnant. I am pregnant. I lift the sheet and look down at my body. My nipples look weird. I bite my lower lip, thinking, my heart filling with terror and maybe a faint twinge of excitement. I'm not. I can't be. A brief moment of relief before the angel voice, now preceded by some sort of harp twang, sings, '*You know the truth*.' This is making me panic. I'm pregnant and hearing voices.

Max gently snores. I whack him awake.

'So, what about Lucy getting married?' I ask loudly.

He smiles, eyes still closed. 'She's the last person I'd expect.'

'Why?'

'Remember her at uni going on about the patriarchy? She's anti-commitment.'

'People change. She's very pro-commitment now. Well, pro- with one man in particular.'

'What's he like?'

'Reuben. Colombian.'

'Ah.'

'He's sexy, into toys.'

'Good on her.'

'Yes, good on her. She'll be pregnant next, I suppose.' I glance at his face.

He opens one eye. 'Guess so.'

'Imagine that. Lucy, a mum.'

'I can't. I'm trying, but I can't.'

'Do you ever wonder what it would be like to be a parent?'

'Nope. I know. Terrible. Not a moment's peace.'

'What? How do you know?'

'Growing up in my family, hundreds of kids always running around . . . chaos.'

'So you don't want kids?' I ask, and he lifts his head a little to peer at me suspiciously.

'We're talking hypothetically here?'

''Course.'

He flops back, laughing nervously, sensing a trap.

'Your answer, please . . . Do you or do you not want kids?'

'Well, *hypothetically* I always thought I don't.'

'Why's that?'

'Because of the planet.'

'Because of the planet?'

'Yeah, like the population is too large already,' he says, gazing dreamily at the ceiling without a care in the world.

'You don't want kids because of the planet.' Of all the answers! He's suddenly become a green warrior? He laughed when I said I wanted to live in one of those eco cave houses for the good of the planet. What an annoying hypocrite he is! I stand up and pace, wearing nothing but a frown. 'Well, that's a bit of a deal-breaker, don't you think?'

'Huh?' He sits up, leaning on an elbow.

'You shouldn't go shagging thirty-something women, then, should you?' I snap. Bits of spit fly.

'Viv, what are you on about?'

'The planet! I thought you were a Catholic?'

'Lapsed . . . Nice muff, by the way.'

'Thanks. Well, other Catholics have loads of kids – in drawers.'

'What?'

'Yes. Because they have so many that they just don't have enough room or beds or cots! I saw that on a documentary where a woman had twelve kids, and that was in Ireland!' I jab a finger at him. I've won.

How can he come back on that? He makes a confused/aghast noise.

'What are you saying? Do you want kids?' He kneels up now.

'Yes! No. I'm talking about principles!' I say, jutting my head at him like a chicken. 'It's all very well going environmental, banging on about the planet, growing a big fucking beard and shagging women left and right with no care for the consequences!'

He actually laughs out loud, and I nearly do too but manage to hold it together.

'"Shagging women left and right"!' he snorts.

I burst into tears.

He jumps off the bed. 'Hey . . . are you . . . ? Come on.' I drop my head and sob loudly, surprising myself. 'Come on.' He leads me to the bed and sits me down. He kneels in front of me, rubbing my legs.

Then I look right into his eyes, willing him to know. They flicker with recognition.

'Vivienne?'

'Yes.'

'Are you?'

'Yes.'

'Pregnant?'

'Yes.'

3

Who's the Daddy?

As we know, the father of your baby will be the guy you had sexual intercourse with at the time of ovulation.

Ovulation occurs halfway through your menstrual cycle.

If you need to ask about your menstrual cycle, what are you doing having sex?

As I did not have sexual intercourse with anyone other than Max Kelly, Max Kelly is the father of my baby.*

* I might not be pregnant.

We decide to get out of the room, walk, get air. Down through winding cobbled lanes we stumble with the news, hand in hand, under balconies dripping with geraniums, towards the sea. We pause to look out over the waves, contemplating our new roles – 'mummy' and 'daddy' – trying them on like expensive, impractical coats. I squeeze his hand, feeling the long, blunt fingers. He scoops up a stone and throws it. We hardly speak as we follow the coastal path out of Cadaqués. There's no beach, only rocky coves. The sea fizzes over small stony islands, making clear pools. It glitters on towards the horizon, shining turquoise and navy. Some of the windows are lit now, and the restaurants on the seafront glow like yellow lanterns. Ahead is a bar that seems to be set into the stone of the cliff. There's music and frying fish in the air. I make for the small metal table out front. He sits beside me and smiles. I look at his brown eyes. He looks steadily back, leaning his elbows on the table, hunching his big shoulders towards me.

'What do you think?' I ask.

'We'd better get ourselves a cot.'

We look away from each other. My thoughts race like a rat in a maze, going over all the possibilities, trying to grasp how the world has just shifted.

Max jerks his head as if he's been hit by a realisation. 'How long have you known?' he asks.

'It really only just dawned on me, at the airport.'

'Huh, that's the kind of intuition you're known for, Viv.'

'I mean, I thought . . . you know . . . but I can't believe it.'

'If you're pregnant, when do you think it . . . happened?'

'It's yours.'

'What do you mean?'

'What do you mean, "What do you mean?"? I know what you're thinking. I never slept with anyone else.'

'You were back with *Rob*, though.' He spits the name of my ex-fiancé.

'I didn't sleep with him.'

'Well, Viv, I hate to have to spell it out for you, but it's not the sleeping part that does it . . .'

'I did not have sexual relations with him.'

'No, but, by God, you did with me, didn't you, girl?' He grins and nods to himself.

'It's your baby,' I say.

'Of course she's mine.' He pulls my chair towards him, kisses me clumsily on the head. 'Ah, she's a blessing, isn't she?' he laughs.

'She? You think it's a girl?'

'Oh yeah. I see myself with a daughter.'

I feel a massive thrill, a jolt of excitement like an orgasm.

'Oh my God. We're having a baby.'

'Obviously we'll need to teach her about art, and she should play the fiddle. She might start a revolution. We'll make a list. Daddy's girl will be number-one priority.'

Then everything is subtly different, the same but more beautiful, like waking in the morning and discovering a sparkling frost has altered the view. I've become like some sort of sacred vessel controlled by an angel within, one that speaks to me. As I listen to Max's voice, my mind seems to float inside with my baby. The ethereal music starts up.

'I suppose we need to do a test,' Max says, bringing

me up short. The music stops with a scratchy-needle noise. A test! It's not confirmed yet, is it? I might not be a sacred vessel at all. I put a hand over my belly.

'*All will be well,*' says the voice, and then, in a harsher tone, '*Eat food now.*'

The waiter brings our food, plate by plate. Sea bass for Max. I pick up a white-eyed sardine by the tail and slice the flesh off its comb of bones. Of all the food I've ever tasted before – and, I'm convinced, ever after – this sardine is the best. Hot, salty and tasting of the sea, eaten beside the ocean, starving.

It's dark when we walk back towards the town. We take the coastal path again and I hear the hush of the waves, but looking across to the horizon I see nothing except blue-black space, as if we're walking along the lip of a great gaping mouth. We're having a baby. I pull Max's arm tighter around me.

'What would you be doing now if I wasn't here?' I ask him.

'Probably I'd be in the internet café with a bottle of vodka obsessively googling you, cursing the amateur rapper Viv Summers from Texas who keeps clogging up my search.'

'And after that?'

'Ah, you know, meet up with a few people, or read, or paint.'

'How could you stand it for all this time? Didn't you miss London?'

'I wanted to be away, Vivienne, that's the idea.'

'I couldn't do it.'

He glances at me sideways. 'I know.'

'So did you find yourself, then?'

'Yeah. I'm a complete dickhead.'

'I could have told you.'

'And I started painting these abstract landscapes. Some of the scenery here is stunning, and you know it's harder to paint a landscape well than it is to paint a person. With a person, you can use some of their character and it lends the work a sort of energy. With a landscape, it's about your eye, the view you take; the character has to come from the artist.'

I narrow my eyes in the dark. 'Is that true, or are you trying to get into my pants?'

Max laughs. 'Both,' he says.

'And are they any good, then, these landscapes?'

'Ah well, that's not for me to say. I sold some, though.'

'I saw the painting of me. I went to the gallery.'

We cross a little square, through the bright lights of the seafront restaurants and uphill along a street lined with gift shops and boutiques.

'I like the way you painted me. I looked cool.'

'Which is a feat of brilliance in itself.' He smiles. 'Someone wanted to buy that.'

'You didn't sell it?'

'I did.' When I gasp in shock, he says, 'What? You'd left me.'

'So you just sold me?'

'Needed the cash.'

'Well, I'll bloody well buy it back! How much did you sell it for?'

'Four grand.'

'Four grand?' I cough.

'The guy got a bargain. It's a masterpiece.'

I think of someone in a mansion somewhere and on his plain white wall, probably over the stairwell, there's me, in an Arsenal T-shirt. I've been sold like a chattel, robbed of my spirit.

'Well, I'll save up and buy it back. I knew I shouldn't have let you paint me. Now I'm on some random person's wall!' I pull away from him, pretending to be interested in some tie-dye balloon pants hanging outside a shop.

'I didn't really sell it,' he says.

'I don't believe you. Look at you. Who knows what you're capable of?' I look at him standing in the path in his 'good trousers' and his crumpled white linen shirt.

He steps towards me with his head to one side as if coaxing a child. 'I turned down two offers.'

'Two offers of four grand?'

He nods. In the half-light from the boutique his smile flashes a crescent of white.

'Is this the kind of business acumen you intend to use to support your child?' I brush past him. He follows, waving his hands as he speaks.

'I'm planning my own exhibition mid-October. You

know the gallery in Westbourne Park that takes pieces of mine? They've agreed to let me take over for a month. The whole gallery will be showing only my landscapes, and if that goes well, it will be a regular thing.'

'So you are planning on coming back to London?'

'I'll have to now you're up the duff. She'd go to any lengths to get her man.'

'I'll stop at nothing. But earlier you were all mysterious about ever coming back. I don't want you doing anything out of duty just because I'm . . . might be pregnant.'

'Actually, I miss the whores and the druggies.'

'And they miss you. So you'll come to Lucy's wedding?'

He pulls me into a doorway and places a palm over my belly. 'Vivienne,' he begins, and then closes his eyes, trying to say something that's difficult to begin. I wait, feeling slightly nervous. 'How do I tell you?' He kisses me. He rests his lips on the bridge of my nose. I press my back against the cool brick. 'Don't you know I'm mad about you? I'd go anywhere as long as I'm with you.' He grins at me crazily. 'I'll have to come to the wedding because deep down all I want is to follow you around . . . licking you. I'll not let you down, or her.' Here his voice cracks a little and he bends to kiss my belly.

I look down at the comb marks in the hair wax he must have slapped on his head and smile.

'None of your Irish blarney, now. Tell me how you really feel.'

He looks out of our little doorway and smiles up at the sky. He leans a hand on the wall behind my head.

'You tell me how you feel,' he says.

I narrow my eyes, pretending to think.

'In my life I've often been glad you exist,' I say.

'Ah, see, succinct.'

'I like what you said,' I say, and stretch up to kiss him.

I take his hand when we walk on and we fall into silence. He loves me. I've got him. I imagine telling Dave, 'I'm bringing him home, boy!' I look up at the sky; it's a clear night with millions of stars. This is a moment I want to freeze-frame, to unwrap at a time far from now, when I'm bored on a slow train in a light drizzle. I imagine Max with his own successful exhibition. I see us playing with our baby, raising her up to the sky; she's smiling, her dimples showing, until Max drops her and then we row about whose fault it was . . . Imagining myself as a mother uncorks a terrible cocktail of emotions; it's thrilling, terrifying and exciting. Being part of something real, having the massive responsibility with no return, ever. When else does that situation arise? Most other things in life you can wriggle out of.

I think of my own mother, how she must have felt being pregnant at sixteen. How she left me with my nana when I was seven. Then a string of thoughts: could I ever leave my child? Why do I want to talk to my mother? Why is she the first person I want to tell, not the lovely nana who raised me? And then with a rush of clarity I know I'm going to contact my mother and tell her and show her *this* is how to have a happy pregnancy. This is how to have a baby. This is how to be a mummy. I want her involved. Her leaving and me being pregnant are the biggest things that have ever happened to me, and they are somehow related. I feel alive with the thought that I'll find her and the certainty that she'll come. We pass by a fruit seller just then. Momentous things are happening, and meanwhile I must eat nectarines immediately.

We return to Max's room with bags of food. Fruit, bread, jam, biscuits, wine and fizzy water. I lie down on the bed, hot and exhausted. Max takes off my sandals.

'Oh, thank God!' I say, as he rubs my feet.

'You've lovely feet.'

'Do I?'

'I don't know how, with all your crazy shoes.'

I prop my head up on a pillow and start on a nectarine, watching him.

'There's a lot to be said for sensible shoes,' I say.

'Really?' He lifts my leg a little. I see him glance at my thighs.

'Like they are actually designed for walking in, which

probably should be the first rule of thumb if you are thinking of a shoe.'

'Not really . . . Some shoes are designed for sex.' He bends to kiss the top of my foot. 'Vivienne?'

'Yeah?'

'Your naked feet are giving me the horn.'

'You might have one of those foot fetishes.'

He's massaging my toes, pushing his fingers between each one, and then he places my foot onto the front of his trousers over his erect penis. I feel a shock run from the soles of my feet up my thighs and into my belly. As he takes off his shirt, I clench my toes over his cock.

He turns his head to the side. 'Vivienne?'

'Yeah?' I say, popping the last bit of nectarine in my mouth and beginning to move my toes up and down.

'Would you take off your dress, please?' I pull it over my head and lean back in my underwear.

'And please will you remove your bra.'

I unclasp my bra. My tits might be sore, but I must say they look magnificent in this lamplight. Are they a whole cup size bigger? I'd quite like a photo of them actually, just so I know they were once this great. Max sits beside me and begins to kiss my shoulders. He trails a finger down my arm. Then I kiss him and we're falling back together. I wriggle further up the bed and he catches hold of my pants, pulling them off. I wrap a leg around his waist and pull him on top of me, wanting to feel him inside me, but he stops, his eyes searching my face.

'Viv, I can't hurt the baby, can I?'

'No!'

'I don't want to poke her in the eye.'

'Don't be thick. You won't.'

'Are you sure?'

'She hasn't got eyes yet.'

'Really?'

'I don't think so . . . Anyway –' I reach up and hold the back of his neck '– come on, Irish. You're so big and hard I've got to have you.'

'OK, I'll do it,' he says, 'since you put it like that.'

4

Pee on the Stick

Los kits caseros de pruebas son extremadamente precisos. Dentro de los siete días de la concepción células de la placenta secretan la hormona gonadotropina coriónica humana en la sangre y la orina. Esto pruebas de embarazo caseras muestra dos líneas azules si usted está embarazada.

Translation by Max Kelly: 'The test is very accurate . . . Er, there's something about a placenta and hormones. You must do it up the bum with your boyfriend and then pee on the stick. If it shows two blue lines, you are pregnant . . . It does say that! Look, pee on the stick.'

Morning and the sun sparkles through every crack in the shutter frames, making halos on the peeling paint. The room is already hot, the smell of damp stone replaced by baked clay and drains. I'm not properly awake but am aware of Max sleeping close by. I glance across. There he is, arms behind his head, sheet gathered around his groin like a nappy. Normally when I wake up, I jump out of bed after a few seconds to turn on the shower, but today I feel as if I've woken on a waltzer ride at the fair and I'm about to be sick in a bag. I lie completely still, trying to think up a strategy. Food is my only hope. I get off the bed and stay low. I scuttle to the grocery bag without retching and sit cross-legged on the stone floor. I grab the biscuits, ripping the packet open with my teeth and ramming two in my mouth; flaky pastry with a synthetic lemon overtone. I take a swig of water and shove in two more. I watch Max's ribcage rising and falling. The fur in his armpits sticks up like a cockatoo's fan. The line of dark hair running down from his belly button under the sheet. His head back, big nose in profile, quite noble. His lips are parted, bottom teeth a bit crooked. His Adam's apple bobs as he swallows.

He turns onto his side. One arm flops over. Now he's facing me with his eyes closed, his black eyelashes making him look as if he's been messing about with make-up. He opens one eye and closes it again.

'What are you, some sort of weird rodent, crouching there, nibbling?' he mutters.

'Get up loser!' I say in what I think is a rodent-type voice. He doesn't move.

I take another swig of water and break off the end of the baguette. The sickness has passed, but I think I should probably keep eating, just to make sure. I unscrew the jam and dip a bit of bread into the jar.

How life can change in such a short time. Only last month I'd decided to live life alone. I was a rock. I didn't need love. Anyhow, now here I am with Max and pregnant. That's about as un-alone as you can get. It's just like Nana says – you never know what's round the corner. Only right now is certain. I chew thoughtfully. I wonder where in the world Nana and Reg are now. I'd like to tell her about the baby. How will she feel about being a great-grandmother? I need her help to contact my mother, Lorraine, who was last in touch to say she couldn't make Nana's wedding as she was touring South America.

Funny isn't it that my seventy-year-old nana is now to be found globetrotting as a newlywed. The last postcard from them was of the Leaning Tower of Pisa.

'It's falling down!' she wrote in biro on the front. Nana and Reg let loose on the world . . . I have a number to call when they get to Egypt next week. I'll break the news then.

Next week. I think about next week. Next week when we're back in London, expensive London, London where I have no job and only three months' rent money . . . and wait, let's chuck a baby into the equation as well.

Oh my God, we're fucked! I put down the jar of jam and crawl towards the bed.

'Max!' I say close to his nose. The eyelashes flicker. 'Max!' I say louder. He turns onto his back again, holding his crotch. I lean over him. 'Max!' His eyes open and he focuses on me with a slow smile.

'God, you are insatiable, woman. Let me wake up, would you?'

'We can't have a baby.'

'Huh?' He licks his lips, tasting his mouth.

'You and I can't have a baby. We aren't responsible.'

He props himself up on his elbows and blinks. His slept-on hair sticks up at the back in a rosette.

'We can't bring up a child. Look at us!'

'Viv, what are you on about?'

'I don't have a job. You don't have a regular income. Where will we live? We need a house!'

He sits up and drinks a glass of water. He sets the glass down, taking a deep breath. 'If you needed a job or a house to have a baby, half the population wouldn't exist.'

'No, we've just got carried away in the moment and we haven't thought this through. I'm in the process of setting up a business and I can barely pay the rent. How much money do you have?'

'Cash or assets?'

'Both.'

'What's on my back.' He smiles, then seeing my face, adds, 'About a grand, two maybe, if I sold the bike.'

'Do you know how much it costs to raise a child? I mean, I'll google it, but I know it's a hell of a lot more than that!'

I unzip a suitcase and take out the first things I can grab: leopard-print shorts, espadrilles and a pink T-shirt.

'What're you doing?'

'There's no internet here, is there? I'm going to the internet café and I'm going to research it.'

'Hold on, Viv.'

I twist my hair up into a bun. 'You coming?'

'Hold on a minute!' He gets up, pulls on boxer shorts and slopes off behind the green panel. The next thing I hear is him peeing from a height and the toilet working up to a flush. He reappears. 'Coffee?'

'Can't we get one at the internet café?'

'It's closed.'

'I don't believe you.'

He shrugs as he fills the tiny kettle. I sink onto the bed. He takes two cups and spoons coffee into them.

'First thing to do is get a test,' he says, glancing at me. He reaches into the fridge. The tiger tattoo moves across the plane of his shoulder. He lifts up a milk carton, sniffs it and pours, topping it off with boiling water. He sits beside me and hands me a cup. I watch a lone coffee granule spin on the surface.

'We'll go as soon as the chemist is open. Then we'll know for sure, won't we?'

'And what will we do then?'

'Then we'll work it all out.' He puts an arm around me and downs the scalding coffee in one. 'We're smart people. We'll figure it out. If we need more money, we'll get some.'

'How? I once read online that raising a baby can cost over two hundred grand.'

'You don't have to pay up front, though.' He nudges me with a shoulder.

'Where will we live?'

'My place, or your place. Babies don't need much.'

'You don't know that. Online—'

'Viv, not all the answers are online, OK? Some things you just have to go with. What are you saying? What'll you do if you think you can't afford it?' He shoots me a glance that hits like a slap in the face.

I look down at my hands. 'Have a baby.'

'Exactly . . . So I'll get dressed.'

We walk to the chemist, through the old town, down cool cobbled steps. Below us, and just visible through the crouched houses, the Mediterranean glitters like turquoise glass. I feel the sun beat heavily on my skin in a kind of rhythm. Max lights a cigarette, letting go of my hand and keeping it out of my way. Of course this is something I should be worried about now. There will be loads of things. I read somewhere that pregnant women should avoid curry, but somewhere else that they should eat it, and what do women in India do with themselves, anyway? I'll research this whole thing online, no matter what Max says. That is, if the test is positive. I mean, we're acting as if I am definitely pregnant, and at the moment we don't know for sure – we're balanced on the seesaw of Fate.

I wonder, if he could choose, would Max actually want to have a baby now? Would I? How could either of us ever answer that question? The issue has come up now, hasn't it? Because of this pregnancy or non-pregnancy, we've taken the idea in, accepted it, so if I'm not pregnant, will we be disappointed? My mind circles, taking pathways and dead ends, as if I'm stuck on one of those decision trees. I'm stuck because I don't know the answer to the very first question.

Is Max father material? Not that long ago, I didn't even consider him shag material, and now the two of us might have made a whole other person. His main motivator, as long as I've known him, has been getting himself laid. Are any of his skills transferable into fatherhood? I wonder. I walk along looking at him and thinking about that.

'Max, how many women have you slept with?' I ask after a while.

He half turns round. 'Why?'

'I'm just wondering whether you'd be any good as a father.'

He frowns. 'Oh. Yeah, I get it – if I've slept with loads, then I'm obviously a very understanding and inclusive person, not to mention persuasive, and if only a few, then I have self-control and virtue?'

'Something like that.'

'In that case, the question to ask isn't how many, but what kind of women have I slept with, since we already know I have no self-control or much virtue,' he says.

'OK, have you ever slept with anyone really fat?'

'Sure.'

'Who was the fattest person you've ever had sex with?'

'Gillian McGuiness. She was fifteen stone.'

'And what happened?'

'She left me after about two weeks.'

'Why?'

'She said I didn't have enough money.'

'You still don't have enough money.'

'True, but I have talent.'

'Who's the weirdest person you ever slept with?'

'Hmm, I once had a fling with a woman who would only do it through a hole in her tights.'

I wrinkle my nose. 'You didn't do it?'

'Of course. Why not? I wanted her to be happy.'

'So you really are inclusive and understanding, but sadly also skint and a bit weird.'

'This works both ways, you know, Viv. What about you? Who's the ugliest person you've ever slept with?'

'You,' I say.

'Bar me,' he says at the same time.

'Hmm, I think it would have to be a guy called Greg who once bought me some Milk Tray. He had these horrible sticking-out teeth and no chin. I ended it by saying I had to revise, but really it was because of the teeth-chin thingy. They just . . . Urgh, no.'

'You lied to the poor fool.'

'I know. I felt very bad about it.'

'And the Milk Tray?'

'Ate them all myself.'

'That story tells me you're selfish, greedy and a liar . . . also shallow.'

'Oh yeah, you're definitely better parent material.'

We've reached the bottom of the hill now and are in the main town. We stop and Max points across a small square to a row of shops.

'Well, we're here. That's the chemist over there.'

We hesitate for a few seconds, squinting into the sun, and then I set off walking purposefully across the cobbles.

Later that morning we return to Max's room with a Spanish pregnancy test. He translates the instructions and I sit on the edge of the bed holding the flat plastic stick upon which both our futures teeter.

'OK, when you've peed on it for three seconds, you get one blue line, right?'

I nod, staring at the little plastic window in wonder.

'That is just to show the test is working. I think it says here if you're pregnant, a second blue line will appear. Would that be right?' He looks doubtful.

'I don't know. Give me that.' I snatch the instruction sheet. 'It says under the two blue lines, "*Si embarazada*."'

'"Yes, embarrassed,"' he translates.

I gawp at him. 'Embarrassed? What?'

He shrugs. 'It must be how they say "pregnant".'

I study the picture on the instructions. 'Right, well, shall I go and wee on it, then? Get it over with?' I stand and make towards the curtained area.

'Wait.' He hugs me. 'Whatever the outcome, I love you, right?'

'OK. I love you as well.' I stare at the stick over his shoulder, break free and walk towards the toilet.

'Wait,' he says.

I stop. 'What?'

'Want me to come with you?'

'No, I'll be OK.' I give him a reassuring pat and slip behind the curtain to follow the instructions to the letter.

Then we sit on the bed holding the test and we wait. A shadow seeps across the first little plastic window. We watch a blue line appear. I look into Max's face. His eyes search mine. The second window is now wet. We watch and we wait and a second faint blue line appears and it gets darker until there is no denying it. There are two bold blue lines.

Si embarazada.

Yes, I'm embarrassed.

5

#Breakingnews

@calicokate I sent my boyfriend the positive test #shocked #delighted

@Brandimoon I gave my mother this cute I love my grandma bib. She cried for like an hour about me missing school

@Lalabinks Put the scan photo on Facebook phone buzzing

@boringedgy I told my boy he's the daddy he left the next day #mistake

So I'm back beneath the grey fug of London with Max and someone else as well – two for the price of one. Waking up in my own bed in my own flat has helped me to properly absorb the news. In Spain, everything was bathed in romance and sunshine; skewed. Now I have the man (he's moved in) and I'm having his baby. Quite a result. I feel like high-fiving myself. Obviously, I'll be the best mummy ever. I'll be smiling a lot of the time and wearing things I haven't tended to before, mummy things like thin-gauge cardigans, big knickers and low ponytails. I'll be firm about some things – table manners, road safety – but mostly I'll be a lot of fun. I think of all the times I've had fun with kids – well, the one time, when I played with my friend Ramona Parker's little sister, chasing her around the garden with sticks. Then she chased me, but she had dog poo on her stick . . . Anyway, I know how I'm *not* going to be: I'm not going to be like my own mother. Be really hard to be worse: even before she left, when we lived in the shitty bedsit together with Uncle Whoever She Was Seeing at the Time, she was unpredictable. I have memories of us – one minute we'd be making stuff with bottles or mobiles out of coat hangers, the next I'd be dumped with the neighbours. She'd be dancing, then suddenly sobbing. Forgetting to get me from school. Angry with me, dragging me, then singing to me, plying me with Jaffa Cakes. Finally leaving me at Nana's with no explanation, to wonder all my life, what did I do?

Hell, being pregnant seems to stir up a lot of emotional debris, and floating on top in a raft of her own is my mother. I can't stop thinking about her. How did she feel with me growing inside her? Did she ever look at me and feel happy?

I wonder how you go about getting on *The Jeremy Kyle Show*. They'd track her down and save me the bother and we could be reunited. 'Abandoned daughter pregnant!' 'Mother who deserted daughter now a grandmother!' Yes, and they'd plug her into a lie detector and make her do a paternity test to tell me who my father is. I need to know these things now for genetic reasons.

Finding my mother is proving difficult with Nana away, but find her I will. I look out of the window, narrowing my eyes. She should know about her grandchild, and she can't run for ever. I imagine how she'll react; I picture her crying and vowing to be in her granddaughter's life as a force for good. A fantasy, I know, but I also know I'd take anything, any insight she can offer, any thin scrap of a relationship without terms or conditions. Forgiveness – it makes me cry.

But no, save your tears, Viv. Stop thinking confusing thoughts about your mother. Concentrate instead on Max and having his baby. I think about all the times in the past when I thought I might have been pregnant, those tense moments, those risks I took and how I imagined it to be. It was a pretty star cloud of a thing, with decorated nurseries and tiny little shoes and silver hairbrushes. I imagined the moment of discovery: hugging the father, who looked a bit like Gary Barlow, crying with joy and dancing about together. When in fact Max and I just sat on that bed in Spain looking at the stick for a good long while. Then he checked the instructions one more time and whispered, 'Whoa . . . shit!'

'I'm pregnant . . . I am pregnant,' I said into the middle distance.

'You are.'

'I am with child.' I started nodding. 'I'm having a baby all right.'

Max clutched my hand, his knuckles turning white as he squeezed.

'Congratulations,' he said.

'And to you.'

We looked into each other's faces in awe and then laughed in sudden gasps and said stuff like, 'Fucking hell' and 'I can't believe it,' and then we booked flights to London.

The funny thing is, when you have this kind of news, you want to act, start building a nest. Everything has changed, but nothing has changed. The sun is in the sky, everyone's going about their business, and there is absolutely nothing to do but wait . . . And obviously research. I'm starting an online pregnancy scrapbook so others can benefit from my wisdom, when I get time. I'm tired a lot – bone-weary, drop-on-the-floor tired. Yesterday I had to chop an onion in shifts because I was too tired to stand up.

But it's good to be back in the Big Smoke. In a way I missed the traffic, the drizzle and the leaflets; there's not enough people giving out paper in other places.

Max has set up the studio to work on his landscape exhibition. That's what we're calling his flat now that we're both living at mine. It's going well. It's been a week of total bliss, just me and Max and Dave – fresh from the cattery and sulking behind furniture. Max is besotted with this baby. He keeps talking to my belly, saying, 'I am your father,' in a Darth Vader voice.

Anyhow, today Christie, my old assistant, and I

are setting up an office for our new company, Dream Team PR. We decided we really need an office to be credible. The thing is, we can't afford an office, so we're going to be crammed into the top corner of a converted warehouse for £500 a month, including broadband, cleaning of common parts and shared kitchenette. I've already contacted our old colleague Mike to ask if he'll come and help with setting up our website. He owes me since I rescued him when he was jilted at his own engagement party. Our first contract is to produce sex-themed crackers for my best friend Posh Lucy's wedding, so we'll be busy today sorting through whips and butt plugs.

Before that I'm meeting Posh Lucy for a breakfast wedding meeting. My objectives for this meeting are:

1. *Tell her I'm pregnant.*
2. *Ask if I can be excused from the sexy pole dancing at her wedding on account of me being pregnant.*
3. *Get her to pay up front for her sex-themed wedding crackers on account of me being skint.*

I think if I'm direct and to the point, it should all go swimmingly.

'I'm having real trouble getting the ice sculpture for the wedding,' says Lucy.

We're in an upmarket organic juice bar she chose.

This isn't like her and it makes me worry – that and her twitchy eye. She sips madly on her pomegranate smoothie with double wheatgrass shot, while ticking off items on her to-do list. I'm playing with my 'veggie medley crush', feeling sick.

'I wanted something phallic,' she continues.

'What like?'

'A cock, Viv. One with champagne coming out.'

'Oh, I see. Yeah, that would be . . . in keeping with the theme.'

'I have two more places to try. You'd think they'd be able to carve just about anything out of ice, wouldn't you?'

'I'd have thought so, yes. Those ice-carver guys! Would you not fancy having, say, a swan, then?'

She ignores me and continues down the list.

'And your sex-themed crackers, Viv – what's in them? I spoke to Christie and she didn't know! You do realise it's next week?'

'Ah well, you see, you have a choice. The edible slogan panties do push the price up a bit unless you go unisex, and it depends what you write on them. We got them to quote for "Reuben and Lucy" with the date, and we're in the final negotiations on price.'

'Viv, I do not want my wedding guests getting a pair of unisex knickers with my name across them. Bloody hell, I knew I couldn't trust you!' She's finished the drink now but keeps on sucking the straw noisily.

'No, you can. You can trust me. As I said, you can

choose. We also have mini penis-shaped bubbles, lube tubes and chocolate boobs.'

'How many things per cracker?' She narrows her eyes.

'Four pieces, not including a joke or a fortune cookie. I've got some here for you to have a look at,' I say brightly.

She waits silently while I place bits and pieces on the table. She opens and sniffs the mini lube tube.

'Bubblegum?' She waves the tube under my nose.

'Mmm, that's, er . . . quite nice,' I say hoarsely.

She examines the edible pants. They're mould-blue with black trim and black writing.

'Actually, these are quite amusing in their terribleness.'

'That's what I thought!'

She arranges the lube, pants, chocolate boobs and bubbles in a line. 'So each cracker will have these?'

'Yup, and a joke, or even one of these fortune cookies if you want.' I slide a few into the middle of the table and we open one each. I read mine aloud: '"When the time comes, say yes."'

She screws up her face. '"Those who tunnel deepest need no eyes,"' she reads, then tosses the paper strip.

'Best of three.' I hand her another cookie.

She breaks it open. '"You are not a cat." What the fuck are these?' she laughs.

'Who writes them? I want that job.'

'Let's have them – they're funny.'

'So all these things will be in a pearl-white cracker, and we'll write the guests' names on in swirly writing.'

'You won't do it, though, will you, Viv? Not with your handwriting.'

'No, not me – someone with nice girly swirly writing. Someone who writes menus on chalkboards in pubs.'

'Good.' She smiles briefly.

'And the cost will be three pounds per cracker. That's as low as I could make it. Special deal for you. You want eighty, so you owe me two hundred and forty pounds, please, and can I have it today so I can finalise the order?'

She takes out her purse and peels off some notes. I'm jealous of/impressed by cash-carrying people. Why am I not one of them?

She watches me closely as she hands it over. 'Don't let me down, Viv. This is my actual wedding day, OK?'

'When have I ever?'

'That time inter-railing when you went off with Fabio.'

'In adulthood, have I ever?'

'You went home early from my thirtieth.'

'I had flu. God, it's amazing how you keep all these details to mind! How is there room for any sane thought in your head?'

'There isn't.'

'I won't let you down, I promise.'

She nods.

'Your wedding is going to be brilliant!'

She smiles.

'Hell, you've even got me pole dancing with you!' I decide on the spot not to try and get out of the pole dancing and to break the news about me being in the family way only after the wedding. She's fragile.

'Yeah, we need to practise that routine again. I don't think you've got the timing of the final swing properly.'

'Actually, I think *I'm* in time with the music. You are the one who's slow.'

'We're supposed to end up on the floor with our left arms up.'

'About that – couldn't we just wrap a leg round the pole at the end?'

'No!' she shouts, and bangs a fist on the orange Formica. A few heads turn. 'I want you to do it my way!'

'O-K,' I say quietly.

She looks out of the window with a huge shuddering sigh. Her shoulders drop, she lets her hands fall open, and I see her eyes are shiny with tears.

'Hey . . . Cold feet?' I ask.

She shakes her head slowly, swallowing a sob.

'Has he?'

'Sorry,' she whispers, beginning to cry. 'It's just . . . it's just I haven't told you about it with everything you were going through, but . . . I'm not pregnant,' she says, as if finally admitting it to herself. 'And we've been trying for six months.'

I slide my chair over, put an arm around her. 'Oh.'

'I got my period today.'

I sit for a while, wondering what to say. 'Is that long enough to try?' I venture. 'Six months. I mean, is there a norm? How long is it supposed to take?' And what am I, some fertile freak who gets pregnant from a toilet? Thank God, thank God I didn't tell her.

She rubs her brow. 'It can happen as soon as you start trying, or it can take up to a year. They don't worry about it unless you've been trying for over a year.'

'Well, then. You don't want to be up the duff on your wedding day anyway, do you?'

'No. It's just for the last six months Reuben hasn't wanted to use anything. He says, "*Amor*, we are two people very much in love. Let Nature take its course."'

'That's quite a good impression of him.'

'Anyway, Nature hasn't taken its course. He's disappointed. I've become obsessed.'

'You have to have a lot of sex. There was this girl at work who was properly trying. She had ovulation charts and wee sticks. She had sex every day. Her boyfriend was terrified of her.'

'We have sex every day.'

'But still . . . You do?'

'Yeah, if I'm not in the mood, he has this ointment and ribbed—'

'Do not go on.' I hold up a hand and she smirks for a second before the worry comes down like a shutter and she's back to mournful gazing. 'Look, let's get things in perspective. You haven't been trying that long. I really think it'll be OK.'

She sighs heavily.

'I mean, I'm no expert, but you look hellish fertile to me. I'd be willing to bet – and put money on, mind – that you'll be up the duff this time next month.'

'Do you really think so, Viv?'

'I do.' She looks unconvinced, turning her head to the window and sighing. 'Want me to sing "Chiquitita"?' I sing the first line.

'No.'

'Want to see how long we can have a conversation using only the lyrics of Smiths songs?'

'We were not cool students, were we?'

'In our own way.' I shrug. 'Want another fortune cookie?'

She miserably opens her hand, wipes her eyes and frowns as she unwraps the paper. '"Your tongue is your ambassador,"' she reads.

'Well, there you are, then!' I say. 'And that's not all – you're getting married next week!'

Christie is waiting beside the huge double doors of our building. She's in work mode, wearing high-heeled thigh boots, black skinny jeans and a bumble bee-striped jumper dress. Her hair is piled inside a straw cap with a pompom. This is understated for her. She waves as a passing truck beeps.

'Christie!' I call.

'Oh, hi, Viv!' She air-kisses both sides. 'How was Spain?'

'Yeah, it was great . . .' I trail off as I stare up at the building. Its red brick walls and huge window frames remind me of a prison. It crouches amid the traffic and noise. Some sort of flyover seems to appear from its roof, spilling cars onto three swirling lanes behind. I look at the front window of our office, and as I do, the light glances off the glass like a wink.

'It's bloody noisy!' I shout into the wind, and she nods.

Then her eyes flick beyond my head and I know someone is behind me. I whirl round and come face to belly with a giant. I look up at the meaty jowls of the man who must be Damon, our landlord.

'Are you Viv?' he says, pumping my hand in his hairy paw. To say he's ugly doesn't do his face justice. It's an incredible face, as if the features were thrown with force and caught in the doughy boxing glove of his head, out of which the eyes now pop and goggle and wiry black hairs sprout at random.

He leads us through the door and I notice the straggly shorn pelt on his head continues down the back of his neck and disappears under his shirt. Once inside the building, he introduces himself and pulls back the cage door of a lift. We step inside gingerly.

'It's very simple. You won't find cheaper premises, but you pay cash up front every month and you have a key and a code for the front door. You don't pay, you're out.' His left eye drifts like a hard-boiled-egg searchlight as he speaks. Christie keeps trying to follow its gaze. He leads us out of the cranking cage towards the door of the corner office. We trail behind with the waft of sweaty nylon. Christie mouths, 'Oh my God,' and holds her nose behind his back as he fiddles with keys at the door. I turn my gaze on the burgundy carpet tiles.

Inside, the office is painted white, and light floods through the huge window. Two desks and chairs form an L-shape, and there are floor-to-ceiling shelves.

'It's perfect, Damon. Thank you. We'll take it,' I say.

'The price includes broadband, cleaner, use of the meeting room and shared kitchen,' he says to the cornices, hands moving as if he's polishing a mantelpiece with two dusters.

'Wonderful. Thanks, Damon. We'll take it,' I say again.

'Toilet facilities are included, but you provide your own tea and coffee and bog roll.'

I look despairingly at Christie, who's already sitting at the desk I thought would be mine. I look back at Damon.

'Pull the cage door shut on the lift or it won't work. The fire exit is out back. Do not use the lift if there's a fire. No staying on the premises overnight. No painting or other permanent decorating of office space without prior permission from me. No animals on the premises without prior permission from me.'

'Damon,' I say loudly before he can draw another breath. He stops. The eye floats. 'I'm pleased to tell you we'll take the office.' I press an envelope in his hand, containing Lucy's money. 'Here's a deposit. We'll drop the rest off when we move in this afternoon. OK?'

He opens the envelope and counts the money. 'There's only two forty here, Viv.'

'Can that be a deposit?'

'Nah, Viv, it's a month up front or no key.'

'Right, well, Christie, do you have any cash on you?'

She empties her bag on the desk. A tampon, a Chupa Chup and a two-pound coin roll across its surface.

'I'd give you this,' she says, picking up the coin, 'but it's my lucky charm.'

'OK. Damon, can you wait while I nip to the cash-point?'

'Viv, if you don't come back with the readies within the half-hour, I'll let the space go,' he says, seemingly polishing windows now.

'We will. We'll be back in a sec. Come on, Christie.'

Out on the noisy, dusty street, Christie's hat is blown off. It sails upwards, lands in the road and is immediately flattened by a truck.

'No, Christie! It's not worth it!' I cry, pulling her back from diving headlong into rushing traffic.

'It's Burberry, Viv!' she shrieks, trying to make a run for it. I struggle with her, eventually managing to grab her about the waist, swing her around using her own momentum and haul her onto the pavement as the flattened hat is caught up in the wheels of a van. Scraps of straw fly.

'Oh!' she whimpers.

'Leave it, Christie.' She lurches forward one last time before slumping into my arms. 'It's over. There'll be other hats,' I shout as I lead her away.

Where the hell is the nearest bank? We hobble around the mirrored curve of an office building, trying to get away from the traffic, only to find a whole other street of mirrored surface. Just then I'm hit by a wall of dizzying nausea and the angel voice starts up with a kind of bossy robot overtone, '*Flapjack now. Flapjack. Get flap—*'

'I think I need a flapjack, Christie! Have you seen a newsagent?'

She doesn't bat an eye at this weird declaration and we turn back towards Old Street station, remembering a cluster of shops there. We scurry along holding on to each other until finally we find a retail oasis and emerge with cash and flapjacks before struggling back again past the hat-carnage scene, where Christie slumps once more into my arms. I pat her back, muttering, 'Don't look,' as I see a pompom roll to the kerb, and then we head on through the heavy doors of our new office building.

We're scared of the lift, but the door to the stairs needs a code to open, and anyway, I'm wiped out by the cash run, so we battle with the cage door. It slides shut with limb-severing force, and we're winched up and down a couple of times before staggering out on the third floor. We open the office door to find Damon seated at the best desk, palms down on the table, as still as a sphinx.

'You made it with two minutes to spare, Viv,' he says.

'I didn't realise you were timing us. I'd have asked for directions.' I smile at Christie, who's smoothing her windswept hair.

'I did say, Viv, "Within the half-hour."'

'Are these offices in demand, then?' I ask. 'I mean, it seems a bit empty round here to me.'

The stray eye wanders slowly left and pops back. He's thinking.

'Do you have the money, Viv?' he sing-songs.

I hand him the cash. He counts it twice before giving me keys and codes and a handbook containing rules and instructions for appliances. He writes his mobile number on the top and underlines it twice. 'Anything you need, Viv, you call that number.'

'I will, Damon,' I say solemnly, and, satisfied, he lumbers out.

Christie spritzes Chloé perfume into the air. She's sitting once again at the desk I would have preferred, but I decide not to battle it out after the hat incident.

In any case, I need to eat a lot of stuff immediately, so I take the flapjacks and settle at the desk with my back to the door.

'Oh my God. He actually had hairy palms,' says Christie.

'No, he didn't.'

'What's *wrong* with him, though?'

My mind shoots to my fears about alcohol abuse and unborn babies.

'Nothing's wrong with him.'

'That weird eye! I didn't know where to look, Viv.'

'He's somebody's baby.'

'What?'

'His mother loves him.'

'Er, he probably strangled her.'

This puts a whole new slant on things. I nibble around the edge of the flapjack while thinking about it. This is the kind of prejudice my baby might have to put up with. This received attitude that humans must look a certain way in order to be acceptable.

'So hold on, do you think that because he looks weir— unconventional, he's a murderer?'

'Ye-huh!'

'You actually think he murdered his own mother?'

'I wouldn't put it past him.'

'Christie, you know what? I hope you never get called for jury duty. Think about what you've just said. You are pretty and young.' She looks pleased. 'But imagine if you weren't. If the genetic lottery hadn't fallen in your favour, would you like to be accused of murder because of how you look?' Her face falls and I'm proud of myself for making her think just that little bit deeper. 'See? Damon is not a murderer, just very, very, *very* different-looking.' She's staring. I smell something not nice. 'Is he behind me, Christie?'

She begins to nod as an almighty thud hits my desk and I jump into the air.

'I forgot to leave the back-door keys,' Damon booms close to my ear. I spin round in my seat and horrifically we're eye to eye. Flapjacks topple. I'm aware of my hands flying to my throat, and a small cry escapes me.

'All right?' he growls, lifting a giant werewolf hand to reveal a bunch of keys.

I nod manically. 'Thank you,' I squeak, and with a gleeful glint in his good eye, he stomps out, leaving me clutching my chest where my heart is trying to escape.

'Like I said . . . weird,' says Christie, calmly taking out her laptop.

We spend the rest of the day setting up equipment and planning a strategy. We're sorting Lucy's wedding crackers and producing a few more as samples to show to retailers, and since Lucy's wedding is next weekend, that's going to be all we have time for at the moment. I think after that we'll soon decide what our strengths and skills are, and which of them are likely to make us the most money, whether it's the public relations side of things or product management or promotions. We have many strings to our bows, we decide, and as long as neither of us is ever left alone with that Damon creature, whom Christie is now calling 'Demon', we think the office could work out well, chiefly because it's cheap.

I decide not to tell Christie about the baby until things take off a bit workwise: I don't want to make her feel insecure about our venture. Actually, I don't want to admit that I'm insecure about our venture. In my more self-sabotaging moments I've seen myself penniless, foraging for roadkill and felting my own hair to make baby outfits. But then I tune in to that angel voice. '*All will be well*,' it whispers, I think. Or hold on, could it be '*All will be hell*'?

No, Christie and I, we've just got to make this work. We've just got to, I think in a *Wizard of Oz*/*Gone with the Wind* way. We are experienced, savvy and clever – I mean, just look at Christie placing an order for the cracker contents in China right now.

'*Duōshǎoqián? Yil? Duōxiè!*' she says, writing on a pad. 'We wan' one hundred!' she shouts in her version of a Cantonese accent. I feel a burst of pride for her and glance back at my laptop, which has finally fired itself into action and shows the results of my last internet search: a birth website. An apple is being pushed through a skeletal pelvis.

'Also one hundred! Same. Same,' screeches Christie.

She dealt with our Chinese suppliers when we worked at Barnes and Worth, so she really knows what she's doing. I hope. Anyway, I have to trust her to do things.

'Thursday, ahh? *Shi. Shi!*' she says, and puts the phone down and starts typing.

'Everything all right?' I ask mildly.

'Oh yeah, they promised we'll get the crackers as soon as. They don't have time to send a sample, so we just have to trust them and go with whatever arrives.'

Hmm, this trusting, it makes me nervous. And wasn't she supposed to order samples while I was away? I look at her, my employee, and think about having a chat about roles and responsibilities, but actually, it's our first day and I don't really know how it's going to work yet, and it may even work out OK without samples. I'll try not to worry. 'Stress is not good for the baby,' it says here. I scroll down the website and click on 'What to expect from an episiotomy.' I open the video link and blanch. Oh, no way. That is not happening! I close the site quickly, inwardly clenching. Jesus, that poor, poor woman. She was . . . and then they just . . . Urghh. What kind of torturous hell have I stumbled into? Surely having a baby can't be that bad or why the population boom? There must be a way of doing it while you read *Grazia* and have a biscuit.

I click on a site with photos of babies dressed as things, and flowers where the centre is a baby's face. They have caterpillars and bees too, and a rabbit. I add them to my pregnancy Pinterest board. I'm about to email some over to Lucy but don't at the last minute, reasoning that if she's upset about not being pregnant, she might not feel like being made to look at pictures of babies dressed as garden wildlife. I don't worry about Lucy: she always gets what she wants. She'll be pregnant soon, and in the meantime I'm actually in the process of growing my very own baby. That is the maddest idea ever. I can't get my head around it, but it doesn't even matter what I think – it's happening right now inside me, like having a parasite. My baby is already fully formed. It has a heartbeat. I gaze at Christie, considering whether to tell her or not, and she looks up and asks, 'Are you pregnant or something?' shocking the life out of me.

'Why do you ask?'

'Just the way you're stuffing your face, Viv,' she says, adding in a hushed voice, 'Have you ever thought you might have a tapeworm? My dog had one. He sicked up the head. There was this head looking around and my dad grabbed it and pulled and it was about a metre long! Honestly, we were all gagging.' I blink at her, imagining the scene.

'Yeah . . . so . . .' She scrutinises me for a bit.

I push the flapjacks away. 'I'd better stop, actually. I have to fit into a very tight dress and dance at Lucy's wedding next week,' I laugh.

'You?'

'I'm a bit nervous about it.'

'Dancing?'

'Yes, Christie, me dancing.'

She purses her lips.

'What?' I ask.

'No, I'm just amazed.'

'Why?'

'You're performing at someone's wedding?'

'Yep. I can dance. I got moves.'

'You're not Lady Gaga, though, are you, Vivienne?'

'No, Christie, I am not Lady Gaga. What's your point?'

'Just that every time I've ever seen you dance, you're a *bit* out of time with the music,' she lectures, widening her eyes and shaking her head slowly.

'Am I? Hold on, when was that?'

'The Hawaiian night at Barnes and Worth?'

'I'd had a lot of rum punch that night, and it's hard to do my kind of dancing to "Agadoo".'

'Your kind of dancing?'

'You know, street dance,' I say, holding her stare and trying not to think about my humiliation the one time I thought I'd nip in for a dance class at Pineapple Studios. I do a head roll, ear to shoulder, ending with a chest pop to back up my argument.

'All I know is, people were laughing at you. "Look at her," they said, "nana dancing."'

'Well, that just goes to show you,' I say vaguely, beginning to pack up.

'What?' she says.

'That nanas can dance great.'

6

The Top Baby Names of the Year

Girls	Boys
Sophie	Harry
Lily	Oliver
Olivia	Alfie
Ava	Jack
Jessica	Thomas

I decide to call into Max's studio on the way home. I find him arranging canvases in a line along the wall, all of them landscapes. He's cleared the portraits to the side and has actually tidied up his crap. There are no more piles of newspapers, the old rags have gone, and the wooden floorboards look swept. The studio seems to vibrate with a different energy, something more organised, and less sexual somehow without the naked women paintings. When I see him crouching there in his old striped shirt and faded grey jeans, I get a flutter inside like a paper fan. I have to stop myself from running in, jumping on his back and shouting, 'Hey, you, I love you!'

'Ah, Viv,' he says, glancing up, 'which one do you like?'

I look along the line. A couple are painted totally in a red brown, and only when you look more closely do you see a kind of landscape within the textures and layers of paint. Others are more literal but stylised with sweeping, curving trees and swelling mountains. I choose one of Cadaqués, a view of the sea between stacked blocks of houses.

'No, no, that's not the best,' he snaps, shaking his head and moving the painting to the end of the row. 'Choose again, and come on, really look this time and try to feel something.'

I go for one of the redder abstracts.

'So how does it make you feel?'

'Calm,' I say. 'Calm and strangely warm.'

'That's good.' He places the painting at the front and stands back with his hands hooked in the back pockets of his jeans. 'See, I'm sorting these for the exhibition.'

I stand beside him, looking at the Spanish views lined up like expensive picture postcards. He puts an arm around me and gives a squeeze, but he stares intently at the paintings. He steps forward suddenly, crouching to swap them around again.

'Ah, maybe I should have painted more of these abstracts, a whole series. These are the stand-out pieces. I really like the way the colour behaves at the edges, and the texture of the paint. The different pigments were actually an experiment. I started with pure powder, but in the end I used acrylic.'

He sits on the floor, leaning back on his elbow, the

long shanks of his thighs out in front. I look at his old paint-spattered biker boots, the leather moulded into the shape of his feet. These are not the shoes of a daddy, and yet they are.

'Acrylic, did you?'

'Yeah. Acrylic gives a true colour, but you can still get some translucence.'

'Translucence, hey?'

I'm standing behind him. He lets his head fall back to look at me, eyebrows raised.

'Yeah, translucence,' he says. 'I'd like to see you in something translucent . . . transparent even.'

'I'm sure you would.'

He reaches an arm towards me. 'Come here.'

I go and sit with my outstretched legs next to his. My trainers reach the top of his ankles. He looks sideways at me and smiles. I stick out my belly, trying to make myself look pregnant.

He places his hand on my thigh and croons to my tummy in a quiet sweet voice, 'Hello, baby . . . This room is where you were conceived. You don't know this yet, but your mammy is a shameless hussy and she bent over that very table . . .'

'And your daddy is a very bad and dirty man.'

He kisses me, gently pushing me back until we're lying on the floor. 'I have an idea. Let's re-enact the whole thing.'

'Erm . . . no, ta. At the moment I'm really only lusting after egg mayonnaise.'

We lie side by side looking up at the ceiling rose.

'This baby controls me, you know. It speaks to me like a sort of angel robot,' I tell him.

He turns his head to the side. He's now looking in my ear.

'Like now it's going, "*Egg mayonnaise, egg mayonnaise, egg mayonnaise . . .*"'

'She is, you mean.'

'Yes, she is . . . like an angel.'

We look at each other. He smiles.

'Angel,' he says dreamily, stroking a palm through the air.

'Angel . . . what, as a name?'

'It's a great name for a bump, don't you think?'

'Say it again.'

'Angel,' he says, again with the hand gesture.

'I like it.'

'You are our little bump. We shall love you, and we shall name you Angel,' he whispers to my belly.

'A boy named Angel,' I say aloud to myself.

'Better than Adolf.'

'Or Judas.'

'Pontius,' he adds, and we leave the studio making a list of historic villains not to name your child, and on the way home we compile lists like this one of names that will make your child stand out from the crowd but not in a good way: Ezekiel, Randy, Jezebel, Hades, Fanny, Dick, Satan . . .

★   ★   ★

Back at the flat, I collect the post. There's a bag containing my dance dress for Lucy's wedding, and there's a note written in a slanted, mean-looking hand.

> Vivienne,
> Called to see you. In London for a short while. WILL RING SOON!
> Rainey
> (Mother)

I stand in the stairwell, suddenly hot. A thud like a low drum begins whacking in my chest. I look back outside the door as if she's lurking nearby. Then I'm holding the note, staring at the disturbing word 'Mother'. What bewitching power that word has, anchored in our hearts and chained to the heart of another woman and another before her, all of them mothers, and now Rainey is yanking on my chain. She wants to see me – my mother, who has never really shown any actual interest in seeing me before. I was going to hunt her down and now she's sniffing at my door. It's too suspicious. What does she want?

'Vivienne?' Max bellows from the door. I put the note in my bag, feeling shaken. The audacity of her. She doesn't know I'm pregnant, but she just turns up for no good reason, demanding to see me, presuming that a) I want to see her and b) I'm available. What about all the times when I needed her? The letters I wrote and the birthdays she missed? I haven't seen or heard from her in three years, and the last time she made unwelcome comments about my hair. But then again, she's here. My mother. I think about a Disney mother, softly spoken and kind and pure fantasy. My mother is not at all like that, but she wants to see me. That's something. I climb the stairs, and by the time I've made it to the top, I'm wide-eyed with excitement. This is the start of something with us. This is it, the big reveal, the reunion. I know it. I can feel it.

7

Doctor (Dis)appointment

You can book an appointment with your GP or directly with your midwife as soon as you know that you're pregnant. Your GP surgery can put you in touch with your nearest midwifery service. Early in your pregnancy, your midwife or doctor will give you written information about how many appointments you're likely to have and when they'll happen. You should have a chance to discuss the schedule with them.

www.nhs.uk

Obviously I'm not going to let my imagination run wild – traditionally my mother has always let me down – however, in my head she's already my birth partner, we're reunited over my pregnancy, and just as I'm becoming a mother, I have a mother of my own to watch over me, to love me even when I'm wrong, to tell me I'm pretty and clever and good. I know this is the fantasy of an abandoned seven-year-old girl, but I have to go through it every time Lorraine appears.

I will stop thinking about her by terrifying myself with this tutu dress and the fact that I'm dancing at

Lucy's wedding wearing it. I say dress but it's more a costume consisting of leatherette corset and net skirt with sewn-in pants looking as if it's made for a child. Surely any grown woman's gusset needs more fabric than that? Any bosom requires more leather? But no, it's size twelve . . . Hell, it makes my skin all red as I drag it on. I close my eyes and step in front of the mirror.

It's worse than I thought, hideous. My boobs look like they're being offered on a tray, and I wouldn't mind so much if they looked OK, but they're wobbly, huge and they hurt. Oh, why do I have to be the best woman for a crazy sex maniac? Why can't Lucy have bridesmaids who wear sateen and flower garlands? I can't pole dance in a tutu! Not sober! What was I thinking? I'll have to tell her I can't go through with it. I imagine Lucy's face, how she looked this morning, how upset she is about not being pregnant and how stressed about the wedding, how angry she can get.

How bad can dancing in a tutu be? It might be fun! I skip off to perform the dance for Max.

'And one and two and three and four. I step in here, grab the pole and spin round.'

'Fucking hell,' says Max from the armchair.

'What?'

'I can see your tits.'

'You can not.'

Max raises his eyebrows in the direction of my chest. I stretch the tutu skirt a bit, trying to pull it up, but my boobs spill out of the top even more. He rolls a cigarette by the open window.

'I'm not complaining, mind,' he says.

'It's just a bit snug, that's all.' I tug at the front of the corset.

'Or does it not fit?'

'Max, shut up, will you? Just watch the dance.'

I go through the routine, concentrating hard. He smokes and smirks.

I switch off the music, panting, and turn to him, hand on hip. 'Well?'

'Very good.' He holds the rolly in his lips and claps.

'I'm knackered.'

'Not surprised – that was a lot of thrusting. It must be hard to get air in your lungs in that corset.'

'Lucy had these specially made.'

'Is that a bit of nipple I can see?'

I flop backwards onto the sofa, defeated. He's right – I've put on baby weight: the dress is too small. I look like a prostitute, and I can't dance to save my life anyway. Yet again I'm about to be utterly humiliated. I press the net skirt down over my thighs and try to sit up without giving myself a wedgie.

I look at Max and he grins.

'You're mean.'

He shakes his head. 'You're mad to do it.' I watch him breathe a long stream of smoke towards the open window. He's aware of being watched and shifts in the chair; he stretches his legs out, resting one boot heel on top of a boot toe. He looks at me and raises his eyebrows.

'I forgot to mention . . . I said you'd be one of the canapé waiters,' I say, deciding to gee him up a bit.

'Did you, now?'

'You have to wear little shorts.'

'OK.' He looks defiantly into my eyes.

'Sparkly hot pants and a bow tie.'

'Bring it on.'

'Now that would be funny.' I laugh at the thought of him hairily lolloping about.

'You look totally beautiful in this light,' he says, leaning forward and staring.

'What would you call this light . . . Terrible Breath? London Gloom?'

'Let me draw you,' he says, stubbing out his cigarette.

'No.'

'I want to sketch you just like that. It'll take five minutes.'

He grabs a pencil and begins to sketch. I watch the tendons in his forearm move as the pencil scratches.

'My mother wants to see me,' I tell him.

He glances up. 'Why?'

'Because I'm a very cool person.'

'No, I mean why now?'

Good question. I hadn't thought of that. She's probably passing through and feels guilty about missing Nana's wedding and thought seeing me might make up for it. She could be about to tell me some life-changing thing. Maybe my father is actually the winner of the Nobel Peace Prize or she might want to get to know me. I retreat from that idea like a snail from a salt cellar; that's abandoned-seven-year-old-girl thinking again. I am a responsible grown woman, a pregnant one, and I was looking for her to tell her about that, don't forget.

'She might just want to say hello.'

He looks up, nods. 'When?' he asks.

'Dunno. She might not even call for all I know.' Hell, I feel upset even as I say that. 'Let's change the subject.'

He sketches in silence, looking up occasionally and narrowing his eyes.

'Did you make a doctor's appointment?' he asks after a while.

'Nine fifteen tomorrow, Dr Savage.' I stroke a hand over my round belly. 'Do you think his name influenced his career choice?'

'I'll go with you.'

'What, in case he is actually savage?'

'He might come at you with forceps.'

'Or get me with the blood-pressure thing!'

'Go after you with stirrups.'

'Stirrups? What?'

'I'll go with you.'

'OK,' I say, wondering when Rainey will call, if she'll call, and if she'd like to go to the doctor's with us.

★   ★   ★

Dr Savage's office is a study in beige, practically windowless and extremely hot. I feel a wave of sickness hit almost immediately after we step through the door. I sit next to the desk, and Max is shown to a chair by the wall, like a naughty boy (which he is). Dr Savage, whose name is Clive I see from the name plate on his desk, has an oval hairless head that looks like it could be inverted and still be a face. He types importantly on a laptop while I study his fleshy earlobe, where the scar from a piercing surprises me and has me suddenly imagining his love life.

'All right, Miss Summers, what can I do for you?' he asks, looking up.

'Well, I'm pregnant,' I say shyly.

'Happily?' He glances from me to Max.

'Oh yeah, delightedly,' Max says. I look at him with his overgrown beard and dark hair all sticking up and feel like laughing, riffing like teenagers in the head-mistress's office.

'Well then, congratulations.' Dr Savage types a line. 'How many weeks pregnant do you think you are?' Seeing my blank-as-a-sheet face, he adds, 'We usually count from the first day of your last period.'

When did I begin my fling with Max? I look at him.

'When did we . . .? Mid-July.'

'That would make you about ten weeks,' says Dr Savage, consulting a colourful wheel calendar, 'which means the baby will be due around about 1st April.'

'Aha. If you're born on April Fool's Day, it means you'll be lucky all your life,' says Max.

'Oh really? Wow. Cool!' I laugh, but Dr Savage doesn't.

'Right, Miss Summers. If you hop up on the table, I'll examine you.'

I lie back while he presses cold, girly hands timidly over my belly, confirms that I'm about ten weeks, and sends us home.

Out on the street, I'm deflated. Shouldn't he have listened to the baby's heartbeat or something? Shouldn't we have some sort of information pack? Freebies? He said he'll 'book us in' and then I'll have an 'allocated person' who'll contact me. We can pay for a scan between twelve and fourteen weeks to check for 'foetal abnormalities'.

What does that mean? What am I supposed to do now? I wonder if he actually knows what he's talking about. I mean, I had to tell him how to deal with morning sickness – he agreed that ginger nuts are good and then started going on about fruit and vegetables. He doesn't know a thing.

We trudge along to the Tube station hand in hand. Dr Savage has burst our bubble.

'April is a lovely time to have a baby,' Max says, nudging into me. 'A spring baby.'

'You think?' I sling my arm around his waist, slotting a hand into the back pocket of his jeans.

'Buds, blossom, chicks, baby rabbits and all that.'

'Suppose.'

'Little birds making nests, Bambis . . .'

'What am I, Snow White?'

'Post-modern ironic Snow White – that's you.'

'*Eat something's flesh now!*' says Angel.

We duck into a café for bacon butties. I get a chicken leg with mine.

'It must be because a lot of women miscarry in the first twelve weeks. They don't want to be wasting time seeing you and testing you and then you go and lose the baby,' says Max, thoughtfully chewing.

'I am not going to *lose* the baby.'

'My mother lost two.'

'Well, I'm not going to.' I lower the half-eaten chicken leg to stare at him.

'And my sister.'

'I don't want to talk about losing babies! Why are you talking about that?'

He takes a slurp of tea. ''s common, that's all.'

I glare at him as he wipes his beard with the napkin.

'Anyhow . . . doesn't matter,' he says carefully.

Now I'm disappointed *and* worried about losing the baby. I wish I'd never darkened bloody Dr Savage's door. I rub my tummy. Everyone but me is so blasé about me having a baby. I'll put something about this disappointing feeling in my online research notebook, in a sympathetic tone to reassure others. I'm just taking a bite of chicken and planning it when my phone beeps a message.

You'd better be coming in soon! The crackers have arrived and Demon is here talking to me – help! Christie xx

I hear Christie's nervous laugh as I struggle from the lift cage, then the rumble of Damon's voice. As I open the flimsy office door, I'm once again stunned by Damon. I resist the urge to cover my mouth in shock. He's standing legs apart, feet squarely planted next to Christie's desk, looking out of the window while delivering a monotone speech about being a Greek Cypriot. Christie tries to concentrate on her computer screen. She winces at me.

'Morning!' I say cheerily.

Damon turns, jolted out of his speech, and fixes me with his good eye.

'I was just telling your friend about my old mum. She lived on this street fifty years . . .'

'Oh, Damon, I can't have you interrupting my staff. Christie won't be able to concentrate with all these fascinating stories.' I start to unpack my laptop.

'Vivienne, you kept me awake last night,' he growls.

'Did I?' I ask, desperate not to hear why.

'I was thinking, did I give her the back-door code or not?'

'Yes, you certainly did.' I sit down at my desk. There's an awkward silence as Damon looks out of the window. I wonder if 'back-door code' is some sort of euphemism.

'Well, I'll sod off and let you work, then,' he declares without moving.

'If you could, that would be super helpful.' I smile and blink sweetly. He starts to lumber out, using mostly momentum to get to the door, where he stops and turns.

'Shame, weren't it?'

I twist in my seat. 'What was, Damon?'

'About Lady Diana,' he says. Then he shakes his head and leaves.

As the door closes, Christie slumps in her seat, clutching her neck with both hands. 'Oh my God, Viv, no word of a lie he nearly gave me a heart attack!'

'He's just lonely, that's all,' I say, switching on my laptop.

She begins marching up and down spraying great jets of 'Spring Breeze' air freshener. 'I can't understand how he can sneak up like that.'

'Did you have your iPod on?'

'No! I just turned round and there he was! Standing right there! I think he might be a ghost.'

'That would be good, a ghost landlord. Would we still have to pay rent, do you think?'

'In blood.'

'Not so good, then.'

'He's like the living dead. Viv, have you stopped to think why there's no one else in this building?'

'No, I haven't.'

'Because he's *eaten* them, that's why.'

I look up and frown. 'Have you been on the Horror Channel again?'

'You mark my words, Viv, no good will come of this.'

'Look, Christie, Damon isn't a ghost, OK. He's just a bit of a strange man. No need to become Mother Shipton.'

Her eyes go wide, staring at the back wall, and her mouth hangs slightly open.

'Is he behind me?' I spin round. Damon is not there.

'See – you're terrified of him too,' says Christie.

I enter into a pact with Christie to meet at the Tube station and always come to work together. Then we make cups of hot sweet tea for the shock and open the box containing Lucy's wedding crackers.

Under layers of shredded paper there are plastic bags, and in each bag there are four massive crackers.

'These are grey,' I say, opening a bag. 'Does that look grey to you?'

Christie takes a cracker to the window and squints at it. 'Hmm, they smell foisty,' she murmurs.

'And huge. Huge grey crackers. They're supposed to be mini. These are bigger than Christmas crackers . . . There's no way that colour could be described as "pearl white", is there?'

'More like "wet-rat grey",' says Christie.

'Where's the fricking brief?'

Christie half runs to her desk and grabs a piece of paper.

I scan down. 'It doesn't describe the colour, just a reference number. Did you check it?'

'No. Did you?'

'No,' I admit.

Shit. Lucy will kill me.

'We didn't check the size either. I never thought to – Technology Paul used to do all that at Barnes and Worth,' Christie says quietly.

'We can't get a new order in time?'

She shakes her head and we sit on the floor among packaging and big smelly grey crackers for a bit, thinking. Lucy's wedding was our showcase. We were supposed to take photos to use as adverts in bridal magazines. We ordered extra, hoping to sell them to party shops. We're about to confirm a meeting with Tease UK, the massive high street chain of sex shops, this month. These were the samples . . . We're just depressingly rubbish.

'Shall we pull one?' she asks.

I hold out my hand with mounting dread. God knows what's inside. This business is doomed. We can't even brief suppliers properly. We pull and the cracker snaps open with a bang and a curl of smoke. The contents slide out onto the floor. I notice with relief that they're all as expected, except the chocolate boobs have a bit of a white bloom to them.

'Right, well, the favours are fine. That's good. What we'll do is save this situation. Somehow,' I say, as

Christie twirls the penis-shaped bubbles between her thumb and forefinger. 'I mean, the size we can't do anything about – we just have to hope they fit on the tables – but the colour . . . Maybe a bit of extravagant-looking ribbon?'

Christie holds a cracker at eye level and slowly turns it. 'I don't know, Viv. Would you want these on your wedding table?'

'Of course I would, especially if they doubled up as place settings and had nice ribbon on,' I say, slowly rolling my hand for her to go with me on this.

'Place settings!' Christie starts to laugh.

'Why not? Write the guests' names on them.'

'But you'd better not, had you, Viv? No one can read your writing. Imagine the mix-up that would cause – no one would have a clue where to sit.'

'That's true . . . Christie, are you able to write without making the dots of the eyes into hearts?' I say, pointing both forefingers at her.

'I'll give it a go.'

I scoff the chocolate boobs and the fortune cookie to stave off sickness while Christie practises grown-up writing. The chocolate has a soapy consistency, but the sugar is welcome – I'm starving. Now, where will we get really lovely ribbon? I start to search online.

'And no eyes in the "o"s, or flowers,' I say with my mouth full, unfurling the strip of paper from the cookie. '"You will be travelling and coming into a fortune,"' I read. 'Hmm, that's uncanny, because we *will* be travelling shortly . . . to a haberdasher's!'

A short while later we leave Dibbons for Ribbons £80 poorer, not counting the bus fare, and go our separate ways, Christie with a calligraphy pen and a list of guest names to practise and me lugging bags of sex-themed wedding crackers to work on at home.

8

Mummy, Dear

Mother *n.* a female parent that has produced or nurtured anything; **mothering** a protective nurturing quality.

At home, I've set up a cracker-titivation table with all the bits and pieces I need and locked Dave in the kitchen after he shredded £10 worth of ribbon. The thing about decorating stuff, I find, is not to overthink it. I'm getting better at these fat bows with each cracker, and this bright pink satin ribbon makes the Monday-morning grey look deliberate. I'll take the best one this evening to show Lucy. I'm going with her to the practice wedding make-up session. If she sees the crackers now it will be less of a shock when she sees them on the actual tables. They are meant to be funny, after all . . . Positive energy, that's it. Then the phone rings and by the time I've found it in my coat pocket I answer out of breath.

'I'd like to speak with Vivienne Summers.' A woman's calm, sonorous voice. Her. I feel a million urgent thoughts rushing. How to be? My heart bungee-dives.

'Speaking.'

'Ah, it's you.' There's a long silence.

'Who's speaking, please?' I say slowly. How will she answer?

'Vivienne, it's . . . it's Rainey. Vivienne?' she almost whispers.

'Hi.'

'Don't you know me?'

I don't know how to answer.

'It's me, Lorraine, your mother.'

I notice the end of the ribbon in my hand is vibrating.

'I'm having a baby,' I say.

'Ah.' There's a pause. I hear her moisten her lips and I try to picture how she looks, gathering scraps of memory from three years ago. She's pretty, I think. 'Can we meet?'

'OK.'

'Now?'

I walk to the sofa and perch on the edge. I'm panic-trapped. Now? Is this a test? That's a pretty small window of time and quite short notice, considering.

'Vivienne? I'm sorry for not being in touch. I understand it's a bit sudden. I've been plucking up the courage to phone for a few days now, but anyway . . . I'm fully prepared for you to reject me. I wouldn't blame you if you did.'

'I'll meet you.'

'Thank you,' she breathes.

We plan to meet for coffee at a place she knows on Portland Street. I jot down the details, feeling like I've swallowed a jack-in-the-box.

I wander to the window curling the ribbon through my fingers. I gaze out at the shops and across to the pillars of flats. My mother's here. She's in this city right now. If I focus, I would probably feel her presence drawing ever closer to claim me like some parent bird. Or not. Hold on, how did she get my number?

I'm lacing my trainers when the phone rings again.

'Vivienne?' It's Nana, sounding crackly, like an old gramophone.

'Hi, Nana! Where are you calling from? Are you having a nice time?'

'We're calling from Cairo . . . What?' she says at the same time.

'I said, are you—'

'Yes, been to the Pyramids today!'

'Was it amazing?' I ask.

'Are we what, love?' Everything I say overlaps with her and I hear my own voice ricocheting. 'Are you there, Viv?'

'I'm listening!' I shout.

'Amazing, oh yes, but a bit scruffy around and about.'

'There was a stinking dead horse!' shouts Reg in the background.

'I'm pregnant, Nana, me and Max are.'

'Nile cruise tomorrow,' she says, 'so we won't ring for a week or so, love . . . But listen – your mother is in London. She wants to see you.' I hear a loud crackle. 'You're pregnant? She's pregnant, Reg.'

'Yes. Yes. Ten weeks. Due in April.' I'm laughing, pressing the phone tightly to my ear.

I think the line has been cut off, but then her voice comes back clear as a bell. 'That's wonderful news, darling,' and then, 'How are you feeling?'

'Happy!'

Another hissing of dead air space and finally the words 'I can't hear you very well . . . Congratulations to you both, and listen – be careful if you meet your mother. Don't let—' before she's gone.

I walk past the café, Eden, peering in, trying to see if she's arrived first. Somehow I don't want to be the one waiting for her. But all I see is my own reflection looking nervously into the huge window. I take a deep breath, turn and stride towards the doorway. The café is pleasant, green, narrow, the ceiling hung with vines and the natural plaster walls with Indonesian gate mirrors. I hesitate by the front desk and then I spot her at the back. She sits at a low table reading a book in her lap. I feel an almost painful thud of recognition. She seems draped in colour, a water-colour left in the rain. Two or three scarves and a long skirt dyed like a stained-glass window, her legs crossed, sandalled foot bouncing, ankle bracelets glinting. I swallow panic, fear, tears. She doesn't look up until I'm beside her table, where I wait for a second with my ears burning. She turns and smiles from her cloud of dark hair. Her small, knowing eyes fix on me; I'm fascinated by the marble flecks of blue and green against the brown.

'Vivienne,' she says gently, and reaches for my hand, bracelets tinkling. The touch feels healing, cool and gentle. She gestures for me to sit opposite her on an uncomfortable Moroccan pouffe thing. Without asking, she pours tea for me from a tall silver pot, and then she sits, head tilted, smiling, like a therapist.

'I'm glad you came,' she says, and then stops. She presses her lips together, rests her hands on the table and considers them. She looks up almost shyly.

'I don't know what to call you,' I tell her.

'My name? Rainey.'

That smarts and we're hardly past 'hello'. I'd wanted to refuse to call her mum, but she's not giving me the chance. I remember how she is: pulling you in and then cutting you off. I'll stay cool, distant, in control.

'How come you're in London?' I ask, trying for a nonchalant tone.

She smiles, showing little pearl-like teeth; I notice a scarlet streak at the side of her hair. She looks really great, I think with weird pride.

'Would you believe it's because of you? I dreamed of you.' I feel myself blush and she notices. 'Does it surprise you to know I have visions about you?'

'I don't know. Not really.' What is she on about? 'So you're in London because you had a dream about me?'

She nods and her eyes sparkle. I take a sip of tea and almost gag – it tastes of sweaty socks.

She smirks. 'Nettle and pandan leaf to nurture your child.'

'And how long are you planning to stay?'

She turns a silver ring around on her thumb. 'You're right not to trust me. All I've ever done is let you down.' She lasers me with sad eyes.

Well, I can't argue with her there, but she's doing the tilted-head smiling again, so I feel I should fill the gaps.

'I wasn't saying . . . I just wondered how long.'

'Well, I'm here for you as long as you want,' she says, reaching for my hand across the table, her eyes bright with tears.

Oh hell, is she suddenly reclaiming me? I know I want her to stay, but I want it on my terms. This was not meant to be her idea.

She notices my discomfort and pulls back. 'Oh, of course. I'm too . . . It's too much for you, I see that.'

'It's just a teeny bit of a surprise you "being here for me" after everything that's happened.' I smile.

She looks towards the door. 'I've made a mistake. I should go.' She speaks into the air, to herself, and I feel a stab of panic.

'Don't!' I blurt, and her gaze darts to my face. I see something in her eyes. Triumph? Pleasure? 'Why don't we just talk for a bit? Tell me about the dream,' I say.

She takes a long drink, leaving me looking at the bottom of her cup, then places it carefully onto the saucer and straightens the spoon. She bows her head and clasps her hands together as if she's praying. Suddenly she throws back her hair.

'For a long time I've known I have the ability to feel the future.'

'Right!'

'In Ecuador, I met a man who loved me, but I knew he'd come to the end of his time here.'

'What? Was he a traveller, then?'

'Of sorts. It was the end of his time on Earth. I often felt this as we embraced. Later, after I'd moved on to visit the Patagonian Lakes, I heard he'd passed.'

'Oh, that's a shame.' Also, freaky as hell. I get a heavy feeling in my gut. Unbelievable how so full of shit she is.

'Then I *felt* you contact me, gently at first but more urgently recently. It didn't surprise me to learn that you are with child. It may even be my granddaughter calling out to me.'

'Hold on – you think it's a girl?'

'I know she is.'

'And what, she's contacting you?'

She shrugs. 'I felt strongly that we three must be together, and so I came.'

I take a good long look at Rainey, sigh through my nose, and decide I'll go along with whatever web of half-truths she's spinning.

'Wow, that's an incredible gift. What's the baby saying now?'

'Vivienne, don't be sarcastic, please. I don't speak with her directly, but I get a sense she'd like you to rest more. Am I right?' I remember this now, how she makes these obvious statements, asking if she's right at the end. It takes me back to some memory, a time when I was with her, and I'm flooded with nostalgia, thrilled to be sitting with her at a table. I want to believe she somehow felt me thinking of her, even if this must be quite a recent gift of hers, because I have needed her a few times before. I believe she felt something, that I felt something too. I'm willing to accept there's a psychic link between mothers and daughters, and now I am both a mother and a daughter, I probably have an extra-strong signal. Maybe she picked up my signal like a mother whale. Who's to say otherwise? We can have a relationship. We will for the sake of my daughter. I look into her eyes, feeling my own fill with tears.

'You are right.' I smile.

She looks into her lap. 'I'm leaving now. You must rest. Would you meet with me tomorrow?' She stands, smiling down at me like a deity.

'Yes,' I say, keen as a convert. 'What time?'

'I'll be in touch,' she says, and as she leaves, I remember how small she is. She seems to float from the café, leaving me star-struck. I'm brought up short when the waiter brings the bill. I look at the total and call him back.

'Excuse me, I think you've brought the wrong bill.' I hand it back. 'We only had a pot of tea.'

'No, the lady who was here with you had the quinoa and lentil salad, the brown rice balls and a large glass of Sancerre,' the waiter points out the items helpfully, and I pay.

Oh, I guess she must have forgotten she'd eaten.

9

Telling Lucy

Women often wait until week ten or twelve before informing anyone of their pregnancy, however, sometimes friends may guess if you feel unwell or refuse alcohol.

www.askthedoc.com

Right, I'm going to tell Lucy that I'm pregnant. I'll find the right moment and tell her, and also tell her that I've met with my mother . . . and that's why I'm dreading seeing her.

Lucy perches on a high stool in the middle of Selfridges looking up at the ceiling while a doll-faced girl brushes brown eyeshadow along her lower lashes. After each application, she hands Lucy a huge mirror and describes the process. Right now Lucy is nodding into the mirror and widening her eyes. I suppress a yawn and wonder about sitting on the floor next to the escalator, but a security guy strolls by and eyes me suspiciously. I try a bit of navy eye pencil on the back of my hand while Lucy gets her lips painted virginal pink.

I hope she's going to be finished soon because I want to tell her about Rainey. I want to be able to say, 'I'm seeing my mother tomorrow.' Lucy will go mad, but I'll explain I have a good feeling about Rainey this time. She will stay, fall in love with me because I'm all pregnant, and have a strong mother-daughter vibe. She'll see that I'm a very cool person indeed and will want to be in my life. Angel needs a granny, a young, interesting and . . . new-age granny. So it won't be like all the times before, because this time I'm in a different headspace. I'm in control. I'm not under her spell anymore, but soon she'll be under mine. Heh, heh, heh.

Lucy is sliding off the chair and buying make-up. I hope she's getting a free trowel thrown in.

We nip around the corner to a tapas restaurant on James Street, where I immediately get stuck into the bread basket. We order a few dishes, and Lucy gets a bottle of wine. How will I get away with not drinking wine? I wonder about nearby topiary.

'What do you think, then? Is this my wedding look?' Lucy asks, fanning her face with her hands.

I examine the mask. 'It's extremely weddingy.'

'Traditional, you mean?'

'Quite a lot of foundation.'

'And waterproof mascara, don't forget.'

'Probably look good in the photos.'

'It'll go with the dress, won't it?'

'What do you mean by "go with"?'

'I mean I'm *properly* made up, aren't I?'

'Oh yeah, she used everything on you. What

is eyeshadow primer, and why do you need it again?'

'Listen, that is essential. Do you realise your eyeshadow could crease at any moment without it.' Lucy pours two big glasses of rosé and takes a gulp from hers. 'Honestly, how shit do I look?'

I hunch my shoulders and squint at her face. She's a crayon-lipped, mauve-lidded, spider-lashed caricature.

'It's not really you,' I offer helpfully.

She pouts stickily. 'But am I kissable?'

'Not so much.'

'Well, you could have said something before I spent a hundred and fifty quid! Now what am I going to do?'

'Take it back.'

'But then I lose the discount on the make-up artist.'

'I'll do your make-up.'

She looks doubtful.

'I've got Chapsticks – in two flavours.'

She laughs and the foundation creases horribly around her eyes.

'Why not? Let's practise tonight,' I say.

'I'm getting my hair done tonight,' she says. 'I'm having a perm.'

'No, Lucy!'

'Just to give it some body.' She fluffs up her fringe.

'Don't you know anything? Lucy, I forbid you from having a perm.'

She laughs again. 'It'll look lovely – bit of a curl.'

'Listen to me. Look in my eyes. Do not mess with your hair. You'll regret it.' I take the last piece of bread. 'What if it goes wrong?'

'A soft root perm, not a bubble perm.'

'You say that as if you know what you're talking about. Then you'll come out like Brian May.'

'Bit peckish?' she asks.

'I've had this tummy bug recently. It makes you feel sick and then suddenly starving.' That's not even a lie, is it?

'Kill it with wine.' She slides the glass over to me.

'Thanks.' I take a sip. 'You seem happier,' I say, changing the subject.

'Yeah, I decided all this trying-to-get-pregnant rubbish was ruining my sex life. I've told Reuben it'll happen or it won't, and now I have to get him to just stop going on about fertility. I'm not even that bothered.'

Tell her you're pregnant now, tell her now, tell her now, tell her . . . I turn my wine glass by the stem.

'That's a lie. I'm so bothered. I'm dying to be pregnant,' she says sadly, 'and so is he, so I feel like I'm failing him and am less of a woman. Anyway . . .'

'It will happen.'

'I know. I *know*. Patience is not my middle name.'

She looks at my face with a small segment of a smile. 'Elizabeth is,' she adds.

'Lucy Elizabeth Bond, you will have a honeymoon baby, a boy named Honey or even Moony. He'll have your knack for straight-talking and Reuben's love of karaoke.'

'Oh, hell, no . . .'

'I had tea with my mother today,' I blurt before we get into the possible features of Lucy's baby or go through the timings of the wedding, which I know by heart.

'No.' She flops back into her seat, disgusted.

'But I have zero expectations.'

'Don't you remember she's the one who criticises you? Says your hair is bushy? We'll spend hours analysing "What did she mean by that? Why doesn't she act like a real mother?"' She does quite a good impression of me whinging.

'Anyway, I've grown my hair now.' I tug at a bit of hair at the back of my neck.

Lucy sighs. 'What does she want ?' She shakes her head, irritated.

'She came to see me. She says I called to her and she felt it. She's going by the name of Rainey.' I smile.

'Oh. My. God. Rainey? Rainey Summers! What, is she some sort of spiritual guru now?'

I nod, pulling a face.

'Tell me you're not going to see her again?'

'I am.' I shrug.

Lucy looks down her eyelashes at me like a pissed-off drag queen, but she doesn't say anything and is easily distracted by a phone app I've got that melds two faces into that of their possible baby. Mine and Brian May's child has the face of a melted chipmunk.

IO

#Wifedat

@**Shaysedo** If she's your best friend and makes you laugh #wifedatgirl

@**littleswagger** If you think about her when you wake up and when you go to sleep wife dat girl

@**IceBabe** She's too good to me #wifedatgirl

@**keilish** If she looks good in sweatpants wife dat girl

@**allofuse** If she's going to be your baby's mother wife dat girl

Lucy Elizabeth Bond is married to Reuben Fernando Candelas Garrido in a bank. Actually, a former bank, gone to the wall and now stripped of its glass barriers and serving mini empanadas and caipirinhas from its polished wooden counters. Lucy looks beautiful in her Vera Wang. She and Reuben hold hands and promise to be honest and interesting in bed from this day forth, and the acoustics send their vows vaulting to the rafters.

Later, the noise of the place is deafening. Max and I shout at each other to be heard above the excited chatter of eighty-odd guests, some in sex-worker gear. Max is looking dapper in his navy pinstripe. He leads the way through the booming crowd backstage to change. I cling to him at the last minute.

'Good luck, baby.' He winks and I drag myself away from his hairy jaw.

And then the moment of truth, stone-cold sober, following Lucy's tiny bottom and newly permed froth of hair out of the back office with my boobs offered up like moulded blancmanges. The boom-tsk drumbeat of the White Stripes' 'My Doorbell' starts up. Lucy turns to me and scowls.

'Remember, Viv, left arm up at the end.'

'Got it.' I nod and we strut into the limelight. Oh fuck.

Lucy explodes into the cleared space and prances impressively around with one arm held showgirl high. Then it's my turn. As I squint into the crowd, I see two girls point and laugh. I take up my position next to Lucy and we begin our routine. I'm concentrating hard, counting my steps. At one point, I head-roll left instead of right. The girls are in hysterics, bloody witches – hands pressed to their throats.

I hold Lucy from behind and we gyrate, sliding up and down the pole to whoops and whistles. This bloody song goes on for ever. I feel a hot pull in my stomach. I'm about to puke. Then we go into our final swing round the pole and slide to the floor like fallen iceskaters. Everyone claps, Reuben rushes forward, and he and Lucy passionately kiss before he drags her to her feet and she raises her arm triumphantly, bosoms heaving. I struggle like a seal pup against the straightjacket of the corset, trying to get up, managing at last to roll onto all fours. Max steps forward finally and offers me his hand. I feel the eyes of those two girls watching me like I'm a freak show. I spin round and pull a 'what's your problem?' face but with a hint of 'please like me' and Max throws his jacket over my shoulders and leads me to the bar.

'I don't believe you just did that, even though I saw it with my own eyes,' he says, blinking in awe.

'I have never been so embarrassed in all my life.' I shade my eyes with my hands and lean over the bar, trying to get my breath back. 'Never. Ever.'

'Buck's Fizz'll be OK, won't it?' he asks, eyes darting to my belly.

I down it in one and it sends me spinning.

'Did it look as bad as it felt?'

He drops his head as the ghost of a smile crosses his face. 'Bad? No, you were gorgeous.'

'Did you see any nipple?'

'Ah, you're a really good sport, Viv!'

'A good sport? A good bloody—' Just then my phone rings in his pocket.

He shows me the display: 'Rainey.' My heart leaps.

'Hello?' I make my way to the door and out onto the street.

'Vivienne?'

'Hi, yes!' I'm keen as mustard.

'It's Rainey. Can we meet?'

'Oh, er, it's actually a bit tricky . . . What time were you thinking?'

'Nowish? But listen, if it's difficult, let's not.'

I imagine leaving the embarrassment of the wedding, kissing goodbye to all my best-woman duties. The thought pops like a bubble.

'Sorry, Rainey, I'd better not. I'm at a wedding.'

'Oh.' She sounds disappointed.

I put a finger in my free ear to hear her better. 'I mean, any other time I would love to, but it's my best friend Lucy's wedding.'

'Lucy.'

'You met last time you were here.'

'Ah, yes, the thin-haired banker. Am I right?'

'Um . . . yeah.' I glance back at the bar. 'I'm her best woman.'

I hear a rush of breath like a sigh or a laugh. 'She won't mind if you pop out for half an hour.'

'What? No, she'd kill me. Can I meet you tomorrow?'

There's a long silence. Then she says something I don't catch as a bus rumbles past.

'Sorry, Rainey – I missed that,' I say, but she's gone.

I turn back to the bar, stung with uncertainty. Will not meeting Rainey be grounds for her to disappear again?

Through the window I see Reuben holding a microphone. After his speech I'd planned to say a few words before he starts on the karaoke. I can't think about Rainey now. I take a deep breath and dive back in. The guests are gathered around the stage, cheering and heckling the story of how Reuben and Lucy met.

I make my way back to Max. He hands me another Buck's Fizz.

'Mostly orange juice,' he whispers.

I take the drink and lean on Max as we listen to Reuben. The speech seems to be entirely based around a giant clay phallus, which he's brandishing at the end of each line.

'I knew she wanted this,' he says, waving the thing in the air, 'but I gave her something bigger!'

I glance behind me to where tables are being set for the wedding meal. The enormous grey crackers look all right in the end: the bright pink ribbon brings out the pink roses of the flower arrangements. Christie's writing is very neat, and the hearts over every 'i' actually add something: it is a wedding, after all. I allow myself a celebratory moment. The tables look great, and Lucy is pleased, even though the ice-sculpture penis isn't erect, but really, what did she expect? It's a luge; they flow downwards.

Reuben is talking and gesticulating. I look across at my two tormentors, one of them in a leather sheath dress, the other a bit nondescript apart from a wilting beehive. Then I spot Lucy to the left of the cleared space, absorbing the shrapnel of Reuben's speech.

'And so let me tell you exactly why I really have this big penis in my hand . . .' More roars and cheers. 'This is a potent fertility symbol! This thing, boy, do we need it! Lucy don't want me to tell you, but for us, the plan is to make a lot of babies and take over the world!'

I look over at my old friend with her perm and her tutu, twisting her hands in her lap. I know she must be hating this. What is he doing, exposing her?

'So far, not so good,' Reuben continues, see-sawing his hand, 'but I tell her we must practise more!'

Lucy shakes her head and smiles sadly.

'Of course! *Amor*, come. Come and take this big fertile cock in your hands.'

She smiles at him, but I think I can see her eyes glisten with tears. 'Not funny, Reubs!' she heckles.

'Yes, come on, *amor*!' coaxes Reuben, and she slowly walks over to him. I can see she's trying to keep her smile in place. Poor Lucy!

She now has to stand there and hold a huge clay penis fertility symbol while he laughs at her. All the pressure she's been putting on herself to get pregnant and now Reuben's idea of funny is humiliating her in front of eighty-odd people.

I turn to Max. 'What is Reuben doing?'

He's been laughing along, but seeing my expression, he adjusts his face from smile to concern. 'Bit close to the bone,' he nods.

'She's nearly in tears. I haven't seen her cry since . . .' When did Lucy *ever* cry, actually?

'Nah, she's all right,' he says.

'I'm going in.'

'No, you don't. Do not get involved.' Max pulls me closer with a forearm across my chest. 'I know what you're like.'

'What we have to do is both hold this fertile cock . . .' shouts Reuben.

'Is that the karaoke machine, do you think?'

'No, Vivienne! Viv!' Max calls as I push to the front. I'll save Lucy. I grab the karaoke mic and hit a few buttons. Reuben and Lucy turn round in surprise as the music starts up and I do the sexy strutting walk I learned from the pole dance as I make my way towards them. I do a twirl as I take the microphone from Reuben and hand it to Lucy.

And that's how she and I came to sing a karaoke duet of 'Islands in the Stream' on her wedding day, almost. Reuben snatched my mic and he and Lucy sang the duet, which is what he must have been building up to with the phallic-symbol routine, so I get the feeling from his glowering looks that I might have ruined the moment.

So it's quite awkward all in all. But then, Lucy had looked upset, although admittedly she seems fine now, dirty-dancing the salsa. As the music dies down, I hover by the stage self-consciously, occasionally doing little side-to-side dance steps, and then Lucy gives me a nod with a wide-eyed look that says, 'It's you!' I've prepared a few words, and even have a couple of prompt cards in my bag. I search the room for Max. He raises his pint and nods unhelpfully. I lift the microphone and my breathlessness is amplified.

'I'd like to say a few words.' My voice echoes sing-songy with emotion. 'As best woman, it is customary . . .' I notice Leather Sheath and Beehive moving closer to the front. 'Er . . . you know, Lucy and I have been friends since freshers' week at uni, when she walked into my halls-of-residence room and *told* me we were going to be. She's like that . . . bloody bossy!' My voice clatters through the room like cutlery falling onto tiles.

I scan the expectant faces nervously. I was going to tell a few hilarious stories about the time we went travelling through Europe and had to escape to Milan after she inadvertently got betrothed to a gypsy leader's son in Greece, and the Christmas party at the deli where we worked as holiday staff and she went into the back room with the relief manager, who liked doing unspeakable things with mini Edams. I think I was going to mention how she went and got my stuff for me from my ex's flat in her VW Beetle named Keith. I look at Lucy and open my mouth to tell those stories, but there's something vulnerable about her that leaves me speechless and unsure. I wonder how bad it would be if I just ran off stage now. Lucy mimes impatience by tapping her foot and looking at her wrist.

'Bossy and posh!' I continue. 'Through thick and thin, that's what she always said. I was the thick.' Lucy nods and I take her hand. 'I have so many stories to tell.' A few people shout. 'But if you want to hear them, see me afterwards, because all I really want to say here and now is that you, Lucy Bond, are the mate everyone wants to have: loyal and funny, clever and kind and honest, sometimes brutally honest, actually . . . but only when needed! Ha, ha! Yes, so . . . my darling Posh Lucy, we've had fourteen years together as best, best friends, through good times and bad, through many a scrape and out the other side. I hereby pass you over to Reuben for safe keeping, and if he fucks up, come get me and we'll kill him together.'

There's a silence followed by uncertain applause.

Lucy leans forward and grabs the microphone. She's probably going to say a few words about our friendship in reply.

'Vivienne Summers, everybody! The only person who quite likes the taste of earwax!'

I glance around, shocked. Why I thought she was vulnerable I'll never know, she's laughing her head off now. I snatch the microphone from her.

'I tried some earwax as a dare one time. I never said I liked it, so . . .' She takes the microphone back and I step from the stage as gracefully as possible, hearing her announce, 'Everybody! Lunch is served, but you only get it after you are photographed taking a shot from the amazing penis vodka luge!'

Jesus, what kind of bonkers wedding is this? Time to escape to the toilet and get out of this straightjacket corset. I spot Max chatting to Leather Sheath, bloody traitor. I grab him and drag him along. We fall into the ladies' toilet. The floor is tiled with smooth stone, and the sinks are green glass bowls lit from below so they seem to float mysteriously next to the bottles of upmarket soap and hand cream.

Max looks in the mirror, talking to himself.

'Kelly, you handsome devil, tell me this – why do you always end up in the ladies' toilet at weddings?'

I start to unclip myself. 'Who knows? There are plenty of other places to have sex.'

'That's your plan?' he says, turning and leaning on the sink shelf.

'My plan is to get out of this tutu, get some food and not do pole dancing, public speaking or karaoke ever again.'

'But that doesn't match up with my plan.'

'Yet again I'm a laughing stock.'

'No.' He smiles.

'People were actually pointing and laughing.'

'In a good way.'

I shoot him a look as I struggle with the tutu. 'Can you help at all?'

He grabs the top of the corset and tugs it down hard and I'm suddenly topless just as the door opens.

'Quickly!' I scuttle into a cubicle, but he hesitates. 'Hurry up, get in!'

We're pressed together and I manage to close the door. Then we wait in silence, his mouth near my ear. Heeled shoes tap into the cubicle next door. I breathe the sweet, beery smell on his breath and feel the edge of his tooth on my earlobe as he bites.

'Hmm, earwax,' he murmurs.

'Shut up,' I whisper.

I put a finger to his lips. He makes his eyes wide. The rim of dark lashes look like eyeliner. His warm sigh over my neck gives me goosebumps. I move my head away.

'Why don't you let me fuck you in here?' he says softly. There is a rustle of clothing from next door.

I hold his hairy face in my two hands. 'Stop. It,' I whisper. 'I'm the best woman.'

'Oh, you are, you are.' He smiles, stroking my bottom.

'Behave yourself!' I hiss.

He shakes his head. I put a hand over my mouth to keep from laughing as he struggles down to the floor in front of me.

'What are you doing?' I whisper half-heartedly.

Max lifts the tutu skirt over his head and I'm pushed forward with my hands against the door for balance as he slides a finger into my pants and pulls them to one side. I look at the ceiling as I feel his tongue. Next door, the toilet flushes and the heels clip-clop to the sink. I look down at the shadow of the tiger tattoo showing through Max's white shirt and notice that his feet are half underneath the door. Whoever it is will see he's down there. Then I feel his beard tickling the tops of my thighs, his tongue and fingers on me and I don't care anymore, even when another set of foot-steps tip-taps in.

'I think there's someone shagging in there,' says a Birmingham accent.

There's shuffling and silence, and then the door bangs closed.

Max appears from the froth of the tutu skirt. He stands up, flashes a smile. 'There's about to be someone shagging in here,' he growls. 'Come here.'

Later, we rejoin the reception. I look at his tanned hand in mine, feeling naughty and cool and happy, and I think I look good in this new green dress that I treated myself to. It's one of those wraparound numbers, low cut but flattering.

As we pass through the tables, I catch a snatch of conversation in a Birmingham accent. 'It was those two in the toilets.'

I look down into the face of Leather Dress. She turns round to watch us walk by. I point at Max and give her the thumbs-up.

Things are looking and sounding a lot more raucous. A fat man in pinstripes is wearing a pair of edible pants on his head. The vodka luge has worked its magic. We manage to slip past it without participating and take our place at Lucy's round table in the middle of the room. Platters of tapas are being served and I'm starving.

'There you are! Have you been shagging in the toilets?' asks Lucy, as we settle into our chairs. 'You've been ages.'

'There's your proof we haven't, then: I'm lightning fast, aren't I, Viv?' Max starts peeling a prawn.

'He's known as "the Under-a-Minute Wonder".' I smile lovingly. 'I was getting changed,' I explain.

'Don't you think all weddings should have at least one incident? Either people shagging in the toilets or maybe a fight,' says Lucy. 'Champagne here!' she calls to a passing waiter.

'I hope I didn't ruin your duet,' I say, stroking her back.

She laughs. 'It was great, Viv, if a bit random.'

'I thought I was rescuing you. I thought . . . Oh, never mind.' I can't say I thought she was humiliated – she obviously wasn't. I was.

'Here, have some champagne.' She passes me a glass. 'The thing about Reuben is, to him sex is just a natural part of life.'

'Of course it is.'

And now tell her you're pregnant.

'We do want to be pregnant, and that's what he was sharing with everyone.'

'Good, then. Wish I was going to Ibiza in the morning,' I say to distract her, and she turns and looks seriously at my face.

'Thanks for everything, Viv,' she says with tears in her eyes. I decide to leave breaking my news until after the honeymoon. It's not all about me, as she often reminds me.

'You're welcome.'

We look at each other in an uncharacteristically

sentimental way until we come over all awkward and self-conscious.

'Anyway, look at you, married!'

'Yes!' She smiles and raises a glass. 'To you, Viv, and to me being married before you. You owe me five pounds.'

'To me. I am amazing.' I take a sip of champagne.

'*Devil nectar!*' screams Angel, and I put the glass down like it's hot. Luckily Lucy has turned back to Reuben.

I take a wedge of cheese and a slice of bread, press them together and, while no one is looking, shove as much of it as I can in my mouth and chew purposely like a cow. I must have food. I must eat a lot of stuff fast. Max puts a hand on my thigh. I glance his way, swallowing and preparing to go in for another bite. He's looking at me funny. His eyes have gone all dreamy. I take the bite.

'All right?' I ask with my mouth full.

He keeps looking at me as if he's never seen me before, his eyes moving over my face.

'Do I have cheese in my hair?'

'I love you, Viv,' he says.

I nod, swallow and put down the bread, looking around for a drink of something that isn't champagne. 'Can you pass that jug of water?'

He pours water into my glass and I take a good long drink, eyeing the tortilla cubes on the platter.

'I love you, Viv,' he says, as I suddenly make a lunge to grab some tortilla.

'Thank you. I'm starving.' I smile. 'Pass the pepper?'

'Vivienne, look at me.'

I turn to admire him. I completely see why girls have always loved this old friend of mine: they think he's hot. He looks like he'd be dirty, and he is! I give his hand a squeeze, feeling totally peaceful and happy.

'Marry me, Viv,' he says.

'What did you say?'

He slides a ring box across the table. 'I said, Vivienne Summers will you marry me?'

11

Angry Cat

Family pets may get jealous. Watch their behaviour and remember even the most docile cat may attack if provoked. Cats and babies have coexisted peacefully for thousands of years.

www.catsandbabies.com

I open my eyes and glance at the window. It's light. It must be about eight. I always gauge the time in the morning by the amount of daylight, but then, I'm quite often late. What am I, a human sundial? I must get a clock. I turn over with the familiar churning of nausea, remember Angel, remember the wedding, the proposal, remember that I said no.

I see Max is not in bed. I sit up, nudging the curled-up bulk of Dave at the foot of the bed, smell the smoky tang of coffee.

'Max?' My voice is croaky and thick with sleep.

'Here,' he says quietly, sitting by the window, sketching, wearing old shorts. He smiles, with an unlit rolly hanging from his lower lip. I run a hand through my hair and watch him. The blind is partly open, showing a band of white sky.

Dave turns onto his back and stretches, his claw mittens snagging the cotton duvet, his curled sage-leaf tongue unfurling in a fishy yawn. I tickle his white belly fur as I look at Max.

'Let me see that?'

He makes it from stool to bed without straightening up and rolls up to me, chucking the pad on my legs – a set of sketches of my naked back.

'Off, Dave,' he says, sliding the cat to the floor with a foot, and turns to lie flat on his back with the cigarette in his mouth.

'They're nice,' I say, curling into him. 'Why are you pretending to smoke?'

'Flavour.'

'I think you'll have to quit.'

'Quit pretend smoking? Jesus, you're hard.'

'Please get me a biscuit. I feel sick.'

I hear him a second later rummaging around in the kitchen. On the bedside table is the ring box and the ruby and diamond ring Max gave me, round as a fish eye, grandma-style ornate, old-fashioned and cool. Max returns with tea and a packet of Hobnobs.

'Thanks,' I say with a comedy lisp.

'You are welcome.' He caresses my back before wandering to the sash window, sliding up the lower half and lighting the cigarette. 'Commitment shy, fucking hell,' he says, blowing smoke out of the window.

'I'm committed.'

He grunts.

'I am.'

He turns, taking a long suck on the cigarette before letting it drop into the alley.

'I love you. I'm committed to you.'

He snorts and turns his back on me, looking down into the alley. 'There's a tramp down here asleep under your window.'

'My last suitor. Waiting for me sent him mad. He now thinks he's a dog.'

'Marry me, Summers, before I go the same way.'

'He's not exposing himself again, is he?'

Max looks out into the alley. 'It's hard to tell. Oh no, it isn't – it's fucking obvious.'

'Memories are all he has,' I say dreamily.

Max slides the window shut. 'Just marry me,' he says.

'Why, though? Can't we just stay as we are? We're happy. We're having a baby.'

'No. Marry me today,' he says, pacing.

'Too soon.'

'Tomorrow.'

'Too soon.'

'In five years.'

'Too soon.'

He laughs. 'Marry me next Valentine's Day?' he says, spinning round and pointing.

'Too obvious.'

'Marry me on the anniversary of Elvis's death.'

'What?'

'Or the anniversary of John Lennon's death?'

'Not on someone's death day.'

'Marry me on Midsummer's Day.'

'When is it?'

'Well, love, it's mid and it's summer.'

He lies beside me on the bed and I curl towards him. How can I explain I just don't want to get married? I love him fiercely. I want to hang out with him for the rest of my days. I just can't face the idea of a wedding. After obsessing over three weddings with my ex, and planning the minute details of Lucy's wedding, the whole scene seems a bit tired, a bit over and done with. I literally could not bear to choose a venue or a bridesmaid's shoe, a cake decoration or a ceilidh band. I'm done. I'm having a baby and that seems the most important thing and all I can cope with.

'See this baby, Max? I'm actually growing it inside me, and I'll push it out of me. That's committed, and you can't tell me otherwise.'

He kisses my hair. 'It is. Rather you than me.'

'So that's enough, right? Ask me to marry you after I've done it.'

He thinks about this. He sighs. 'Just wear the ring.' He leans across me and grabs the box. 'Be engaged to me.'

'I hate long engagements.'

'Wear it for me. Look like someone loves you.' He balances the box on my tummy.

'OK. But will you ask me again after?'

'I'll ask you again every day for ever.'

My second meeting with Rainey happens that morning by accident. I'm walking towards the row of shops near my flat when I see her. My eye is drawn to the shape of her. I feel a kind of silent shout in my chest as I recognise her hair, and her style, the long scarf, turquoise and green like a swirl of sea. I call to her and she turns with a knowing look on her face as if we'd arranged to meet. I jog over to her across the road, and as I get close, she opens her arms and pulls me into a jangling silver and rose-scented embrace.

All my words fall over themselves with relief that she's still here, and I offer to buy us breakfast. She wants a gluten-free muffin and coffee, so I get them to take away and we walk into a little square park.

'It's amazing to bump into you like this. I only came out to get breakfast,' I say. She smiles into the air. 'We've started this bad habit on Sundays, getting croissants from the café,' I jabber.

'I like this area,' she says.

'So expensive. I live in the scruffy bit.'

'Alone?'

'With Max.'

'The father of your child. I'd like to meet him,' she says. She places her feet down like a dance, her toes spreading in the sandals. Step, pause, sway, step. I dawdle beside her.

'Oh, well, I'd like you to meet him.' I smile at the thought of Max.

'Why do you live with him?'

'Er, I love him. He makes me happy . . . It's the usual thing, et cetera.' I smile at the side of her face, looking for her meaning.

She keeps her eyes fixed on the path in front of her feet. 'Love,' she sighs. 'Vivienne!'

'What?'

'I'm surprised. I thought you'd be more realistic, with your background.'

'Nope. Die-hard romantic.'

'Have you asked yourself what's special about this man that makes you want to turn over your whole life to him?'

God, this is a bit of a downer. I'd like to explain the full complement of feelings, the many reasons why I'm in love with Max, but I'm not going to dissect them and pin them out for her approval like a rat in a biology lesson.

'He's always in a good mood,' I say.

'Huh,' she marvels at that. 'Is he a simpleton?'

'He's just, you know, very positive. You should meet him. You'll fall in love with him. I can't understand how the whole world isn't in love with him.'

'Please!' She indicates her stomach. 'I'd like to keep my coffee down.'

I laugh and she steps up the pace and moves towards a crescent in the path where there's a bench. I follow, sitting beside her while she throws crumbs of muffin for a gang of pigeons. One has a club foot and a limp, but she makes no allowance for that with the crumbs and it doesn't get any.

'So when do I get to fall in love with this demi-god of yours?'

'Well, are you free today? Now, even?'

'I'm stranded, actually. I have had to leave my hostel,' she says, crumbling the muffin into pieces, 'but I'm not ready to leave London.'

I feel a spike of panic and have to remind myself that I'm in control.

'Why do you have to leave the hostel?'

'Tiresome reasons. Apparently it's for travellers, not for stayers. They have big signs up all over the place.'

'But where will you go?'

'Madrid, I think. I have an unfinished affair there.'

God, so what then? She just travels around the world having affairs? How forward-thinking and bohemian. 'Of course, I could go to Madrid today. I have hospitality arranged, but I felt something between us. I'd like to stay for a while to see how that pans out. Have I imagined it?'

I try to hold on to a relieved laugh in my chest. I know I'm falling for this powerful-magnetism thing, but I can't help it. I really think it's Angel bringing us together. I've been thinking about her and she's felt it.

'I don't think you've imagined it.' I turn to her. 'There is definitely something. It's never been there before when you were here. Could it be to do with my pregnancy, do you think? Oh, what am I saying? I don't know!' I take a breath, looking out at the flower beds before grabbing her hand onto my lap. 'I'd absolutely love you to stay longer. I want us to know each other.'

She smiles at her hand as she gently slides it back onto her own lap. I notice the yin and yang tattoo on her inner wrist as the bangles slip.

'The sad part is,' she says quietly, 'that it's out of the question. London is prohibitively expensive, especially now I haven't a place to stay.'

'You can stay with me!' I blurt. 'It's only a one-bedroom flat, but there's a sofa bed.' Her eyes shine as she turns to me, those beautiful green and blue flecks like jelly slivers. She's curious, head tilted to the left. I immediately feel exposed. 'I mean, you don't have to. I'm not trying to, you know, tie you down. Ha ha. No, I understand. Madrid. Unfinished affair. Wow.'

'What about your lover?'

'Oh, he won't mind,' I say, thrilled to have a lover, who is Max.

'Well, if you're certain,' she says casually, watching the pigeons.

'Of course. You go to the hostel and get your things and I'll—'

'I have everything with me here.' She lifts a quilted cloth shoulder bag.

'Oh. Oh, well, even better,' I say as I stand up.

This is blowing my mind a bit, I'm not ashamed to admit. I go over my plan to seduce Rainey. This new development fits with my plot to keep her around so she can be a good granny. What's more, it's time we understood each other for better or worse, and if she's staying with me for a little while, so much the better. I'm fully in charge, controlling it.

'I'm really pleased you're staying,' I say. 'We can finally get to know each other.'

'Vivienne, in many ways we are each other. Am I right?'

I glance at her and nod, realising I don't know her from Adam.

Wandering back through the park, I begin to feel like a little girl who's invited the whole street of kids round for a go on the SodaStream. I should have checked with Max. I glance at Rainey and she looks up with her sparkly, smiling eyes. I have to take a risk – nothing ventured and all that – and Max will understand. Anyway, it's my flat and Rainey will only stay for a little while. They'll get on like a house on fire. What could go wrong?

When I open the door of the flat, I'm hit by the smell of shit. Dave's crouching in the litter tray, tail twitching, staring innocently.

'Oh, sorry, Rainey. Er, the cat, it's a bit smelly.' I flap the door a little, but she slips through with one sideways step and stands in the narrow hall corridor staring at Dave as he half-heartedly scatters litter granules. They ping against the radiator. He turns, steps out of his tray, shaking one back paw, claps eyes on Rainey, recoils and hisses as if she's Nosferatu.

I smile apologetically, but her eyes are fixed on Dave, who's now backed against the wall, spine arched, tail puffed, growl-hissing.

'What a horrible cat,' she says.

'He's not normally . . . I don't know what's got into him.' I swing my bag at Dave and he scarpers under the coffee table.

'Viv?' Max calls from the living room.

I nod Rainey in the right direction and we step into the room, where Max, in shorts and nothing else, is strumming his guitar in front of the television with the usual unlit cigarette dangling from his mouth.

He looks up at Rainey and smooths his wild hair down a bit. 'Oh, hello,' he says.

'Max, this is Rainey Summers, my, er—'

'I'm Vivienne's birth mother,' says Rainey.

'Unbelievable – we just bumped into each other,' I say, moving to switch off the television.

Max carefully sets down the guitar and stands towering over her. 'Nice to meet you,' he says, offering her a hand to shake.

She smiles but keeps her hands in her sarong. 'I never shake hands because of cross-contamination,' she says.

'Max Kelly,' he says, pulling back the redundant hand. 'Pleased to meet you.'

'That's an Irish accent. Am I right?'

'Dublin.'

'You prefer London?'

'Women keep me here,' he says, catching hold of me as I tidy up. I'm swung off balance and my hand brushes his tanned stomach, low where a line of dark hair disappears. 'Whoa, there, girl – she can't get enough of me!' Max laughs, and Rainey snaps her eyes away.

'Rainey, would you like tea?' I say.

She shakes her head, her eyes moving around the flat and over Max and then to me.

'Cava?' asks Max, and she smiles coyly.

'Well, only if you're having some.'

'I always have a glass about now on a Sunday.' He swaggers off to the kitchen.

'No, he doesn't,' I explain, in case she thinks he's an alcoholic, but she just shrugs and sits in the shabby leather armchair taking in the flat. I scan it myself, looking for anything odd – underpants hanging from the ceiling light maybe – but of course it's just my not-very-cool flat: cheap wood laminate and whitewash with the usual low-level messiness.

'I feel this space has good energy,' Rainey declares finally. 'Which room will be mine?'

'Er, there aren't many rooms as such, but this sofa folds out into a bed.'

'Ah, OK, but I'll need a room of my own. I'm not being selfish, but there are certain rituals I like to perform before bed and in the night that will require total privacy, and I couldn't tolerate an animal in the vicinity.' Her gaze falls to the coffee table, where Dave softly growls in the shadows, eyes glowing like green coals.

'Hmm, that might be tricky . . .'

'The rituals are essential. Some of the mantras will help to ensure the safe arrival of a new life.'

'Oh, I see,' I say, thinking about giving up my bed. I suppose the sofa bed could be more convenient for us at the moment, as I do keep needing the toilet in the middle of the night and I'd be nearer the bathroom and wouldn't disturb Rainey.

Max returns, now wearing a soft cotton shirt and carrying two glasses of cava but nothing for me, I notice.

'I'll have juice,' I tell him, and he turns on his heels back to the kitchen.

'What line of work is your lover involved in?' asks Rainey.

'Oh, call him Max,' I laugh. 'He's an artist.'

'A successful one, mind,' Max adds, as he returns with orange juice. 'I've an exhibition coming up next week.'

'I'm deeply interested in native South American art myself. I was a collector for a short while.'

'Oh yeah?'

'The painter Hernán was a favourite of mine, and I sold many of his works to interior designers in the US.'

'I don't know his work. What kind of artist is he?'

'A dead one. He was shot in Bogotá, Colombia, in 1989. A great shame. His work was easy to sell since he tailored it to suit the interior trends of the time.'

I know Max will hate that idea, because art is a kind of communication with the soul; it's about provoking an emotional response and not to do with interior design. Something like that, anyway. I shoot him a look, but he's listening politely to Rainey's impromptu art class, nodding and smiling along. After a while I have to pee, so I leave them just as Rainey accepts a top-up of cava. I hear her giggling. What a relief they're getting on so well. I nip to the bedroom and pick up clothes, shoes and books. I strip the bed and open the window. I gather up my make-up bag and a pot of hair bobbles and earrings from the dressing table. I empty the condoms from the bedside table, and the book of sexual positions – a joke present from Max. We only tried one, a kind of human knot that made us both fart a lot. I look around. The room looks pleasant enough. Certainly nicer than any hostel could have been. I wonder how much room Rainey will need for her rituals . . . Will she have to jump around or swing stuff? I hope she will stay. I hope she'll be impressed with me, proud even, but I'll settle for just being able to say I know who she is. I dump the sheets into the laundry basket and go back to join them.

'And you're going to be a father,' Rainey is saying. The empty bottle of cava is on the table.

'Yeah.' Max nods, opens his arm out for me and I flop next to him, folding up my legs.

'I'm really feeling you're not prepared for the birth. Do you know what to expect?' she asks, glancing at us.

'Oh, I'm only just getting used to the fact that I'm pregnant!' I glance at Max and laugh. 'Nope, I am not at all prepared for the birth. Are you, Max?'

'Well, from what I've been told, it hurts,' he says, and he smiles and pats my arm.

'Not necessarily,' says Rainey, gazing into the middle distance as if seeing a vision. 'I met a woman in the Australian outback who birthed a baby just walking along, and she'd never had sex.'

'Immaculate conception?' asks Max.

'Artificial insemination,' says Rainey.

'Oh!' I snigger.

'Yes, she was walking to the shop to get those . . . What do you call those brown biscuits you only get in Oz . . . ? No matter. She was going to buy some when she felt something dribbling down her leg, and then whoosh! The baby just washed out. It just surfed right out on its own waters.'

'I've heard of those painless labours,' I say, fascinated.

'And the child – Cody she named him – went on to be the Cottesloe Surf Champion of 1999 and 2000.'

I shake my head with a look on my face that says, 'Unbelievable.'

'Well, I hope I have a labour like that! Painless, I mean, not on the way to the shops.'

Rainey picks up the empty bottle of cava and puts it down again.

'Will I get you another drink?' asks Max.

'In a moment. When I gave birth, aged sixteen, to Vivienne, it was the worst ordeal of my entire life.'

I glance around uncertainly.

'An awkward, bony thing she was.'

Max turns to smile at me.

'I laboured for hours, but she was hooked in like a coat hanger.'

I gulp uncomfortably. 'Oh, I remember Nana saying I was a difficult birth,' I shrug. What does she want from me? Should I apologise?

'What would she know? She wasn't there.'

'She told me she was with you.'

'You were anterior, had to be ripped from me in the end. I was in post-traumatic shock, of course, but nobody had heard of it then, so I was discharged after a week, alone with a child and just a child myself . . .'

'You went home, though? To Nana's?'

'They were ashamed of us, Vivienne – kept us in that back bedroom.'

'I thought you shut yourself away and left me with them.'

'I struggled to feed you even though I had infected milk ducts.'

'Nana always talked about how she bottle-fed me.'

'She can't remember, Vivienne. She makes it up.'

I think of Nana carefully answering my childish questions, always making Rainey seem good, better than the truth.

'Sorry for your pain,' I say stupidly, and Rainey stares at the coffee table as if in a trance. 'Shall we make lunch?'

'Yes!' says Max, standing quickly, and we scuttle off to the kitchen.

'Jesus, your mother is a fucking lunatic!' Max whispers, eyes wide, shoulders hunched.

'I know, but think of her as kooky. She's . . . you know, alternative.' I take a pepper out of the fridge, thinking about soup or maybe ratatouille. I remember buying a courgette. 'Anyway, you gave her the cava. She's probably hammered.'

'She nearly bit my hand off when I offered booze. Oh, she can handle it, all right.'

'Yeah. Can you, though?'

I start chopping an onion, feeling ever so slightly irritated with him.

'Hernán the interior-design artist,' he scoffs, leaning with both elbows over the draining board.

'I knew that would annoy you.'

'Why do people talk to me about art when they don't know what they're talking about?'

'I think it's something about you. Maybe it's your open face, your questioning expression?'

'Yeah . . .' he says, missing the sarcasm.

'Look, I want you to like her,' I say, pouring some oil into a pan and banging it on the gas ring as the stove ticks and a crown of blue flame springs. I fry the onions. 'So will you please try?'

'I'm trying,' he says, turning down the gas. 'Did you not notice?' He kisses my shoulder. 'And I'll keep trying.'

'Thank you very much,' I say, pressing my head back into his chest.

'I am not calling her Rainey, though.'

Next thing, we're shocked by a terrifying wail. We turn and run towards it. Max gets to the doorway of the kitchen first, holding the doorframe to swing himself round. I follow, pushing him in the back, straining to see.

Rainey is on the sofa holding her ankle where three thin red lines are beginning to pinprick with blood.

'That thing attacked me!' she gasps over her shoulder, glowering towards the coffee table where the tip of Dave's tail swishes.

Max drops to his knees and fishes under the table. He drags Dave out by the scruff of his neck; he's puffed up to twice his normal size and hissing as if Rainey is Beelzebub.

'Dave! What the hell's wrong with you?' says Max, carrying the growling furball to the bedroom.

I get a tissue and Rainey dabs at the scratch.

A moment later we hear the door close and Max returns, shaking his head. 'He's never done anything like that before.'

'Are you OK?' I ask Rainey.

'I can't stay here with that brute.'

'Well, he's never like that normally . . .' I look at Max, appealing for back-up.

'You know, he's quite playful. He might have been going after one of your bobbles there.' Max waves a finger at the edging of tiny orange pompoms at the bottom of Rainey's sarong.

'It went for me. It made sure you were gone and then it pounced. You can't have that animal near a pregnant woman, never mind a baby. It's clearly gone mad. You'll have to put it down.' Rainey speaks to her wound, dabbing at the skin and wincing.

I look at Max. He pulls back his head, disgusted.

'We'll . . . we'll talk about it later, Rainey. We'll sort something out, don't worry . . . Shall we have another drink?' I look at Max and widen my eyes.

'I'll get us some wine,' he says.

'Do you have any brandy?' asks Rainey. 'For the shock.'

That night Max, Dave and I are jammed within the narrow metal frame of the sofa bed, Dave purring like a lawnmower. We've . . . Well, actually, I've decided that he's going back to Max's studio in the morning. It's for the best. He was only here by accident. I mean, I never planned to have a cat, and the way he behaved today whenever Rainey came near was an embarrass-ment, yowling and hissing like that.

Max is starting to snore. I lie looking up at the glass ball light-fitting above our heads. It turns anti-clockwise in the draught and back again. I can make out our window reflected in the weak lemon glow from the street. I wonder who it would hit if it fell. I comfort myself, thinking it would be Max, and with his big, tough Irish head, the damage would be minimal. He took it quite well when I broke the news about Rainey staying. He said he's happy if I'm happy, and then he didn't say much, just drank and listened to her. She has a lot of stories, but of course she's spent her life travelling: she knows a lot of things.

I look towards the bedroom, at the strip of light between the floor and door. My mother is in there. She's in my flat. I smile. I'm pleased, like I have a secret precious thing, wrapped in special paper, inside a pretty box – something I've always wanted. She's here, finally, and I will make her fall in love with us. The strip of light disappears. I imagine her settling down to sleep.

Max turns over; his hand rests on my belly. I look at the tanned hand, the raised veins, and then I close my eyes. Vivienne Summers, you are becoming a mother, a wife and a daughter. Wow.

12

Dog-Tired

Take a power nap. In early pregnancy, I was so exhausted by lunchtime at work that I physically needed to sleep, so I did, in the sickroom bed . . . Dawn

Whenever I start to feel drowsy, I down a bottle of water and it wakes me up. Becca

When I feel my eyes starting to droop at work, I do some gentle stretches at my desk. I go to yoga, so I know a few that I can do sitting down. Any movement helps to liven you up if you're tired. Lisa

www.babyandme.com

I gaze at the lined-up traffic from the office kitchen window as the kettle boils. Some guy in a silver Audi unwraps a stick of gum and drops the crumpled wrapper onto the road. It's a still, grey day, but the wind cartwheels his litter the length of three cars.

Why is it permanently windy here? I make three teas, squeezing the tea bags in each cup. Damon hasn't turned up yet, but it's only a matter of time before his heartbeat sensor kicks in and he realises there are life forms in the building and locates us. I pour milk into the tea. Across the front of Damon's mug it says, 'Not just a pretty face.'

When I get to the office door, he's already hovering by Christie's desk. I hand him the tea wordlessly and he takes a sip as I check through emails. I can hardly concentrate on the screen I'm so tired. I didn't really sleep on that tiny bumpy bloody sofa bed with Dave purring and Max snoring in my earhole all night like a whistling rasp. Max left early with Dave in a box and I was able to tell Rainey that Dave was gone, offer it to her like a gift to show how accommodating we can be and make her stay longer. Also without the cat, she might move onto the sofa bed and I can get my bed back. It was great to see her first thing in the morning, though. We've never stayed together in the same house since she left. I sort of hung around her door until she called out asking for warm water with lemon. I had one as well and we sat sipping like any other mother and daughter facing a new day. Except weirder.

'I like your look today, Christie,' Damon is saying. 'Very Autumn/Winter 2012.'

I glance across at Christie. She looks like a cat burglar, all in black – velvet dungarees, Doc Marten boots and a Smurf-like knitted hat; her hair falls in a plaited rope of platinum blonde.

'Are you not a bit warm, though?' I ask, patting my head.

She ignores me, continuing to bat her heavily

mascaraed lashes at Damon, who's talking her language.

'It's all about black leather this season, ain't it?' he's saying.

'I know. I'm saving up for a trouser suit.'

'Hello! If we don't get some work done here, there'll be nothing to save up,' I say, widening my eyes at the screen and chuckling sarcastically to myself. I delete a few messages. Then I find one from Michael. He's free this morning and can call in if we like. I quickly reply, saying yes, please. I hope it's not too late. I want him to help me with my internet research and talk through ideas with him about selling our crackers online. Actually, I want him to build us a website for free. Damon is on the move.

'All right, look, girls, I got to go – I got work to do. Catch you later, all right?'

'OK,' I smile.

'What time?'

'What time what?'

'Shall I catch you later?'

'Er, probably we won't be available for catching later.' I grimace.

'Oh, you have the look of Lady Di when you do that face.'

'What?'

'Doesn't she? When she looks up like that?' he appeals to Christie, who wrinkles her nose and shakes her head. 'OK, see ya, Lady Di.' He waves a palm the size of a spade and closes the door slowly.

'Jesus, we're going to have to factor in at least ten minutes every morning for this fuckery!' I slam a drawer closed for effect. I'm overtired, nauseous and I'm the boss around here.

'Awww, you know, that's the first time I've felt all right with him. I think you're right, Viv – he is just lonely.'

'Look, Christie, shall we get the pictures of the wedding crackers Photoshopped for our website, do you think? Michael is coming in today and we have that big Tease UK meeting coming up. Actually, can you please put a menu together – you know, with all the different cracker contents – and work out the costs?'

'All right,' she says, sulkily tilting her head and then disappearing behind her screen.

I yawn and stretch. God, I'm tired. My eyes feel like two dry marbles rolling in sand. I google 'tiredness in pregnancy': something about a comfy bed, a milky drink, a calm home. I scroll down. Aha! What's this? 'Ask your boss if you can install a camp bed at work for cat naps, play music at regular times throughout the day and dance with your bump to re-energise.' I imagine mentioning camp beds and cat naps to my old boss, Snotty. That would be hilarious. But now I'm the boss, so it's camp beds and musical interludes a go-go, starting now. I click on Spotify and blast out 'If You Wanna Come Back' by the Vaccines. Christie frowns over her laptop.

'Dance time, Christie!'

She gets up, comes around her desk into the space where I'm throwing shapes and joins in with slow jerking movements, her face deadpan. When the track ends, we go back to our desks.

'Ohhh,' I sigh, as I sit down, pink-cheeked and a bit out of breath. 'That's better.'

Just then I hear a noise like a bluebottle made of metal trapped under a board. Christie and I look at each other. It starts up again, in three bursts, a really horrible, unbearable sound.

'What the hell is that?'

'Is it a fire alarm?'

'That would be a continuous ring . . .'

'Someone's buzzing us, Viv,' she says.

We look at the wall where the plastic intercom box vibrates.

'Of course! It must be Michael.' I rush to lift the receiver. 'Dream Team PR. How can I help you?'

'Hi. I'm looking for Vivienne Summers.'

'Speaking?'

'Hey, doll face, it's Mike.'

'Michael, Mike . . . Come up to the third-floor corner office.' I press every button on the plastic box and hang up nonchalantly. I wipe my palms down the front of my trousers, smile and open the door. The lift clanks and groans. I hear the cage door crash open.

'Mike? This way,' I call, already getting a whiff of patchouli, and then there he is, wearing his shiny grey suit and synthetic shoes. His hair is slicked off his thin white face, giving him a widow's peak Dracula would be proud of. He's kept the strange facial hair, I notice, complete with rat-tail beard. He stops when he sees me, then breaks into a kind of robotic dance ending in a handshake.

'Great to see you, Mike!' I say overenthusiastically.

He points a finger-gun at Christie and fires. 'Baby doll, hiya,' he says, and she smiles from her desk.

'You look great! How are you?' I ask.

'I'm well, Viv.' He nods knowingly. The last time we saw each other was his disastrous engagement party in Soho, when his fiancée (my other former boss, Mole) didn't turn up and I had to get him home. He cried and propositioned me, but it's all in the past.

'So would you like tea, coffee?'

'No . . . I think we can get straight to the coalface.'

'OK.' I motion for him to sit at my desk and I take one of the non-swivel chairs. He bounces his legs, leaning back. 'Well, Michael, there are a couple of things I want to pass by you,' I begin, and then I tell him about the sex-themed crackers while he takes notes, draws arrows, exclamation marks and what looks like a bum on his pad.

At the end he double-thumps a fist over his heart and says, 'I'm on board.'

'Well, just to be clear, it's a piece of freelance work we're offering here, not a job.' I smile.

'Look, you need me. I need a job. Let's put our skills on the table and make a party.'

'We do need you, but there isn't a party or really a job.'

'You're looking at a highly skilled web designer and talented programmer here. Guys like me don't rock up every day.' He jiggles in the chair.

'We don't have any money, though,' I say, 'or customers.' God, when I put it as baldly as that, it's actually terrifying.

'I'll tell you what you do have, though – po-ten-tial. With me on board, you will fly, guaranteed.'

'Yeah, I'm sure, and don't get me wrong, I'd love to have you, but I was talking about a piece of work for us. We just can't pay you for more, or really pay you. At all.'

He raises his arms, making a cradle for the back of his head with his hands, and smiles. I look at him and he raises his eyebrows. His little black eyes flick from my face to the door.

'Why aren't you at Barnes and Worth anymore?'

'Personal reasons.' His knees begin to tap together.

'Because of Mole?'

He sighs. 'Marion, yes, she who threw my heart down like a scrap of offal for the wolves.' Christie pulls a face over the top of the laptop. I adopt what

I hope is a concerned/interested face. 'And now she's all like "I want to see you" and I'm like "The relationship is dead and buried, sister, after that engagement humiliation" and she's like "I have to have you. I must have you," popping up at the office and bawling her eyes out. Following me, sending love notes with bodily hair Sellotaped in. So I left. I'm nobody's sex toy, Vivienne. I'm not into sexual harassment. That's just not how I roll.'

'No, that's understandable. The thing is, Mike, unless you can work for free until we get some clients—'

'I'm in.'

'In what?'

'I'll work for you for a month for free, and if you get a client, you pay me, but if you don't, I'm gone.'

'Why would you do that? A talented guy such as yourself could have a top job like that.' I snap my fingers.

'I like you, Vivienne. I never forget a good turn. I remember what you did that night in Soho. I was in bits at my own engagement party and you were the one who got me home.' He narrows his eyes and I swear I can hear spaghetti-western music.

'It was nothing . . .'

'The way you put me in the taxi and your thoughtful engagement gift – I still use that spice donkey, by the way, for my fish food. Well, I'll always remember what you did that night.'

'Ha, ha. Really, it was nothing . . .'

'I know, but I'm down on my luck and I need something to do. Just one thing, though?'

'What?'

'When you pay me, it's fifty pounds an hour and that's mates' rates, and if you don't pay and I go, I take down any sites I've built and all my design property.'

'Done,' I say, offering my hand. In a month, if we have no clients, we won't be needing any sites or design property. The craziness of this situation is strangely liberating.

'Well then, let's ride this thing until the wheels fall off!' he says, and we high-five to seal it.

13

Correct Nutrition for Building a Person

Yes! Muesli, wholemeal bread, raw organic vegetables, tofu, fresh fruit, poultry, cooked white fish, yoghurt, nut spreads, fresh well-cooked eggs.
No! Processed food, fatty food, salt, sugar, unpasteurised milk and cheese.

Your Baby, November issue

I return to the flat just after six, hoping to have time for a rest. It's the opening night of Max's exhibition this evening. I'm going down to the gallery later to be supportive. I'll probably stand beside him and smile lovingly at him, that sort of thing. I can't wait, but my legs feel like lead. If I could just lie down for half an hour . . . As I kick off my shoes, I'm hit with a cloud of pungent incense, and I step into the living room to find Rainey sitting cross-legged on the floor next to a tiny silver bell. Her hands rest on her knees, thumbs and forefingers pinched together like little 'o's. Her grey silk harem pants are low cut, and she wears a short, fitted Indian-style top, showing a swathe of loose belly skin. The furniture has been rearranged – the sofa is now against the far wall, and the television is covered with a green patterned sarong – and there's a huge cheese plant by the kitchen door. I walk past her, but her closed eyes don't even flutter. I wait in front of her. The sun streams a halo around her hair; her eyelids shimmer pale green; she silently mouths some sort of chant, her lips repeatedly making the same shapes, nostrils flaring with each in-breath.

'Hello?' I say softly. No response.

I flop onto the sofa and lie on my back. My legs throb. I raise them up onto the arm of the sofa. I lift my shirt and undo the improvised hair-bobble fastening on my trousers. The skin of my belly is taut for the first time in my life. There's a noticeable bump now, I think, if you really look. It looks like a baby rather than too many takeaways. A baby growing in there! How incredible is that? I hold both hands over it and breathe out, long and slow, trying a bit of meditation myself. After a few goes, I turn my head back to Rainey. Her lips move quickly. I squint at her, trying to lip-read. Amber beaver? Satin amber beaver? Big brown beaver? I don't know. I kind of wish she'd open her eyes now and make me a cup of tea and maybe a sandwich. What has she been doing all day, I wonder, apart from rearranging my flat and buying big cheese plants?

I look at the ceiling, thinking about that green wraparound dress I wore at Lucy's wedding. I'll wear it tonight. I think it suits me. It fits.

'Ommm,' Rainey says quietly. 'Ommm.' Then she picks up the silver bell, it tinkles prettily, and her eyes snap open, the colours like galaxies, whole universes in there. 'Vivienne.' She smiles.

'Hi.' I lift a hand to wave and let it flop. 'I am absolutely knackered. My clothes don't fit. My work life makes no sense at all, even to me. I must have tea and something to do with cheese.'

She stands, seeming to draw herself up by her head, and disappears into the kitchen on her dancer's feet. I feel relaxed and heavy, teetering on the edge of sleep. She returns, handing me an orange-coloured drink. I take a sip. Carrot juice, quite nice.

'With proper nourishment, you won't feel tired or sick,' she says, dropping like a severed puppet onto the floor beside me. 'The women of Patagonia don't suffer in pregnancy like Western women, mainly due to their diet.'

I close my eyes and laugh to myself. 'Oh, what do they know? They aren't running businesses selling sex crackers, are they? They're just sitting around, occasionally going on foraging duty.' I lift up my head to peer at her. 'Thanks for the juice, though. What have you been doing today?'

'Viv, you're an idiot if you don't take nutrition seriously.'

'I do take nutrition—'

'You think it's all flimflam.'

'Flim—'

'You think I'm full of mumbo-jumbo.'

'No.' I sit up, confused.

'You are wrong about Patagonian women, but anyway . . .' She looks away. The side of her mouth twitches.

I don't know what to say. We sit in silence for a few seconds.

'Well . . .' I begin.

'You asked what I've been doing today. I've been sorting out the flow of chi in this apartment,' she says, glancing sideways at me.

'Thank you. That's very . . . It looks really cool. I like the big old plant there.'

'And you may like to know I've stocked the fridge with vegan power foods to nurture the baby. Have you had any cravings?'

'Cravings? Yeah. I have a strong yen for cheese, but also meat and chocolate constantly.'

She tuts.

'You need protein. I'm making my vegan tofu stir-fry for supper.'

'Wonderful . . . Ah, thing is, I'm going out. It's Max's opening night at the gallery, so I think there'll be nibbles there.'

'Nibbles? Well, OK, then, Vivienne, you know best,' she sighs sadly, getting up and floating away.

'No, I don't! I don't know anything! Please can I have the tofu?'

She half turns and looks at me with pursed lips.

'I want tofu!' I cry, and that's a sentence I never thought I'd say.

It's chilly out and already getting dark. Piles of leathery leaves are gathered by the kerbside, and I shiver in a denim jacket that won't meet over my breasts. I take the Tube to Westbourne Park and, following Max's directions, find the gallery a couple of streets away, on the corner of a street filled with expensive-looking houses. It's small and exclusive, beautiful with shiny green paintwork and huge sparklingly clean windows. A poster of one of the red-brown abstracts is displayed on the door: 'Max Kelly' is printed in plain black capitals, 'Mountain and Plain. Reception for the artist Monday 15 October, 8–10 p.m.'

Seeing that poster, I feel suddenly vulnerable for him and for me, as if we ourselves are on display, open to inspection and therefore rejection. I smooth down the front of the magic green dress, check my flicky black eyeliner in the glass, hoping I'll be worthy, and then open the door. A bell rings softly and I hear voices coming from another room out of sight, up a couple of steps. I smell polish and coffee. I move to inspect the row of abstracts hanging on the white-painted brick wall in front of me, my brogues tapping on the solid oak floor. The paintings are well lit, the shadow and light picking up on the layers and textures. I peer at the information. '*Solo*, Max Kelly, acrylic on canvas, £2,000.' Then somewhere I hear his voice, followed by his big loud laugh. I follow the sound, up the steps, into another small gallery and there he is in his gallery uniform: long legs in black jeans, black crew neck that was drying on our kitchen radiator yesterday, mad black beard trimmed, wild hair combed and gelled into submission, looking so achingly cool and lovely that I suddenly feel I've no right to him and should shuffle back into the shadows and leave him with the beautiful people. One of those beautiful people has her porcelain hand on his forearm right now, her cherry-red lips close to his ear. He's looking at the floor, all smiles, listening. He nods and takes a sip of champagne.

He lifts his head. 'Ah,' he says, and his dark eyes glance her way and then they turn onto me and it's like being plugged into a power source. 'Viv!' he says, and flashes his chipped-tooth-pirate smile. 'Excuse me,' he says to the beauty, and he walks over to me with his big bear walk and puts his arm around me. 'You OK?' He kisses me, squeezes my shoulder. 'What do you think?'

'Amazing,' I say, and he nods excitedly. I turn to him, putting my face close to his, trying to shut out everyone else. 'I fancy you like mad. I'm so proud. You are getting it later fo sho.' I look at the crinkles at the corner of his eye, the handsome groove his smile makes on his cheek.

'Are you OK to hand out drinks to people?' He pats my bottom.

'Show me the tray.'

'Champagne or orange juice, all up here. Come on, I'll introduce you.'

I follow him back to the group, arranging my face into a polite smile, aware of the interest of the beautiful girl, who I now notice looks familiar. I see her eyes slide down to my shoes and back to my hair, and when she looks away, I check her out. Long, glossy dark hair, short curled-under fringe, amazing eyes, better flicky eyeliner than mine, red heart-shaped mouth, skinny, midnight-blue tunic dress, unbuttoned to show lace undergarment, shiny gold leggings, studded ballet pumps.

'Vivienne, this is Lula,' Max introduces us. 'Lula's one of my models.'

'Oh yes, hello! I thought you looked familiar.' I smile. 'I recognise you from the painting, only now you have clothes on, of course. Ha, ha! Nice dress, by the way.'

'Hi there,' she says, and looks at Max in a way that I don't like – proprietorially.

'Lula, please be nice to Viv,' scolds Max flirtily. I look to the next person in line and try to ignore Lula. Why wouldn't she be nice to me?

'Guy,' says Max to a tall man who has the look of Chewbacca, 'here's my girl Vivienne Summers.' The man shakes my hand. 'Vivienne, Guy owns the gallery.'

'Good to meet you, Vivienne,' he says.

'Thank you. Nice to meet you, and thanks so much

for having Max's exhibition here.' Is that an OK thing to say, or do I sound like Max's mother?

'He's a great talent. We're lucky to have him.' We stand smiling at each other for an awkward moment. I feel hot. Max is distracted by another man and has his back to me.

'He is a great talent,' I repeat.

'He is, he is,' says Guy.

'So have you had the gallery for long?' I ask.

'About four years now.'

'Good, good, and who cleans your windows?'

'Uh, just a local guy.'

I laugh, but Guy doesn't. I gaze around the room.

'And how's business? They say art is recession-proof, don't they?' I ask. Yes, good one. Luckily Guy is a pro: he talks about art and his gallery for a long time, filling in all gaps with little stories until I'm called away to sort the drinks and I don't have to ask any more questions, which is good because the only thing I could think of was to ask for the window cleaner's number.

Max is mingling with guests in the main room while I hand glasses of champagne to people, nice people, and try not to get into a conversation with anyone. I can't think of a single thing to say. It's nerve-wracking. I'm worried I might just blurt out something shocking, and also the damned tofu stir-fry is repeating on me.

Each time I pass Max, I try to catch his eye, but he's always deep in conversation about paint/emotion, et cetera. I know he's trying to sell paintings, but I'd thought we'd be more together. As it is, I'm actually a waitress here. It's really filling up as well. I make a loop with my tray and go by Max again, thinking I'll just get a sniff of him or maybe a quick feel, but there's Lula standing with him. They're talking to a little elderly lady and laughing, and Lula has her hand on Max's arm again. As I approach, Max takes a glass of champagne from my tray, gives it to Lula, winks at me, and carries on chatting. I open my mouth, beginning to say something. Then, seeing his shoulder turned towards Lula, I close it again.

I know he has to schmooze, but why does she have to hang off him? Why isn't she giving out the drinks and I can be the one who does the hanging-off? I linger next to them, shooting looks at Lula, but she ignores me knowingly out of the corner of her eye, and then I have to circulate because someone at the back is saying, 'Where's that funny little waitress with the drinks?' I go around the room for most of the evening, and every time I pass Max, she's with him. I feel a ball of fury growing inside.

Eventually the crowd begins to thin and I've handed out the last bottle of fizz. My very bones feel heavy. I'm sitting in the little back office, with my puffy ankles up, thinking about undoing my bra, which is really digging in.

Max bobs his head around the door. 'There you are. We're off for a curry. Come on.'

'A curry? What, now?' I pull a face. I thought that was it. I thought I'd done my supportive bit and was looking forward to having Max all to myself again, and also to having a right go at him about his flirting/ignoring.

'Everyone's starving.'

'Who's everyone?'

'Me, Guy, Lula . . .'

'I don't want to.' I look away and rub my ankle.

He sits opposite me and takes my feet onto his lap. 'Come on, beauty – you have to.'

'No, I don't.'

'You do because I need you.'

'Why, are they short of waitresses at the curry house? Or do you need me to serve drinks to your lover!' I know this is completely jealous, over the top and not at all what a cool chick like me should be saying, but I've lost control. He smiles and looks down.

'My "lover"? What are you on about, Viv?'

'Old wasp hips in there. Don't tell me there's nothing between you two.'

'You mean Lula?'

'She's all over you.' I shake my head bitterly. 'What I can't understand is why you brought me here. Was it to humiliate me?'

'Viv, stop being a total loon.' He actually laughs then, in my face.

'Loon, am I? Might I remind you I'm the loon

who's having your baby!' I hear my own voice screeching, then hearing laughter from the gallery, I shout-whisper, 'I'm the loon you proposed to!' I take my feet off his lap, making a show of putting on my shoes.

'What are you doing?'

'I'm going home! I'm not your muggins!'

He says nothing. He watches as I fasten laces and straighten myself up. I'm about to flounce out, but I imagine myself heading home alone, leaving Lula to comfort him. A little sliver of doubt makes me hesitate. I stand staring at him and he stares at me.

'Vivienne,' he says softly.

I shake my head and look away.

'Come on, Viv – you know I only have eyes for you.'

'Funny way of showing it,' I mutter sulkily.

'Come for a curry. I'll hold your hand the whole time.' He stands behind me now and rubs my neck. I let him. 'We won't be long. You know you love curry . . .'

'I don't feel good,' I snap.

'Poppadums? Little tray of pickles? A pakora?'

I don't answer. He kisses my shoulder.

'*Get pakora now. Get onion bhaji now.*' Angel has woken up.

'Don't be jealous,' says Max.

I turn to face him. 'I am not jealous!' I say indignantly,

pointing at my own chest, but I look at his eyes and glimpse our friendship and our love and realise I'm very jealous indeed of the willowy Lula and I will concede that I might even be overreacting. Question is, how can I get out of it now?

'Viv, you have no competition,' he says, holding his palms out to the side, like he's pleading with a knife-wielder.

'Huh! She's your muse!'

'No, you're my muse,' he says.

'Am I?' I ask, thrilled.

'You know you are.'

'I was once upon a time, but maybe now that you've conquered me . . .'

'You always have been and always will be.' He smiles.

'Well, then –' I wince and bang my forehead against his chest '– sorry.'

'I shouldn't neglect you,' he says, stroking my hair.

'Tonight was your big deal.'

'Such a big deal and no sales.'

'There will be sales. You're a great talent, Guy said.' I kiss him, but he doesn't respond as usual; he breaks off first.

'I'm a very, very hungry talent,' he says, 'so will you please just come for a curry?'

We leave the Star of India close to midnight and I've learned a couple of things:

1. *People who are drunk are not hilarious; rather, they are repetitive and loud and only think they are hilarious. I obviously believed Max was an absolute scream because I was always drinking when he was. Now pregnant and sober, I see the light.*
2. *Lula is thick as mince.*

We get home and climb the stairs to the flat with Max trying to sing 'I'm in the Mood for Love' and me shushing him. After I unlock the door, I turn round and hold my hand over his mouth.

'Shh, shut up. Please do not wake Rainey,' I say.

'Rainey, Rainey, give me your answer do,' he sings. I close the door. 'What're you doing? Let's go to bed. I'm going to give you the spanking of your life.'

'I'm not opening the door unless you promise to be quiet.'

'OK, O-K,' he says.

I turn the key and open the door a crack. He draws a huge breath in as if he's going to shout and I spin round, holding the key up to his face like a weapon.

'Joke!' he says, grinning and swaying.

We stumble inside, me supporting Max, him repeating, 'Shh!' I steer him into the living room and set about organising the sofa bed with Max watching.

'Viv, Viv, Vivienne!'

'What?'

'Can I go to the toilet, please?'

'No.'

'Come on! I have to pee.'

'Go on, then, but be quiet,' I whisper.

He clomps away. The door bangs, then a shout – something like 'Ho!' – and then a screech.

'What in the name of unholy hell!' Max is bellowing.

I run to the bathroom. Rainey stands under the fluorescent light clutching a hand towel to herself, her hair wild, her face covered in some sort of white cream.

'Fuck me, I thought the place was haunted!' laughs Max, swaying and unzipping his fly. 'By a mad, naked she-ghost!'

Rainey shoots me a mortified look and flees the bathroom.

'Sorry!' I call to her bare bottom as she slams the door.

14

The Thoughts and Opinions of Rainey Summers

Deodorant gives you cancer.
All food should be braised in water or raw.
Smoking roll-ups means you are on the road to drug addiction.
All life on Earth is spiritually connected.
Meat is destroying the planet.
The spiky plant named George in the bedroom was killing good energy flow with its dagger leaves.
Money grows on trees.

Time flies when you're having fun. The sofa bed now fills us with dread. Thinking about it, I realise it's never been a very good sofa and is actually the opposite of a bed, in that it's almost impossible to sleep on, especially with a six-foot-two Irishman. I hate everything about it: the creak of the unfolding springs, the baggy fitted sheet and the mean, thin scrap of mattress. But as I explained to Max, it's only for a short time, and I think he sees that having Rainey here with me is important since I must have some kind of relationship with her before Angel is born, hence it's worth all the discomfort.

Rainey has taken it upon herself to ensure that I have the correct nutrition. She's preparing snacks using crushed-up rice crackers, nuts and molasses, and putting them in my bag with notes saying things like, 'This is a really lovely day – congratulations!' I won't say I don't sometimes crave a bacon sandwich, but on the whole I feel a lot healthier. We've managed to have a couple of talks and I think we're getting to know each other. Not close enough to ask who my father is or to find out why she left, but we'll get to that.

There is a little bit of an atmosphere developing between Rainey and Max. Yesterday when he refused to eat the braised lettuce with mung bean stroganoff, she suggested he go out and find himself some Irish stew. Then he asked if she might feel happier staying somewhere else, and I had to tell him off and make him say that she is very welcome, because Rainey locked herself in her room and started chanting. I think Max is under a lot of pressure and worried because he hasn't sold any of his Spanish paintings. I'm trying not to think about that, though. I know he is a great talent, and today I have an important meeting with Tease UK, and also Lucy is back from honeymoon. I'm meeting her for dinner, and this time I will definitely tell her I'm pregnant. There's never going to be a right time, and I think I'm starting to show anyway. To be honest, it'll be a relief to be out of the flat for an evening.

The head offices of Tease UK are in Guildford. Michael, Christie and I take the train down from Waterloo, going through the products, the costings, looking at the market until we feel that the people at Tease are in on the opportunity of a lifetime. Wedding crackers are going to be huge.

'Who are we meeting with, man or woman?' asks Michael.

'One of their buyers, Sarah Marshall.'

'Well, that's good. There is nothing I can't sell to a girl.'

He sits opposite me tapping a pen against his pointy little teeth. He's in his one and only suit – pale grey, slightly shiny – with a thin purple tie. Christie sits beside him in a demure gold dress with a Peter Pan collar. She seems buoyed up by his enthusiasm, or else she's just taken something in the toilets: she's wide-eyed and alert in a new way.

'Ha! What do you think their offices will be like? Do you reckon there'll be a bondage room where they test all their products?' I ask, smoothing down the skirt of my coming-in-very-useful green dress.

'No,' says Michael, holding up a hand, 'I've got it. Their waiting room, right, will be furnished entirely with their range of furniture: cunnilingus hammocks, ass-thwacking stools and bondage beds made up in their own range of black satin bed linen.' He waves an open palm in an arc. 'And all the light fittings, yeah, will be made entirely from dildos.'

'And will there be naked dwarf slaves running about?' I ask.

'Hey, whatever floats your boat,' says Michael, sitting back.

Christie does a little breathless laugh through her nose. 'And there'll be a desk and Sarah will be sat at it!'

'I fucking hope so, Christie – she's meeting with us!' says Michael, and titters in his strange way, ending in a bray.

'No, I was going to say she'll be sat there hand-cuffed.'

Michael frowns, then sniffs and takes to gazing out of the window. I smile reassuringly at Christie.

The meeting actually takes place in a shabby out-of-town office block. Sarah Marshall leads us to a gloomy meeting room, a small cordoned-off space with polystyrene tiles on the partition walls. Sarah is quite overweight, but her brown V-neck top is slim. She leads us up a few steps and sits breathlessly at the table. I notice the pointed toes of her high-heeled boots are misshapen, sticking up like the ends of two organic turnips. There's not a harness or a sling to be seen; it's just dry and grey and slightly dusty in here. A scribbled note stuck on the wall reads, 'Leave this space clean and clear of clutter, thank you!' and underneath someone has written, 'What you looking', which is absolutely maddening, because

I keep reading it over and over and wondering what it means.

'Before we start, let me give you a brief outline of the kind of company Tease UK is,' says Sarah, as if reading a script in a very camp voice. 'Tease UK started as one woman's dream of bedroom fulfilment in the late 1990s and very quickly mushroomed into the multi-national company you know today.' I raise my eyebrows to look amazed, even though we read this information already, on their website. 'We have fifty stores in the UK alone, with plans to double that number by the end of the year, and last year we had an annual turnover of just under fifty million.'

'Well, you're impressing the shit out of me right now!' says Michael.

Sarah stops for breath and glances at him with the hint of a smile. 'We manufacture a lot of our own products, but occasionally we do buy from other companies. We're interested in sex toys, lingerie and party accessories, but we also look for innovative bedroom furniture design and sex-themed bed linen. Now it's over to you guys to tell me how you think your product fits in to our vision,' she finishes, pressing her lips together carefully.

I feel my heart bump up against my ribcage in shock. It's me. I'm on.

'Thank you, Sarah, for that informative outline and for giving us the opportunity to meet with you today,' I begin, noticing her eyes flicking from me to Michael, her lips remaining pressed as I introduce our products. 'What we have to show you today is a range that I think will fit very well with your party accessories line,' I say, taking out a holdall and placing my hand on the zip.

I go through our planned sales pitch, although we ad-lib a little. Christie gushes over the photos of the crackers on a wedding table. Michael pulls a cracker with Sarah so she can get the full experience. He blows the bubbles from the mini penises at her while she's looking at the profit margins and she bats them out of her face with a little giggle. Then she says she'll let us know, thanks us for coming, and escorts us out into the windswept, traffic-tangled overflow of Guildford.

As the train drags us London-bound again, I run through the meeting in my mind. Our presentation was OK, I think. We were professional and yet not too dry. We were approachable and yet on the ball, and now we'll have to wait and see, but I hope to God they buy. I hope they do. Under the table, I cross my fingers, and putting my hand near to my tummy, I realise that I'm completely starving and look down the aisle for the buffet cart.

'Did you see that girl?' asks Michael. 'She wanted me.'

'You mean Sarah?' asks Christie.

'Yeah, I mean Sssaraaah. I love big women.' He jiggles in his seat.

'I don't think she wanted you – how could you tell?' Christie scrunches up her face.

'I pick up vibes,' he says, wiggling his fingers in her face. 'From you, nothing.'

'What about me?' I ask, and he does the finger thing in my direction.

'Very weak, hardly anything.'

'Who here fancies a cream tea?' I say, spotting the man with a trolley.

'Viv, you're not on the Orient Express. "Cream tea?"' scoffs Christie, and she's right: I end up with a paper cup of weak tea and a bag of Mini Cheddars.

'Probably for the best, though,' she says, as I cram as many Mini Cheddars into my mouth as will fit and, when they suck all moisture from my tongue, take a slurp of tea.

'How do you mean?'

'Well –' her eyes shoot to my waist '– you know.'

I put down the tea. 'Go on,' I say.

'You've put on a bit, haven't you?'

I stare at Christie until she starts to fidget.

'I mean, you still look OK . . .' she begins.

'For your information, Christie, I'm having a baby,' I say proudly.

'What, you're . . .?'

'Up the duff,' I nod.

'So you've . . .?'

'Got a bun in the oven,' I say.

'But how . . .?'

'Well, what you have to do is somehow get live sperm. I did it by the traditional method, but you don't have to nowadays . . .' I begin to explain.

'Vivienne, are you having a baby?' interrupts Michael, pulling out his iPod earphones.

'Yes! Look, gather round, team. I am having a baby in April. The father is Max. We're engaged.'

Christie looks at my left hand, at my face, and then closes her mouth.

I carry on with the Mini Cheddars.

'How's the morning sickness?' asks Michael.

'Well, I find it OK if I just keep eating,' I say with my mouth full.

'Sepia,' says Michael, nodding knowingly.

'You don't want an Aries baby, Viv. Wilful they are, selfish.' Christie shakes her head, worried.

'You don't get to choose, Christie. That's those zodiac teddies you're thinking of.'

'Couple of drops of Sepia 30 will sort sickness out.'

'I didn't know you were into homeopathy,' I say to him.

'No!' says Christie, turning to study Michael. 'I would have sworn you were straight,' she says.

'Tee-hee,' Michael says sarcastically, pressing his fingers to his lips. 'Ha, ha, bonk,' he says without smiling. 'I am literally laughing my head off.'

15

Facebook

Eve Summers Greetings from Santorini! Viv, you must come here one day. It is the most romantic place. Reg started quoting love poems, but the spinach falafel has given him terrible wind and it put us off a bit. It has been an amazing trip, but I miss you so much – more since hearing your news. We just can't stop talking about you and the baby and what a happy ending it is when you thought you'd lost Max. We both think you're having a boy, and Reg thinks Lawrence would be a lovely name, after Granddad, but you know, Granddad hated being Lawrence and was known as 'Lol', and I said you can't saddle a baby with that in this day and age, lol. See what I did there?

I hope you are managing OK with your mother. Don't forget – no matter how charming she can be, she's really a completely selfish cowbag. As long as you know that, you'll be fine. I'll call soon.

Lol (lots of love) your ever-loving Nana x

Thursday at 4.21 p.m.

Lucy rings that afternoon and suggests we meet at the well-being centre just off the Edgware Road and 'go from there'. When I ask about the honeymoon, she says she can't talk, she has work to do and she's sure I have as well, and she'll see me at six-thirty.

That's why I'm mooching around the reception area of this centre of well-being, picking up and putting down leaflets and wondering if the spherical water feature is actually a new-age drinking fountain. Against the wall is a sofa and side table where a little oil burner spits and hisses menthol vapour. Tinkling music rises and falls. A staircase to the left is signposted 'Reception.' I peer up before turning back to the door and looking down the street for Lucy, but there's no sign of her. A bus that had been blocking the view of the pavement opposite moves off and a huge McDonald's restaurant is revealed like a spaceship, all glass and lights. Someone familiar is in there.

Is that . . . Rainey?

Is that her? I can't really see her face, but the hair, the red streak, the turquoise and green scarf, it bloody is. Rainey is sitting at a window seat in McDonald's finishing off a burger, eating as if she's ravenous, taking great shark bites.

'God!' I whisper, and my breath steams the window. My heart leaps with the betrayal of it. My mind casts around for an explanation as I stare. That fraudster! That liar! She crumples up the burger wrappings, still chewing, and makes to leave. I rush to the door of the well-being centre, planning to confront her, but as she leaves the restaurant, another bus whooshes in and one rumbles out of the bus stop and she's gone, leaving me thinking I imagined her.

'Vegan, my eye,' I mutter, glaring after the bus, but then Lucy appears, pulling gurning faces through the window. We hug on the doorstep. Over her shoulder I scan the street for Rainey, but she's vanished.

'Miss Summers!' declares Lucy.

'Ah, I can smell the sunshine,' I say into her perm-frizzled hair. I pull back to look at her. Her face and arms are golden and smooth; her teeth seem whiter, eyes sparklier. The dress is new: I know all her clothes and I haven't seen that before. 'Was it great?'

'Dude, it was sublime!'

'It lived up to the brochure?'

'All I'll say is that every evening we watched the sun set over the beach, drinking champagne in our private jacuzzi.'

'Wow.'

'Wow is right, and we really got into tantric sex, and I'm not joking, dude, he made me come with his eyes.'

'But how did he get . . . ? What?' I have a mental image of detachable eyeballs.

'Anyway, dude . . .' She drags me over to the sofa and I wonder where she picked up this new 'dude' thing. We perch on the edge of the seat and Lucy places her hands on my knees. 'Guess what? I'm pregnant!' she squeaks. 'I mean, it's early days – I'm only just pregnant, four weeks – but I'm so fucking happy.' She thumps the sofa.

I'm just drawing breath to congratulate and hug her when she grabs my hand and starts dragging me up the staircase. 'Come on, I have to register for the pregnancy-yoga class here: it's the best in London, and if you don't book early, there's no chance of a place.'

We register and Lucy doesn't question why I would want to too, presuming that I want to support her, I guess. She's so excited about everything that I can't find a way to tell her my news.

Out on the street, we talk disjointedly as if we're being washed down rapids: bobbing up for air and shouting things. She says, 'Let's eat some lamb tagine!' and I shout out, 'I'm engaged!' and we whirl around, with her saying, 'I'll be pregnant at your wedding!' and me saying, 'I told you you'd be pregnant!' and her shouting, 'You're engaged!' We end up in a cute, crazily tiled little Moroccan place she knows, and she tells me the full eye-popping details of the honeymoon, which I'll summarise for you here: they did it under a beach towel, underwater, underground, up a tree, up the bum, up against a wall, and upside down.

'Isn't it weird being out and not having wine?' she asks. 'You can have some, though, Viv. I'll just sniff it.'

'Actually, I can't drink either,' I say, watching her.

She looks up sharply. 'Because . . .'

'Because . . . I'm pregnant too.' I pull a goofy face.

She looks at me and blinks. Her eyes glisten. She sniffs. 'Oh!' she says, and fans her face with her hands. 'Sorry, I'm really happy. I'm just so happy.'

I smile as if only just realising it's true – I am pregnant. I am happy. In my mind's eye, I'm extremely slim, wearing a long floaty cardigan and spooning custard into a cherub.

'How many weeks?' Lucy asks.

'Er, fourteen or fifteen? I'm rubbish at knowing,' I say.

'So have you had your three-month scan?'

'No. When I booked in at the doctor's they offered me that, but you have to pay, so we decided not to.'

She looks doubtful, then worried.

'I'm not private like you. You probably already had a scan,' I laugh.

'Not yet, but soon. Hold on, you conceived three months ago?'

'About that.'

'Is it Max's?' she whispers.

'Oh yeah, definitely – don't worry.'

'You were pregnant at my wedding?'

'Yeah.' She's going to praise me now for being such a great mate and going through with the pole dance.

'But, dude, you were drinking?'

'I had two champagnes all day.'

'You can't take risks like that! No alcohol.'

So maybe not praise, then.

'Well, you know what? It was my best friend's wedding and it was fine,' I tell her.

She takes a sip of her mineral water, eyeing me thoughtfully. 'I can't believe it.' She shakes her head. 'I thought you were acting weird. Well, weirder.'

'Hmm.' I lean back. 'It's getting hard now – this dress is the only thing that fits.' I stick out my bump and she gasps at the size of it. 'This'll be you in a few weeks,' I tell her.

'Oh God –' she stares at my belly '– you look like you're smuggling a giant Easter egg.'

'I'm what they call "glowing". Look, what do you know about maternity clothes? I need to get me some of those! Cheap ones, mind,' I add, and we decide to go shopping, and she says she'll buy some things too that I can wear now and give back to her when she's beginning to show.

'Joint maternity clothes,' I say. 'Brilliant.'

'My style, though – I know what you're like.'

I agree because I know Lucy thinks I have crazy dress sense. This all stems from the time I started sporting this brown paisley flannelette shirt – Lucy doesn't get irony, or anything without a collar to stick up. In any case, if she's going to buy clothes for me, I'm on board.

'So my mother has moved in with us.' I drop this in casually.

She shakes her head, then bangs her forehead into

her hands. 'You won't learn, will you? I can't say anything to you. You're like a stubborn bloody mule.'

'Neigh,' I say, knowing that's the wrong sound. What do mules say? Shouldn't I know these things in my position as mother-to-be? 'She is so fucking annoying! But on the plus side, Max and I are embracing a vegan lifestyle, and we're really learning a lot about South America.' I'm not telling Lucy about McDonald's – I'm still taking it in myself. Seeing Rainey today has made all the small irritations and minor annoyances of having her to stay come together in a big ball, and right now it's hard to swallow. I must swallow the ball. I must.

'Aggh, I can't listen. She just . . . doesn't deserve it!'

'No, look, I have a clear plan. I'm going to get to know her now before Angel is born. Even if she is a pain in the arse.'

'She's poisonous.'

'Even if she's poisonous, and it will either work, which is great because then she can be in the baby's life, or it won't, which is also great because I'll have stopped wondering about her.'

Lucy glowers.

'She is my mum.'

'I know. You know what, dude? I have a mum too, but she doesn't move in and start banging on about Guatemala.'

'Your mum's never been out of Cheltenham.'

'No,' says Lucy thoughtfully. 'Anyway, that isn't the point.'

'And your mum bangs on about other things, like you marrying Aaron Baton-Bum.'

'Baton-Bailey, yeah . . . and she hasn't met Reuben yet either.'

'Right, so you can officially shut up about mums . . . dude.' This dude thing is catchy.

'Yeah, fair enough,' says Lucy, looking worried.

I smile to myself, imagining Mrs Bond meeting Reuben. Talk about cat and pigeons.

I get home at about ten-thirty in a very good mood, so excited to be pregnant at the same time as Lucy. She's really proper and thorough about everything, so that will keep me right. I mean, I would have never thought about pregnancy yoga, and now look – I'm only enrolled in the best class in London! As I take off my shoes, I hear low voices coming from the living room. Max and Rainey are talking. Hearing Rainey's sonorous tones, I feel a fresh flash of irritation – that shape-shifter! I'll ask if she enjoyed her *beef*burger at *McDonald's* and I'll do inverted commas with my fingers.

I open the door and find Max sitting holding a cigarette out of the window, a can of beer in his other hand, and Rainey, mid-story, on the sofa. She turns her head and gazes at me but continues speaking. I flop into the armchair, rubbing my feet.

'You can't say there isn't a spiritual connection, Max,' says Rainey. I glance at him and he gives me the glad eye. 'I helped for a time in a little children's hospice in Argentina—'

'Oh yeah?' says Max, taking a drag and blowing it outside.

I watch him, liking him, especially his forearms.

'And José, a little boy I befriended, kept a pet mouse. Of course, he wasn't allowed to bring the mouse into the hospice, but every time he was well enough to go home, he played with that mouse incessantly. People would say to him, "*Dónde están le souris?*"'

'"*Souris*" – that's French, isn't it?' asks Max.

'Anyway, José became gravely ill and entered the hospice for the last time. On the day he died, his family went home and sat in the boy's bedroom, where they found the little mouse dead in his cage.'

'No way,' says Max casually. 'And what's your explanation for that? The mouse couldn't go on and committed suicide?'

'There is no explanation, Max,' smiles Rainey sadly, and looks to me. 'The story merely illustrates that we're connected spiritually to animals.'

'Christ! So sentimental – it's like watching *Bambi*,' says Max. 'So if you're so bothered about animals, what about Dave? He's a fine animal and you put him out of his own home.'

'That cat is a very damaged animal with bad energy.'

'OK, so he's a bad cat,' says Max proudly, 'but if a

mouse is supposed to be spiritually connected, don't tell me my cat isn't.'

'He's connected to you, I suppose. Same energy,' sniffs Rainey. The insult spins across the floor and crashes between them like a china plate. I swallow the ball.

'I think you're a beacon of positivity myself,' I interrupt, trying to inject some light-heartedness.

Max barely glances my way before turning back to Rainey. 'OK, so let's get this straight – you think all animals are connected to each other, except the ones you don't like, such as me and Dave. Are you high or what?'

'Are *you* high?' she asks nastily. 'That would explain your paranoia.'

'I wish I was, and then I might be able to understand your gibberish.'

'What about eating animals?' I throw in, before a full-scale row erupts. They glare at each other for a moment before Rainey drags her stink-eye look away.

'Should we, you mean?' she asks, and I nod, meeting her gaze. 'Absolutely not.'

'I see, I see.' I think about saying, 'Ha! Well, that's extremely interesting, because I saw you necking a beefburger earlier this evening, so what have you got to say to that?' but I don't. I just say, 'Hmm,' thought-fully.

I later ask myself why I didn't confront Rainey. These are the reasons I think of:

- I didn't want to escalate the bad feeling developing between Max and my mother.
- I'm a cowardly person who only wants us all to get on really well and love each other.
- I'm afraid I would fly off the handle and I'm afraid of upsetting my mother and losing her again.
- I want to give her a chance to admit she occasionally jumps off the vegan wagon like a joyous vampire.
- I don't want to believe she is a liar.
- I don't know what to say.

'I don't understand how anyone can pollute their bodies with toxins,' Rainey continues and sighs deeply.

'You weren't saying that the other day when you were knocking back the cava,' snorts Max and gives a huge laugh.

She fixes him with a patient stare. 'And do you think smoking out of that window prevents toxins from reaching your unborn child?'

'Yeah, I think so, and you're OK with it, aren't you, Viv?'

I'm not OK about Max smoking – I want him to quit and he knows it.

As I hesitate, Rainey gives a triumphant little smile. 'Of course she's not OK with it!' she says.

'Well, I'd rather you didn't smoke, Max. I don't want you dying of cancer and ducking out of parenting duties. Ha, ha.' I look from Max to Rainey, but they stare at each other like a pair of fighting cockerels.

Max drops his cigarette into his empty can, places it on the windowsill, and closes the window.

'It's time to rest, Vivienne – you look weary,' says Rainey, gracefully getting up.

As she passes in a fragrant waft, she places her hand on my leg, pressing lightly for a moment in a gesture of reassurance, and I have to fight the urge to cling to her and sob wildly into her neck, begging her to tuck me in, stroke my hair, read me a story, get me a milky drink, et cetera. *Get a hold of yourself, Vivienne.* It must be neediness brought on by vulnerability because I'm pregnant. I shake my head, look at my hands.

'Goodnight, Vivienne,' she murmurs.

''Night.' I smile.

'Goodnight, *Lor*-raine!' Max calls after her.

We hear the door click closed and, a few seconds later, the ritual chanting.

'Don't call her Lorraine,' I tell him, and he starts to laugh, palm over his beard.

'What?'

'Suicidal mice!' he says, and goes over to struggle with the squeaky fold-out mechanism of the torture bed.

'I know – she is one crazy fruit loop.' I sigh. 'I was kind of hoping we'd all get on, for a while anyway. I really think she cares about me.'

'I'm trying, darlin', but I don't know how she hasn't been strangled by now.'

'Can you try any harder?' I smile, contemplating the sofa bed and wondering if my tolerance will hold out.

Rainey is infuriating and I know it's unfair to ask Max to put up with her, but I just need to keep her a bit longer, long enough to cement something between us. I'll have to find a way, try harder to make them get on.

'God, I'm tired.' I feel the dead weight of my body slung like a sack of porridge into the chair and my bag is pressing into my hip, but I can't even be bothered to move.

My phone buzzes a message, three short vibrations through the bag into my thigh, and I force myself to fish it out. A text from Lucy.

Dude, r babies r going to b best friends!

I answer.

Dude, they r going 2 get married!

As I press 'send', I notice I have a voicemail from Sarah at Tease UK. I look at Max. He's pretending to be a suicidal mouse; my smile fades as I listen to the message.

'Hi, Viv. It's Sarah from Tease UK calling. Just a quick message to say thanks for coming in today. Lovely to meet you all. I presented your products to the rest of the buying team, and unfortunately, although we really liked the idea, we feel it isn't for us at this time. We will keep your details on file, however, and will be in contact if circumstances change.' Here she clears her throat and slips out of the reading-a-script voice to a sort of low half-whisper. 'I wonder if you would ask your IT freelancer, Michael, to give me a little tinkle. I have a couple of projects he might be interested in. Thanks, Viv. Bye.'

I feel disappointment like a giant hand pressing down on my head. My heart clatters under my ribs.

'Fuck it,' I say to the ceiling.

Max frowns. I replay the message and hand him the phone.

Later, we lie together, him curled behind me, his mouth near my ear. I listen to the tick of the radiator, and the occasional rumble of a night bus on the main road. Thoughts come into my head and fly off again, taking my whole insides with them.

'You all right?' asks Max, his voice buzzing on my earlobe.

'No.'

'What you thinking?'

'Just . . . how do people make a living?'

'That's a morning thought. Think night thoughts.' He strokes a hand over my belly. 'Think about Angel.'

'Terrifying.'

'No,' he whispers.

'We don't have any money.'

'But we'll get some.'

'Just like that?'

'Yeah.'

I turn over to face him, make out the shape of his profile in the dark. 'Aren't you worried?'

'Nah.' He lifts an arm and I rest my face against his ribs. I put a leg over his thigh and wriggle into him. 'Careful,' he murmurs.

'I'm not scared of you.'

'Oh, you're not?' He puts a hand on my bottom.

'How are you not worried?'

'Shh, don't think.' His hand circles.

I try to think of the bigger picture, things bigger than me – stars, death, elephants and where his hand is heading. I shift myself up on top of him and kiss him slowly.

'I'll take your mind off things. I have special and ingenious ways,' he says.

'You reckon you could?'

'Almost definitely,' he says, sliding both hands up my back.

I'm sitting giggling on top of Max, about to take my mind off things when the overhead light snaps on above our heads. We freeze. I cover my boobs with my hands as Rainey pads through to the kitchen wearing my velour dressing gown. When she's out of sight, I fall flat against the mattress, pulling the covers over us. She comes back through with a glass of water.

'Could you not ever knock?' Max shouts. She turns off the light and closes the door without an answer. I listen to her footsteps and her door closing, clutching a sheet up to my chin. Max slides me across the bed towards him.

'I can hear her, so she must be able to hear us.'

'So?' he says, kissing my collarbone and moving down.

'So we can't do it now,' I say, tapping him on the head.

He appears from under the covers, hair sticking up with static, and rolls onto his back. His erection makes a tent of the sheets.

'What will I do with this, then?' he says.

'I don't know. Think of something horrible.' We lie on our backs. I stare up into the grainy darkness. 'Has it gone?'

'Almost instantly.'

'What did you think of?'

'Your mother.'

16

#Ifallelsefails

Right, it is now time to take matters into my own hands. I've woken up bouncing with energy, not at all sick. We are going to start the day positively and everybody will be cool. I hum to myself as I set the table for breakfast. Max is confused, as he usually eats children's cereal with water, from a Tupperware tub, standing up.

'This morning I've decided we're all having a lovely family breakfast together,' I announce as Rainey saunters in wearing a purple and yellow kaftan in almost see-through material. Max is already sitting at the fold-out dining table, with his triple shot of coffee, sulkily reading the paper.

'I don't eat wheat—' begins Rainey.

'I know you don't, but I've made you a lovely fruit salad and sprinkled it with seeds, see?' I show her the bowl as I put it on the table.

'No fruit for me, thank you, dreamboat,' says Max without looking up from the sports section.

'No, for you, my love, I'm making a bacon sandwich.' I smile lovingly and ruffle his hair. Is this a bit like dealing with adolescents?

I go to the kitchen to get the sandwich and my banana and toast. I'm going to be a great mum if I can handle these two. The whole flat smells of coffee and toast and bacon, morning show on the radio, red autumn sun flickering through the blind; we're like a breakfast-juice ad in here, except we don't have juice and no one is talking to each other, but you know what I mean. I go through to the table where my mother and fiancé sit in silence.

'So what's your plan for today?' I ask Rainey.

'My "plan"? We are corporate, aren't we?' she says, picking the kiwi out of her salad. 'Of course I don't have one.'

I smile sweetly. This family breakfast is going to involve a nice conversation if it kills me.

'What about you, darling?' I ask Max.

He looks up, grinning. 'Well, *darling*, I'm going to the studio, and after that I'm going to see Guy.'

'Guy?' asks Rainey.

Max glances over at her. 'Trust me, you don't know him.'

'Oh, I'm not remotely interested in the sad snippets of your life. I was just trying to make conversation,' she says.

'Good,' I say, looking at Max's lowered eyebrows – he looks like he's just been stung on the nose by something he didn't see coming. 'Then I might come with you to the studio this morning,' I say to distract him. He drags his daggers back from Rainey and looks at me, his face softening.

'Grand,' he says.

'I'll just have to call work.' I smile.

'I may have to leave for Madrid this afternoon,' says Rainey, pushing aside her full dish of fruit. I try not to stare – that fruit cost me nearly a fiver in Marks & Spencer.

'What . . . but why?' I say desperately.

'I'm in the way here. You clearly don't have time for me, Vivienne.'

'I do. I have time.'

'No, you don't,' says Max.

Rainey puts her head to one side and smiles sadly. 'You're very busy. I see how it is.'

'But don't go to Madrid yet. Let's have lunch today. I'll meet you.'

Her eyes flick from me to Max and down to her lap. 'No, I think I need to move on,' she says.

'You're probably right,' says Max.

'How about I meet you at Baker Street Tube station? There's a vegetarian restaurant down the Marylebone Road. We can talk.'

She sighs, tilts her head the other way and says, 'Uhm,' while sighing again. 'All right, I'll meet with you, Vivienne, but nowhere special – I have very simple needs.'

Max's laugh is muffled by the huge bite he's taking of his sandwich. He wipes brown sauce from the corner of his mouth with the back of his hand.

'Something amusing you?' asks Rainey.

He nods, chewing, and points at her. He mimes laughing, holding his ribs. He looks her in the eye, rams the last of the sandwich in his mouth and saunters to the kitchen with his plate.

I smile, nervous as a knock-kneed goat in a temple. Rainey looks at me with exaggerated patience, pressing her lips together.

'I might . . . I'm just going to get dressed, then,' I say, pointing to the bedroom.

She nods. 'Do, Vivienne, but please God, not that green dress. It really doesn't help you.'

It's one of those crisp late October days, sunny, blue skied, with just the right amount of red and orange leaves floating about – a perfect picture of autumn. I'm walking hand in hand with Max to the studio in my spot-sponged green dress, looking at my belly in shop windows. I happen to think this dress really does help me, skimming as it does over my small bump. I'm proud of pregnant me. I like to think there are two of us in here and one of us has to look after the other one and that's why I asked a man to give me his seat on the train. The funny thing is he just got up. He didn't ask for scan pictures or a doctor's note, didn't speak, just stood up and let me sit in the indentation warmed by his bottom. Max, in his unzipped biker jacket, hung his hands over the bar above the seat and looked down at me. He's quiet because:

a) *We've just agreed he should sell his motorbike in Spain rather than bring it back, and he loves that bike like one of his own limbs. It was his idea to sell it. I merely agreed and said it was 'sensible', which I now know is a word he can't stand and something he never, ever wants to be.*

b) *I missed the chance to pack Rainey off to Madrid.*

By the time we get to the studio, he's feeling better. Dave runs to the door as we open it, trying to escape. Max lifts him up to the ceiling, saying, 'Flying cat,' holds out his front legs, points him towards me and says, 'Cat escaping explosion,' puts Dave round his neck and says, 'Scarf cat,' while Dave glares murderously. Max asks Dave what he wants for breakfast, takes him to the kitchen, and scrapes fish mush onto a saucer.

In the whitewashed studio, there are four really amazing sketches of me taped up on the wall and a huge painting on a canvas next to them of me wearing the tutu, looking miserable. I examine the painting. I love it. I'm always amazed and surprised at his talent. It's incredible that someone I know can paint like this. Up close the slicks of paint that make up my limbs and face and spilling-out breasts are yellow, purple, blue and grey, but when you step away, they cleverly make up the shadow and light of my skin. My face is half turned moodily, and I have smudged eye make-up. The thing is, this painting is a zillion times better than any of the landscapes. I can't tell Max that, though. He comes into the room with coffee.

'You don't want one?' he asks, and I shake my head. I can't stand coffee anymore, or the smell of mangoes, or the drag marks lips make on spoons of yoghurt.

Max looks at the sketches and the paintings, standing beside me. 'I'll tell you something, this work is way stronger than the landscapes,' he says, and then he laughs.

'What?'

'Guy has a whole gallery full of fucking landscapes he can't sell.'

'He will sell them, though. I mean, they're not the kind of things you snap up on impulse, are they, landscapes? People need time to view them and think about them. These are great, though.' I stroll along in front of the sketches.

'I want to do a whole load of paintings of you pregnant, but I'll do them from photos,' he says. Then he downs the coffee in one and gasps, wiping his hand over his beard. 'So, Viv, when are you going to get rid of your mother?'

I turn to face him. 'That again.'

'I googled her. She's no vegan hippy. She's a

businesswoman importing and exporting stuff in Colombia.'

'I know.'

'You know?'

'I know she's not vegan, anyway – I saw her in McDonald's.'

He shakes his head. 'She's so full of shite.'

I sigh heavily and slump onto the floor. 'I told you, it's complicated. I don't really even know her. The last time I saw her was for, like, one day, three years ago, so this is the longest I've ever spent with her, as an adult anyway. I wanted to get to know her . . .' I trail off, bored of saying it. I look at him. I smile, but he doesn't. He leans against the wall, ankles crossed, listening.

'Why?'

'Why what?'

'I can't see why you want to get to know her.'

'It's hard to explain . . . It's because I'm pregnant. I want to know my own mum. When you're pregnant, you start to wonder about your own flesh and blood. I don't know. I know it isn't working. I know. But if it was your family, I'd really try to like them.'

'I wouldn't ask you to like my family – they're all nuts.'

'I know! Why don't we visit your family? We could go to Dublin.'

He frowns as if confused. 'Why would we do that?'

'I want to meet them, and we'll get away from Rainey for a bit.'

'But how much longer is she staying, Viv?'

'I'll speak to her. I'll ask.'

'Tell her,' he says, and when I glance at his face he's very stern-looking. 'She can't stay for fucking ever, can she? She's doing my head in with her theories and her stories and her "I don't eat wheat" and her "Why don't you paint something to match the sofa?" And she has you dangling like a yo-yo.'

'Not really.'

'You're her puppet.'

I pretend to be a puppet. He remains stern-looking.

'I can't stand it.'

'I know what I'm doing – see, I'm indulging her.'

'Tell her to go.' He shakes his head.

'I will tell her. When we have lunch today, I'll say just another week. One more week – can you handle that?'

'I know she's your mother and all, but I can't live with her.'

'A week?'

'I'm having fantasies about clubbing her to death.'

'One week, Max.'

'Apart from her being a witch, the place is too small. I want our bed back. I want you back to yourself, not stressed about her.'

'Seven days!'

'OK,' he says finally, tilting back his head, staring at the ceiling. 'I can never refuse you anything.'

'Good, then give me a thousand pounds.'

He digs in his jeans and pulls out a crumpled fiver. 'Here, don't spend it all,' he says, and I get up to kiss him goodbye. The kiss is about to turn into a full-on snog, but I break off, suddenly starving with a strong desire for one of those yoghurt and granola tubs from Pret A Manger. I whip the money out of his hand and make for the door.

'See you later,' I say over my shoulder.

'Either she goes or I do!' he shouts as the door closes.

17

Never Call Me 'Mummy'

There are mythical images of 'mother' in stories from around the world; Mother Earth, the Wicked Stepmother, the Fairy Godmother. Some of these stereotypes might influence your perception of the role. You may begin to reflect on your parents, the way they brought you up and how you feel about your upbringing as you progress through your pregnancy.

www.askthedoc.com

The great thing about being your own boss is that you can choose to work from Pret A Manger all morning if you like. I'm meeting Rainey nearby, so I don't have to schlep across London and back. I have my laptop and my phone, therefore I have my office. I love it when life is this easy. Give up the struggle, I say.

I already rang Christie to tell her I'll be in later this afternoon and asked if she was OK with Damon, who I could already hear in the background going on about his old mum. She said she was fine. I asked her to email every major retailer we know and get a sales meeting. Michael wasn't even there, but I guess if you're working for free, you get to turn up whenever. I settle down to researching wedding favours, hen-night gimmicks and a 'circle of life' thing for pregnant women where you answer questions and follow arrows that lead to the answers, which seem to be 'Take time out', 'Enrol support' or 'Let go.' No matter which answers you give, you always get to these three solutions. It's absolutely maddening, actually. I break off from work only once to order a soya chai latte, which smells like fermented trainers, but before I know it, I've spent the whole morning dicking about on the internet.

I meet Rainey in a kind of veggie canteen with booths and chalkboard menus. There's an open kitchen with a salad display and a grill for the huge mushrooms they make into burgers here. Brick-shaped white tiles cover the walls, and over every table hangs a shiny brass flying-saucer light. It's busy, but I manage to get a booth table near the toilets at the back. She dances in with her aura; people notice as she floats past in her flowing purple and yellow robes. I'm transfixed. I know she's tricking us, trying to make us believe in this role she's playing, but I want to suspend my disbelief until the end of the performance, whenever that might be – I want to find out what happens. Instead I have to cut it short. I feel a pounding in my guts. Is this going to be our showdown? Will I be able to get the answers I need and tell her to go? My throat feels dry, and now she's at the table, sliding into the booth in a cloud of cool, fresh outside air.

'Hello, Vivienne. You look as if you've seen a ghost,' she says, arranging fabric and scarves and her hair. Then she studies me. 'I think it's that nondescript hair colour – it really drains you. Do you feel OK?'

'Well, I did.'

She gathers up the three card menus, shuffles to the relevant lunch list, her eyes moving over it. 'Do you know what you're having?' she asks without looking at me.

'Not yet,' I say, watching her. What is it about her? I like her and I can't help it. I like her hair and her straight nose, her little hands with the bangles. I want her to like me.

'Hmm,' she says, reading the menu.

'They don't do beefburgers, if that's what you're looking for.'

She looks at me, the pupils of her eyes narrowing to pinpricks.

'I saw you in McDonald's, Rainey – you don't have to pretend to be vegan anymore,' I murmur.

She watches me for a few long seconds. Then she looks down at her hands.

'And Max wants you to move out,' I continue.

'I see,' she says. 'Well, what that artistic rake wants is of no concern. It's your flat. What do you want?'

'It's our flat, Max and me together. I'm sorry, Rainey – I said you'll go in a week. It's difficult. It's a very small space, and with you in the main bedroom . . . I mean, I don't sleep well on the sofa bed.'

She spreads her hands flat on the table and clears her throat with an 'ahem' sound. She takes a deep breath. 'Look, I'll come out with it. I'm in a lot of trouble, Vivienne,' she whispers, and looks up into my eyes like a snake charmer. I start blinking as if I'm staring into a hot wind. 'If I tell you something, will you swear not to tell a soul?'

'No! It depends what you tell me.'

'I can't tell you unless you swear.' She presses her hands together in a prayer position and points them at me.

'All right, I swear. I won't tell anyone.'

'Solemnly swear.'

'I swear on my mother's life,' I say sarcastically.

'No, I don't feel I can trust you.' She shakes her head, eyes closed.

'Well, it's up to you,' I say, looking away.

'All right . . . I was involved with a married man whose wife is the daughter of a very powerful drug dealer. She found out about us. He stole a whole load of money and disappeared, and I received death threats. It got out of hand. I had to leave Colombia in a hurry, and I can't stay in hostels, because that's the first place they'll look for me, and I can't stay at Mother's, because that will be the second place they'll look for me. Then I met you and, well, no one knows I had a daughter, so . . .'

I make word shapes with my mouth, but I'm totally speechless.

'I just need to lie low for a few months, and your place is so perfect, so unlikely a place for me to be. And no, I'm not a vegan, and no, I'm not particularly spiritually connected to animals. I just wanted to seem appealing to you. I remember you always loved animals. Didn't you collect those little pottery woodland creatures?'

'What?'

'That little hedgehog and the squirrel?'

'So let me get this straight. You are on the run from a drug dealer who wants to kill you?'

'I think they'll give up looking for me in a few months.'

'What were you going to do in Madrid?'

'Madrid fell through,' she says, shaking her head impatiently.

I lean back against the leatherette bench, trying to take this in. The waiter appears at our table. Rainey orders curly fries and a Greek salad.

'Did you not think? You might have put me and Max in danger? Or Nana?'

She laughs. 'You're not in any danger – don't be dramatic. They want me, that's all,' she says.

'A fricking drug baron is after you!'

'This is exactly why I didn't tell you the truth in the first place. I knew you'd overreact. Look, all I need is a place to stay for a few months. By then they'll have forgotten about me and I'll move on.'

'I don't know what to say. Are you for real?'

'Oh, it's very real, Vivienne. Look, OK, I'll go. I'll find somewhere else. I'm sorry I dragged you into this, and if they catch up with me, if I end up murdered in a ditch, it won't be your fault.'

'So you might get murdered, but we're not in any danger?'

'They're not after you. Look, I'll leave.'

'What?' Oh my God. I rub my eyebrows. 'Where will you go?'

'I don't know. I don't actually have much money left until I can get some wired over to me. But listen, it's not your problem.'

The waiter brings drinks and seems to take an age arranging the table. I sit watching her and wondering what to do. Rainey has always had a vivid imagination/ is a liar. I don't believe half of what she says and it drives me crazy to be lied to, letting her think I'm some gullible fool, but there's always that chink of doubt, isn't there? Didn't I promise myself that I'd put up with whatever she does for the sake of knowing her finally?

'Well, obviously I'm not going to turn you out onto the street.' I was thinking this, but I've gone and said it out loud.

'No, don't trouble yourself, Vivienne,' she says sadly.

'Are you telling the truth?'

'I am many things, but a liar I am not,' she says, looking into my eyes.

'But you didn't feel my unborn baby calling to you, did you?'

'No.'

'So it was a lie, then?'

'Well, I may have exaggerated a bit, but I definitely felt something pressing me towards you.'

'And was it gun-shaped?'

'Oh, Vivienne, please.'

'I can't believe this. You didn't come to London to see me at all! Why should I help you? You left me to fend for myself and I was only seven,' I say, and feel my lip wobble.

She watches me carefully. 'I'm just your mother, that's all, and I didn't leave you to fend for yourself – I left you with Eve,' she says, then thinks a bit and adds, 'OK, I see what you mean. You might as well have fended for yourself.'

'She loved me at least! Why do you always have to slag her off?'

She purses her lips, shrugs.

'You told me never to call you "Mummy". Remember that? Why did you leave?' I release a gaggle of caged emotions and old hurts. They clamber up my windpipe until I swallow them down again. I must get a hold of myself; these childish feelings of abandonment are clogging up my thinking. I look at Rainey. I want her in my life, but there's such a lot of pain to grapple with. I'm pregnant and emotional; I can't think straight. I need to talk to Nana. Things would be clearer if she was here. Why is she on a stupid world tour? I suddenly get a huge surge of missing Nana and fight the urge to cry.

'I was a child, Vivienne,' she says, and looks away.

'Not when you left. You were twenty-three.'

'Let me tell you something – age has nothing to do with it. Some people are eighty and still children inside. I was thinking I'd wake up one day and be grown-up, be ready to take on my responsibilities, but it never happened. There's no training to being adult; you're suddenly just doing it.'

'You were never grown-up enough to care about me?' I ask, feeling emotion prickling behind my eyes.

'I remember the day you were born, Vivienne,' says Rainey softly. 'I danced you out. I just danced around the room to Bob Marley and then you were suddenly in my arms, a little pink bundle smiling up at me.'

'Well, for a start, newborn babies can't smile, and secondly, I thought you said I was stuck in like a coat hanger?'

She blinks and looks off to the left. 'Ah yes, you were for a bit before that. It was a long time ago now.'

'Huh.' I laugh and shake my head in disbelief. 'You are such a liar.'

'Storyteller.'

'What's the difference?'

'One is bad.'

What can I do? What should I do? She's my mother and I can't tell her to go. I need time to think about this, but there is no time. If she can't stay with me, where will she go?

'What Bob Marley song was it?'

'"Three Little Birds."'

One of my favourites. 'You can stay, Rainey,' I sigh.

'Really?' She reaches for my hand and squeezes it.

'Stay as long as you need.'

'But you can't tell anyone about what I told you, not even Max.'

'You're not really in a position to be making conditions,' I say.

'Without that promise, I'll have to leave. He's unsympathetic to my cause.'

'You'll have to respect Max; you can't keep nagging him, and stop over-explaining things about art. He's an artist. It's very annoying.'

'But you won't tell him?'

'No.' I grimace, and she comes around the table and hugs me. She has never spontaneously hugged me before. There in her arms I feel a wave of relief and compassion. I'm in the unique position of being able to help her. We'll be closer. I've done the right thing. I squeeze my eyes shut and think about the generations of my family – my baby, me and my mother – all stacked together here and now on this bench like Russian dolls.

18

Congratulations – You're Pregnant

Cracker contents: anti-stretch-mark body cream, emergency chocolate, a badge, support socks, nail polish for toes while you can still reach them.

I arrive at work mid-afternoon with an uneasy feeling blooming, a bit like I've accidentally given away a favourite irreplaceable vintage handbag to the charity shop and then seen them selling it to someone for 20p. I've given away something precious. '*Your integrity,*' pipes up Angel. Who knew babies could be so astute?

No, no, no, what I need to do is rebrand this feeling, make it about being a marvellous, generous, selfless, loving daughter.

That's better, but then every time I think of Max, my stomach hurts. I'll speak to him. I'll make things work somehow, but right now I have bigger fish to fry. As I open the office door, I hear Damon's voice.

'Who here knows about Moomintrolls?' he says as I stand in the doorway. Michael is sitting on my chair with his feet up on my desk, Christie is at her desk wearing some sort of patterned quilted two-piece skirt suit with her hair in a messy bun, and Damon is leaning against the partition.

'Oh, all right, Viv?' Damon says.

'Damon, hello,' I say, and Christie looks up over her laptop. Michael spins his chair round to look my way, grinning. 'So what's been happening today? What deals have been done? What meetings organised?' I ask.

'Mike's been sorting me out about my aquarium,' says Damon.

'Has he?' I look at Michael, who nods knowingly while rocking his legs side to side.

'I need more bottom-feeders,' explains Damon.

'Yeah, get yourself a couple of false julii corydoras. Easy, peaceful, nice to look at. A bit like you, Viv,' says Michael.

'Ah, you with your saccharine words. Now shift off my desk.'

He shuts down a couple of sites, then stands behind the chair holding the back of it for me to sit. The seat is strangely over-warm and smells of patchouli. 'Right, so moving on from Moomintrolls and aquarium bottom-feeders just for a tick, who here has got us a sales meeting?'

'We are in at Belle Peau on 29th November,' says Christie with her hand up.

'Belle Peau? Upmarket lingerie,' I say, writing it into the office diary and circling it so it looks more substantial against the acres of white meeting-less space of the week-to-view page. 'I'd have thought they'd be a bit too upmarket for sex crackers.'

Christie shrugs. 'It was hard to get a sales meeting for sex crackers with any of the mainstream retailers,' she says dejectedly.

I get a sinking feeling. I gaze out of the window at the shuttered-up building opposite. I thought we'd have an order by now, ready for Christmas. Maybe it's time for me to face up to it: this whole shebang is going down, taking the last of my redundancy money with it. Unless . . . maybe we can do something drastic. We must be doing something wrong. Is it the product? Is it apathy? Are we inept? What? Is our product appealing? Can it sell, and if so, who would buy it and how and where? Should I have thought of all this before?

'Right – Christie, Michael, my desk now,' I say in a bossy manner.

Christie totters over on hoof-like shoes with a notepad and the lens-free specs she wears in order to look like she has some clue. Michael takes a step closer to me.

'What about me?' asks Damon.

'All right, you too, since you seem to have nothing better to do.' I beckon him with a flapping hand. 'So, Tease UK are out. They don't think the crackers will sit with their range, which loosely translated means they don't think they'll sell.'

'Weird, I thought I'd got a twinkle off of that chick,' mutters Michael.

'Oh, she asked for you to call her,' I snap.

He narrows his eyes. 'Shabbah,' he whispers.

'Anyway, obviously that's very disappointing, so I think what we need is a brainstorming session,' I continue.

'Ideas shower,' corrects Christie, somehow setting off Damon's funny eye.

'Whatever. Let's think about the product. Is it good enough?'

'No,' says Michael.

There's a silence while we look around at each other and take in this unfathomable truth. Christie snort-laughs down her nose.

'Well, then. Good. That we've realised. Because. Then. We have the opportunity to make it better.' I slump into my chair with the weight of the knowledge that our product isn't good enough. 'OK, so come on – what's wrong with it?'

'No one wants it,' says Michael, showing why no one really invites the IT guys to creative meetings.

'Let's have a think. What *do* people want?' I make a rolling motion with my hand, staring at Michael. His eyes dart around, looking for an idea.

'Umm . . . sexy underwear?' asks Christie.

'In a cracker. The cracker packaging is our USP. Unique selling point,' I explain to Damon. 'Maybe we need lots of different types, not just a sex version – maybe a romance one?'

'A night-in one?' says Christie. 'It could have choc-olate truffles, a romantic-comedy mini disc and a bottle of Malibu.'

'Another version, two hundred Lambert and Butler, a case of Breezers and some nasty porn,' says Michael.

'What about extending the wedding crackers?' I say, ignoring him. 'We could have the romantic one, the sexy one, the one for the kids?'

'Or a Lady Diana one,' says Damon, getting excited.

'Yeah, fan crackers. Anyone who has fans can have a cracker . . . Occasion crackers! So births, divorce, civil partnerships . . .' I say, writing it down.

'Coming out of the closet!' gasps Christie.

'What would that have in it?' asks Michael, and she looks doubtful.

'Doesn't matter, Michael – we're just coming up with ideas,' I say, getting into it.

'Yeah . . . I think you need to look at the transitions people go through in life. Nearly every life transition could have its own cracker,' says Damon, waving his hands in the air.

I point at him with my pen. 'You are a genius, my friend,' I say, and his great head wobbles with pride.

I look from Michael to Christie to Damon, with ideas madly whirling in my head like snowflakes.

'Transitions . . . being born, going to school, leaving school . . . er, starting your period . . .'

'Congratulations on menstruation!' Michael announces, doing a little dance. 'What'd we put in?

A hot-water bottle, a packet of aspirin and some bloke to snap at!' He guffaws at Damon, who ignores him.

'Going travelling, getting married, first job – it could be massive!' I shout and bang the desk.

'Getting divorced, getting repossessed, death of a pet or death of anything,' says Christie, shaking her head with the flow.

'Well, we can't shrink away from reality, can we?' I say, wide-eyed.

We go through the rest of the afternoon filling five pages of foolscap with ideas, and even when it gets dark, we carry on. Eventually Damon has to lock up the building for insurance purposes, but we're all so full of it we decide to move down to the Old Fountain for dinner to try and come up with a shortlist and possible contents over scampi and chips. These are only ideas, mind. We know some of them definitely do not have legs.

Wedding 1. Romantic (Loveheart sweets, heart confetti, dance card, Kissy Lips lip balm, floating lantern)

Wedding 2. Sexy (penis bubbles, edible pants, lube, choccy boobs, sexual-positions card)

Congratulations – you're pregnant (stretch-mark cream, big knickers)

Congratulations on your new baby (teddy bear, sleepsuit, booties, bath and body lotion)

Congratulations – you're out of the closet (club listings, Gay Pride stickers, novelty pants)

Congratulations – you've passed your driving test (mini champagne, number plate, furry dice)

Congratulations – you've lost your virginity

Congratulations – you're single

Boys' and girls' night in (various possible contents – depends on price)

~~*Diana memorial crackers*~~

I'm at the bar feeling very positive about our venture when I notice it's eight o'clock. I'll have to make this my last orange and soda, and get along home to face the music. I feel immediately low, remembering my promise to Max and subsequent conflicting promise to Rainey. I know how Max feels. Of course I'd like Rainey to find herself a nice little flat somewhere nearby. The novelty of her staying with us has long worn off. It's been a month – she should go and leave me and Max to our lives and our baby. I know enough about her now to see she isn't suddenly going to become the loving mother I crave. I have a loving nana instead. Rainey is intolerable, and she won't change, and why should I expect her to? I should just let her go. But how can I make her go, into the possible death grip of drug barons? I know it's unlikely, laughable even, but what if? I imagine my own shocked face in the news under the headline 'Daughter Turns Mother over to Drug Barons.' I can't do that, can I? Asking her to leave is something I might regret for ever. I'll just have to put up with her a while longer, while subtly helping her to leave of her own accord. Max will understand if he loves me.

I turn with the drinks and walk back to our table, where Christie looks to be getting on with Michael. She's chewing the arm of her glasses and gazing at him; he's leaning back against the bench with both arms spread out mid-air, lecturing. Damon is staring into space like a gargoyle and gritting his teeth. No, hold on, he's smiling – teeth pointing one way and his lips another. I snake my way back through the tables, thinking:

- *This group of people are all here because of me.*
- *These are the people upon whom my livelihood depends.*
- *These people and 'transition crackers'.*

I take a deep breath and suck up that terror.

19

Pregnant Warrior

@poshluce Yoga class with @vivsummers wellbeing centre six pm #excited

@vivsummers @poshluce what if I fart like a monkey? #worried

@poshluce @vivsummers #firstworldproblems

@vivsummers @poshluce another pressing concern, clothes don't fit belly

@poshluce Shopping for maternity clothes with @vivsummers after yoga then dinner? #mytreat

I sit cross-legged on a sunlit wooden floor. My hands rest on my knees. Next to me Lucy sits in the same position, wearing expensive-looking grey leisurewear. Around the edge of the room, other women sit like us, all different sizes, colours and styles, all cross-legged. Music plays, a chant in Urdu. We breathe and we wait. I sneak a look across the room. You'd think pregnancy would be a bit of a leveller in the attractiveness stakes, that we'd all have huge bellies and big bums, but no, those skinny girls who look good in everything – you know the ones who speak to you in changing rooms, who say, 'That's lovely,' and look you up and down when you're shoe-horned into something, while themselves sashaying around in hot-pants playsuits – they look great pregnant as well. They have neat, cute little bumps, and their arms, legs and bums remain tiny, and they all hang out at antenatal yoga classes wearing cashmere hoodies in pastel shades with matching leg warmers.

A lovely little fairy with long grey hair arrives to teach us. She sits in the middle of the semi-circle of women in the quiet sitting position and begins to chant, and some of the women join in. Lucy's lips move, mimicking the words as if she knows what she's saying, so I do the same. The woman opens her eyes, presses her long fingers to her chest, and says she's Dita. She twirls her fingers a lot like ET as she welcomes us and asks us to introduce ourselves one by one, say where we are with our pregnancies, if it's our first one, and to share our experiences.

This is excruciating. I hate the 'introduce round the circle' thing. The pressure gets to me and trips some sort of alter-ego. I end up becoming someone else. Once, at a work training thing, I was surprised to find I had a lisp when I spoke. Another time, instead of introducing myself, I told a joke and laughed in a cackly way. I only half listen now: I'm paralysed with terror, nodding and smiling, while dreading my turn. One woman named Mary, who's quite mannish, with hair like a baby doll that's been through the boil wash, tells us she's twenty weeks pregnant and it's her first baby.

'Ah, Mary, well into your second trimester, and have you been massaging your perineum?' asks Dita.

Christ on a bike! That's a bit personal, isn't it? I mean, surely what you choose to do with your own perineum is nobody else's business. I look nervously over at Mary, thinking she might be too mortified to answer, but no, she's waxing lyrical about it, going on and on about the type of oil she uses and how she sometimes puts some into her vagina and sometimes Colin does it for her. Colin? Who the fuck is Colin? Presumably her partner, who has nothing better to do, and not some ubiquitous service called Colin that we can all call on. 'Call on Colin.' Oh, a tongue-twister! Urgh, what will I say if Dita asks me about my perineum? She's coming. She's coming. Think, think!

'Ladies, it's vitally important to massage your perineum to keep it nice and stretchy and elastic so that you don't tear,' says Dita, nodding around the room. I inwardly clench.

Dita turns to the next woman, who has a history of pelvic-floor problems. I keep looking at Mary in amazement as she settles back into her quiet sitting pose. She feels my eyes, looks up and smiles.

Lucy is now talking about her birth plan and asking if Dita could recommend a doula to help with labour, and all the women are nodding and commenting. Lucy is a complete pro at this. Lucy is already thinking about labour? Lucy has a birth plan? Oh, now I feel very bad. She's what – five or six weeks pregnant? I'm much more pregnant than her and I'm not sure I know what trimester I'm in. Trimester wasn't a word I'd ever used until today, or perineum, or doula. Dr Savage didn't prepare me for this! Nor did any midwife. Of course, I realise now that I've been a fool. If I'm going to have a baby, I need to know the correct technical language. I should know what to call my own equipment, shouldn't I? Otherwise, what questions can I ask? 'Dita, I'm concerned here. Are you telling me the baby is going to come out of my foo-foo?'

Argh, now it's my turn. Dita is looking expectant. I feel myself blush to my hair roots.

'Hi. I'm Vivienne Eliza Summers, BA hons,' I say in a strange sing-songy American accent. 'This is my first baby, I'm nearly twenty weeks, and I've been having a lot of discharge.'

'Hmm, what colour was the discharge, Viv?'

Oh shit, I don't know – I just made it up to have something shocking to say. Now what? Now what? Lucy is looking at me aghast.

'Kind of whitey-blue?' I whine without pronouncing the 't'.

'And is there typically a lot of it?'

'Oh, loads. Erm, not much,' I say meekly in my own voice.

'It may be reassuring for you to get checked over by your doctor.' Dita smiles. Her teeth are beautiful.

'Really? My doctor? Old Dr Savage! Honestly, he knows nothing about babies,' I say, hoping others will relate, but no one makes eye contact.

'Neither do you,' hisses Lucy.

'Wha—?' I begin, but thankfully Dita has moved on to the lady beside me, who's having twins. Now Mary is looking at *me*. She rolls her eyes. I stare her down. What does she know, anyway, with her great baggy perineum?

As we go through the class doing eagle and cow arms, nourishing the pelvis and lengthening the spine, I resolve to learn this pregnancy jargon. I'll have books and information at my fingertips and specially designed Tupperware. I'll get involved and become a pregnancy know-it-all. And I realise now it's all Max's fault that I know almost nothing. I've been going along with his lackadaisical attitude – him with his 'Everything's going to be all right' and 'Women have babies all the time . . . in war zones.' Well, look where that's got me. Humiliated in yoga. Not pregnant warrior, more pregnant loser.

Lucy and I try on maternity clothes after class: it's late-night shopping on Oxford Street. In Gap, they let us take as many items into the changing rooms as we like, which is good because who wants the hassle of trying on four things, calling for the changing-room assistant and getting no response, then having to get dressed in your own clothes again so you can try on more things? Not us. Also, there's a whole maternity section.

I emerge from the changing room in a black jersey maxi-dress with wizard sleeves, and Lucy pops out in a striped rugby shirt. She scans me, a wrinkle appearing between her brows.

'I'm getting this,' I say, and swing the arm material.

'When would you wear it?'

'Anytime. It has "day to evening" written all over it. You just accessorise accordingly, don't you?'

'Do you?' she asks, picking at the sleeve hem.

'You'll look great in this as well. You should vamp yourself up a bit,' I say, remembering we're sharing the maternity wardrobe.

She pulls a face. I use the curtain tie-back as a belt/necklace in an attempt to demonstrate versatility. 'Evening,' I say with it around my neck. 'Daytime,' I say and drop it.

'Erm, no,' she says.

'Yes, Lucy, this is a really useful dress!'

'If you go to a lot of Harry Potter do's,' she laughs. 'Dude, you look like a snake that swallowed an egg and got bat sleeves.' Lucy has never got the hang of analogies.

'Oh, ho, ho. That top is a no too, then,' I say, and she looks at herself in the mirror.

'I think it's quite cute, for the weekend.'

'Do not turn up that collar!' I say. She does.

Thus we go through every maternity collection on

the high street with the end result being two different sets of maternity clothes – her collection of bags is huge, mine not so huge. To be honest, we were deluded thinking we could have a shared wardrobe: I'm cool and edgy and not-trying-too-hard sexy, and she's corporate Home Counties with a sickening leaning towards cutesy – she bought a top for herself in H&M that came with a matching sleepsuit for the baby.

Later, perched on high stools at a health-food eatery in Soho, we plan our children's wedding. We think even if we both have girls or both have boys, our offspring could still be married, reasoning that this, in some ways, could be cooler than the traditional set-up.

I'm just swallowing a mouthful of beetroot and alfalfa California roll and pinning on a 'Baby on board' badge – that Lucy helpfully acquired for each of us for when we're commuting – when she asks about my wedding.

'Have you set a date? Because I want to know how pregnant I'll be. Remember I'm due on 20th June, so it can't be a month before or after that, otherwise I won't be able to be your best woman.'

I have never asked her to be my best woman – she presumes a lot of things.

'Oh, it won't be in the summer. Um, maybe in September?'

'Dude, are you trying to punish me for something?'

'No.'

'September? I won't have had time to lose the baby weight, and I want to breastfeed for at least six months.'

'Oh. Yeah. Well, we haven't actually set a date. I'm not really thinking about weddings for a bit, not until after the baby.'

'But you should book somewhere. Do you have a venue in mind?'

'Nope. I'm planning it all after the baby.'

'OK, but don't come crying to me when your dream venue is booked up for the next two years.'

'"Dream venue" is not a term I ever want to hear again,' I tell her.

'What about your birth plan?'

'I . . . have a plan for the birth.' I nod unconvincingly.

'You don't, do you?' she laughs.

'I'm . . . I'll probably squat,' I begin, raising my voice as she bursts out laughing, 'and I'll have some music, probably Bob Dylan.'

'No clue,' she says, and shakes her head. 'Have you enrolled on any NCT classes?'

'NCT classes. I'll google that. I will! I have some clue – I've been researching online.'

'What, your Pinterest page? Dude, it's full of babies dressed up as bees!'

So begins a lecture from Lucy about all the things I should have done by now. Quite a lot, it seems, and she goes on to tell me about her cure for morning sickness, which is to eat a lot of Orange Maid ice lollies.

'I've been to midwife appointments!'

'And were you listening?'

'Yes. I'm booked in. I have leaflets.'

'Dude, have you even read one leaflet?'

'And I have a twenty-week scan next week, and I plan to ask a lot of questions at that.' She opens her mouth to speak and I talk over the top of her. 'A lot of questions. More questions than answers,' I repeat until she's quiet. Then I feel sorry for quashing her enthusiasm. 'Anyway, let's hear your birth plan so I can copy,' I say. She's pleased and tells me in detail about her natural water birth using HypnoBirthing techniques, and how she's keeping an open mind in case medical intervention is required because there's this one girl she knows at work who laboured too long at home, had some sort of prolapse, and now has to wear her fanny in a sling. I wonder about a transition cracker for that situation.

Lucy goes off to the toilet and I check my phone. A text from Max: Down the pub – call in on the way back? Just wanged your mother around the head with a pan. Think she might be dead – oh well.

This is the kind of text that could be incriminating later if Rainey gets nabbed by drug barons and we can't explain her whereabouts. I delete the text, tutting to myself, and when Lucy returns, I say I'm tired and we leave.

I take the bus home, staring out of the window and thinking hard about a solution to the fiancé-hates-mother puzzle. I haven't found a way to explain to Max that Rainey is staying for a while longer. Last night wasn't the right moment, and this morning he was rushing out and so was I, but the more time that goes by without telling him, the more I feel like I'm actually lying to him. I'll tell him tonight. I know he'll be pissed off, but I also know he loves me so he'll understand. Of course he will.

The Crown is a huge, sprawling pub with pool tables and large flat-screens showing round-the-clock sport, and it's also our local. I spot Max at a little table near the window. He's wearing a red woolly scarf of mine knotted twice, a Minnie Mouse T-shirt and grey trousers. He's halfway down a pint. I decide not to get a drink, thinking that after I tell him about Rainey we'll be leaving pretty quickly. He stands when he sees me and holds out an arm. I hug him.

'Can I get you a drink?'

'I'm tired. I'll just wait for you to finish yours.'

'Like your badge,' he says.

I flick it and smile, pulling up a stool opposite him. 'You OK? How was yoga?'

'Uh, you're supposed to massage my perineum.'

'Anytime,' he nods.

'Very accommodating.'

'I'm in a good mood. I sold a landscape,' he says, and waves his clasped hands.

'Ah, that's brilliant.' I feel a surge of relief. 'Which one?'

'A little one. Only a thousand, but at least . . .'

'We can eat.'

'Yeah.' He holds my hand.

I take a deep breath. What I'm going to do is look him in the face and say something like, 'I've agreed to let Rainey stay for a few months. Don't ask me why, because I can't explain, but if you love me, you must understand. I need your support on this matter. Thank you for listening.'

I take another deep breath and say, 'You killed Rainey, then?'

'Ah, I only dream of it,' he snorts.

'Don't you think killing her is a tad harsh? Couldn't she just have niggling discomfort, like getting a nasty yeast infection?' I ask, leading up to the big speech.

'OK,' he says. 'I can go along with that, or how about she has to have extensive root-canal work involving a lot of wiring?'

'Become allergic to mascara? Develop a bald patch maybe?'

'I suppose it could be OK if she got all of those things and underwear blisters and . . . anal fissures,' he says with a gleeful look in his eyes.

'Though we mean her no real harm.' I frown, checking.

He laughs and so do I, and I end up having half a

Guinness with him for the iron content and to celebrate him selling a painting. He's really happy. We're having fun. And somehow I don't get round to telling him about Rainey staying for as long as she likes.

20

Daddy Quiz: Proof that He Knows Less than Me

Is a pelvic floor:

a) *That new-fangled poured-concrete surface useful in kitchens?*
b) *A band of muscles that stops your womb from falling out?*
c) *A guitar band with punk leanings?* √

Is a doula:

a) *A chest plate used in fencing?*
b) *A person who assists a woman in pregnancy and birth?*
c) *A kind of face cloth or towel handed round in Turkish baths?* √

I feel a pulling sensation, and there's a sound like straining timber. My limbs are stretched unnaturally; things are cracking. A bitter wind blows through my bones, and when I look down, my lower half is made of Lego and I have an enormous hole between my plastic legs.

'Her pelvic floor's gone,' tuts a hooded nurse-type figure, handing me an armful of screaming Beanie Babies.

'Can we rebuild her?' asks a doctor who looks a lot like my granddad, although he sold vending machines when he was alive.

'No. Not ever. Never, ever will she be the same again,' wails the nurse, and her face shrivels in on itself like an old peach.

I wake up in a sweat on the sofa bed, clawing at my own legs.

I'm alone, cocooned in the quilt. I turn onto my back and try to reassure myself. I still have a pelvic floor and I'm clenching it for all I'm worth.

'Clench, hold, release, repeat,' I say to myself.

Then without warning I start to feel incredibly horny. Now, this is a new thing. The women at the yoga class last week were discussing it and they said it's to do with having more blood in your body than normal. This must be what men feel like all the time. How brilliant. Sadly I can't do anything about it. Max left early for work, and anyway, my mother is already banging about in the kitchen. I can hear her singing in Spanish. Today is the day of my twenty-week scan and the beginning of my pregnant know-it-all phase. After the scan, Max and I are looking at baby equipment, researching what we need and then seeing if we can find it cheap second hand. I found out about the NCT – it stands for 'National Childbirth Trust' – and I booked Max and me on to a class next week. Even though the group is halfway through the course, the woman on the phone said we could sit in. I reach into my bag and fish out a list I wrote on the bus after seeing Lucy the other day, smoothing out the paper of the old receipt it's written on.

Birth plan? Bob Dylan/water/massage?

Hypnotist!

Doula

<u>NCT – to make friends!!!! Will be lonely after baby and know no one!</u>

Pelvic-sling thing?

Epidural/gas and air

Baby pouch

Buggy – research

I cross out the NCT part and add 'maternity clothes' to the bottom of the list and cross that out as well to give myself a sense of achievement. Then I nip off to the bathroom to get ready.

I meet Max at the hospital and we sit with another couple and their little boy waiting for our scan. I smile at the pregnant woman and she slides her eyes away from my wizard sleeves. The boy is wearing a little baseball cap, which he keeps flinging to the floor. I try not to look at him because two hideous green candles of snot are hanging precariously from each of his nostrils.

'Mackenzie!' the woman says. 'Mackenzie, pick that up now!'

The man she's with is super thin and nervous as a whippet. Every time he swallows, his Adam's apple trembles like he's crying inside. His eyes are pleading something like, 'I'm no more than a boy myself. Release me from this hell.'

Max reads the newspaper, occasionally patting my leg reassuringly until Mackenzie climbs on top of the magazine table next to Max's chair and starts to jump up and down, knocking into Max's sports section and getting his attention.

'Mackenzie!' the woman starts up again. 'Come here. You're getting a belt in a minute. You won't have no telly!'

The boy continues to jump, flicking magazines and papers over the floor with his feet.

Max puts a hand on the boy's shoulder, pressing him down mid-jump. 'Hey, your mammy wants you,' he says.

'Shut up, shut up, shut up,' sings the boy, flinging his hat. It lands in Max's lap and he picks it up.

'This is a really nice hat. Thomas the Tank Engine. I've been looking for one like this.'

'Mine!' squeals Mackenzie.

'Go to your mammy,' says Max, and hands her the hat.

She smiles a smile that says, 'Thank you. I love you. I need a father for this child and would give you lots of filthy sex.'

'You big poo,' says Mackenzie, getting down from the table.

'You're a bigger poo, and you have a poo hat,' says Max, squinting menacingly and pointing, and at that moment the woman's partner turns and takes a good, long, unfriendly look at Max. I feel Max squaring up his shoulders next to me, so I take his hand and place it on my tummy.

'Can you feel something there?' I ask. 'I feel a little flutter.'

Then thankfully the other couple are called in for their scan. The woman ignores my smile as she passes.

'Bye, Mr Poo Head,' says Mackenzie, as he disappears around the corner and Max waves his fist.

After they're gone I stare at Max.

'What?' he shrugs.

'Can we not even wait for a scan without you starting a brawl?'

'He was asking for it. He'd better not show his weaselly little face around here again.'

'He was about four.'

Max leans back in the hospital chair, staring straight ahead, and then he yawns massively.

'And in other news, Mr Poo Head . . . I'm undergoing a transformation that is nothing short of miraculous here.' I indicate my belly with the backs of my hands.

He bear hugs me. 'I adore you, my precious jewel!' he shouts. 'And you,' he says to the bump, and then I definitely feel a kick like a soft wingbeat inside.

Later we leave the scan room clutching each other in excitement, our eyes brimming with tears, not able to believe what we just saw. First the screen was black, and then there was a grey swirling blizzard, and then there was a baby! It was like spying. The baby was relaxing on her back, sucking her thumb, doing her own thing, and we watched her and measured her and talked about her. I say 'her' because we're certain it's a girl, even though we decided not to find out the baby's gender. We heard her little heart beating, we counted her toes, and we now even have a picture of her.

We leave the hospital high as balloons and go straight into the first department store we can find that has a baby section. There's a whole floor of stuff and still more stuff hanging from the ceiling. We stare around at this strange, colourful new world in amazement.

'You don't know this yet, but we need a Doodle Baby playmat with interactive mobile, mirrors and squeakers,' I say, checking the price and putting it back.

'Oh, one of those. Yeah, that's a must,' says Max, and it's a moment before I realise he's being sarcastic. 'And look – a baby nest. We need one of those to trap her in. No, no, even better look at this!' He's found an activity centre on wheels and starts pressing buttons. 'We can shove her in that and watch as she becomes enraged by these high-pitched nursery rhymes on repeat mode and tortured by these flashing lights coupled with her inability to move . . .'

'He's a cheerful man.' I smile to a woman shopper who's backing away.

'And it vibrates,' he continues, switching on the vibrating seat and making the beads on the tray rattle. 'Jesus on acid.'

I turn my back on him and head over to the gift section. Here there are Peter Rabbit moneyboxes and solid silver rattles, my-first-year photo frames and baby sock bouquets, but there's nothing like one of our congratulations crackers. Our 'New Baby' cracker could come in hot pink or blue stripe and contain useful stuff like a special dummy that makes the baby sleep on demand or bath oil that transforms mothers to fully made up, with good hair and dressed in leggings and a chic tunic. Something like that, anyway.

I put down a silver-plated hairbrush and wander off to the buggy section, where there are carriages of every conceivable style and colour. A young salesman approaches as soon as I touch the handle of a Biggedy Buggidy and asks about my perfect buggy criteria. Never before have I been required to consider this. I have a think while stroking the spotted canopy of a Ladybird City Bug.

'Erm, I'd like to be able to see the baby as I go along?' I ask apologetically, and he immediately wheels out three contraptions with clip-on bits and runs through their features. Max saunters over.

'This model, sir, is the four-wheel drive of the buggy world. It's a deluxe off-roader with suspension, and it folds down at the touch of a button to the size of a laptop – great for popping into the car boot or on a train or in a restaurant. Its aluminium frame makes it super lightweight, so your wife can lift this easily in and out of the car.'

'Ah, don't worry about that. She can lift a hell of a lot more than she looks like she can,' Max says, pointing up and down with his finger at me. Then he yawns.

I listen carefully and occasionally take notes as the sales guy talks me through an egg-shaped capsule on a wheeled tripod, designed to keep the baby out of the way of traffic fumes, and a pram-type affair that flips over and becomes a pushchair as the baby grows.

'And does that one keep the baby out of traffic fumes?' I ask.

'It suspends your tiny mewling newborn at just about exhaust-pipe height, I'd say,' Max interrupts with a pleasant smile.

Eventually bewildered, the sales guy wanders away, leaving us to have a think.

I punch Max on the arm. 'You weren't even listening to any of that, were you?'

'Neither were you,' says Max, snatching the note-book out of my hands and reading the list. '"Traffic fumes, laptop, eight hundred and fifty pounds"?'

'Look, it's our duty to know about this stuff. One day, in some class or something, I know I'm going to feel rubbish for not knowing about the parasol function of the Caterpillar Off-Road Sprint.'

'I'll bet you a hundred quid you won't,' he says.

'Aren't you interested in the Days Away Travel System With Car Seat?'

'Well, now, let's see. "Interested" is too strong a word, I think,' he says, rubbing his beard.

'You're not excited by one-finger manoeuvrability, then?'

'Well, I'd rather have a blow job.'

I shake my head and walk off tutting, and Max follows, calling out, 'I'm here, though! I'm with you.'

'And how I wish you weren't,' I mutter, and he laughs.

In the end we decide our first purchases should be a Moses basket and a sling baby carrier. We jot down the names of the leading brands so we can search eBay later, and I insist on buying a pack of tiny white sleepsuits with matching hat and a book called *Forty Weeks and Counting Down*. Then, boosted by that small purchase, we drift into the department store's café and moon over the first pictures of our baby.

Max takes out a scan photo. It's a close-up of the baby in profile, and he holds it up next to his head and tries to make the same pose, and then I'm extremely worried. As I look from him to her picture, I realise our baby definitely has Max's nose. I try to tell myself things might change over the next few months – she might lay down some cartilage or something, but flicking through *Forty Weeks and Counting Down*, it seems this might be her actual nose. At twenty weeks, she's fully formed, poor love. Shall I tell Max he might have made our daughter ugly? I'm just about to when my phone rings and flashes up 'Lucy', and when I answer, she's crying.

I get up, walking out of the noisy café to hear her better, and stand with one finger in my ear frowning out of the window. She's so upset I can't hear what she's saying.

'What's happened?' I manage to ask as she takes a breath.

All I hear is her rhythmic breathing as she sobs.

'Is it Reuben?'

'I'm bleeding,' she whispers. 'I'm bleeding loads, Viv.'

21

Reasons for Bleeding

In early pregnancy you might get some light bleeding, called 'spotting', when the foetus plants itself in the wall of your womb. This is also known as implantation bleeding, and often happens around the time that your first period after conception would have been due.

www.nhs.co.uk

Lucy is pale as the moon and red-eyed when I let myself into her flat. She's sitting with her legs wrapped in a towel on the floor, leaning against the wall, and staring into space.

I put down my bag and slip out of my coat, not taking my eyes off her. I get on the floor, sitting in front of her, and she slides her gaze to me.

'I just read in a pregnancy book that sometimes you can get bleeding and nothing is wrong with the baby,' I say gravely, smoothing her hair.

'It's out,' she says. She looks stricken and confused. I notice her hands are covered with dried blood. 'There was this lump of purple skin in my pants.'

I move to sit beside her. 'But bleeding can be normal,' I say, my certainty wavering.

'It's in the toilet,' she says, and swallows slowly. 'It just slid out.'

'The . . . the blood?'

'And . . . something else. I felt it slip out,' she says, and she looks at me with wild eyes. Then her face contorts and her shoulders start to heave.

We hold on to each other. Her fingers press into my forearm and she cries like I've never seen her cry. She keeps lifting her head and gulping for air.

'Hey, Lucy. Hey, babe,' I try to console her, rubbing her back as I look around the flat. There's a rusty smell of blood, and Lucy's work trousers and pants lie by the bathroom door, next to a red footprint. I wonder how long she's been bleeding and how much blood she's lost.

'Lucy, Luce, listen to me. Did you ring Reuben?'

'He's on a business trip.'

'OK, so did you ring the doctor?'

'I can't get through,' she wails, and shows me where her phone lies next to her.

'I'll try, or do you think we should get you to hospital?'

She lets her head fall back against the wall again. 'I don't know,' she says miserably.

I really don't like the colour of her now, so pale, almost blue. I pick up the phone and press 'redial'. I get up and walk past the open bathroom door. The bathmat is red and the toilet bowl is streaked, like a horror-film scene. I dare not look into the bowl. I walk back to Lucy, listening to the recorded messages, pressing options, and then I get to speak to a doctor, who puts me through to the hospital, and they ask how many sanitary towels she has needed to use within the last hour. I hand the phone to Lucy, who answers questions quietly with a yes or a no. Then she hangs up.

'They want me to go in for a scan,' she says in a flat, dull voice.

I don't know what to say. It seems likely with all this blood that she's lost the baby, but what do I know? I feel my stomach turn. If they want her to have a scan, does that mean there's some hope? It's just a relief she's not dying. I look at her and nod.

'Will you come with me?' she asks.

'Of course I'm coming. What do you need . . . ? I'll get us a taxi.'

'They want me to bring the . . . whatever came out of me,' she says, and her eye sockets seem to turn darker. I glance towards the bathroom. 'They want to do tests.'

'But how will you get it and take it? How?' I jabber, trying to stop myself from openly shuddering.

She gets to her feet and pads to the open-plan kitchen, leaving me staring at her bare blood-streaked legs beneath the towel. She reaches into a cupboard and takes down a large plastic box. She opens a drawer and fishes about among utensils, eventually bringing out chopsticks. She places them on the counter next to the plastic box and looks at me, her face deathly white.

'Mate, I don't think chopsticks . . .' I shake my head.

She reaches into the drawer again, this time bringing out a slotted spoon, and places it solemnly down on the counter. We look at one another, our eyes snagging on each other's.

She walks towards the bathroom holding the box and the spoon in her bloodied hands. Then she stops at the door.

'I'm not doing it,' she tells me, and for a sickening moment I think she might hand the equipment to me, but she places it down on the counter. She leans on the counter and rests her head in the crook of her arm. Her foot smears a fresh new drop of red on the tiled floor.

'Shall I just flush it?' I ask, but she doesn't answer.

I take her to the bedroom and make her lie down on a towel, trying not to look at the chair in the corner where her maternity top and matching sleepsuit are draped, the little, flat, empty striped sleepsuit waiting there for nothing. I feel a lump in my throat. She closes her eyes while I pull a cover over her.

'I'm going to clean up the bathroom, OK?' I say, and she nods. 'And then the taxi will be here and we'll go to the hospital.' I stroke her hand as a tear slides down into her hair. 'It's going to be OK, Lucy. You're OK,' I tell her.

She opens her eyes and looks at me. 'But my baby, Viv,' she wails, and her face crumples.

22

Losing It

Fifteen to twenty-five per cent of pregnancies will end in miscarriage, most often between weeks six and twelve.

Forty Weeks and Counting Down

It's dark outside and cold when I leave Lucy. I hail a cab and it pulls up outside the Portland Hospital with tyres hissing on the wet tarmac.

I tell the driver the address of Max's studio in Kilburn Park and he makes a U-turn, passing a busy restaurant. I glimpse a scene of cool London, girls in bars instead of in hospitals.

Lucy's doctor wanted to keep her in overnight and perform a procedure in the morning to make sure she doesn't get an infection. Lucy's scan showed a dark, empty coffee-bean shape where her baby used to be. No heartbeat and no baby – no viable pregnancy, they said. It seems she miscarried. I hate the word 'miscarried', with its implication that she's to blame. I hate that she's not pregnant anymore, and I hate that she's sad. Part of it is selfishness. 'It just slipped out,' those horrible words she said. What if it happens to me? I feel a tear spill as I place a hand over my belly. Poor Lucy. Who understands how it feels to carry a baby? Who can I talk to? Who knows everything? It was Lucy. I'm then awash with loneliness and wishing for all I'm worth that she'll be pregnant again and soon.

I look out of the window at busy Baker Street station as we pull up at the traffic lights; I gaze at the red reflection on the shiny road and try to focus on the fluttering movements of my baby. I can't face that yoga class without Lucy, that's for sure. In fact, all the exciting classes and shopping and learning just seem pointless now.

'*All is as it should be,*' whispers Angel.

I struggle up the stairs to Max's studio, heavy and soon out of breath, and after a while he opens the door to see where I am and skips down to help me up the last flight. When we get behind the door, he hugs me to his chest. He smells of cooking, like frying onions.

'How're you doing?' he asks, and in the scruffy little entrance hall, I tell him about Lucy, my face pressed against him, speaking into his shirt. He doesn't say anything, and when I've finished, he leads me through to the studio, offering me some stir-fried chicken he made. The studio looks cool, lit up with his collection of tatty lamps. Some jangly world music plays. The canvases are stacked away. I look at my reflection in the large dark expanse of window; my pale face seems to float above the black dress. I look away around the room and notice a half-bottle of wine and a glass. Max brings a plate and I realise I'm starving. He sits across the room, picks up a pencil and begins to sketch while I eat. Dave sits at my feet offering his friendliest face, all purrs and hopeful blinking. Max sketches, occasionally taking big slugs of wine. It feels peaceful. I'm glad he doesn't talk about Lucy.

I get up and take my plate to the kitchen, returning with a glass of water.

'Do you not want a glass of wine?' asks Max.

'No,' I say, and down the water.

'Pretty rough evening,' he says.

'Terrible. Sad.'

'I'm staying here tonight,' he tells me. I lie down, resting my ear against the arm of the chair. 'Stay here with me.'

'OK.' I feel I could fall asleep in seconds. I don't really care where.

He walks over, the bottle of wine and a glass dangling from one hand. I look at the long toes of his bare feet. He takes my hand and I follow him to the bedroom. I watch as he pulls the pea-green curtains closed. We lie on the bed together. When he kisses me, I taste the wine, a deep red berry tang on his lips. We don't speak. I move my mouth away from him and he stretches to kiss me again. Our teeth tap together. I listen to our breathing as he moves over me and pushes up my dress. I lie completely still and watch his face. His hair and beard and eyebrows dark like the hollows of his eyes. The dim light from the open door falls on his cheekbones and the curve of his shoulder. His lips part as he moves and I glimpse the white of his teeth.

He drops down onto his forearms and touches my nose with his. 'Think about this,' he says, 'think about us,' and he moves a hand between my legs.

I link my hands behind his neck, concentrating on the sensation of his fingers on me and feeling him inside me, and feeling the muscles of his shoulders moving.

Afterwards he pulls the sheets up to his waist and sits back with his wine. I watch him. Something about the way he is makes me relax. He's calm. The bulk of him somehow makes everything seem easy and better.

'You bit me on the ear,' he says, rubbing it.

'It's my latest craving, Irishmen's ears,' I say, stretching up my arms. I glance sideways. He sips the wine moodily. I roll onto my side and rest my chin in my hands.

'I'm staying here until your mother is gone,' he says. 'When is she going? You said a week.'

I get jolted out of the peaceful feeling. I'm not prepared for the big speech.

'Soon. She hasn't found a place to stay yet,' I lie.

'Viv, she's not looking. Any fucking idiot can find a place to stay in London.'

'She can't go just anywhere, can she? Anyway, she will be gone soon.'

I watch him. He looks away. I realise suddenly that I've been hoping that this situation would just go away, that somehow we'd all start to get along, that they'd love me enough to make it work, and we'd end up being a happy family. Max is glowering into space, obviously thinking about Rainey.

I touch his arm gently. 'You can't stay here. You live with me.'

'I live where I like,' he snaps.

I don't like the way this conversation is going. I get up and pull my dress down.

'If we're going to talk about this, let's not do it when one of us is drunk, hey?' I say quietly and start towards the door.

'Neither of us is drunk, Vivienne!' he shouts.

I go into the studio and stand there not knowing what to do, while he pulls on his jeans and follows. 'Don't fucking walk off!'

'I'm trying to get rid of Rainey, OK?'

'No, you are not,' he says, glaring.

'If you stay here . . . it's like leaving me. I know she aggravates the shit out of you. She aggravates the shit out of me, but she's going.' He shakes his head angrily. 'She *is* going, Max. I told her she has to go, and she will, and meanwhile I'm pregnant with your baby and I need you with me, helping me! Not fucking sulking.'

'I do not sulk!' he shouts, throwing his hands in the air dramatically. 'I don't need to sulk!' He walks away.

'Do you know what you are?'

'Oh, I think you're about to tell me.' He turns to me, pulling a mad, angry face.

'Fucking selfish!' I point at him now. I'm on a roll and he's swaying uncertainly. 'I'm having a baby, OK? You might think it's nothing, that women do it every day, but it's a pretty big deal to me, actually, and it's not good enough you smoking out of windows and going on about blow jobs in baby shops and making me . . . upset!'

He scratches the back of his neck and frowns. 'I was joking about the blow job . . .'

'Do you know I read in the paper today that Harold Pinter used to fill every room of the house with flowers for Antonia Fraser?'

'What?'

'Yes, and when I read that, I thought, how romantic! I've never been treated that romantically. You treat me like your mate or something!'

'No . . .'

'Yes, you do!' My voice wobbles as if I might cry. He steps towards me, but I hold up a hand.

'I'm the one who wants to get married,' he says, jabbing his chest.

'So do I!'

'You don't. You won't even set a date. Am I not

good enough for you? Am I not rich enough, is that it?'

'Don't you dare say that.'

We glare at each other. He looks away first.

'I love you and that's all,' he says quietly. 'Maybe I've been a dick.'

'You have been a dick, a selfish dick,' I say, and he looks up sharply. 'An unsupportive, selfish dickhead. Babyish too.' I like insulting him. I smile.

'Well, then I'm sorry, Viv.'

'Yes, well, just, you know, be better!'

'Am I not supportive?' He shakes his head. 'You mean everything to me. All I want is to be with you and do my painting.'

'Well, you just described your life. That's what you do.'

'I mean make a living painting.' He looks into the middle distance, thinking. 'My da always said, "You'll never make a living painting pictures." He thought I should be a painter and decorator. I want to make some money, Viv. I want to support you and the baby.'

'Your dad's wrong. You're the only one who's earned a penny this month.'

He walks over to the stacked canvases and picks one out, leaning it against the wall. It's the painting of me in the wedding tutu.

'Guy is closing my show early,' he says.

'Why?'

'Not enough sales.'

'But doesn't it take time?'

'No, Viv. It wasn't successful.' He takes out his plastic wallet of tobacco and starts to roll up a cigarette, leaning on the chair arm. If he wants to smoke out of the window, I'm going to be fine with that, I decide. He watches me as he licks the paper. 'I've decided I'm going to get a job.' He turns to me, half smiling. 'Do you think I'd make a good postman?'

I shake my head.

'No?'

'You'd be the worst postman ever.'

'Ah, you're right. What about a courier? I could get my bike back.'

Shit, he's really thought about this. He's actually considering a job other than painting. I feel my heart pull – it's just too sad. He's only ever been interested in art. All the way through university he worked hard at it. He loves it and he's so good. It's what he was born to do. He puts the roll-up cigarette away in the pouch and closes it.

'You're an artist. The only other thing you've ever done profitably is make bongs from household objects,' I say.

'Not true – I once worked as assistant to a dog groomer who said I had talent. I was good at cleaning the arses.'

'Oh yeah, and I suppose there's your recent business idea of knitted companions for the bereaved?'

'It was crochet companions.'

'Look, Max, we still have options. We can get rid of my flat and live here, and I'm on the brink of a deal at work, I know I am. We've been doing a lot of thinking about the product and we have another sales meeting coming up,' I say, trying to sound confident.

He smiles sadly. 'I can't paint. I feel like I've lost my edge, lost my passion,' he says, and looks off to the left forlornly.

'Can't you divert some of the energy you use to hate Rainey?'

He laughs and stares at his feet.

'Max! Fucking hell, snap out of it. You don't have the luxury of losing your passion. We need you, so you'll have to just get on with it. You're a great artist.' I take out all the canvases and line them up. They're all me in different poses and in different phases of pregnancy. 'You can't sit about wondering if you're good enough. Just accept that you are – look.'

'I can't *sell* any of those – you don't like paintings of you sold,' he says.

'I've changed my mind. Sell me. Paint some more and sell them. Put on another exhibition.'

'Guy won't want another exhibition of my stuff.'

'There are other galleries.'

He sighs.

'You can't give up – you're too good.'

'You love me, don't you?'

I leave a pause and pretend to think about this. 'Yeah, I suppose I love you,' I say resignedly.

'Hey, Viv, will you marry me?' he asks. He walks over, puts his arms around my neck.

'Yeah,' I say.

We kiss and go back to bed. I curl up next to Max and hold his hand, feeling rocks in my heart because I've lied to him good and proper now. I've told him Rainey is looking for a place to stay when in fact she's making herself at home, settling in for a few months. 'Stay as long as you like,' I told her, and I can't un-tell her, can I? Shit. Shit. Shit.

'You all right?' asks Max, putting his arm over me.

'I'm just thinking about Lucy,' I tell him, and I think about Lucy. I hope she's asleep now and not staring at the moonlight through the curtains, like me.

23

#Slowlyslowlycatchymonkey

During pregnancy you could find yourself being irritable and impatient. It is important to think about your own needs and take time to understand how you feel. Try to tune in to yourself to discover what you really need.

Forty Weeks and Counting Down

'What's occurring, people?' asks Michael, moon-walking in backwards, ten minutes late for our Belle Peau briefing.

The boiler has broken, so Christie and I are wearing coats and pretending to smoke using pens and our visible breath as props. Christie now gives up trying to do smoke rings and pulls the funnel neck of her mohair jumper dress over her nose.

'Jesus, it's colder than a witch's tit in here,' says Michael.

'We're just going through the website, Michael,' I say. 'You've done such a great job. It really looks perfect. I love the build-your-own-cracker option too.'

'I thank you,' says Michael, joining us at the little office meeting table. 'That's what you don't pay me for.' He puts up the hood of his old duffel coat.

'So, for Belle Peau, as well as the website, we're showing the cracker samples in different colours so they have something to handle, aren't we?'

'We have the tangerine and the pearlised pink and the grey,' confirms Christie.

'The lines we're looking at are: "I'm Attracted to You", "Sexy Bride", "Out of the Closet", "Still a Virgin", "Like a Virgin", "Not a Virgin Anymore", "Suddenly Single", "Girls' Night Out", "Hen Night" and "I Love You, Valentine".' Michael and Christie nod sagely. 'I got these Belle Peau panties to use for one of the samples.' I take the scant scrap of peach satin and black lace from its tissue-lined box and Christie gasps.

'Oh my God, they are gorgeous.' She takes them, fingering them in awe.

'Just seeing those in a female hand is giving me a twitch-on,' says Michael.

Christie giggles.

I give Michael a stern look. 'Those cost seventy pounds – don't put your greasy fingermarks on them.'

'Not greasy, Viv, warm and dry,' he says, wiggling the fingers of his right hand.

'Right,' I continue. 'We have to decide which product to put in with the pants – there's the upmarket scented candle, the luxury lollipop or the massage oil.'

Just then Damon bursts in holding a spanner, managing to look even more disconcerting by wearing a woollen hat with a peak and leather earflaps, accentuating his brow overhang and flapping jowls.

'Is that radiator on there, Viv?' he booms.

I reach out a hand but detect no warmth. 'Sadly no,' I say, and he stomps over to feel for himself at the bottom near the pipes, wafting around a peculiar smell that reminds me of a pet gerbil I once had called Bubble, who fell in the toilet and drowned.

'So, this cracker will retail at a hundred pounds,' I continue.

'Then definitely put the massage oil in. I mean, it looks like the most value, and also you're led to believe that by buying it, you're either going to get rubbed down with it yourself or you're going to get to rub this oil all over a loved one,' says Christie gravely.

'You know what? I agree with you, Christie. Very insightful. Well done,' I say.

'What transition is it?' asks Damon from under the radiator.

'"I Love You, Valentine" or "Sexy Bride". It needs to be an occasion to spend that kind of money,' I say, feeling the end of my nose turning numb. 'Damon, is this building going to be heated today? Because I don't think we can work under these conditions.'

'Keep wrapped up and you'll be all right, or dance around a bit.'

'Dance around a bit?'

'Yeah, have a little jig about,' he shouts over the clatter of spanner on pipe.

'Damon, mate,' Michael calls out, and the hammering

stops, 'it's mid-November, yeah? Viv's pregnant. Her baby's trying to lay down fat and grow eyelashes. It needs to be warm.'

I have to say Michael's in-depth knowledge of pregnancy is becoming a bit spooky, especially when he says it's all based on fish-breeding. He squints at me now as if I'm something in a tank.

Damon appears, on his knees, and lays down the spanner.

'All right, all right, I know what this is leading up to! Free rental of the office space as compensation. What say I give you the rest of November free?'

Christie and I look at each other. This hadn't occurred to us. She raises her eyebrows and nods.

'On one condition.'

'What's that, Damon?' I ask.

'Fifty per cent of the business.'

'What? No way,' I say, setting my mouth into a firm line.

'Then I'm out,' he says.

'No, Damon, we're out. I'll tell you what – we'll go to a café for the rest of the morning because we have a very important meeting to prepare for this afternoon. If the heating isn't fixed by tomorrow, you'll give us two weeks' free rent for the inconvenience of being freezing, not to mention the loss of revenue.'

Damon drops his head in defeat. 'All right, Viv, you win,' he says.

Christie holds up her hand to high-five me, but I'm

already packing up our equipment. Damon glowers under his hat like some kind of weird troll.

Then Michael puts his face close up to Damon and turns a finger round near his own ear. 'Don't you know she's loco?' he says. Then he sucks his teeth, turns and saunters out.

Belle Peau's head office is in Soho. It's above their flagship store, which drips luxury from every padded hanger and puts you in mind of saucy mistresses and bordellos. Upstairs in the office, the walls are papered in purple flock, and there's a sweet heady fragrance of red roses.

We meet with the buyer, Sebastian, who's tall and thin with an upsweep of grey hair like a feather and a voice with a whistley 's'. He seems to use more words with an 's' than normal. He likes us. He wants to give us a break. He likes our products, thinks it's a fabulous concept, but in his mind's eye he can't separate crackers from Christmas, so he wants us to quote for luxury festive crackers for next year, and in the meantime he'll share our website with the rest of his colleagues. We leave, walking back through the scented dream world of silky French knickers and lace teddies, and then out onto the shiny pavement of a wet and windy already-darkening afternoon.

We stand for a moment looking around as if we've just been beamed down. I try to process the meeting. What just happened? We should be cheered by the fact that he actually wants us to quote, even if it is next Christmas. The trouble is, by next Christmas we'll be toast. Across the road, I spot the glowing lamplights of a pub inviting us and, since our office is out of service, we settle in there for the rest of the working day.

The atmosphere at our table is gloomy. Christie is talking about getting a better-paid job delivering pizza, and Michael is already applying for work. I wonder if I should do the same, but then I'm pregnant, aren't I, and no one is going to want to employ me. In any case, I don't want a job, I want to run my own business, and if Belle Peau are interested in the product, well, that means something. Businesses take time to set up and turn over a profit. I'll find a way to make it work. I'll get a loan or something.

I look at Christie gazing into space with her head at an angle and Michael rocking his crossed legs on one foot. I need to deliver a rallying speech and fast.

'Slowly, slowly catchy monkey,' I say, raising one finger wisely.

'You what, Viv?' asks Christie.

'Slowly, slowly catchy monkey, Christie! It means things take time. We must be patient and concentrate, and then we'll get what we want.'

They both mull this over. Christie's lips move as she repeats the phrase.

'We need a buyer quickly, quickly, though,' Michael points out with the kind of insight he's known for.

'We do, Michael, and that is where you come in, my friend.'

They both sit up a little now, interested.

'Me?' asks Michael.

'Yes, you. You are irresistible to women, self-proclaimed albeit. Well, let's put that to the test. Let's *capitalise* on that.'

Christie looks at Michael anew with a puzzled little frown.

He leans forward and starts chewing imaginary gum, eyes narrowed. 'Go on,' he says.

'Barnes and Worth,' I say, and lean back triumphantly.

'Oh no. No way,' he says. 'You've got to be joking!'

'I have never been more serious.'

'I won't go crawling back to that Medusa!' he spits.

'Michael, Mike. Don't look at it as crawling back. All I want you to do is influence her a bit and get her to buy some transition crackers, pronto, like.'

'You mean Mole?' asks Christie, for whom the penny has yet to drop. 'Our old boss Mole, who was engaged to Mike and then was sexually harassing him?'

'Was it sexual harassment, though, or was it just a bit of fun?' I say, not liking the sound of myself ethically but getting over it by thinking of a big fat order from Barnes and Worth.

'Vivienne, that sister haunts me day and night.

Before I left Barnes and Worth, right? She gave me a CD. Of course I played it, thinking it must be some of our get it on songs. Do you know what was on that CD?' he asks, and we shake our heads in unison. 'A lot of banging and her crying for twenty minutes.'

Christie looks at me and gulps.

'People grieve in different ways, Mike. Some are more socially acceptable than others.' I shrug.

He giggles sarcastically, ending with a totally straight face. 'Viv, two words: Forget. It.'

'Yeah, just hear me out. She wants you, and we want her to place an order,' I say, pushing his pint of beer closer, 'and if she places an order, I'll be able to pay you – it's win-win. It's about leverage and low-hanging lemons and that.'

'So let me get this straight – you want to dangle me like wriggling bait above the enormous toothy jaws of that she-devil, my sworn enemy, so that she'll place an order?'

'Well, that's it in a nutshell,' I say.

'Er, not even legal. That's harassment. You're using my sexuality to ensnare.'

'Yes, OK, I am. But women are subjected to this kind of thing all the time and no one bats an eyelid, do they? You're just making it a teeny bit more even. And we won't actually let the she-devil get the wriggling bait, so . . . no biggie. Anyway, it's our last chance. It's harassment or foraging for roadkill to eat.'

'This won't even work,' tuts Christie. 'How will it work?'

'It works like this,' I say, smoothing out the air with a hand for effect. 'We get a meeting with Mole at Barnes and Worth, and we let Mole – I mean Marion – believe that if she places an order, she'll win favour with the lovely Michael. A big order, mind – we're not throwing him into the lion's den for nothing!' I catch his horrified expression and add, 'Or at all, really.'

They both stare at me for a long moment and then Christie shakes her head. 'It's not like you, Viv. You're not the Viv I know – since you fell pregnant, you've gone all hard,' she says, eyeing me sadly.

I consider this, picturing myself as some sort of lioness: predatory, dangerous, willing to risk anything to provide for my young.

'Needs must, Christie. Needs absolutely must,' I say looking at her baffled face.

24

Emotions

Early miscarriage may feel like you are losing part of yourself and you may experience intense emotions. You could be angry or feel a sense of injustice. This is part of the grieving process. You might feel confused or guilty. All of this is a normal response.

Forty Weeks and Counting Down

That evening I visit Lucy. She's home alone until Reuben returns from his business trip, and has been told to rest in bed for a couple of days. On the way, I buy flowers, cartons of fresh soup, chocolate and trashy magazines.

She looks wan sitting up in her big white bed. Everything in Lucy's flat is pristine and white; that's what made the blood seem so shocking. I glance in the bathroom. I did the best clean-up job I could in the time I had, but I'm worried there might be a spot I missed. I don't see anything except shiny white tiles.

She looks crossly at the magazines, tapping the front-cover caption above the photo of some beautiful A-list film star.

'What I don't understand is, why does she always have to have "Unlucky in love" plastered above her head? Isn't she a frigging billionaire?'

'How are you feeling?' I ask.

'Been listening to a lot of Portishead.'

'That bad.' I take her hand, arranging the engagement and wedding bands so that the beautiful diamonds are at the front.

'The hospital were very good, very reassuring. Dr Morgan said these things happen for the best.' She smiles wistfully. 'He said there's no reason why I shouldn't be pregnant again in a couple of months, if I want to be.'

'Do you?'

'Reuben will want to. I do. God, I want to get pregnant straight away. I can't believe I have to wait a whole month until I even ovulate. I want this over with.'

'I know you do—' I begin, preparing to say something about grief taking time.

'I don't want to talk about it, Viv,' she snaps.

'No. You just need time to—'

'So don't mention this to me ever again, OK?'

'OK.' I nod decisively.

We sit and think about that for a while. The radiator in her bedroom ticks. The maternity clothes are gone from the chair. I look at her and she glares back like a wounded cat.

'When's Reuben back?'

'Tonight. He cut his trip short because of . . . this.'

'He'll look after you, then?'

'I thought I was OK, but I need him here. I do.'
She looks at me for a moment before shaking her head
and dissolving into tears. I pull her into my arms. 'Am
I a failure as a woman?' she sobs.

I squeeze her tight. I gaze at the ceiling while she
cries, my heart breaking for her.

'Of course not,' I say, smoothing down her hair. 'Of
course not. This happens all the time, babe.'

'I'm old. I'm too old,' she wails, desolate.

I pull away so I can see her face. 'Hey, hold on, you
and I are the same age!'

She gives a snotty laugh. I find her a tissue.
She blows her nose and takes a long, shuddering
breath.

'It just happens sometimes, at any age.'

'You're right.' She nods. 'I know.'

I pat her leg. 'Want some soup? I have cream of
mushroom or pea and ham?' I ask, showing her the
cartons. She points at the pea and ham. 'I'll just go
and warm it through for you, pet,' I say in a nana
voice.

I heat the soup in the microwave, where Lucy does
most of her cooking. Her hob is showroom clean, and
I don't know if she even has any pans. I take in a tray
with a bowl of soup and a slice of bread and butter.
She slurps the soup bent over the tray, and then she
wipes around the bowl with the bread.

'Look at you, the Cheltenham princess, eating in

bed, mopping up with bread – what would your mother say?'

'My mother,' Lucy sighs. 'She's never forgiven herself for having a daughter who refuses to be interested in ramekins.'

'But *why* aren't you interested in ramekins, Lucy? They're so great.'

'I wanted to go home pregnant when I introduce Reubs to Mum.' She adds sadly, 'A double whammy.'

'You still can,' I say, and her shiny eyes flick to mine, then to my bump and away. I feel bad for still being pregnant.

'What about *your* mother? Tell me she's not still with you?' she turns on me.

'Yep, still with me, and before you say anything, you should know I've told her to stay as long as she needs, because she's in a bit of a situation, and I want you as my friend to understand and support my decision.'

Lucy pulls back her head, looking puzzled. 'God, that's a bit of a prepared speech. What situation is she in?'

'One that requires my help.'

'Another Rainey guilt trap, I bet,' she sighs. 'How is Max liking it?'

'They hate each other.'

'I bet he's pleased about her staying as long as she likes, then.'

'He doesn't know that bit.'

'Viv!'

'I'm going to tell him. I'm telling him today.'

'I thought you two were madly in love. How can you keep secrets from him? I mean, what in God's name possessed you to say she can stay, anyway?' She shakes her head.

'It's complicated.' I look away. Sometimes I wonder when Lucy assumed this big-sister role. It irritates me because I've always tried not to judge her or offer unsolicited advice. 'Yeah, I've dithered, left it too long without telling him already, and the longer I leave it, the madder he's going to be.'

'Dude, this is going to end badly.'

'No, it won't.'

'Yes, it will,' she insists, raising her eyebrows.

'It won't, because I have a plan I think might just work.'

'Let's hear it,' she says in a bored voice, pushing away the tray. I put it on the floor.

'Well, it's a skeleton plan at the moment . . .' I pause for effect. 'If Max and Rainey start to like each other, he won't mind that she's staying longer, will he? What I want is a family. If we can all get on, she'll be around when the baby is born. In my mind's eye, I see us all at Nana's chatting over some shared task, like shelling peas or peeling potatoes, or some other food preparation. Perhaps we'd even dust off the waffle-maker . . . Anyway, then Reg pops in with Pimm's for us all, and how we laugh . . .'

'What would you be laughing at?'

'Eh? Oh, I don't know . . . at life, love and the universe . . .'

'That is not a plan; it's a bloody fantasy,' says Lucy, and my vision disappears into thin air along with my dreamy smile. 'Viv, you can't sort this out using your usual misplaced optimism.'

'Anyway,' I say, and fiddle with the edge of her bedspread, 'I shouldn't discuss it with you – you're blinded by rage at the moment.'

She shakes her head in disbelief. 'OK, just for argument's sake, if you do want them to get on, how are you going to make them like each other?'

'Well, I thought I might organise some sort of shared experience, like that team-building thing you went on at work.'

'You're going to take them paintballing?'

'Ice-skating, pottery-painting, something like that.'

'It won't work.'

'I know,' I say gloomily, and turn to look at Lucy. Her eyes move over my face.

'If you want to make them behave, you need to use emotional blackmail. You need to use the baby. They're both emotionally invested in the baby,' she says, and I immediately love her completely, for being so clever and manipulative.

'That kind of thinking is why you're where you are today, Lucy Bond.' I shake my head in awe.

And right there and then the plan to get Rainey and Max to at least tolerate each other is hatched, and it starts with taking them both with me to my very first National Childbirth Trust class.

25

Our very First National Childbirth Trust Class

28 November 10:47

From: margaretnuner@nct.co.uk
To: viviennesummers@dreamteam.co.uk
Subject: local classes

Dear Vivienne,

Thank you for your interest in the National Childbirth Trust. The NCT is the leading charity offering information and support throughout pregnancy, birth and early parenthood. I'm pleased to say that there is space for you in our Tuesday class at the St John's Wood surgery at 6.30 p.m. on 4 December. We are quite a few classes into the course, however, and this week we are preparing for birth, just so you know what to expect. It would be a very good idea to attend this class with your intended birth partner or partners.

I look forward to meeting with you then.

Best wishes,

Margaret

It could work. To prevent either Max or Rainey backing out, I didn't tell them the other was coming. I'm not the kind of person who goes around manipulating situations, but in this case I'm willing to give it a go. Rainey is meeting us at the doctor's surgery at six.

When Max and I arrive she's standing outside. They clock each other, eyes glittering with hostility like warring street cats.

'Oh, he's here,' Rainey says, and visibly sinks into her yellow felt coat. She's wearing a floor-length skirt of many colours.

'Father,' sneers Max, pointing to his chest. He guides me towards the main entrance of the surgery.

'Given up smoking, have you?' she fires at his back.

I turn and give her a stern look while reaching for her arm; the three of us cannon through the door together.

In the little waiting room, a semi-circle of about four pregnant women and their partners look up at us mildly. The leader of the group pops up from behind the receptionist's counter with refreshments. She's about fifty, tanned and blonde in a 1960s way. She smiles at us.

'Hello. Welcome. I'm Margaret,' she says to each of us as she shakes our hands.

'Max Kelly. I'm the father,' says Max formally and a bit too loudly.

Some of the seated group break from their con-
versations to watch.

'I'm Vivienne,' I gush. 'I emailed you. I hope you
don't mind I brought my mother along.'

'Not at all,' says Margaret. 'We welcome the perspective of those who have done this before.' She smiles
at Rainey, who squints in a knowledgeable way. 'Please
take a seat.'

We turn to the group. There are two free chairs
beside each other and one on the edge of the line. I
make for the pair of chairs and Rainey quickly sits
beside me before Max has even moved away from the
counter. He takes off his battered leather jacket and
hat, smooths his hair back, and quietly takes the spare
chair. I wait for him to look at me so I can smile
encouragingly, but he concentrates on the class, briefly
acknowledging the man to his left, then leaning forward
with his elbows resting on his knees and hands cupped.

Margaret brings her chair to the front and begins
by saying that this week we are concentrating on the
birth and working on our own individual birth plans,
but before we do that, she asks if anyone has any
questions that have arisen since last week. A woman
across from me raises her hand. She and her partner
are super-sized in bottle-green tracksuits, dwarfing the
rabbity couple beside them. Together they represent
a heavy wall of flesh. She is only marginally smaller
than him, and her head is the size of a bucket, with
features seemingly drawn on. Her oiled black hair is

slicked back into a thin plait that snakes over her shoulder and ends curled in her lap like an adder.

'Yes, Kitty?' asks Margaret.

'Yeah, I've been getting a lot of pelvic pain and I was wondering if I should stop hand-shunting the steam engines now I'm seven months.'

What the hell did she just say? I smirk at Max, but he ignores me, turning his hat around in his hands, looking up under his brows.

'Me and Paul work on the miniature steam railway,' Kitty says to the group by way of explanation.

Margaret thinks Kitty should stop hand-shunting, but adds that exercise is good for pregnant women, that we need to be fit for the birth. Then she asks Rainey if she agrees. There's a pause. I turn slightly to see what Rainey's doing and see she's thinking.

'Having travelled extensively around South America,' she begins with her eyes closed, 'I've had the privilege of witnessing many births. Often the women were literally toiling in the fields when they went into labour. Some gave birth and carried on.'

Oh no. Please not another fricking 'birth in the fields' story. Not here. The girl from the rabbity couple scrutinises me as if I'm an odd specimen. She and her husband are wearing power suits. I feel inadequate and inappropriately casual in my maternity leggings and smock.

'Yes, it's good to remember, ladies, how incredibly privileged we are to be having a baby in this country at this time,' nods Margaret, and Rainey nods too and is about to open her mouth again when a tiny-boned, frightened Indian girl asks if a person can be too small to give birth.

I glance across at Max, wishing I was sitting with him. He doesn't make eye contact. He's chewing a matchstick and watching Margaret, who answers that our bodies are designed to cope with birth, and then she tells us to couple up with our birth partners and take a birth planner. Rainey gets up and snatches a sheet from the pile. I feel a small thrill that she's here and involved. I've dreamed of something like this for years, of her caring for me, helping me. She returns to her seat and begins reading out the questions. I lean forward and motion for Max to come over.

'OK, Vivienne, what are your plans for pain relief in the first stage of labour?' she asks.

'Paracetamol, lavender bath, bit of relaxing music,' I say confidently. I've been reading *Forty Weeks and Counting Down*. I know what I'm doing.

'Already discounting a TENS machine? O-K,' says Rainey.

What's a TENS machine? I have no clue. Luckily Max has appeared. He hovers uncomfortably for a bit before bending down to the man in the seat beside me.

'Hi, there,' he says in his polite voice. 'Would you mind moving up one place so's I can sit next to my partner?' he asks.

The man looks around, surveying the seating arrangement, then refuses to move because the birth video is on in a minute and he and his wife – Jane, I think he said her name was – chose these exact seats so they could get a direct view of the television. Max gives a small nod, then turns towards the television and moves it slightly so that the seat to the left of the man now has the most direct view.

'Can I sit down next to my partner now?' he asks, and the couple move up, muttering something about punctuality and seating allocation.

I put a hand happily on Max's knee. You see, this is exactly what I wanted. The three of us together, concentrating on our baby. I feel very special. I'm a sacred vessel again.

'Are you considering a water birth? If so, have you booked in at a birth suite where these are provided?' continues Rainey, reading in a staccato voice.

'No, not considering one,' I answer.

'Vivienne, I think you should – water is Nature's anaesthetic.'

I don't want a water birth. I don't like water; my hair goes funny even in a slight misting of the stuff, and I want to look good in the photos.

'Are you sure?' asks Rainey.

'Positive.'

'I'll put yes down and you can decide nearer the time,' she says.

'She said no,' says Max.

Rainey closes her eyes, holding the pencil in mid-air. 'One of us here has actually experienced birth. Am I right?' Her eyes snap open and she gazes into space waiting for an answer.

I glance at Max.

'So what?' he says. 'She said no – put no.'

'Vivienne, I'd urge you to keep your options open,' says Rainey, ignoring him.

'All right, put yes,' I mutter, resigning myself to frizz-ball hair. I look at Max and press my lips together. 'We don't know what it's going to be like, do we?' I say with a shrug. I feel his thigh muscle tense under my palm.

Next up is the birth video. A naked sweating woman is squatting and holding on to a rope with both hands. She's rocking and moaning, deeply concentrating. I look across at the innocent faces of Kitty and Jane and Rabbity Woman. I can see the wide eyes of the Indian woman shining in the flickering light. We're all going to have to do this: these babies are going to have to come out of us somehow.

On screen, the woman is kneeling now and leaning on a chair. Her thighs are streaked with blood. Then suddenly there's a shocking close-up as she opens like some sort of seed pod and a tiny furry head appears. Twinkly music is playing. A man steps up and wipes the woman's brow. She whispers, 'Thanks,' and smiles. Come on, if she's smiling, how bad can the pain be? I mean, you don't smile if you're in agony, do you, unless you have some weird fetish? The midwife speaks low and calm. It all seems quite peaceful, but then the woman lurches forward and cries out a long 'Huuuuh' before slumping onto the chair. She doesn't rest for long. Suddenly she's crying, 'Ah, ah, ah, ahhh!' She heaves and something slippery shoots into the arms of the midwife, the umbilical cord unfurling like a blue aniseed twist. Then the woman smiles; she laughs and cries as she cradles a crumpled purple baby in her arms.

I realise my mouth has been hanging open. I gulp as I look back at the faces of the women in the room with a spike of terror in my heart. Soon something similarly wild and brutal is about to happen and it's going to involve us. This is serious shit. I sit wide-eyed and motionless as Margaret snaps on the lights. She explains in a grave voice that the woman giving birth in that video had absolutely no pain relief at all.

There's a long silence as we take this in. Margaret then changes her tone to bright and breezy, and asks us each to think of a concern, something that may have been niggling us, anything at all. Rainey raises a hand.

'Yes, I've been worried about how stress levels of the mother affect the unborn baby,' she says, head on one side.

Margaret invites her to expand.

'I'm worried that my daughter, Vivienne, is under

too much pressure to earn money because her partner is unable to keep them.'

'What?' I begin to interrupt. 'No—'

'He's an artist, you see, and his recent exhibition failed,' explains Rainey.

'I'm not under pressure!'

Max snorts and throws back his head.

'What? It did fail, Max. Surely you can't deny that? I went to the gallery. I spoke to Guy.'

'Shut up, Rainey!' I say, shocked. What the hell is she doing?

Max turns to look at Rainey. His eyes are blazing. I press my hand down on his knee. Please don't let there be a fight. I glance around. Everyone is watching, fascinated.

Max slumps down in his chair, lets his head fall back, and stares up at the ceiling.

Margaret begins a spiel about avoiding stress in pregnancy. I glare at Rainey and shout-whisper, 'Stressed? I'm stressed all right.' I mouth, 'Because of you,' pointing at her. She's deliberately trying to undermine Max and I just do not understand it. I can't see why.

Max leans forward again, elbows on knees. He smiles nastily at Rainey but doesn't speak. I take his fingers and squeeze.

Just then the Indian woman raises her hand and asks if it's possible to pay up front for an epidural on your due date, before you even feel a contraction and then keep topping it up until the baby is born. We all strain forward to hear the answer to that one. (The answer is no. It's a cruel world and women bear the brunt.)

Later, as we make our way home in the dark, Max and I link arms. Rainey walks ahead, scarves billowing and swirling with autumn leaves.

'She's been a total witch,' I say. 'Are you all right?'

'No. I'm fucking furious.'

'I bet. Thank you, though.'

'For what?'

'Being supportive, not rising to her.'

He looks at Rainey's retreating yellow back. 'If she was a man, I'd give her a smack in the mouth,' he says loudly enough so that she turns round.

'Do you have something to say to me?' she asks.

'Ha, do I have something to say? Er, yeah, I have quite a lot to say to you.'

'Well, come on, better out than in.' She smiles. She looks like she's enjoying this.

'What did you think you were doing in there, Rainey?' I ask.

'Does the truth hurt? Would you prefer to sit about pretending you're a successful artist?' Rainey goads.

'That's enough!' I shout.

'I don't have to pretend anything!' he spits.

'OK. Well, how many landscapes have you sold?'

'None of your business.'

'One! And that makes you successful, does it? Don't forget I know the art business.'

'Ah, you don't know what you're talking about.' He waves her away dismissively, but then spins back to her. 'And another thing, what the hell were you doing talking to Guy? Stay the fuck out of my business.'

'It's an open gallery. I went to find out if you could support my daughter, and frankly the answer is no! Your work has no edge, and your problem is, you can't handle the truth.'

Max hesitates and then turns and walks away, raising a hand.

I glare at Rainey. 'Why are you being like this?' I ask.

'For you, Vivienne,' she says.

'For me? Well, don't bother!' I shout, running to catch up with Max.

'I'll help her find somewhere to live. I'll hurry her up,' I tell him, and I will bloody well tackle Rainey. She'll have to go if this is how she's planning on behaving. She's humiliated Max. I can't bear it.

'I can't live with her up my arse. I'm moving into the studio.'

'Please don't. I don't know why she's being like this. She's got to go.' He walks on, shaking his head. 'I'll tell her,' I call after him.

'When, Viv?' he shouts over his shoulder.

'Soon, really soon. I promise.' I run to catch him up. 'Will you trust me to sort it out?' We stand in the residential street looking at each other. He breathes out clouds of silver under a streetlamp. He turns and kicks a wheelie bin, setting a dog off barking inside a house.

'Please, Max? I'll deal with her.'

'I can't live with her.' He says it like a warning.

'I promise I'll deal with her.'

'OK, Viv,' he says dejectedly. 'OK.' He nods and his anger disappears as quickly as it started, like the strike of a match in a gale.

26

Your Cervix (and Mine)

A short time before labour commences, hormonal messages in the body will ensure that the wall of your cervix begins to thin and shorten. This process is known as 'effacing' or 'ripening'.

Forty Weeks and Counting Down

Ripening is happening inside me. I am ripening and I feel sick.

At work the next week, I find myself googling 'dealing with difficult people', and make a list of strategies to use on Rainey. Apparently, what you have to do is remain calm in the face of provocation. I'll tell that to Max because I can't believe how calm he was after the disastrous NCT class and how patient he's been since. Then you have to think about things you like about the difficult person and try to focus on those. For example, the night after the NCT class, she made dinner and she apologised for attacking Max, and he said, 'Don't mention it,' so that was a good thing, even if Max and I couldn't stomach the tapioca dumplings she'd prepared and had to go out later to stuff our faces with pizza.

But I have to face defeat; now she's driving me mad.

She's a slippery customer and I have totally failed in my quest to make a proper family for Angel, I think gloomily.

One of these dealing-with-difficult-people tips says you may have to avoid the difficult person. Get them out of your life and surround yourself with lovely, positive, shiny happy people. It's not inclusive, but I'm doing it: I'm telling Rainey to go.

In many ways I wonder why I haven't done it already. I've been cross enough and got close a few times, but when it comes to the crunch, I can't bring myself to throw her out. I was hoping she'd go of her own accord without a struggle. I know her drug-baron story doesn't hold water; I mean, she doesn't seem to be in hiding or anything, and doesn't wear a disguise on the way to the shops. Unless the guys who are after her aren't very efficient drug-baron types and keep getting distracted by sparkly things in shops and missing out on nabbing her?

Oh God, I just can't throw out my own mother, even if she's so irritating it makes me dread going home, even if the way she has of pronouncing foreign words super-correctly in the middle of sentences is *très* annoying.

But what if I let her stay, like a very old incontinent dog that's gone smelly and can hardly walk but you can't get rid of for sentimental reasons? After all, I made her a promise that she could stay, just as I promised Max she'd go. When I think of Max I know she has to go. What about Max? He was hurt by her and I told him she'd be gone soon. There's no way out of this. I'll tell her today. The trouble is, when I think of her leaving, my heart becomes seven years old again and seems to pull loose of its moorings as if she has it on a hook. I know telling her to leave will be the last thing I'll ever get to say to her. I'll never see her again; she won't come back.

I close down the search and concentrate on work. The atmosphere in the office today is frosty even though the heating has been fixed. I'm being viewed by Michael and Christie as some sort of Dickensian evil-boss figure who subjugates her workers out of greed. I wouldn't care but Michael has agreed of his own free will to a Barnes and Worth meeting, but he said if the meeting fails, he'll be gone. I've just drafted a very sweet email to Mole asking if we might present our range to her, and I include Michael's name before mine in the sign-off. I click 'send' without a trace of guilt.

'The trap is laid. Now we wait,' I mutter.

'God!' gasps Christie in horror.

'Oh, sorry – did I say that out loud?' I press a finger over my lips.

Christie gives me a dirty look as she heads over to the printer. She's wearing shiny trousers with a peacock-feather pattern and a royal-blue shirt.

'You look really nice today, by the way.' I smile, but she ignores me. I look across at Michael scowling at his machine. I reach into my desk and take out the chocolate advent calendar I've been saving. This will cheer them up. I shake it so the chocolates rattle. 'Ooh, look – I bought us an advent calendar and it's already the tenth, so we have nine chocolates to scoff!'

Michael looks up. 'Ten chocolates,' he corrects.

'I ate the 1st December chocolate already.'

'Without us?' asks Christie. 'When did you?'

'Sometime back in November,' I say, and they stare cruelly. 'I had to – my cervix was ripening . . . or something,' I say, and Christie clutches her throat in disgust.

'Viv, if your cervix was ripening, you'd be dropping a sprog, not stealing chocolates from the proletariat,' scoffs Michael.

I look at him and decide not to cross swords with such a creepy pregnancy expert. People are upset enough, and besides, he always wins. I wish I could just swallow *Forty Weeks and Counting Down* and absorb all the information that way instead of having to read for hours on end about cervixes thinning and being pulled up like socks.

'Anyway, who wants a choccy? Look – there's a little bell, or a snowman?'

'No, thanks,' says Christie, sashaying back to her desk.

'Suit yourself,' I say, and shove two snowmen in my mouth.

I read through my emails feeling more and more despondent. There is not one reply to any of my meeting requests. I suppose that's better than an inbox full of rejections: there's still a very slim hope of a meeting, an anorexic hope. I think about Sebastian at Belle Peau. How he said he'd look at our website. I open our website. It looks great. Michael really is very good. I bring up Belle Peau's website, and realise it's too fancy and difficult to navigate. It could do with redesigning. It could do with a few of our products on it as well . . .

'Stop the train! I've got it,' I say, holding up a palm as I stare at the desk, mentally formulating a plan. 'Michael, how easy would it be for Belle Peau to put some of our crackers on their website?'

'Cinch,' he says.

'I'm going to ring Sebastian and ask – no, beg him to put something of ours on the website before Christmas. Would you be able to do the design for them? That could be a sweetener.'

Michael starts up rocking in his chair and tapping his teeth with a pencil at the same time. 'I just need the codes,' he says.

'And, Christie, could we get hold of the stock in time to fulfil the potential orders?'

'If I speak to China today.' She shrugs.

We all look at each other for a long moment, and then I nod solemnly into their eyes and pick up the phone.

On the bus home shuddering along the Euston Road, I think about the work situation. I gaze at the lit shop windows as we slide by, all piled high with the kind of gifts I used to put together when I worked for Barnes and Worth. I dreamed up so many seasonal gift sets; there wasn't a single holiday or occasion that passed without one. They all sold really well. This cracker idea is just an extension of gift sets; therefore I reckon I can do it. I can make it work. I still have it. I spoke to Sebastian for nearly an hour today, and although it was nigh on impossible not to copy the whistley 's' – especially when saying 'Christmas' a lot of times – he went for it! Two crackers from us are to go on his website by the end of the week, and he was interested in having Michael redesign their whole website in the new year. We'll have a scramble to get all the logistics in place, and it may not even bring in any money, but at least we have some interest, a possible customer. Our first bit of good news.

I feel like celebrating and think of maybe picking up a bottle of cava on the way from the bus, and some orange juice to mix mine with, but then I remember I promised myself I'd speak to Rainey about moving out and suddenly feel my happy mood evaporate. As the bus hisses to a stop, I text Lucy to see if she's free to meet for a quick drink.

My back aches. My legs are swollen. I'm tired. I rub my pregnant belly, feeling a rounded bit under my ribs. Is that a head or a bottom? I wonder what it will be like to be a mum, to be responsible for another person. I look up at a commuter holding a newspaper. The headline is about a missing girl.

There's a story about a knife-crime victim. What kind of world am I bringing a baby into? I think about Rainey as I watch people get off and onto the bus, struggling with bags and enormous rolls of wrapping paper. Christmas is not a good time of year to send your mother packing, is it?

I let that thought settle and melt into a puddle of guilt as my phone beeps a message. Lucy.

Viv, we're on the way to Cheltenham. My mum died.

27

Facebook

Eve Summers Greetings from Kuala Lumpur! It's so hot here you could cut the air with a knife and fork, but they have the most lovely orchids. We've visited the Petronas Towers, which are the tallest twin towers in the world, but didn't go up as Reg is scared of heights. I've worked out how to upload pictures on the Facebook now, so watch this space. We're India bound in a few days. I hope for your sake that Lorraine has moved on.
   Today at 4.22 p.m.

Vivienne Summers Hi, Nana. I've seen the Petronas Towers on television. Someone was getting married to them. (It's a known syndrome apparently.) Lorraine is still here and Max isn't happy. I'm going to have to tell her to leave. I didn't think she'd stay this long – she never usually does. Anyway . . . advice?
   Tuesday at 6.16 p.m.

Eve Summers I'm not sure if I'm too late to give advice, but tell her straight to her face and make sure she understands what you're saying. She is very good at missing the point and then loans become gifts and you've agreed to things you can't remember discussing. Don't let her make you feel guilty – she's good at that too.

Tuesday at 6.31 p.m.

Back at the flat, I'm thankful no one's home. It's perfectly tidy and clean since Rainey moved in, and that's something that can be said for her: she's a neat housemate. (But has to go.) I ring Lucy and afterwards sit and think about Lucy's mum. It's funny the bits and pieces you remember about people. There was this one time she came to our house and went on and on to me about how to peg washing on the line, tops by the hem, not the sleeves, jeans by the legs. She cleaned our stained coffee mugs with bleach and frightening vigour. I found her handbag on the sofa with a half-bottle of vodka in it.

Of course, Lucy losing her mum has added a new layer of guilt to the Rainey situation. Lucy was never close to her mum; I mean, who gets married without even telling their parents? But now she's devastated. She thought they'd have a relationship one day, thought that having a baby would bring them closer. She'd hoped that her emotionally unavailable mum would be a really good grandma. Now she'll never know. Now she's in Cheltenham spending Christmas filling bin bags with her mother's things for the charity shop. It's too sad.

However, I'm a woman of strong resolve. There's no point in being sentimental: I'm telling Rainey to leave. So what if Lucy's sad news has made me appreciate the fragile beauty of the precious mother-daughter relationship? So what if it's cold outside and nearly Christmas? God, I feel bad. I go off to take a shower, and when I return to the living room, there she is hunched on the sofa looking pained. I wade in anyway. No time like the present for throwing out your mother.

'Rainey, I need to talk to you,' I say decisively, and she raises serious eyes to meet mine.

'Thank God you're home, Viv. I have something to tell you,' she says, bringing me up short.

'Good. Right then, well, you go first.' I bow my head to listen.

'I've found a lump.'

'What?' It takes a few seconds to take this in and in that time my thoughts race through irritation that her announcement is so dramatic it trumps mine, fear that she might be dying, relief about not having to tell her to leave. I can't now, can I?

'Under my arm. It hurts.' She massages an armpit, wincing.

I sit beside her. 'Let's have a look.'

She positions my hand over a grisly ball beneath the skin at the side of her breast.

'Quite big, isn't it?' she breathes, turning terrified eyes onto me.

I feel around the sides of the lump, but it moves each time I press, making me queasy.

'There's definitely something.' I nod, tucking my hand under my leg. 'Have you just noticed it?'

'I've had it a while, but it's grown.'

'You should see a doctor.'

'I've just been to your Dr Savage. I got an appointment with him straight away.'

'And?'

'He's very worried. They're putting me in for tests.' I study the lines of her face. I can't see Dr Savage worrying about much – it must be serious.

'When? What tests?'

'I'll probably hear next week, but it's nearly Christmas, so a lot of the cancer docs are away.'

There, she's unleashed it, the C-word. The bones of my chest ache.

'Cancer,' I say, staring into space. She has a lump. A lump means it could be cancer. Cancer – that terrible, wicked, sly thing that takes people away. I feel pretty bad about nearly throwing her out now. If she has cancer, she could be leaving for good. I'm surprised to feel a tear roll down my face and quickly wipe it away.

'What did you want to talk about?' she asks.

'Nothing. It's not important.' I turn my back and think about Lucy losing her mum and imagine losing mine.

'It's OK me staying a bit longer, isn't it, Viv? Just while I wait for the tests?'

28

#Terriblecarols

@**jaslolee** Have yourself a shitty little Christmas
@**Gazzmund** Jingle bills
@**RebsRhab** Little Saint Prick
@**tucksmonster** Silent Shite
@**gazeldag** Baulking at a splinter in me hand

I wake up on the sofa bed on Christmas morning with zero enthusiasm and lie there in a listless C-shape, feeling sorry for myself and gazing at the cat scratches on the side of the armchair. Because we're skint, Max and I said no presents this year. What seemed like a very good idea in November turns out to be a shitty idea on Christmas Day. Of course, I didn't mean no presents. What I actually meant was a stocking full, especially as I'm doing all the hard work of carrying our baby, not Max – after all, *his* pelvis isn't threatening to uncouple itself when he walks, is it?

It's freezing in here – I can see my breath rising to meet the hastily Sellotaped tinsel on the ceiling. I sit up and, reaching to my left, turn on the Christmas-tree lights. The tree is kitsch white, with luminous baubles. It was in the sale at the supermarket and I thought it would be cool – I thought I'd do this whole winter-wonderland theme, with a lot of white pompoms and reindeer and silver twigs, but I didn't get round to it and now that tree just pulls all the hope out of me. I look down at Max asleep with the quilt pulled up to his ears. He looks too big to be sleeping in this bed. Rainey asked me not to tell Max about the lump. I explained she's not very well and re-assured him that she's really searching for a place to stay and will move out after Christmas. He looked at me with disappointed resignation but has since become Mr Supportive. I couldn't fault him: quitting smoking, hardly drinking, not punching Rainey. They've now reached a sort of understanding; they circle each other trading insults, but it never turns into a full row.

I've given Christie three weeks off on half-pay to save money while we don't have much to do, and Max and I are planning to visit his family in Dublin for New Year. All in all, I'm hopeful that things between us can move positively forward from here and with careful refereeing we can reach a satisfactory resolution. Jesus, I've got to stop reading those mediator websites – I don't even sound like myself in my own head anymore.

I look at the white winter sky framing the blind. Christmas morning in London town. Somewhere a church bell is ringing. I feel the soft flutter of the baby moving inside.

'Things will be different at Christmas when you're here, Angel,' I say, and stroke my belly, feeling little kicks against my hand. 'What? Of course we'll have a real tree! Yes, and presents! Oh yeah, babies get them, what are you on about? Babies get the most! And you'll have a little Christmas outfit . . . You could be a snowman or a mini Santa . . . No, I don't think they do stars for babies . . . Oh, in Mothercare? Did you? OK, then, and your daddy . . . Yes, that big Irish man you've been hearing . . . Ha, ha. No, he isn't that bad! He'll make us all a big dinner with champagne and Christmas cake.' I smile.

'Oi, Little Match Girl, pipe down, will you? I'm sleeping here,' Max says from under the covers.

I slide under until we're nose to nose. 'Merry Christmas,' I say.

'Merry Christmas yourself.' He smiles.

'Where's my present?'

'Ah no, see, I knew you'd do that!'

'I *want* a present. It's Christmas, you fecking miser.'

'It was *your* idea not to.'

'I don't care. I want one.'

'OK, here, I've got something for you,' he says, taking my hand and putting it over the erection straining against his boxers. I kiss him and he's just beginning to slide a hand up my T-shirt when we hear the bedroom door open and shortly afterwards Rainey walks in.

Max raises himself onto one elbow. 'Ah well, if it's not one of Santa's little elves!'

I sit up. Rainey is standing by our bed wearing a green shiny kaftan and holding two parcels wrapped in reindeer paper.

'Season's greetings,' she says, handing me one of them.

'Thank you, Rainey. The first gift you have ever given me,' I say in awe.

'Apart from the gift of life.' She smiles, raising her eyebrows. 'And compliments of the season to you too, Max,' says Rainey, handing him the other parcel.

'Thank you, Lorraine,' he says, and rips off the paper. Inside is a scratched pink plastic pig that oinks and hoovers up crumbs, or at least it did before it lost its batteries and battery cover. 'That's, er . . . I don't know what to say. What did you do, open eBay, slam your head on the keyboard and buy the cheapest thing that came up?'

'Oh, something about that pig reminded me of you.' She smiles sweetly. 'Open yours, Viv.' I tear the paper off a box containing two squashy rubber balls. I look up quizzically. 'Birthing balls,' she explains. 'Squeeze them rhythmically through the pain.'

'How useful. Rainey, you really shouldn't have,' I say, trying them out. 'Would you like a go, Max?' I ask.

'No, thank you, my love,' he says with a forced smile.

'Oh well, cup of tea, anyone?' I say.

'I'll make it,' says Rainey for the first time ever, and

Max narrows his eyes suspiciously. She disappears off into the kitchen.

'Well, that's very nice of her. Maybe she's been visited by the ghosts of Christmas,' I say. 'Anyway, I got you a little something. I know we said we wouldn't, but . . .'

He rolls his eyes as I hand him a shoebox wrapped in newspaper and leftover ribbon.

'Ah, now I feel really bad,' he says, ripping it open. 'No, I don't – single malt! A woolly hat! And what's this? Pralines! It does not get any better.' He puts on the hat, takes a good slug from the whisky bottle, wipes the top and passes it to me with a big smile.

'No, thanks,' I say, feeling as if I'm in a shelter for the homeless. I stare at him expectantly.

'What?' he asks, stuffing in a chocolate, and it dawns on me that he's kept to our bargain. I can't believe it. He hasn't got anything for me on our first Christmas together. My throat tightens with self-pity just as he starts to laugh. He reaches down and brings up a white knitted stocking. 'Merry Christmas, baby,' he grins.

I snatch the stocking off him. 'I thought you'd kept to the deal,' I gasp, holding it to my chest in relief.

'Viv, come on. I'm not stupid.'

'You can be, sometimes.' The stocking is full of goodies I've been hinting about: ribbed grey maternity tights, posh mascara, Chanel nail polish, silver and pearl dangly earrings, mint Matchmakers and a minia-ture bottle of champagne.

'Thank you.'

'Come and give us a Christmas kiss,' he says, lifting the quilt.

'No.'

'Give us one of those Matchmakers, then.'

'No way.'

'Give me one or I swear to God I'll take them from you.' I hold them in the air, but he pulls my arm down easily. There's a tussle, he pulls me under the covers, I try to kick him, but he emerges with the Matchmakers and my knickers. By the time I struggle up, Rainey is back with the tea.

'My God, your daughter is a strong one. It's like wrestling a conger eel,' he tells her, and starts dipping Matchmakers into his tea.

She settles on the armchair with a look of disgust.

'I have a little something for you, Rainey, from me and Max.' I reach under the bed and hand her a soft package – it's a scarf from Liberty. I found it half-price in the pre-Christmas sale. She opens it, holds it out, then quietly folds it back into the paper.

'Thank you, Vivienne,' she says.

'Do you like it? I thought I'd go for warm colours. I know you have a lot of blue and green.'

'Yes, well, there's a reason for that.' She smiles and I smile too, thinking, what an ungrateful cow. Everyone knows you should accept any gift gracefully, then ask for the receipt later.

'So it's Christmas Day! I say let's jack up the heating

and break out that Baileys. I got a Marks and Spencer turkey crown with *some* of the trimmings at a knock-down price, and they had Christmas puddings and mince pies on a buy one, get one free, so . . . happy days!'

'I have something else, for both of you,' says Rainey, her voice hushed and serious. She walks out towards our bedroom. Max and I look at each other, frowning.

She reappears sliding a large flat rectangle. The front is covered in reindeer paper. The back is open, it looks like a canvas. She slides it my way.

'Wow, this looks expensive,' I say.

'It was for what it is,' she murmurs as I rip off the paper to find one of Max's landscapes. I look up at Rainey and catch something shining in her eyes; what is it, triumph?

Max springs up from the bed. 'It's one of mine!' he says, glaring at the painting.

'Correct,' smiles Rainey.

I'm sitting between them holding up the canvas. 'Er, I love it!' I say uncertainly.

'Oh my God. You bought that to humiliate me,' Max says, nodding knowingly.

'I intended it to be a thoughtful gesture. I didn't mean to upset you,' says Rainey, po-faced.

'I'm not upset. I'm blazing,' scowls Max, pulling on his jeans.

'I know money is tight. This is my way of helping

out. I didn't get a discount either – Guy made me pay full price,' she tells me.

'We don't need your charity,' says Max.

'You're just too proud, aren't you?' She turns on Max. 'You can't stand that it was me who bought the one and only painting you sold!'

'Listen, woman, just stay out of my business, all right? I don't need you buying my work back for me.'

I'm stunned, sitting on the sofa bed looking from one to the other. Rainey turns to appeal to me. 'Vivienne, I only wanted to help,' she sniffs.

I shake my head. What exactly was she thinking? She must have known Max would go ape shit over this. The one painting he sold was purchased out of charity. I feel gutted for him.

'If you wanted to help, why didn't you just give us the money?' asks Max, pacing now.

Oh yeah, good point. Also, how come she's got the kind of wedge to buy a painting?

'I wanted you to have some hope. I wanted you to believe the public would buy your work, Max!' she cries, her voice breaking dramatically.

'Like fuck you did,' he says, and throws the canvas, sending it clattering down the corridor.

'Without me, the whole exhibition would have been a complete failure.'

'Did you not hear me when I told you before? I

don't want your kind of help. Stay out of my business!' he roars.

'What business?' she scoffs. 'I don't see anyone clamouring for your work. I mean, where are they?'

'Shut up, Rainey!' I cry. I feel Angel kicking madly. We're upsetting her with all this shouting.

'So what? Failed exhibition, lack of buyers, gallery – my concern, not yours. Got it?'

'Hey!' I shout, and they both turn murderous eyes on me. 'It's Christmas Day – stop it.' Max scratches the back of his head and looks at the floor. Rainey stares straight ahead, looking as if she's holding a small ball inside her mouth. 'Look, you shouldn't have bought the painting,' I tell her.

'I thought I was helping,' she begins.

'You've humiliated Max.'

'If he wants to react badly, that's up to him.'

'I love the painting, though,' I appeal to him.

He makes a pissed-off noise.

'And it is Christmas Day and I don't want everyone fighting. It might be our only Christmas together,' I say, thinking of Lucy's mum and cancer fears and feeling my throat tighten.

I can't catch what Max mutters. It sounds like ''kin hope so.'

'Oh, don't get maudlin,' snaps Rainey.

'Can't you just apologise to each other?'

Rainey turns away.

'I'll apologise when all Hell freezes over,' mutters Max.

'OK then, well, merry fucking Christmas.' I stalk to the bathroom, where I sit on the toilet pressing the heels of my hands into my eye sockets until they hurt. This is such shit. How am I going to get through the day? A few moments later Max follows holding the malt whisky. He takes a massive couple of swallows and holds the bottle out to me.

'Medicinal,' he says. I shake my head and look away. 'She did that deliberately, to make some big point about what a pile of wank my work is.'

'It doesn't matter,' I say.

He looks at me thoughtfully and takes a deep breath and sighs. 'No. It doesn't matter,' he says.

I shrug.

'You matter.'

'I didn't hope for much today, just that it might go all right, but it's already turned to a fucking pantomime.'

'Oh no, it hasn't,' he says in a pantomime way, and grins.

'You're supposed to be the Prince Charming.'

'I am the Prince Charming,' he says, taking another swig of whisky. 'Shall we dance?' he growls, wiping off his mouth and offering his hand. I take it and he pulls me close, nuzzling my neck, singing, 'Merry Christmas, baby, you sure do treat me nice,' and fumbling with the tie of my pyjama bottoms until I giggle.

'Prince Charming never tried to feel girls up in the toilets.'

'Oh yeah, he did it all the time,' he murmurs.

'Merry Christmas, Nana!'

'Same to you!'

'Where are you?'

'Phuket *then* India we decided in the end. It's absolutely boiling. It's hard to believe it's Christmas, but the hotel have put a little tinsel tree in the foyer. Is she still there?'

'Yes. We're just heating up the turkey crown and I wish you were here.'

'Can you talk?'

'No, no, not really.'

'Is everything going all right?'

'No, not so much.'

'Rows?'

'Yeah . . .'

'You and Lorraine, or Max and Lorraine?'

'The last one.'

'Ho! Good on Max! Listen, I have to go – it's the receptionist's phone and costing us an arm and a leg. Try to have a good Christmas, darling. See you soon.'

'Miss you . . . Nana, are you still there?'

The line crackles and dies.

'Charades!' I say, clapping my hands. Later that afternoon I'm still doggedly pushing for a good Christmas

Day. Rainey and Max have polished off the Baileys, a bottle of wine and are now halfway down another. I managed my miniature bottle of champagne with our miniature lunch and now settle onto the sofa with a cranberry and lemonade while Max rubs my feet. Rainey bought cheese and crackers, and she lays them out on the coffee table.

'In Bogotá, we played a game called "Best of, Worst of" at the end of the year. Let's play that,' she slurs. While we try to think up excuses, she says, 'I'll go first, and the subject is "the worst Christmas ever".'

The Christmas after you left me, I think, a thought that flashes in so quickly I worry I might have spoken it.

'It was here in London,' continues Rainey. 'I was helping in a soup kitchen and I befriended a young addict. He literally had the face of an angel.'

'What, glowing?' Max interrupts.

'On Christmas Day, he died in my arms.' She stares into the middle distance, remembering. 'And do you know, when I left that shelter, there was the brightest star I've ever seen shining right above it.'

'Police helicopter looking for the addict.' He turns to me, grinning.

'It really was the most beautiful star, sort of latticed.'

'Sure the smackhead didn't spike your tea?' asks Max. 'And this shelter, how much like a stable was it?'

Rainey smiles sadly at him. 'There's a lot we don't know in life.'

'There's a lot we don't know in life and other

platitudes by Lorraine Summers,' Max says to himself.

I grab the remote and turn up Jona Lewie on the stereo, nodding along in my paper hat. Turns out Max's worst Christmas ever happened after he and his father drank a bottle of cheap brandy together, went temporarily blind, and had to stay in the pub for the day and miss their dinner. I don't tell them about mine, a Christmas Day of waiting, looking out of the window for my mother. I look at Rainey, rosy-cheeked with drink now.

'Vivienne, put your shoulders back when you walk. If you waddle about like that, your spine will go permanently S-shaped,' she comments as I clear away some glasses. I straighten into an L. 'That's better. You shouldn't be working either. Isn't it time you gave up doing . . . whatever it is you do?'

'Run a business,' answers Max protectively.

'She should be thinking about the baby. Only three months to go, Vivienne, and we get to cradle your little one in our arms!'

How come she's come over all maternal? Must be the booze.

'Yeah, we'll send you a photo,' says Max.

'I'll be taking plenty of photos of my own,' says Rainey, obviously planning to be around.

'Er, let's change the subject,' I say. 'Look – there's a Bond film starting in a minute.' I glance at Max and he flicks on the television with a frown.

'How's it going with the accommodation search?' he asks Rainey. She gives him a withering look and says something like, 'I wouldn't know,' but I interrupt, speaking loudly to drown her out.

'Do you know, I think I got us a box of Quality Street!' I say. 'Would you mind getting them, Max? Quick – the film's starting.'

We watch television for the evening and I manage to divert any further confrontations, feeling the last of my Christmas cheer fading like a scattering of city snow, turning instead to dirty slush, the kind that leaves tide marks on your boots.

29

Happy New Year

Resolutions

Viv Summers
Remove mascara before bed
Be organised and assertive person
Drink water

Max Kelly
Drink a wider variety of whiskeys
Dedicate life to worship of Viv

Max's family live in Ballyfermot, a suburb of Dublin. I remember the area from the last time I came here, as a student. His parents own a 1960s house, white render and red paintwork, off the main street.

'Turn right after Iceland,' Max tells our taxi driver.

As we walk to the front door, the large bay window gives a view of the entire family assembled in the living room, a welcome party sitting around in a half-circle. There are loads of them, and they are the best-looking family I've ever seen. A great cheer goes up as Max walks through, shouts and squeals follow, finally a hush as I step up. There I stand alone – Englishwoman, unmarried and pregnant in a house full of Catholics. I raise a hand to wave, think better of it, and fiddle with my hair instead.

'Everyone, you remember Vivienne.' Max pulls me by the hand further into the room and I feel my face burn with all those eyes on me. I'm not a shy person, but I fear my weird self may surface, speaking in a bad Irish accent and asking them if they can do River Dance. 'Here's my da, Declan, my mammy, Bridget. That's my eldest sister, Claire, and Siobhan, my little sister. There's Kathy, my baby sister, and I don't know who all these little chislers belong to.' He leaves me and starts chasing a gaggle of kids around. I smile lovingly at him, thinking, 'Get back here, you bastard!'

'Take the weight off, Vivienne.' Declan shows me a chair between Siobhan and Kathy. 'Sure, we're harmless really, apart from these.' He swings a finger between the two girls. I smile at them in turn. Declan stands over us, flashing the same pirate smile as Max. He looks good, roguish, still fit, fancyable.

'When's your babby coming?' asks Siobhan with a friendly smile at my belly.

'Oh, erm, April. We're engaged,' I tell her, showing the ring, and she congratulates me. 'Do you have kids?' I ask, thinking I should know.

'My three are the boys with Max and the sulky lady there.' She points to a teenage girl sitting prettily on the arm of the sofa.

'You look like sisters,' I say.

'That's Yasmin. I fell with her at eighteen, sure didn't I, Kathy?'

'She did.' Kathy is another dark-haired stunner with red lips and eyes like summer skies, cornflowers, faded denim. Max is now chatting to Bridget. She keeps hugging him, kissing him and letting him go.

'Look at little mammy's boy with the big beard,' calls Siobhan, and he breaks free and comes over.

'Viv, whatever these tell you about me is all lies and insinuation,' he says, and kisses his sisters. 'What's happening?'

Declan pulls Max into an embrace, slapping him on the back. Max looks to be a foot taller than his dad. Declan then goes off to get drinks, wiping at a tear. Kathy tells Max she's working behind the bar at O'Shea's and seeing someone called Sean who's a total ride. Siobhan's left the cousin of their neighbour (whom she only married last year) and she doesn't give a shite because he's a gimp who's away in the head. They seem to all talk at once, leaving me time to sit back and take it in. I keep looking across to Bridget, and every time she seems to feel my gaze and turns and smiles almost shyly. I watch Claire, who I think is the eldest sister, as she rounds up the children and sends them to wash for lunch. She's more gamine then the others, with auburn hair in a sleek tight bun; her head looks like a shiny hazelnut. Declan returns with cut glasses of champagne.

'Oh, no expense spared for the prodigal son,' says Siobhan, rolling her eyes.

Max takes two glasses and hands one to me. I take a sip, waiting to feel sick, but it slips down nicely.

'I shouldn't drink really,' I say.

'Sure one or two won't hurt,' says Declan, fixing me with the twinkliest eyes. 'Lunch is nearly ready. Do you want to see your room?'

We're in Max's old bedroom, now redecorated: rose-print walls and muted pink carpet. There's a shelf with some of his old books and a great big double bed with a camberwick bedspread.

'Oh my God, a real bed.' I fall flat on my back onto the pillows. I could cry with relief thinking of the cruel collection of springs and foam we've been used to sleeping on. I close my eyes, listening to the sounds from downstairs: calling voices, kids shouting, banging pots. Music starts up loud and then is turned down.

Max lies beside me. 'What are they like?'

'How come your family are so good-looking? You must be sad you got the only ugly gene.'

'Funny girl now, are you? Watch it or I'll leave you to fend for yourself down there.'

I smile without opening my eyes. 'I fancy you more seeing you with your family. You look more gorgeous and swaggery than ever here, and they love the bones of you, which makes me love you even more.'

He takes my hand and gives it a squeeze.

'I've got a crush on your dad as well. Could be hormones.'

'Everyone falls for me ol' fella.'

'How do I make Kathy and Siobhan think I'm great? They're so cool and lovely and pretty.'

'Pair of witches they are.'

'Your mum hasn't spoken to me, though.'

'She will and you'll be sorry.'

'Oh shit. Am I the evil English girl who's ensnared you?'

'She'll be giving you the third degree.'

I roll onto one elbow and look down at him, panicked. 'What shall I do? How shall I be?'

'Just be yourself.' He smiles.

Lunch is a meaty lasagne with salad and baked potatoes and bread and butter, served at a big old kitchen table. There's red wine and beer. Claire is smoking at the back door, watching as the food is dished out. She tuts as Declan fills my glass with wine.

'She's pregnant, Daddy! Not everyone is as fond of a drink as you.'

'Sure, she's giving out to me about the drink already and I'm only half cut,' Declan confides to me.

Claire puts her cigarette end in the bin and brings me a glass of lemonade. 'Now,' she says, setting it down, 'your big day won't be long coming, will it?'

'The first of April.' I smile at her, but she's off, sorting out the kids' plates. I glance around the table and across at Max, sitting opposite, already tucking into a huge pile. Here he is with the weight of his family around him like an assembled power, an army of lookalikes to take for granted. I so want to be part of it.

'So, Max, your exhibition, was it successful for you?' Declan asks.

'No,' he says, shaking his head and finishing a mouthful. He takes a gulp of wine. 'Unmitigated disaster.'

'That's a shame.'

'You're telling me.'

'So what'll you do now? Get a job?'

'No Da I'm still painting. I'll look for another gallery.'

'I don't know, I'm only your ol' fella, but would you not be better off getting paid work?'

I shoot a glance at Max. He's calmly eating, looking at his plate and nodding.

'Selling art won't get you far up the road, son, and soon with a mouth to feed.'

The whole table falls quiet now, as if they know this particular impasse well and are settling in for a fight. Max puts down his fork and leans back in his chair. He smiles while his eyes burn with indignity. I hear a thudding and realise it's my own heart drumming through my chest.

'The thing is,' I begin in a cheerful tone, 'Max is a great talent who's had work displayed in the Royal Academy, London.' I see Declan taking a breath to argue, so I continue quickly, raising a finger, 'Most great artists have suffered unsuccessful exhibits, but you wouldn't tell them to get a job: Picasso as a car fitter or Monet as a software analyst? He, he, no! Artists have a gift to give us: they raise society to new levels and *must* not be allowed to do anything else, because without art or music, we're just animals. Someone famous said that, I think. With art, we may be in the gutter, but we're looking at the stars.' I blink a couple of times at their stunned faces, take a sip of lemonade, and give what I hope is a friendly little smile.

'Oscar Wilde,' smiles Max.

'I take what you're saying, Viv. It's all well and good, but how'll you make ends meet, Max?' asks Bridget.

Max gives her a hurt look that says, 'You too?'

'Well, I run my own business,' I pipe up again. Why did I go and say that? Now I'll have to explain all about transition crackers and seem even more bonkers.

What follows is a full-on debate. Every one of them chips in with an argument and counter-argument through the lasagne, two more bottles of red and a Key lime pie, through work, finance, culture and that 'shower of savages', the government. Declan is the main antagonist at one point, taking us all on and saying it's the fault of the capitalist regime that he can't sell any antiques. By the time we get to coffee, we've reached no firm conclusions that I can grasp, except that Max thinks he's the 'cat's pyjamas', I'm a 'right one, fair play to me', and they love nothing better than a bloody big argument.

On New Year's Eve, we go with Siobhan and Kathy to Downey's bar, where there's a good atmosphere and karaoke later. I'm in the wizard-sleeve number, but I forgot to pack any costume jewellery so can't accessorise and feel a bit like the pint of Guinness Max is throwing down his neck: black with a bulge in the middle.

'By rights we should have taken you to Temple Bar in town, but it'll be rammed and we'll not get a taxi,' Kathy tells me.

I'm transfixed by her stick-on eyelashes, so long and black over her blue eyes she has the look of a blinking doll.

Siobhan is concentrating on filling out a karaoke card.

'What'll we sing?' she asks, sliding a finger down the list.

'"Islands in the Stream" is Viv's favourite,' says Max.

'Oh, no, I'm not singing,' I say.

'Is she any good?' asks Siobhan, ignoring my protests.

'Oh yeah, brilliant,' says Max in a comically strangled voice.

I take a sip of my lime and soda. I'm so sick of lime and soda.

Max moves closer, sliding a hand up and down my thigh. 'It's OK, baby – I won't let them drag you up.'

The master of ceremonies takes the microphone and announces the first singer, a drunk-to-the-point-of-staggering middle-aged guy singing 'I Will Always Love You'.

'Hard choice,' nods Kathy.

The man hits the first note flat.

'Jesus, what an eejit,' laughs Max.

'He's a bit like you, I think,' I say, and his hand on my thigh squeezes and slides some more. Why didn't I put on a shorter skirt? In Ireland, I thought we'd have some time alone, but no such luck, and being pregnant makes me want him all the time.

'Will I put the three of us down for Destiny's Child – you know, the *Charlie's Angels* one?'

I shake my head and lean in to whisper, 'Siobhan, I can't sing a note, but Max will.' When I lean back again, I find I'm sitting on his hand. I don't move, though, and taking this as encouragement, he moves his fingers around.

'If Max sings *Charlie's Angels*, I'll wet my pants,' shouts Siobhan.

'It'll be like when we made him to do the nudey run,' says Kathy.

I look at him, waiting for the story. He smiles his gorgeous smile; the fingers move on me; I am dying for him.

'They dared me to run and touch the fence in the nip,' he says in a bored sing-song voice.

'The nip?'

'Naked. When I did it, they locked the door and called the razzers.'

'He made a holy show of himself banging on all the windows with his gooter dangling,' laughs Kathy.

'I hope your next shite is a hedgehog, Kathy,' says Max.

The next up for karaoke is a girl in a pink cowboy hat. The girls don't like her because she's an awful skank, so they turn round to scowl through her rendition of 'Killing Me Softly'.

Max leans in for a kiss while they're not looking. 'Sit on my knee,' he says. 'I'll let you have a feel what you're getting later.'

'But I want it now.' I look into his eyes, thinking, Happy New Year to me.

'Come on.' He nods towards the door.

Out under the black and stars, our breath comes in white clouds and we walk away from the muffled karaoke beat, huddled together for the short walk home. The pavement is frosted; we leave a zigzag of footprints while he's telling me what he's going to do to me. When I giggle, my teeth freeze.

'Shh, shh,' he says, opening his parents' front door, and we tiptoe into the narrow hallway.

'That you, Max and Viv?' calls Bridget, and we wait.

'It's me, Ma!' he calls, showing me the huge erection pressing against his jeans, pointing at me, then pulling his coat over it. He opens the door to the sitting room, motioning for me to stay put.

'Will you not have a drop with us?' I hear Declan ask. I study the swirly pattern of the brown shag pile, while he tells his parents I'm feeling a bit tired so he's brought me home for a rest.

'Goodnight, Vivienne,' Bridget calls.

'Goodnight! Sorry – just a bit tired with the baby,' I answer.

'Oh, I know how it is!' she says, and then Max is back in the hall chasing me upstairs by smacking me on the arse.

I fall onto the bed giggling and he falls on top, propping himself up with one arm.

'Talk Irish to me,' I say between kisses.

'I'd eat chips from your knickers,' he says with a grin. Then he's slipping out of his coat and fucking me with my dress ruched up and his trousers half down, and I'm laughing and yelling, 'Yeah, buck me!' and wanting him to do it for ever.

We lie on the bed afterwards and watch from the window as the New Year fireworks crackle across the sky.

'Happy New Year, sexy,' he says.

'Same to you.'

He suddenly moves to pull off his jeans, shoes and socks. Then, giving me a good view of his arse, he rummages in his coat pocket for something. He rolls back onto the bed, dangling a pretty silver locket.

'For you,' he says, laying it against my chest.

I scoop it up and run a finger over the engraved flowers on the front. On the back is engraved 'My heart.' I look at him.

'I love you so much.' I smile and then burst into tears, because I do and all kinds of crazy hormones are racing around my body.

He wipes my tears and takes the locket.

'See there, you put my picture on one side and Angel in the other and wear us over your heart.'

'You are romantic, after all.'

'But don't let on,' he says.

30

Entering the Third Trimester

The last three months of pregnancy, known as the third trimester, can be a tiring and uncomfortable time, with backache, shortness of breath, varicose veins and frequent urination to deal with, but it is still important to stay positive.

www.babeeandme.com

7 January 1:07

From: marionharrison@barnesandworth.com
To: viviennesummers@dreamteam.co.uk
Subject: Re: Meeting

Dear Vivienne,

Thank you for your email requesting a meeting with the Barnes and Worth gift-buying department. We have provisionally scheduled a day to meet with our suppliers on 4 March and could meet with you at 11.30 a.m.

If this time is convenient for you, would you please confirm who from your company will be attending so that we can ensure refreshments are adequate?

Best wishes for a happy and prosperous New Year,
Marion Harrison

7 January 1:20

From: viviennesummers@dreamteam.co.uk
To: marionharrison@barnesandworth.com
Subject: Re: Re: Meeting

Dear Marion,

We here at Dream Team would be absolutely delighted to
attend the meeting at 11.30 a.m. on 4 March and give you the
opportunity to buy into our exciting product range. The whole
team will be coming along: myself, my assistant, Christie
Thompson, and our IT consultant, Mike Clarke. (I must say
he's really looking forward to seeing you in person instead of
just gazing at that framed photo he keeps on his desk.)

A happy New Year to you! One filled with joy and the
love of a good man.

Best wishes,

Vivienne Summers

I'm just about to click 'send', but doubt stays my
hand. Is my reply a bit much? Is it less dangling
Michael as bait and more promising him as a done
deal? Is it . . . lying? I go to delete the line about the
photo, but I'm distracted by a bit of streamer falling
from the office ceiling and accidentally press 'send'.
Ah well.

I look around the silent office. No one will be back to work until next Monday. I try to imagine my colleagues on holiday. Damon will have seen in the New Year with his old mum, I suppose. Christie will have been on the guest list for some achingly cool hipster party, probably so cool and 'out there' that the usual party conventions were sniffily bypassed and they all ended up sitting around on crates in a cavernous warehouse somewhere. I shudder to think what Michael has been up to in his free time – he said something about an evening in involving masturbation and maybe a single lace glove.

I think about my New Year with Max. On New Year's Day we went into Dublin and wandered around the sights; then even more of his family came over for a buffet. I met his aunty Hilda, who's slightly deaf and insulted almost everyone with her straight-talking. They all had a skinful and a rowdy sing-song. I loved being part of Max's clan. I can't remember a better time. Rainey claimed she spent New Year 'giving something back'. Apparently she befriended the local homeless man who thinks he's a dog and decided to take him to a shelter for the night to comfort him while he whimpered through the fireworks. It's not great to be home. It's like leaving a warm seat by the fire to stand in a cold kitchen. All my worries and concerns lie in wait; not one problem has gone away by itself, as I'd hoped. I sigh and flick through my mental to-do list:

1. *Resolve Rainey situation to satisfaction of all parties.*
2. *Make failing business into international success.*
3. *Have easy, pain-free birth.*
4. *Have happy, fat, easy-to-care-for baby that sleeps a lot.*
5. *Lose all baby weight and become slim and tanned person who says, 'I can't put weight on running after this baby!' like the woman I overheard in Boots.*
5. *Marry Max (small, informal, gorgeous retro dress, English-country-garden theme?).*

All quite straightforward, then. 'A lot to do,' I tut to myself as I shut down the laptop and pack it away. I'm relieved that we have the meeting confirmed with Barnes and Worth, even though I'll be less than a month away from having the baby. I lock up the office door, feeling OK, hopeful even. And then I arrive home.

Rainey is sitting on the sofa with her feet tucked up, a look in her eyes like a dog who just stole the roast. Something is wrong; I walk in warily looking from her towards the kitchen before putting down my bag.

'Where's Max?' I ask, and she nods towards the bedroom.

'Sorry,' she whispers, and turns in her lips.

I hurry down the little corridor with a sudden sense of unease. He's packing.

'Hi,' I say.

He looks up with a jerk of his head. 'How're you?'

he says, and goes back to shoving a checked shirt into a side compartment of his backpack.

'What are you doing?'

'I'm going home, Vivienne,' he says quietly.

'What, just for a bit or . . . ? You're packing quite a lot of stuff.'

'No, I'm pretty much getting out of here, darlin'.'

'What? Why? What happened?'

'What happened?' He swings the pack onto his back and walks right past me into the living room. I follow. 'You know what happened.'

Rainey now turns casually in her seat to watch us. 'I only said—' she begins, but Max interrupts, turning to me.

'You told her to stay as long as she likes,' he says, and I glance at Rainey. 'Didn't you?'

'What? Hold on, it wasn't like that. I just said while she was looking . . .' I trail off, looking at the fury in his eyes. 'Yes, I did. I said . . . I told her that.'

'And you lied to me,' he says, jerking his head forward in disbelief. 'You told me you were dealing with the situation. You said she was going. You lied to me loads of times. Why?'

'I was trying to make it work. See, I thought—'

'You lied to me!' he roars.

'I didn't want to lie,' I begin, but he shakes his head as if my words are buzzing around him.

'I think you should just calm down,' says Rainey, getting up.

Max takes a step towards her, his eyes flashing. 'Listen here, woman, let me tell you this – there's no use in you bleating to me: you can't rule me or control me like you do her, OK?'

Rainey blinks at him, her hands hanging limply by her sides. Max turns and looks at me before opening the door. I don't see our connection in that look; I see only hurt there.

'Please, Max,' I say, as he walks out. 'Don't go,' I cry in a panic, following him out onto the stairwell. What the hell is happening? I catch hold of his hand. 'I'm sorry,' I say.

He looks down. 'I can't compete with your mother anymore, Viv. You've chosen her over me.'

'No, I have not! Max, I love you.'

'Not enough to tell me the truth.' He shakes his head. 'There's no trust when you lie to me like that.'

'I'll go back in there and make her leave!'

'It's not about that now; it's about you and me. I have to be able to trust you.'

'You can trust me!' I shout, hurting my throat.

'No,' he says, and looks at me coldly.

'So you're leaving me, are you?' I hear my voice crack.

'I need to get out for a bit,' he says quietly. 'Maybe you need time with her to get her out of your system, I don't know.'

'Well, then I can't trust you, can I? I can't trust you

to stay when things get tough, so good – better to find out now than when we have a baby! Go on, then, if you're going!'

'Viv, I'd stand by you for ever, through anything, but you let her come between us and you've done that before. If you'd told me the truth . . .'

'The truth! Truth!' I say, impersonating him. 'I'll tell you now!'

'But you've had every chance to tell me, to stand up to her, but you chose to lie. To me!' He thumps his chest, angry again. We stare at each other.

I scratch at the top of my head. 'You can't love me if you'd do this,' I say, feeling a sob choke me like a wad of wire wool. I start to take off the engagement ring and a thump of fear hits me in the chest. What am I doing? How is this spiralling so badly out of control? A quiet, reasonable thought in my mind points out that this might be a bad and stupid thing to do, but right now I don't care.

'I love you, Vivienne. That's why it hurts. I'd never lie to you.'

'You'd better have this back,' I say, handing him the ring. 'You don't want to *marry* a liar, do you?' I give him the ring and he shakes his head sorrowfully. 'People who love each other don't just fucking walk out, Max!' I scream.

'People who love each other don't fucking lie,' he shouts back, and takes off down the first flight of stairs.

'Don't ever come back, then,' I yell after him stupidly, and I lean over the stair rail crying.

He turns and looks at me sadly. Then I watch him go, a flash of battered leather jacket turning the bottom of the stairs. The door slams and I sink to the floor.

31

January Snails

Eve Summers Hello, Vivienne. Happy New Year from Goa. It's beautiful here, but I've been eaten alive by mosquitoes all over my face and my eyelids have swollen to the size of golf balls. Reg says we'll rent a house in Kerala, but between you and me, I'd be happy to come home while I can still see. I picked up a couple of beautiful sarongs for you – useful for discreet breast-feeding? Darling, I really miss you. Please direct-message me and tell me what's happening.
  Thursday 4.41 p.m.

During the long, slow days following Max's departure, I spend a lot of time slouched on the sofa contemplating the web of shadows moving across the laminate floor. Outside the window, the cold slab of white sky threatens snow. Rainey keeps walking in and delivering lectures, something about self-reliance. I half listen. I watch my belly move as Angel kicks and turns. I now know why people say they have the blues; this exactly describes me. This is not the hot, hysterical struggle of heartbreak I've experienced before; this is something different – dull, cold and numbing, like being locked in a freezer. Everything is colourless and empty; there's no clowning around or loud laughs, rude sex, beards or big boots, nothing to look forward to.

But if he so much as shows his big Irish face here, I'll kill him. I don't even know if I'd let him come back after he left me so easily. Thinking along these lines drives icicle daggers into my heart.

I spend a lot of evenings watching soap operas with Rainey. She munches bowls of crisps and falls asleep peppered with crumbs.

A couple of torturous days later he rings.

'How's the baby?' he asks.

'Heavy,' I say in a flat voice.

'How are you?'

'Fine. What do you care?'

'I care a lot,' he says, and my heart leaps like an enthusiastic puppy.

'So are you seeing anyone?'

'Don't be stupid!' There's a pause. I hear him breathing into the phone. 'Why did you say that? We're not broken up.'

'Er, you walked out and left me . . .'

'Did you or did you not tell your mother she can stay as long as she likes?'

'That's not the point! You left me.'

'*Because* you told your mother to stay as long as she likes! Why *do* you lie to me, Vivienne? Is it a condition or something? What other lies have you told, eh?'

'What do you mean by that?'

'I mean, how the hell can I trust you?'

'You obviously can't!' I shout, and hang up.

The phone immediately buzzes with his name. I bury it under a cushion, staring straight ahead until it stops. I walk over to the window and look down into the street. I start to imagine a life without him, raising our baby alone. It makes me want to cry. My eyes get red and itchy. I throw myself on the sofa and try to cry just as Rainey appears.

'What's wrong with your eyes? Are you allergic to something?'

'No,' I snap.

'So what shall we do today?' she asks, as if we're on a package holiday, choosing a boat trip. She's been very chirpy since Max left.

I look to the side, away from her, sliding my hand over the sofa cushion. 'I need to do sitting and staring today.'

'You did that yesterday. Don't take this personally, Vivienne, but I really think you are too reliant on others for your own happiness. You need to understand that other people will always let you down, always. You should expect it, especially from a man.'

I let my eyes trail over her as she stands by the sofa with her hands on her hips.

'That's actually quite funny coming from you,' I say.

'Oh, I let you down. I know you think that and you're right! But let's not dwell on things we can't fix.'

'Why not? I fancy a right good dwell. Why don't you make us a brew and tell me about my father?' Her eyes skitter away to the window. 'Why won't you talk about him?'

'Why do you want to drag all that out into the light and pick through it?'

'Oh, I dunno. Maybe I'm curious about half of my genetic make-up. Just tell me and I'll stop asking.'

'There's nothing to tell,' she sniffs. 'He was just a boy. We were messing around.'

'What was his name?'

'He didn't even know I was pregnant, and if you're thinking of tracing him, you can't – he died in a car accident.'

I glance at her as I take this in, another bond severed. I'm now almost totally anchorless, I think sadly.

'Am I like him?'

'Only a bit. Same bushy hair,' she says, waving a finger up and down.

'What was he called?'

'Arthur Poole,' she announces with an embarrassed shrug.

'What did you like about him?'

'I can't remember.' She shakes her head. 'He was older than me – he was nineteen, and I was fifteen. He was the youth club leader. Arty, we called him. All the girls were mad about him, but he liked me, and one night we went behind the clubhouse, and then I was pregnant.'

'How romantic.'

'It wasn't.'

'Why didn't you have an abortion?'

'Because I didn't face up to being pregnant and by then it was too late.'

I hear this, feeling something like a punch in the chest. I came into existence because she was too late. I slipped into life under the net. Go, me!

'And you never told anyone about him?'

'I was underage.' She sinks onto the armchair.

'And how did Nana react?'

'They were upset.' She nods.

'But they didn't kick you out or anything?'

'No. They were angry at first but supportive, I suppose.'

'You said they put you in the back room. I thought they must have driven you away.'

'No, Viv. I left of my own free will,' she says, looking into my eyes.

'Are you telling the truth? I never know anymore.'

'I left of my own free will.'

'Well, everyone does.' I shrug, feeling a wave of sorrow engulf me. Why does everyone I love leave me? Why? Am I so unworthy? Now I've lost my father as well . . . poor old Arty!

'When did my father die? I'd at least like to visit his grave.' I picture myself in a black headscarf placing a single rose by a forgotten headstone somewhere windswept.

'Uh, I don't know . . . sometime in the 1990s. Don't be sentimental, Vivienne. Self-pity is an ugly emotion.'

I gaze into space. The gloom seems to hang like smoke. God, I miss Max.

'So anyway, I thought I'd take you shopping in the sales for baby things, if you like,' she says.

'You haven't got any money,' I remind her. Hell, this little heart-to-heart has made me feel terrible. I'm running with the 'I'm unworthy so everyone leaves' theme, adding evidence, and it's really gaining momentum in my brain. I wonder what the point of human love is when it only ever brings pain.

'I've had some cash wired through.'

'Cash wired through? Where from? I don't want to spend your ill-gotten gains on my precious baby.' I imagine myself raising Angel alone. We'd be content, poor but honest.

'I want to buy you a Bugaboo. I saw a lovely lime-green one in John Lewis's window. It has a matching bag. It would make me happy to buy that for you.'

I look at her with narrowed eyes and she nods encouragingly. I really want one of those Bugaboos and she knows it. She caught me looking through the catalogue. I wonder, if I let her buy me that, what are the consequences? Will I be betraying Max? We were bidding for a cheaper version on eBay, but it was a boring beige and the hood was a bit torn.

'Max and I were buying one,' I say half-heartedly.

'Max! He's left you. He's gone. He's let you down.

Am I right? You don't owe him anything. You sitting here alone out of some misplaced sense of loyalty isn't going to bring him back now, is it? Better to forget him and go shopping.'

'I'll get my coat.'

That afternoon Rainey returns to the flat with the Bugaboo baby buggy in 'lime zest', and I meet Lucy at Oxford Circus. We take a walk down Regent Street, towards Piccadilly. She's supposed to be in mourning, but she's wearing a bright pink beret, and although she seems sad and quiet, she's not as broken as I'd expected.

We mooch about the ground floor of Liberty.

'Purses. My mother loved purses. She had about twenty, all with odd coins and lists and stamps in,' she says, trailing a hand through a display of leather coin pouches. 'All this stuff we collect and then one day we're gone, but the stuff is still here and someone has to sort through it and shove it in a bin bag.'

I smile sympathetically.

'Sorry, that's a bit of a miserable thing to say,' she sniffs.

'No, it's not. You're allowed to be miserable.'

'The thing is, I'm not miserable. I should be. I always thought I didn't know my mum, but the truth was that I did know her – really well. There just wasn't much to know. She wasn't this deep person keeping it all in; she was as light and see-through as a cobweb.' She looks at me, surprised. She squirts a perfume tester onto a card, makes a face and puts it down. 'Even her death was simple – went in her sleep, no fuss.'

'That's how I'm doing it,' I say.

'You?' She squints at me. 'You're far too dramatic for that; you'll be eaten by a tiger or something.'

We walk back out onto the busy pavement.

'So your dad met Reuben?'

'All dad really said to him was, "Bad timing, old son," just before we left.'

'Huh.' I link her arm with mine as we face a flotilla of Spanish schoolchildren. I think about Lucy's father rattling about in their big family home. 'Parents,' I say sadly.

Lucy suddenly turns on me. 'I hope you haven't got all sentimental about Rainey because my mother died,' she says, and so I spill the whole story about Christmas and Max leaving and Arty dying until we're nearly at Piccadilly.

'Shit. So your peace plan backfired massively, then?'

'Yep, and don't say you told me so.'

'You and Max will be fine.'

'No, we won't. He left me.'

'Not really. If Rainey left, he'd come back.'

'I don't want him back.'

'Well, that's sorted, then. Congratulations – you now live with your mother.'

'She's being very nice, actually. She bought me a Bugaboo.'

'But what will you do for sex?'

I laugh and look sideways at her. Her cheeks are red. She smiles; her teeth are wet and creamy white.

'It'll be all right,' she says. 'At least you're pregnant. Me and Reubs are still trying. Oh God, I have to tell you this! The other morning it was the perfect time in my cycle to conceive, but I had a train to catch for this urgent meeting and had to dry my hair, so I told him to get himself ready to come while I dried my hair, and then I just sat on him at the end.' We turn left into Leicester Square. I walk with my head down, taking this in.

'What do you mean, you "just sat on him at the end"?'

'You know what I mean.'

'You never cease to amaze me.' I smile. 'Look, I have to rest for a while – there's only so far I can waddle without needing the toilet, anyway.'

We find a café and take an outside table underneath a heater.

'I'm completely alone,' I moan, flopping down.

'You're not alone; you're just annoyed,' she says. 'Have a non-alcoholic mulled wine.'

32

Weepy and Anxious

As you advance towards the end of your pregnancy, you may just be beginning to comprehend that you will soon become a mother. You may be more emotional and sensitive and you could even find yourself weepy, anxious or excited about the birth or worried about what kind of parent you will be.

Forty Weeks and Counting Down

It's Monday morning and I'm a basket case. In the split second I wake up, I forget Max has gone. When I remember, I prop myself up on an elbow and stare at his pillow, with a dull ache in my heart. I imagine him waking up where he is, in the studio, making a coffee, looking out of the window, murmuring my name, sighing, scratching and shaking his head sadly. I look towards my silent phone. Should I ring him? I think of another long day without him and pick up the phone. What shall I say, though? I could insist that Rainey leaves, but he already said it's too late for that, or it's not about that anymore, or whatever he said. I can't follow him to the studio: he told me not to. I did lie to him, but I've apologised, and at least I didn't leave him. I stare at the phone. I bring up his number and then the thing rings in my hand, the display flashing his name.

'If I hadn't rung, would you ring me?' he asks.

'Nope.'

'You're hard as nails.'

'Why would I ring you? You left me. Come back to me and we'll have a chat.'

'Ah, so you're still doing that whole "he left me" thing? OK, well, I'll pop over when you're ready to take some responsibility for your actions.'

'I take responsibility. I said I'm sorry!'

'Well, then I'm sorry too.'

'What for?'

'Good question! What am I supposed to be sorry for? Being a gullible fool?'

'Look, Max, I can't deal with this shit anymore, OK? I'm having a baby and I need a grown-up to help me, not a spoiled brat who walks out on me. So you just ring me when *you* are ready to take responsibility for *your* actions, dickhead!'

'Oh, name-calling, is it? Very adult!'

'Go away!' I hang up on him.

He calls back immediately.

I answer in a weary voice. 'Are you ready to talk nicely?' I ask.

'Don't be a baby, Vivienne. I rang to talk to you.'

'Baby, am I? Goodbye,' I say airily.

'Don't you ha—'

I hang up and throw the phone. It skitters across the laminate. *I'm* acting like a baby? I stare into space. I rock on the edge of the sofa bed, chewing on the side of my thumbnail. I stick out my bottom lip. I go and get ready for work.

I arrive at the office before anyone else and despondently rip down the Christmas streamers, leaving short, flaccid strands Blu-tacked in each corner of the room, where they'll remain until next Christmas . . . but who cares? I won't even be here by then, the way things are going.

I turn on my laptop, and as if to confirm this gloomy prediction, I find an email from Sebastian at Belle Peau saying our crackers are not doing well for him and cancelling our previous deal to have them on his site. He said he'd probably had one glass of sherry too many when he agreed but that we should meet up and discuss ways forward in the New Year. I look at the office calendar. It's bloody 4th February already. January has been a total wash-out. I've hardly been at work since Max left. I rattle out a reply, pointedly wishing him a happy New Year and asking for a meeting. It's better to act dense in these situations, I've always found.

New Year! Stupid whistley bastard.

At nine forty-two Christie arrives, wearing a black leather trouser suit and heels covered with spikes.

'You come straight from the fetish club, then?' I

ask, nodding at the shoes. She turns an ankle towards me, showing them off.

'Look and learn, Viv,' she sighs.

She hums to herself as she carefully removes the jacket and hangs it on her chair, switches on her laptop, cleans the screen with a special wipe, and arranges a Danish pastry next to her keyboard. Her lips are shiny red and her hair is pulled to the side in a backcombed ponytail like a fox's brush. She looks up.

'Fancy a cup of tea?' she asks.

'Go on, then,' I say. There's no point in reminding her that we start at nine. We're almost bust, so her work habits are soon to be someone else's concern, I guess. I search despondently through our website, looking at the samples for the Barnes and Worth meeting. I think we'll just take the whole range for them to pick through and dress Michael up in a gimp suit. Christie returns with the tea.

'God, you're massive now, aren't you, Viv?' she says, setting down a milky mug. 'How far along are you?'

'Thirty-three weeks.'

This means nothing to her. 'That's a really big bump, really wide! You're huge, Viv!' she says.

'Don't you think I know that?' I snap. 'I'm supposed to be big – there's a whole other person in here.'

'OK, then,' she says, raising her eyebrows at her screen.

'And my back is killing me,' I add, hoping for sympathy.

She doesn't answer. I watch her, but she doesn't look up. Am I unreasonable? Snappy? Am I a baby and a liar? A bad person? I would have said not, but actually, what do I know?

'Hey, Christie, I haven't really seen much of you since we've been back. You never told me about your break. What did you get up to?' I ask mildly.

'I never went away.'

'The Christmas break? Tell us what you did.'

'Oh, it seems ages ago! I went to this wicked New Year's Eve do, Viv. You should have come. It was mental. It was on a farm!'

'Mental.'

'At midnight we all went out into a field and balanced on these round hay bales and you had to try and run on top of them while someone pushed.'

'Mental,' I repeat.

'What did you do at New Year?' she asks, smile fading.

'Oh, you know, not much. Take That came over and we had a bake-off.'

'Oh.'

'Yeah, Gary Barlow really messed up his Victoria sponge, but his lemon meringue was the best you ever tasted.'

'OK, Viv, whatever.' She sips her tea.

'Actually, I went to Dublin to meet Max's family.'

'Oh, Dublin. Did you sing "Tell Me Ma"?'

'Yes! Do you know it?'

'I always end up singing that in Dublin.'

I look at her and nod encouragingly, waiting for a Dublin story, but none is forthcoming.

'So, anyway, Belle Peau have dropped us.'

'What?'

'Sebastian just emailed,' I say, whistling the 's'.

'His loss,' she says, whistling hers.

'Actually, it's very much our loss. Things are looking a bit tricky. If we don't get that Barnes and Worth thing . . .'

'We're up shit creek without a boat,' she says.

'Without a paddle,' I correct.

'But we still have a boat?'

'Yes, but we're heading for the rapids without a paddle, so we'll soon be matchwood.'

'Unless we get washed into the shallows,' she says hopefully.

'Even if we do, there's a waterfall ahead and we'll never make it. Barnes and Worth are our only hope. They're the sticking-out branch that we must grab hold of.'

'Oh well, I've applied for a job as a beautician anyway,' she says, examining a nail.

'You've already applied for a job?'

She nods her head with a serious expression. 'I need a secure job, Viv – I've booked Ibiza.'

'What about us? Me and you, the Dream Team?'

She wrinkles her nose and giggles as if it's all been a silly joke. 'Dream Team,' she says.

'And we still have the Barnes and Worth meeting. When they place a massive order, we'll need you. You're the only one who can speak Cantonese!'

'I'll probably be gone by then, but they speak OK English in the factory. Don't worry – I only do the Cantonese to keep them on their toes.' She smiles and pops a piece of Danish into her mouth.

I feel all the energy suck out of me. I'm instantly depleted. I slump forward, laying my hands across the desk. I take a long, shuddering breath, then drop my head and cry loudly into the crook of my arm.

'Oh, what's the fricking point, anyway?' I whimper into my jumper sleeve.

'I know. I sometimes think that,' she says.

I glance up, wiping my eyes. There she is, gazing at her screen, munching away without a care in the world, while I am about to lose everything. I'm facing a very uncertain future charting a course as a single mother, probably having to *live* in that zingy-green Bugaboo, while Christie, that faithless deserter, is saving her own skin like a rat leaving a sinking ship. Also, I can't seem to get away from these sailing analogies. I sit up and bang the desk, suddenly full of rage.

'Let me tell you something – you would be a terrible beautician, Christie!' I say, wagging a finger at her. She looks up, shocked. That's got her attention. Good. 'Beauticians have to be empathetic to people. They have to do things like wax old ladies' beards and spray nude fatties with fake tan, you know! They have to be tactful!'

'I am tactful, Vivienne,' she says, wide-eyed.

'You wouldn't know tact if it kicked you up the bum!'

'*You* wouldn't!'

'What? I'm the *epitome* of it!'

'As well you might be, but you're not very tactful,' she says, flicking her ponytail over her shoulder.

'Do you know I've been paying you out of my savings?'

'So?'

'So where's your loyalty?'

She shrugs. We stare at each other. A red flush is rising up to her ears. What am I doing? I know I can't make her stay here if she wants to go. I look at her wide eyes and suddenly feel sorry for her. I'm taking out all my frustrations on her and it's not her fault. It's Max who's left me. He's the faithless deserter. I take a deep breath.

'Oh, look, I'm sorry,' I say. 'Sorry, Christie.'

She lifts her nose, looking sideways at me.

'It's just I'm under a lot of pressure at the moment, but I shouldn't take it out on you. I hope you'll stay and see us through the meeting, and then whatever you decide to do is, of course, fine. You'll be a great beautician. You'll be great at whatever you decide to do.'

'Really?'

'Really.' I smile.

'Aw, thanks, Viv.' She giggles, as forgiving as a Labrador. 'I couldn't do what you're doing, though.'

'How do you mean?'

'Well, having a baby. I'm too selfish to ruin my figure, and I couldn't stand never being able to earn the same once you've got a baby, because even if you go back to work, you've got to spend half your wages on childcare, and then you always have to rush off to pick up the baby, and then you're constantly knackered because the baby won't go to sleep.'

'No. Well, that's right,' I say, feeling tears welling again. 'I'm just popping out for a bit.'

I go and stand outside on the fire escape. The freezing wind soon dries my eyes; it snaps at my nose, lifts my hair, and throws it in all directions. I gasp for breath as I try to pull myself together.

It's all right, I think. Everything is going to be fine. We will get a huge order from Barnes and Worth. Max will let me off for my barefaced lying. Rainey will begin to act a bit like a parent.

'*Who are you trying to kid?*' asks Angel.

'And if not, I will deal with it!' I shout. The words fly off into the rushing air. I turn and stand against the railing with my arms held out to the side like Kate Winslet in *Titanic*. 'I will deal with it!' I shout, shaking off a page of airborne newsprint that catches on my arm. I lift my chin to meet the wind, and out of the corner of my eye I see someone moving. I glance to the left, at the building opposite, where a small gathering has assembled at the window of an office. A few jump and clap when I look over. Then they push a thin man in glasses to the front of the window. He holds up a sign that reads, 'Will you go out with me?'

I don't know why, but I look around to make sure he means me. I point to myself and he nods. I pull a face and shake my head and they all fall about laughing. I feel sorry for the skinny man; he must be the butt of all the office jokes or something, poor guy. I turn to go, but I see he's scribbling something else, so I wait while he holds up the new message.

He holds it up, smiling. It reads, 'Go fuck yourself, fatty.'

33

Mother Knows Nothing

When one mother watches her daughter becoming a mother, the mixture of pride and love, sadness and nerves may be confusing.

Forty Weeks and Counting Down

I arrive home that evening and Rainey meets me at the door holding a bottle of Merlot and a glass. A ragged dark red line of wine has formed on her dry lips.

'Vivienne, welcome home. Want wine?' she asks, as I struggle out of my coat. What I want is to lie down in a dark room.

'No, thanks. I'm pregnant, remember,' I say, irritated.

'I've made us a casserole. Would you like mashed potatoes with it or rice?'

I head for the sofa. There is a delicious garlicky smell coming from the kitchen and I realise I'm starving. The living room is spotless: Rainey has cleaned up again. She's packed away the depressing Christmas tree that I started on, then left half undecorated with its white top sticking out from a wrapping of baubles like a half-peeled banana. She's replaced the tree with a vase of slender daffodils and some candles. The lamps are lit and it's warm and cosy in here. I drop my bag and lie flat on my back with a sigh of relief. Rainey comes over and arranges a cushion under my head.

'There. Is that better?' she asks, smoothing my hair. 'It feels nice to look after you,' she says, leaving 'Such a novelty' unsaid but hanging in the air. This is starting to feel weird. I feel like a pet.

'What a relief to lie down,' I groan. 'I'm so tired.'

'I told you, you should be resting, not working and trudging around London. Am I right?'

'You are so right. What about all those toiling-in-the-fields women? Did you say the same to them?'

The side of her mouth twitches. 'That's different – they're used to it. Mash, did you say?' She sings as she goes into the kitchen.

I find my phone and hold it on my chest. No missed calls from Max. This thing with us is getting serious. This is too long for a tiff. It's officially more than a tiff. What's he been doing today? Has he thought about me at all? Doesn't he miss me? Doesn't he care about Angel? I stroke my belly. It feels as if something is jammed under my ribs.

'We miss him, don't we?' I sniff, and wipe my eyes just as Rainey returns with a drink for me.

'You're not crying, are you?' she asks, placing the glass on a cork coaster.

I shake my head.

'You *are* crying,' she says. 'I hope those tears are not for that big Irish blockhead.'

I shake my head again and root around in my bag for a tissue to blow my nose.

'He's not worth the salt of your tears, Vivienne.' She presses her lips together.

I try to smile.

'I know you think you loved him. You thought you were some rock chick and he was your bohemian artist and the world was just going to open its arms to you because you were so adorable together.'

What is she talking about? I never thought that at all.

'But love isn't like that. You will always be let down. I could have told you,' she continues. 'I should have warned you he'd be gone at the first sign of trouble. And now he has! He's gone and left you with a baby on the way. It's the same the world over, Vivienne. That's what men do, and Irish men? Well . . .'

'It isn't like that,' I begin. 'Max wouldn't—'

'Don't be so naïve! It hasn't dawned on you yet, has it? I might as well tell you . . . He's already on to the next victim. Lula, is it?'

I sniff and wipe my tears. Eh? Lula? What has she got to do with this?

'Next victim? No, Lula's just one of his models,

and I am not naïve, thank you very much. I've lived a good successful life without you so far, you know. I'm thirty-two,' I tell her, all the while feeling very uneasy about Lula. I feel that name like a blade between the ribs. Lula with the bewitching lips and slim thighs? Lula with the glossy hair and the sexy laugh?

'Well, she rang here looking for him. I told her he'd gone for good and she's welcome to him. I said she could have him to herself from now on.'

'You what?' I sit up now. 'Lula rang here? You said what?'

'Yes, she rang today. She was upset, asking for Max.'

I feel sick. I rest my head in my hands. It's our student days all over again, the girls in tears ringing to speak to Max. Has he just reverted? Am I now one of those girls?

'You had absolutely no right to tell her he's gone for good. He has not gone for good! She can't have him,' I shout, feeling tears spring to my eyes at the thought. 'What did she say?'

'She was crying. She asked for him and hung up when I told her he'd gone.'

Can I believe this? I can't believe what Rainey says: she hates Max and would do anything to put him down. This is Max, my love, the man who loves me, my friend. I think back to the night at the gallery, Lula with her hand on his arm, how he stood next to her all night, but then I think of him proposing to me, telling me he loves me. *Then* I think of his face when I gave back the ring. I lied to him. What if I've pushed him into Lula's arms?

I take the phone and press his name. Rainey watches.

'Hello?' says a velvety female voice.

'Who's this?' I snap.

'Vivienne? It's Lula,' she croons with a laugh in her voice. I hang up.

Rainey raises her thin eyebrows.

'She just answered his phone,' I whisper.

'I told you,' she says, triumphant. 'Am I right?'

'But . . .' I stare into space. I don't believe it. Max wouldn't go off with Lula. He loves me, but then I wouldn't have believed he'd leave me, and he has.

'They're all the same,' says Rainey. 'Why do you think he never liked me? It's because he knew I was on to him. Men like that, they don't want a strong, independent woman like me around. I've seen his type before, all sexy smiles and wild hair and blarney! Then boom – they're gone like rats up a drainpipe!'

She's getting quite excited now, quite loud, but I'm only half listening. Despite everything that's happened, I know Max wouldn't do anything like this; he's my friend. He'd tell me it was over before he'd cheat on me. There must be a simple explanation, surely.

'He has a real aggressive streak too,' continues Rainey, pacing. 'Can't stand to be criticised, won't be told anything – everything has to be his way or the highway. His foolish pride will stop him from ever being successful, you know. He was jealous of me and my artistic expertise.'

'Rainey, shut up! You don't know the first thing about him, and I'll tell you something – you're the cause of this mess!' I say as my phone rings, flashing up his name. I hesitate.

'Don't answer it,' Rainey spits like a wild thing.

'Hi,' I say, ignoring her.

'Viv, it's me. How're you doing? You just rang. Are you OK?'

'Why is Lula answering your phone?'

'We're working. I was making tea, so she got it for me.'

I think of him happily painting and chatting and making tea while I'm here heavily pregnant and pining for him. It makes me wild with rage.

'Tea, was it?'

'Yeah . . . tea,' he says uncertainly.

'I see, I see. So why was she ringing here today in tears, then? Why did she ask Rainey for you?' I look up at Rainey, who's hovering nearby, and wave her away angrily.

'Ha! I bet Lorraine just couldn't wait to tell you that! What, d'you think I'm fucking Lula now?'

'I don't know. Are you?'

'Fuck's sake! This is what I mean. There's no trust!'

'Why was she crying down the phone for you?'

'She's pregnant. She doesn't want to be.'

'Who's the father? Tell her to ring him! Or are you . . . ?'

'No! I am not the father. What do you take me for, Viv? What's happened to you? She's a friend of mine, right? She needed to talk to me because we were meant to be working.'

Oh my God, what have I become? Accusing Max of all sorts. A tiny part of me wants to just say how sorry I am and beg him to come home, but now I'm wild with jealousy.

'Well, I'm supposed to be a friend of yours and I *am* having your baby, so you should be here,' I wail, and then I start to cry. I can't help it. I've had enough of this shit-with-shit-on-top situation, and everything I do just makes it worse, and I don't even know how it happened really.

'Ah, don't cry.'

'I don't know how this has happened. I don't understand why it's like this. I love you. How are you not here with me?'

'You know why.'

'Because I lied to you? I'm sorry! I made a fucking mistake, so you need to decide – are you going to forgive me or what?'

'Huh! Your usual "just let me off" approach isn't

going to work, Viv. I can't live with her. I don't know
how you can either when she puts you down all the
time. I can't stand it,' he says.

There's a long pause. I listen to him sigh, his
breath crashing into my ear.

'I thought you said you'd walk through fire for
me. What happened to that? I thought putting up
with your mother-in-law would be nothing to you.
Thanks a lot.'

'If you'd ever *asked* me to, I would have put up
with her. Instead you lied to me, you sided with
her, you made some sort of pact with her, and you
always choose to be loyal to someone else instead
of me!'

'Are we talking about what happened with Rob?'

'Yeah, if you like. You went back with him when
you'd started something with me. Now you're
choosing her over me. You're doing it again, Vivienne.'

'I had good intentions . . . I was just trying to do
the right thing.'

'So what?'

'That doesn't even make sense!'

'It does to me.'

'What about you and me?'

'Yeah, Viv, what about you and me?'

'I asked you first.'

'I didn't lie to you. I didn't scheme behind your
back. I didn't break off our engagement. You did. I

don't hang up every time we talk. So what about you and me? Do you want it or not?'

'No!' I shout, and then I hang up.

I wait. He doesn't ring back.

34

Not so funny Valentine

Max,
    I think you are very mean to leave me as well as being wrong. A lot wrong actually about most things. But I realise I am not perfect and see how it may seem to you that I've betrayed you or some such shite. The fact is I miss you and I am the one having our baby so can you come back and help out with that and we'll sort this other stuff all out later when I'm less needy? I think this is the best solution all round.
    Yours truly,
    V.E. Summers

I scribble this in a valentine's card, one with a photo of a kitten hanging in a sock with 'Stuck on you' across the top, and then throw it in the bin when he doesn't ring back. Then he doesn't ring back some more. A week passes by and he doesn't ring. I want to talk to him and say something like, 'Look, this is stupid . . .' but I don't.

Then a card arrives from him on Valentine's Day. A handmade card, a beautiful pencil sketch of pregnant me, asleep, and inside is written:

Vivienne,

Come to Uno's tonight at 7.

M x

I put it on the table and keep glancing at it and picking it up again for a long time, flooded with relief and excitement. He loves me. He wants to see me. I look at his handwriting and black thoughts begin to circle, overpowering my forgiving heart. It doesn't say he loves me, does it? Or that he's sorry. He probably wants to meet to tell me why I'm wrong all over again, and I don't care what he says about trust and lies and whatever else he thinks; I'm pregnant and that is a 'get out of jail free' card if ever there was one. He should forgive me. He should be beating down the door, showering me with flowers and chocolates or something, not summoning me mysteriously. He shouldn't have left me in the first place, and he knows where I am if he wants to see me.

I wander into the kitchen and find myself staring at a fridge-magnet gift from Rainey. 'When the going gets tough, the tough get going' it says above a picture of a grinning chimp. She's taking the 'be tough and get going' approach with her lump. A mammogram showed up a shadow, she says, and further tests are needed. Worrying about her and being driven mad by her has helped to distract me from the empty ache of missing Max.

Still, my heart reasons, I feel dull inside, muffled, as if I'm looking at the world through a thick layer of ash. Not being able to talk to Max makes everything worthless as shit. I miss him so much I've developed a twitch in my eye. He makes my day. I always check my ideas with him because the way he looks at the world makes total sense. He finds a way to laugh at things. I miss his big, loud laugh.

I stick Max's card on the fridge, slamming the grinning chimp over the lovely sketch. I'll go to Uno's tonight and I can't wait to see him.

The day at work is a drag mostly involving me staring at my PowerPoint presentation for Barnes and Worth with a sense of doom. I make up a slide entitled 'Likelihood of Getting Back With Max' and put in a pie chart with 'likely' being ninety per cent, 'unlikely' five per cent and 'anything could happen' being the rest, and then I do another with 'unlikely' being ninety per cent.

There's a brief interlude after lunch when some really gorgeous sample crackers arrive. We lay them out by Christie's desk and get excited by the bright colours and the finish of the card. Michael sets about taking pictures of the 'New Baby' range and Photoshopping them onto pictures of happy new parents holding tiny cute offspring. When he shows me, I tear up with longing for Max and my baby and our little family. Michael gives me a tissue and a lecture about hormones in the third trimester running wild and making you do crazy stuff.

I leave early, saying I'm not feeling well, and nip into H&M's maternity section on the way home. I pick up a low-cut maternity dress in midnight blue to wear tonight. Just as I'm walking out of the shop, Rainey calls. I press 'ignore'. I need to concentrate on tonight and not be distracted by her latest drama. I make my way home to take a long bath, and I'm relieved to find she's out.

Rainey is still not back later when I head out to meet Max. I leave her a note. I'm pleased with the dress. It accentuates my mahoosive boobs, and the silver locket draws the eye right to them. My black eyeliner and messy ponytail say, 'Not-trying-too-hard sexy', a look I work hard at and only occasionally pull off.

Uno's is chock-full of couples at tables for two with candles twinkling in jars. I look around for Max, and then when I lay eyes on him I have to compose myself. He looks completely gorgeous in his old denim shirt. He stands as I approach and kisses me on the cheek. I get a whiff of him and my traitor heart flips with longing.

'Hey, Viv.' He smiles.

'Hi.'

I sit and a few moments pass. What is he doing, just sitting there smiling? I fiddle with the napkin, spreading it over my lap. I avoid looking at his eyes:

they make me think of sex and I know I'll lose all composure.

'You look fantastic,' he says.

'Thank you, I try. You look good.'

'Thanks.' He nods.

'Welcome.'

The waitress brings two glasses of Prosecco and a rose, dumping them down on the table, like she has fifty times already this evening: they're complimentary with the booking, a valentine's gimmick.

'Cheers.' He raises his glass to mine and we chink.

'Why did you summon me? To apologise?'

'I invited you so we could talk without you hanging up on me. Pretty relieved you came. It's fucking great to see you, baby.'

'Oh,' I say airily, looking around at the table arrangements, trying to stop the corners of my mouth turning up into a massive smile.

He rubs the back of his hair, messing it up, as if wondering how to handle this.

'Also I have a proposal for you,' he says.

'Another one?'

'Come and live with me.'

I'm saved from answering immediately by the waitress bringing bread and olives and tap water in a fancy bottle. I look at Max as she slides the menu in front of him and he looks at me. Our eyes and hearts connect like old friends.

'It makes sense,' he continues.

'Does it? How?'

'We have a bed at mine, for a start. We can be together. I miss you. You know you miss me.'

'I thought I was a big liar who puts other people before you?'

'You still are, and I'm the guy who fucks off at the drop of a hat. Nobody said we're perfect.'

Here I want to look up at the ceiling and laugh and say, 'Oh thank god!' But I'm gripped by a terrible stubbornness and its forcing me to stick to the principle and not give in to my heart. I'm pregnant and he chose to abandon me rather than support me. I can't just forget about that.

'Well, it's a lovely idea, but I can't.'

'Why not?' He frowns.

'Because my mother is staying with me, and the reason she's doing that is so we could get to know each other after all these years. As I explained, I have a need to get to know my mother before I become a mother myself, and I had hoped you would understand that and support me, instead of accusing me of choosing her over you, instead of making me choose.'

'I did, I do. The woman's a witch.'

I shake my head. 'I expected you'd support me by staying with me no matter what she's like.'

'What can I do? I can't live with her. You swore she

was going. Meanwhile telling her she can stay for fucking ever.'

'Not for ever. Look, she got ill.'

'Of course she got ill!' He throws himself back in the chair, shaking his head. 'Are you really that gullible?'

'Maybe.'

'She manipulates you. She puts you down, Viv.'

'Well, anyway, in other news the baby is fine, although my pelvis is shagged.'

'Viv, I didn't leave you. Can't you see why I had to leave? You lied to me for her.'

I sigh. I'm confused and exasperated, and he's making all these strong arguments as to why I'm a gullible fool and totally wrong, but he doesn't know what it's like to have a mother like mine, does he? He doesn't know anything.

'I think you were right when you said I need time to work out my relationship with Rainey,' I say, adding, 'without you,' to hurt him. Why not? I'm hurting all over.

'Well then, you made your choice,' he says sadly.

'There shouldn't be a choice,' I swallow, and look away.

The rest of the meal is horrible – prickly but polite conversation – and I insist on going halves on the bill to piss him off. We walk out of the artificial valentine's bubble into the icy wind of a February night.

'Well, goodbye,' I say, stoic as a wartime heroine.

'Vivienne . . .'

I touch his hand, kiss his cheek and turn away, walking into the wind, letting it smart my eyes to hide the tears.

35

Forty Weeks and Counting Down

Work burdens can be difficult to bear – stress is tiring, so you will need to plan extra time just to relax, spend time with your partner, and discuss any concerns. It is better to get your worries and doubts out into the open now.

Forty Weeks and Counting Down

Bloody *Forty Weeks and Counting Down* is right about everything. You might get a powerful craving to eat soap. Look it up and there it'll be: 'In week thirty, some women have a powerful craving for soap.' It's so accurate I want to catch it out. I thought, surely no one else in their thirty-seventh week likes to bite cotton wool for that dry, squeaky feeling? I look it up and there it is! I throw the book down. Spend time with your partner, it says. I'd love to. I stare into space, brooding, overcome with a dark pessimism. Since Valentine's Day things have become alarmingly civilised and unemotional. He calls, we talk politely. It's worse than not speaking. I try to insult him just to get a rise out of him, get him to show some emotion, but he doesn't react. Is this the death knell for us and our hot passionate love? I need to talk this through with a close friend.

'Lucy Bond speaking.'

'It's the death knell for me and Max. We've become polite.'

I hear a weary sigh. 'You know what I think.'

'You think he's right.'

'Yes he is right and he loves you, so just go round there and give him a blow job. Death knell!'

'Even though he left me and I'm pregnant?'

'Viv, just go round there and sort it.'

'Not while there's breath in my body. Anyhow, I can't can I? Perineum failure.'

'You're pathetic,' she laughs.

'You try walking without one.'

'I would but I'm at work, Viv. I have to go.'

'OK, you hang up first.'

The line goes dead instantly. I look at the time. Six forty-five and she's already at her desk. Wow. I think about calling Max, but don't. I get up and make tea.

Rainey is still asleep and I don't want to wake her. She's been for more tests on her lump and has been slightly frosty with me for avoiding her calls while she's battling with possible cancer. She tells me they still can't say if it's cancer, although a quick Google search tells me she should know by now. I asked her what tests she'd had, but she was vague, muttering something about 'the one with the needle'. I think if she's had that test, we should know the results very soon.

I hope she is OK because I need her to move out and I won't feel guilty about it. As Lucy explained to me, lots of people love their mother, but hardly any of them want to live in a tiny flat for months with them while pregnant. It's my guilt that's keeping her here, says Lucy, which is crazy, because Rainey left *me* all those years ago. Why should *I* feel guilty? Lucy says it's because inside I feel it's my fault she went away and now I'm trying to be the perfect daughter to prove that I can make her stay. Lucy and her tinpot psychology. It got too confusing to fathom in the end. I make the tea feeling down, thinking thoughts like 'Everybody leaves me' and 'I don't even like my own pyjamas.'

I'll have to pull myself together, though. This isn't a great frame of mind to be in today, because today I'm facing Barnes and Worth. I shuffle off to get ready for work.

Damon has offered to take us over to the Barnes and Worth's Baker Street head office in his van, so that we don't have to struggle with all the samples on the Tube. I sit in the back seat wearing my wizard-sleeve maternity dress, marvelling at the circumference of Damon's hairy neck as we crawl through the London traffic. Michael is up front, wearing his pale grey suit and a new navy tie. He's slicked his black hair back and even added an extra bead to the end of his straggly beard. He's looking sharp for a weirdo. Beside me is Christie, my wing-woman, wearing a shocking-pink satin playsuit more conducive to a night out clubbing than a career-defining business meeting, but as I said in my earlier pep talk, we have to be the best version of who we are and that's all we can do, because that's who we are. I think I made a point, anyhow. Sliding around in the back of the van are boxes of sample crackers. They look good. We went with five key colours with contrasting ribbon. So we're good to go, we're all set, and we're all looking forward. The only thing that's missing is some action-film-type music.

'My old mum used to know Bette Barnes of Barnes and Worth when they were market traders together,' Damon tells us as we pull up to unload by the revolving doors.

'How old *is* your old mum? Barnes and Worth were market traders in the 1800s, Damon,' I say.

'Oh yeah, of indeterminable age, she is,' he says.

I turn and look up at the tall building with a shudder, counting up to the thirteenth floor, where we used to work. The last time we were in this building, I quit and Christie was sacked by the very person we're meeting with today. I square up my shoulders and blow out a breath. I'm facing down the fear.

'Right, come on, Dream Team!' I shout, turning back to the van to grab a box.

Michael climbs down, smooths his suit and does a

little boxer's dance on the pavement, sparring with the air.

'That's it – stay loose. Looking good,' I tell him.

Christie totters round the back of the van holding up a bright pink cracker tied with a pea-green ribbon.

'Look, Viv, see what I did?' She motions to her pink playsuit with pea-green sash. 'I *am* a transition cracker!' she says, smiling delightedly.

'Oh yeah!' I say, and gulp. How the hell are we going to pull this off? And what will happen if we don't? I waddle to the back of the van to get a box, but Damon stops me.

'I'll park up and help you in with these boxes, Viv,' he says.

I don't know what to say. I hesitate. I definitely do not want him to come into the building.

He clocks my reaction. 'Or are you scared I'll scatter the crowd with my breathtaking beauty?' he asks, one stray eye searching the sky.

'No, that's great – help with the boxes.' I nod, ashamed, and we go through to the marbled foyer to wait our turn.

There are other companies waiting for sales meetings: one neat husband-and-wife team, edgy as hens, with a crate of rusty wire hearts, and various suited groups with briefcases. Here we are in the thick of it. Michael is sweating slightly despite the air conditioning and I pass him a tissue to wipe his forehead.

'She's not going to eat you, Michael,' I tell him.

'You don't know her, Viv. She once went for me with a dentist's drill during foreplay,' he says into his lap, and Christie turns to me, wide-eyed, mouthing, 'Oh my God.'

At that moment Damon exits from the revolving doors holding two boxes. I give a discreet wave to his good eye and he lumbers over.

'Just pop them down there, thanks, Damon,' I say.

'So this is it. This is where it all happens!' he declares, hands on hips.

'Yes. We'll be OK from here, thanks,' I say, eager to usher him out before Mole appears to collect us, but it's too late. Here she is, sliding herself sideways through the security gates. A coil of nerves tightens around my chest like barbed wire. Nerves or it could be heartburn: I've been getting that. I moisten my lips and check Michael. He's transfixed like a mouse facing a python.

Mole is swathed in maroon linen. It appears as if lengths of fabric with ridged seams have been sewn and knotted together at random and she's found a hole to pop her head through. Her mouth is dark maroon against her pale shiny skin. Even the sprinkle of moles across her cheek look maroon. Her pale blue gaze covers the foyer before coming to rest on Michael. She looks at him hungrily. Her eyes pin him down like two laser beams. I glance to my left, where he stands spellbound and stupefied by her. His statement facial hair quivers.

'Be cool,' I whisper, and pinch him on the thigh.

I step forward a little and extend my hand. She drags her gaze away from Michael and enfolds my fingers in a clammy handshake. She looks to Damon and then to Christie and back to me.

'Wow. Dream Team. You really are,' she says, raising her eyebrows.

Eh? What does she mean by that?

'Hi, Marion,' I say warmly. 'May I introduce our driver, Damon. He's just leaving, and Christie you know, and of course Michael . . .' I trail off.

There's a moment of awkwardness while Mole and Michael just look at each other. This is some weird energy between them.

'I'll wait in the van, then, Viv,' Damon interrupts, and I nod impatiently.

'Well, now,' croons Mole. 'Shall we go up?' She gestures with a chubby hand and we follow her to the lifts.

'You look very nice today, by the way,' I say. 'Have you lost weight?' I'm shameless: clearly she hasn't lost any weight; if anything, she's heavier than before.

'No,' she chuckles. 'I've put on a few pounds, actually,' she says, looking at Michael, who has a thing for big women. He fingers his beard and smiles at her, and she colours slightly.

We ride a couple of floors in silence.

'Congratulations to you, Vivienne,' says Mole suddenly.

'You look very big.' She motions towards my belly. 'May I touch?'

'Yes, of course.' I smile and try not to cringe as she strokes a hand over my newly popped-out belly button.

'How many months pregnant are you?' she asks. Her breath smells like poo.

'Thirty-seven weeks. They count in weeks,' I tell her, surprising myself. Birth seems scarily imminent.

'Working right up to the bitter end?' she asks.

'Oh yes! I could pop any minute, as they say!'

'Hopefully not in our meeting, though,' she says, hastily removing her hand.

'No, no, bunged myself up!' *Shut up, shut up. Just stop now!*

Thankfully the lift arrives at our floor.

She shows us to a meeting room and Christie and I begin arranging the crackers in order. We're starting with some of the more usual transitions – 'New Baby', 'Sexy Bride', 'New House' – having decided to keep back 'Out of the Closet', 'Fetish' and 'Hen Night' for later.

'How have you been?' I hear Mole murmur in Michael's ear as he sets up our presentation.

'I'm well, Marion,' he says, looking sideways at her.

The Smart Board buzzes to life, lighting up the gloomy room, and we wait as Michael prepares the presentation and then I'm away. I feel a flutter of nerves as I begin the pitch. I go through the background research – the numbers of people getting married, the birth rate and divorce rate – and our rationale, and then I hand Mole a cracker to pull. I choose the 'Fetish' one, deliberately, knowing she'll ask Michael to pull it with her.

'Michael, would you like to pull a cracker?' she asks coquettishly. It's really quite sad to see. He obliges and a pair of our trademark edible pants, a blindfold and some foldaway handcuffs slide out onto the table. Mole picks up the pants.

'I remember these,' she says, opening the packet. 'Edible pants.'

'That's right.' I smile as she slips the blindfold on Michael. He sits there with his mouth slightly open like a fish. 'Er, there's also a little leaflet of knots in there, should you wish to tie up your partner,' I add chirpily.

Christie and I go through the costs and the retail prices, and Mole questions the profit margins. She handles each cracker, lays them out in a line, and then she blows out a breath like a whale and says no.

We're all still smiling as she says it, until one by one it dawns on us and our smiles drop and shatter like icicles from a roof.

'It's a shame, because I really like this product. Great ideas. The crackers look beautiful, but we'd have to launch it. I feel the investment will be too much for the gifting budget and will leave us short for our classics. People expect a pop-up brolly from us. We are the destination store for toiletry bags and lavender talc, but fetish crackers? Not so much.'

I feel as if a big rock has been placed over my lungs. I'm casting about, thinking of something to say.

'I appreciate what you're saying, Marion, but I don't think you need to see it as a huge launch. You could start slowly, with perhaps just "New Baby", and see how they sell through,' I say, raising my eyebrows into my hair and smiling crazily.

She picks up the baby-blue cracker and sorts through the contents.

'Could we choose what we put in?' She frowns at a tiny pair of sock/slippers.

'As long as we can supply it,' I say. 'I know these are in demand. A lot of my friends are pregnant and having babies, and they all say there's a lack of cool gifts for new mums. Also, the whole American baby-shower idea is trending big time over here.' I don't have any friends who are pregnant, and the closest I have ever got to a baby shower was chugging vodka from a baby's bottle with my old neighbour.

'Hmm, no, I can't see it working . . .' she mutters to herself.

Michael has actually stopped jiggling. He's pushed the blindfold up onto his head, giving him the look of a kung fu warrior. He licks his lips and turns to look her in the eye.

'Now listen, Marion, I'm not here for shits and

giggles, all right? I want something from you and you have the power to give it and vice versa, quid pro quo and all that.'

She moves her chair round and studies him.

'What are you offering?' she asks huskily.

'You well know what I can offer,' he says, and her face lights up like a landscape when the sun breaks through, 'but I'm asking for something here and now and this is a one-time-only deal.' He gestures to the crackers. 'I know what you want, Marion,' he growls, 'and you know I can give it to you, but what are you going to do for me?'

Christie's eyes dart from Mole to Michael and back again. I feel as if we've stumbled into some live porn theatre. I'd expected Michael to turn up and look keen, but he's taking this whole idea to a totally different level.

He stands and places a hand on her shoulder. She briefly closes her eyes. 'You can discuss it with the girls. I'll be outside waiting for your decision,' he says and saunters out, whistling casually.

As the door closes, Mole seems to snap out of some kind of trance. She looks at her notes. 'I do see a market for the product, but . . .' she muses.

'The thing is, we package the crackers in printed shelf trays, so I think it could stand up alongside the other gifts,' I say.

'OK, I'll take five hundred,' she says, glancing towards the door. 'Email me how you think they'll be split, but I'll need two hundred "New Baby", a hundred pink, a hundred blue, sale or return to start with.' She shakes her head, making notes. 'You can leave. Send Mike in here,' she says.

We look both ways up and down the corridor for Michael. He steps into view from behind a pillar like a gunslinger.

'Well?' he says.

'Five hundred,' I say. 'Not enough, and fucking sale or return. Shit. Can't you go and shag her over the desk or something?'

'I'm not a piece of meat for women to peck at like carrion, Vivienne,' he says.

'I know, I know, but wow, your sexuality certainly was potent in there . . . I thought I'd need a fire extinguisher at one point. I was sure you'd blown her mind. I thought she'd go for at least a thousand. Damn, we were so close!' I peek sideways at him to see if blatant flattery is working.

'Go back in,' he tells Christie, 'and say these exact words: "Drill and hockey mask". But tell her to add another zero.'

'Drills and masks? No, Michael! Don't sacrifice yourself—' I begin half-heartedly, but Christie is already through the door.

Later, Christie, Damon and I wait for Michael in the Dog and Gun, one of our old after-work drinking spots. Christie is sucking up an orange Bacardi Breezer through a straw. I have a lime and soda – it's the only soft drink to have when you're pregnant that's not sickly sweet. I always have lime and soda now. I'm even sicker of lime and soda than I was before.

'Where is he?' I sigh. I'm getting worried. Michael has been ages. 'What did she say again, Christie?'

'I went in, right, and I went, "Michael says, 'Drill and hockey mask, and add another zero.'" Then she goes, "Send him in," and I came out.'

'Send him in for what, though?' I ask, having visions of Michael turning on a spit somewhere with an apple in his mouth. If he's in any kind of uncompromising position, it's totally my fault.

I look up at the clock. It's half one. He's been gone an hour. By two I'm despondently listening to Damon telling Christie about the knock-off designer gear they sell down the market when the pub door is thrown open and Michael swaggers in. I jump up and wave him over. He gets to the table and does a short robotic dance ending in a spin. He grins, showing his little sharp teeth.

'Am I the man, or am I the man?' he asks.

'What? What happened?'

He sits down, bouncing his knees together.

'Five k in the bag,' he says deadpan, and holds up a hand to high-five us all. He smooths back his hair. 'Fuck me, I need a case of Breezers.'

'What did you do?' I ask.

'You wouldn't believe what I did if I told you.' He

smiles and picks something off his tongue. 'I don't want to give you nightmares.'

'Oh Jesus, don't tell me,' I gulp. 'Thank you, Michael. Well done.'

'No, thank you, Viv – I'm back with her!'

'What, you and Mole?' asks Christie, looking hurt. 'You said she was evil.'

I've thought for a while that Christie might have feelings for Michael. She's been acting weird around him. Crikey, Michael! Is no chick immune?

'The course of true love never did run smooth, baby doll. Now, who's going to get me a drink?'

I wait at the bar and look back at our table. I hear Michael exclaiming, 'Five k!' They're laughing. I feel a burst of excitement. Thank Christ we have an order! Not any order but a massive one with a major retailer, a retailer with stores nationwide. This will make us. This will give us leverage with other companies too: they'll all want transition crackers! The whole world will clamour for them.

I take out my purse to pay for the drinks and my silent phone lurks there at the bottom of my bag like a dead rat. No messages. No missed calls. What's the point of good news if there's no one to share it with?

I pick up the phone and check if it's working; sometimes it loses signal and then I don't get my messages immediately. The signal has never been stronger, a great mocking full grey rainbow of signal. I find Max's number and tap out a text message.

I miss you. Can we talk?

My thumb hovers over 'send' and then I press it before I can think about it anymore.

I go back to our table and hand Michael his drink.

'She was the most beautiful woman in the world!' Damon is saying.

'Oh God, please not Lady Di again?' I say, sitting down.

'I've seen more meat on a butcher's pencil,' Michael argues.

And so a debate ensues about female beauty and who embodies it the most. I'm just about to make a very valid point about personality shining through smiles when I'm distracted by a text message buzzing in. It's Max.

Meet me at gallery 8 in a half-hour x

A kiss? A kiss means he's forgiven me. Or is a kiss a way of saying, 'End of message'? Is that a friendly peck or something else? Either way I'm instantly over the moon. I can't get out of here quickly enough.

'Where is gallery 8?' I ask the table, and discover it's a very cool art gallery and café in Hoxton, and that to be there in half an hour, I should have left ten minutes ago.

But hold on, stop the train! I'm here celebrating with my team; I can't just go running because he wants to see me. He left me. I'll jolly well text the boy back saying if he wants to meet me, he'd better get to the Dog and Gun in ten minutes, but then as I think that,

I imagine another row and another day of not seeing him, and I'm up, pulling on my coat. Christie and Michael look up expectantly.

'I have to be somewhere,' I tell them. 'You guys take the afternoon off, and have a drink on me,' I say, remembering I only have five pounds in cash. I throw it down anyway. 'Well done today!' I run/walk across the pub carpet, fastening my coat as I go. 'See you all tomorrow!' I call over my shoulder. 'Well done again! Dream Team! Yay!' I double-pump my fist at the door and leg it for a taxi as fast as my bump will allow.

36

Weird Tits

One of the first changes you notice when you are pregnant is a change in your breasts. They become fuller, often increasing in size by two cup sizes. Now is the time to invest in some pretty maternity and feeding bras.

Baby and Me, February 2013

The taxi pulls up at gallery 8, a tall brick warehouse with large metal-framed windows. In the rush to get over here, I didn't get cash to pay the driver. I look through the lit gallery windows with a hammering heart. What to do? If I ask the driver to turn round and take me to a cashpoint, it could take ages and I'm already twelve minutes late. Telling myself it will be the perfect ice-breaker, I decide to borrow cash from Max. I compose myself and walk up to the gallery, battle with the large glass doors – because it's one of those with a pull handle on the outside even though they push open – and step inside onto the cool polished concrete floor. I see lamps, a coffee bar, a display of arty greeting cards, but I don't see Max anywhere. There are a lot of young people in ironic retro knits and coloured skinny jeans leafing through classy books and magazines. I look up to an open balcony, leather sofas, art, more art, no Max.

Then I hear a wolf whistle from somewhere behind me. I spin round.

'Hello,' he says, and he smiles.

I'm struck how tall he is and dark and actually very handsome. I'd forgotten about all of that while I was building my case against him. Before I can say anything, he hugs me. His arms circle my shoulders, and my face gets pressed into the scratchy wool of his jumper. I try to tell him about the taxi money.

'Don't say anything. Just let me hold you,' he says, kissing the top of my hair.

So now I'm stuck. I move my eyes to the window, where the cab driver is now unfolding his newspaper. The meter is running. I glance down and see directly into the pocket of Max's Crombie coat. His wallet is nesting there with a twenty sticking out of the side. If I just reach down, I could get that. I drop my head, which allows an extra few centimetres' reach. Max squeezes me closer in response. I stretch my fingers and I have the note, but the wallet comes too.

'I missed you so much, Viv,' he begins. Then he jolts. 'Wait, are you trying to *rob* me?' He steps back, leaving me holding his wallet dangling from the twenty.

I pull out the note. 'I just need this,' I say, dropping his wallet back in his pocket, and I go and pay the taxi.

As ice-breakers go, it was a good one. Instead of being all guarded and serious, we were straight into how much money we owe each other.

'I'll add that twenty to the ten you took the other week,' he says when I return.

'I'll knock that thirty off what you owe me for cattery charges.'

'I didn't put Dave in the cattery, you did.'

'Because you left him with some druggie neighbour.'

He stops and flashes a smile. 'Right now, you look the most beautiful you've ever looked,' he says. 'Let's go back to hugging.'

I take a step up close to him and he bends to kiss my face. He waits with his lips close to mine. I bump my forehead on his chest, and then I look at him and remember how in love with him I am. Damn his sexy brown eyes. He kisses me again and I kiss him back, until I start to feel weak at the knees and have to sit down. He buys me a cup of tea; it comes in its own pot, which actually becomes a mug. This café is extreme coolness.

'So why did you bring me to this godforsaken place?' I ask.

'I want to show you something.'

He leads me up the stairs to the gallery. There are battered leather sofas. There are bronze sculptures of human body parts scattered about like dissected limbs. The title of the exhibition is 'Human'. There's a 'mind' section with a blue glass brain that lights up in different places in response to recordings of music or voices, and then we go beyond a partition, to where a new title reads, '"Forty Weeks" by Max Kelly.'

There are about ten paintings of pregnant me. Me wearing a tutu, me asleep, me stretching my back and looking out of the flat window, naked me, half-turned me, massive-bellied me, pissed-off me, smiling me and first-thing-in-the-morning me. Underneath each painting is the number of weeks I'm pregnant. I look pretty dog rough in some of them, but they are beautiful paintings; even I can see that. He is a talent, just as gallery Guy said.

'What do you think?' he asks.

'I can't believe it.'

'It's all I've been doing since I left, just crying, calling out your name, ripping at me own hair and painting pictures of you for this exhibition.'

I turn to look at him and he looks straight into my eyes with a knowing, loving look. 'You like?'

'I love. It's amazing,' I say, peering at the paintings. 'Do my nipples really look that purple?'

'Yeah, "Weird Tits" we call you.' He smiles and I laugh. 'I already sold two—' he begins, but I lunge at him and throw my arms around him.

'I love you so much,' I say into his coat collar, 'and

I've been wrong and I'm really sorry and I want to stop this polite shit and be us again.'

'I'm sorry as well. I want that. Come back with me?' he says.

Back at his studio, we just hang out. It's exactly like before, as if we haven't just spent over a month apart. I'm leaning on his chest on the sofa, and he's making Dave appear to headbang along with Bob Marley by waving cheese.

'We were so stupid,' I say. 'We nearly broke up.'

'I had no intention of breaking up with you, stupid,' he says.

'Let's not go into it. I've learned my lesson – you are more stubborn than a barn door, but I can't stand to be away from you.'

'Thick as a barn door, that's me.'

'But I'm addicted to you, Kelly.'

'Magnets, babe.' He nods. He struggles with his jeans pocket, pushing me forwards. I move to sit up at the other end of the sofa. He brings out my engagement ring, handing it to me between his thumb and forefinger. I look at his face. He nods towards the ring. I take it.

'I want to marry you. I've always wanted to since the day I first laid eyes on you, so will you please just put this back on your stubby finger and make me the happiest man alive?'

I take his hand and place it on my belly where Angel has begun to kick like mad suddenly.

'See, she wants you to marry her daddy and make an honest baby of her,' Max says.

'Two against one.'

I push the ring down my finger; at first it gets stuck on a wave of skin, but I manage to get it on. 'So,' I say, holding the ruby up to the light.

'So,' he says.

'Three Little Birds' is playing on the iPod; I remember Rainey's story about dancing me out. I think of a frightened sixteen-year-old having a baby alone. I think of her turning her back on me and taking off at twenty-three.

'This was Rainey's birth song,' I tell him.

'So she says, but then she's a pathological liar.'

'I want it to be my birth song. Put that down on the birth plan.'

'What birth plan?'

'The one we're going to write.'

He reaches over to the upturned crate/occasional table and grabs a pencil and an old envelope and scribbles it down. 'Vivienne, I'm sorry I left you,' he says, and kisses my hand. 'Especially because she left you.'

'You think I have a thing about being left?'

He turns my hand over and kisses my palm. 'Hmm,' he says. 'Maybe, definitely.'

'I just want a happy ending. I've always wanted a

happy ending since I read the Ladybird version of *Cinderella*. You know the one where she has the three dresses?'

'What are you talking about?'

'A happy ending.' I reach up to play with his hair.

'If you want Rainey around, I don't mind.'

'You do.'

'I mean, I can't stand her. Ah, that's too strong. No, it isn't. And I don't trust her. I don't like to see you trying so hard with her when she lets you down, and I'd like to have sex without her walking in.' He smiles.

'Sex? What's that?'

'You know the thing with the thing, where I . . . and you . . .' He makes shapes with his hands.

I stare off into space with narrowed eyes as if trying to remember.

'Doesn't ring a bell,' I murmur.

'I know she's your mother and everything . . .'

'But?'

'No but.'

'I wanted her to love me. Stupid huh?'

'Do you think she does?'

'I don't know what she thinks or what she wants. I tried so hard with her because I was scared of losing her again, I suppose. It sounds pathetic really, but now I'm not scared. I don't care. I choose you.'

'You still are scared.'

'Nope. I'm strong and I'm fine. I'm not even going to call her.'

'Rainey Summers speaking.'

'Hey, it's Viv.'

'Hello, Vivienne.'

'You OK?'

'Is that what you rang to ask me?'

'I . . . wanted to tell you I'm staying for a couple of days with Max.'

'Oh,' she says quietly. There's a pause. I can hear a game show blaring in the background. 'I made a casserole for us.'

'Sorry. I should have rung earlier.' God, I'm glad I missed the casserole – it would have been my third in a week. There's only so much I can take.

'So you're back with him, are you?'

'Yeah.' I pick at my sleeve hem. Why do I feel guilty about it?

'For good?'

'I hope.'

'Might I ask why? After everything he's done, everything we talked about?' Her voice is tight with anger.

'Look, thanks for all the advice you gave. I'm not ignoring it. In some ways Max is an artistic rake, and he definitely can be irresponsible. I'm not sure about foozle, but whatever, I love him. I have to forgive him. I'm just not happy without him, you know?'

'No, I don't know.' She sighs heavily. 'He'll never change, Vivienne, if that's what you're hoping for. He will chew you up and spit you out! He'll let you down,' she says, and I suddenly get a glimpse of this inter-stellar coldness about her; she doesn't know how to love. She won't forgive, and aren't love and forgiveness almost the same thing? She can't forgive, even herself; she's hard inside like the pit of an olive.

'Well, anyway . . .' I begin.

'Vivienne, I found another one,' she blurts suddenly. There's a sawing sound and it takes me a moment to realise that she's crying.

'What?'

'In my breast. Well, more in my armpit.'

'Have you had it checked?'

'I rang your surgery – I'm going in the morning.'

'What time?'

'Eight.'

'I'll come.'

'I don't want to bother you.'

'I want to come.'

'Do you?'

I hesitate for a split second. 'Of course,' I say, and then there's an awkward silence.

'I'll speak with you tomorrow. Goodbye, Vivienne.'

She ends the call. I sit staring for a moment with the phone in my lap. I can't leave her to face this on her own again. I'll have to go home. Max won't like it, but I have to do what I have to do.

I look down at my belly. 'You've gone quiet all of a sudden,' I say, and lift my hand to admire the ring, back in its rightful place on my finger. And then I wet myself all over the sofa.

37

Waters Break

Before labour, usually when the birth is close, the sack of fluid surrounding your baby will break. This happens as labour begins. There could be a rush of fluid, a puddle or a dribble.

Forty Weeks and Counting Down

'Viv, this is not wee. It smells like *mushrooms*,' says Max.

'My wee always smells funny. If only I'd done those damned pelvic-floor exercises, I wouldn't be incontinent.'

'There's quite a lot of liquid here.'

'Fuck's sake, Max, don't you think I know that?'

'I mean, it's all over the couch.'

'All right! I already loathe myself.'

'Just saying.'

'Ah God, I'm doing it again!'

'Go to the toilet!'

'I'm going. Don't follow me. What are you doing?'

'Viv, I think your waters have gone.'

'Don't be stupid.'

'Do you have any pain?'

'I'm not due for weeks.'

'No contractions?'

'Oh. Ohh.'

'What? What is it, pain?'

'Ah God, Jesus, fucking hell!'

'Don't lie on the floor!'

'No, it's OK, it's OK. It's passed. It might be wind.'

'Viv, darlin', you're having the baby.'

'I can't – it's not tiiime. Ah shit! Fucking ow!'

'OK, pass over the controls. I'm in charge.'

'What? What are you doing?'

'Come on, we're going to hospital.'

38

Oh, Baby

The baby is ready to be born. Giving birth is one of the most difficult things a woman might go through and also it could be the most fulfilling and liberating experience of your life. Are you ready?

Forty Weeks and Counting Down

I am on all fours in the examination room, staring at a calendar showing Daniel Craig in tiny pants, as a lemon-faced midwife checks my cervix. That damned cervix, I knew it would get me in the end, and all because I kept skipping that chapter about 'effacing' in *Forty Weeks and Counting Down*. I am a fool. What is she doing rummaging about up there? It feels like she's taking out my bowels with a crochet hook.

'I'm not dUUE yet.'

'You're about thirty-seven weeks by your dates, and you're in labour all right, but only five centimetres dilated,' she says. She has a brutal vibe about her.

'I couldn't give a rat's arse. Get your hand out of

my fanny,' I say. Actually, I only think that. What I say is, 'Thank you very much!' and my voice has become so high-pitched I sound like a squirrel. Max and I are 'booked in' and then I'm left to die in a sterile birthing room. Terror streaks through me; I strip naked and run circuits. I'm a babbling nervous wreck flapping around the room like a wild animal. I get into the bath, but I can't stand to be still. I get out and run some more. This is definitely not what was on my birth plan. This is not an ideal situation.

Max watches me calmly. He has read *Forty Weeks and Counting Down* and he knows what to say.

'You're doing well. That's it,' he soothes, and I'd like to take out his eyes with a rusty screwdriver.

I drop onto all fours, desperately trying to remember the yoga, the NCT, anything useful. The pain comes in waves. At the brink of each wave, just as I am desperate to be decapitated, the pain suddenly stops. Like some terrible torturer, it prowls the room only to come at me moments later as a new wave begins.

Lemon-Face appears, smelling of coffee; she casually wipes cake crumbs from the corner of her mouth. 'Let's have a look at you,' she sings, and I dart away behind the bed. I eye her from under my sweaty hair as she snaps on surgical gloves. 'I just need to see how dilated you are,' she says, looking sympathetically at Max.

'Oh, I'm dilated all right, and I don't need you to

tell me that.' I point a crooked finger. 'What I need from you, lady, is drugs,' I snarl.

Max leads me away from the bed. 'Viv, be calm. The midwife needs to see if you're dilated,' he says.

'You'll be dilated in a minute if you keep . . .' I drop to all fours, felled by another contraction.

She wheels over a canister labelled 'Entonox,' which is hooked up to a rubber tube.

'Have some gas and air, Vivienne.' She smiles, shoving in a plastic mouthpiece. 'We'll just wait until this contraction passes and then I'll have a look,' she says.

'She's just going to wait for the next contraction to be over and then she's going to examine you, Viv,' explains Max.

I take out the mouthpiece and say, 'I'm not fucking deaf,' in my new squirrel way.

'I know you're not Keith,' says Max, shaking his head quizzically at Lemon-Face.

I can't repeat myself because a new wave hits – I bite down on the mouthpiece, not getting any relief. Then, as the agony passes, I collapse and lie on the floor.

'OK, I'm just examining you now,' says Lemon-Face, and the torture of her hand inside me makes me vomit. She stops. 'I think you're nearly fully dilated, but that's very unusual for a first-time mum. I'll just have another look,' she says.

I move into a squat position and grab her by the

forearm. 'If you try to do that again, I will take you down.' I nod quickly so she knows I mean it. 'Understand? I will kill you and destroy everything you hold dear.' Another wave of pain is starting up. I grab the mouthpiece and bite on it hard, trying to convey danger to her with my eyes. I know how to do it: I've seen the haka.

'OK, no worries. Oops – we didn't turn this on!' she says, twiddling with a knob on the gas and air canister. What a witch!

I break off the gas mid-contraction to scream, 'Bring me drugs, you evil crone!'

Max steps between us. 'I'm really sorry, but I think she's taken a dislike to you. Maybe you'd better leave,' he says apologetically. 'Is there someone else?'

'I'll just give you a little breather then. I'll pop back in a bit,' she says.

'No offence,' says Max.

'Oh, none taken.'

Ah, the gas and air! It helps, like quilted pants would help if you're being repeatedly kicked up the arse. It muffles that top note of searing pain. But then the pain ramps it up a notch for a good hour or so. I ride the waves until I'm finally beaten and want my nana.

'Oh no, this is a mistake. I'm not meant to be here. I can't do this!' I cry, and vomit into a cardboard tray. 'Jesus, please God kill me now!'

That contraction dissolves slowly. Look, women do this in war zones, in fields. They are doing it right now behind enemy lines. They've been doing this since the start of humanity. So why in the name of God did no one tell me not to? And here it comes again. I hear a sound like a tortured animal. It's me. The pain is changing now, moving.

'Vivienne, do you feel pressure in your bottom?'

Oh Christ, Lemon-Face is back, or maybe she never went away, that trickster. I shake my head at her vigorously.

'Vivienne, you're all right. I'm here to help. Try to calm down. Do you feel pressure in your bottom?'

I nod. I pant. Yes, good, panting helps. I feel pressure all right, in the sense of my tailbone being snapped off. I take out the mouthpiece; strings of saliva fall.

'Drugs,' I beg, then suck back on the gas and air before the next wave hits.

'It's too late for drugs, Vivienne. You're having this baby now. Do you feel the need to push? I'm just going to attach the monitor and have a listen to the baby's heartbeat.'

What is she talking about, too late for drugs? Is she even qualified? Then I'm pushing like mad and I can't help it.

'That's it – nice strong push,' says Lemon-Face.

Max kneels in front of me. 'Go on, Viv. I love you so much. You're doing really well,' he says, stroking my claw of a hand.

I drop my head and get to work trying very hard to get this baby out of me. The pain has changed to something I can deal with. It feels more bearable now that I can channel it into pushing. Lemon-Face is counting back from ten with each contraction. She listens to the heart monitor and frowns.

'Vivienne,' she says quietly, 'I think the baby could be in distress. Have you been told about episiotomy? I might have to make a little cut in your vagina to help the baby out.'

I lift my head to look at her concerned face. Her act doesn't fool me. I know I'm looking into the eyes of a psychopath.

'What's that you say?' I ask sweetly. I need to change my approach. Easy now – try to be polite: she's packing a scalpel. But there's no time for a discussion. The next wave of pain knocks into me like a wrecking ball.

Right, this is it; the witch isn't going to cut me! With the next contraction I bear down into the ground with everything I've got and the whole universe yawns open, revealing the wisdom of the ages for a blinding moment. I'm connected to the ancients. I'm primal, I am!

'Uhgaaaaaah!'

I feel a stinging, a nipping, a burning.

'That's it! Well done – the head's out. With the next contraction your baby will be born.' I glance at Max. He's gone white and his mouth hangs open. He looks like he's going to be sick.

Another wave is building. Come on, girl – you are powerful beyond belief and you can do this thiiiing!

'Woaaaah!'

I feel pinching heat, burning like pepper, and then it's out of me, a baby! A slippery, red, squirmy alien being passed back to me like a rugby ball.

'It's a girl,' says Max. 'Is it a girl?'

The baby looks like a skinned rabbit, with dark hair and a squashed face, an expression as if she's just been very rudely awoken; she gives a little squeaky cry.

'Ah, congratulations – you have a daughter,' says Lemon-Face as she places her on my chest. 'What a quick birth! Only three hours.'

'Is that quick?' I ask.

'For a first time, yes. So well done.' She smiles. 'We'll wait for the placenta to be born, shall we, or do you want the injection to speed it up?'

I decide against more pain. No injection.

I absolutely love Lemon-Face. Her name is Rita, and she is the greatest midwife that ever lived.

I look into the red, scrunched-up face of our daughter and her slate-grey pebble eyes lock onto mine with a strange knowing look, as if she's been sent here to sort my shit out.

'Hey, baby. We're your parents,' I say, and look up at Max and I'm terrified for us all.

39

Questions for Rita

Where can I buy the gas and air?
How soon can I be injected with strong contraceptive medicine?
Will I ever walk the same again?
Why is my baby cross-eyed?

Rita and I are discussing our worst fears as she finishes up the stitches. Being torn apart in childbirth used to be my number-one fear. Now I realise it's a mere trifle; I'm high on relief and gas and air.

'I've worried a lot about spontaneous combustion,' I ponder, 'where all that's left of you is a lower leg in a slipper.'

'Big ships – just the thought that it could sink without a trace,' she says, and snips off a thread. 'There. All done. We'll get you into bed – you must be exhausted. I'm finishing my shift now, so I'll tuck you up and say goodbye.'

'Oh, well, thank you so much, Rita. Sorry again about being rude to you.'

'I've heard worse,' she says putting a pillow behind my back.

'As if I'd try to kill you or harm your family! I love you so much. I'll never forget you, Rita.'

'Good luck with everything. She's gorgeous.'

I look at my baby girl sleeping in a plastic tank next to me and I know I'm mighty, a warrior who just earned her rite of passage into a new club, the Womanhood Club. I'm high as a kite.

That evening I've settled into a private room as there are no beds free on the ward. The walls and floor are painted pale pink, and the curtains are the colour of sticking plasters. I can hear footsteps, a creaky door opening, a woman screaming. Max brings me a cup of tea and a cheese sandwich. I eat gazing into the tank at this new person we made. I keep expecting her real parents to come and take her away.

'She's tiny. What was she, six pounds? Look at her funny hair.'

'She has the look of Clint Eastwood.'

'She's just a bit crumpled. Did you text everyone?'

'Lucy and your workmates, couldn't get through to your mother, but I got through to mine, and by the time she and me sisters had finished yapping, I ran out of battery. I'll put the details on the Facebook later.'

'Facebook.'

'That's what I said.'

'You said "the Facebook".'

'What'll we call her?' he asks.

I look at his face; he looks red-eyed and tired. He smiles crookedly.

'I really like Evelyn. It's Irish, and then she could be Eve like my nana.'

'Why not call the child the name you want her to be called?'

'Angel.'

'She is Angel, isn't she?'

'Would it be OK when she's fifty? Can you imagine her in a boardroom shaking hands going, "Hello, I'm Angel Kelly-Summers?"'

'Absolutely.'

'Baby Angel.' I stare into space feeling things like bliss and love and hope and peace.

The next morning I press the bell with a picture of a nurse on it. A midwife I've never seen before arrives; they change like the wind around here. The nightshift lady who helped me breastfeed was really lovely; we had quite a spiritual conversation about life and death and new generations.

'All right?' asks this new midwife whose badge says, 'Kate Redman.'

'Oh, is the other midwife gone, then? The Indian lady?'

'Indian lady?' She seems puzzled.

'Shahan, was it?'

'Oh, you mean the night janitor? Yes, she went at five.'

Night janitor? The woman milked me like a goat.

'Everything all right? How's baby?' she asks.

'She's been sleeping a lot.' I turn to look at Angel, who is lying on her back, oblivious, frog-legged, tiny starfish hands by her ears.

'Long may it last!' chuckles Kate Redman. 'So why did you buzz?'

'I think they forgot me when they were serving the breakfast.'

'No, love, there's tea, toast and cereal in the common room – it's just out to your left,' she says cheerily, heading for the door.

'But I really fancy bacon and egg,' I say.

'Don't we all!' she laughs as she leaves.

Oh fuck, I have to get up and walk so I can eat. The painkillers have worn off and I'm not an all-powerful goddess anymore. Never was, in fact. I'm a girl in a hospital gown who feels like she came last in an arse-kicking contest. My undercarriage is a war zone, and what's worse, I didn't have an overnight bag with me, so I have no pyjamas, make-up, eye make-up remover or toothpaste. I sent Max home to get it. He swore to me he'd be back first thing. I'll text him in a minute. I slide off the bed, wincing, and pull on my wizard-sleeve dress. A quick look in the mirror shows a wild woman. My hair is matted and my eyes are black with exhaustion and day-old make-up. I must eat.

I shuffle off to the common room trying to keep my perineum taut, which is a lot harder than you think.

I make a beeline for the toast. It's cold and floppy. I scrape about four plastic pots of butter onto a slice and two marmalades. I take a bite as I turn round. There are two wholesome, blonde ponytailed girls in pyjamas and velour leisure suits staring at me.

'Morning!' I say with my mouth full. 'Good birth?' They both immediately study their cuticles. 'Hold on, I'll just get a tea and join you.' I turn back to the tea urn and pour out a mug, and then I butter another slice of toast. When I look round, they've gone. Rude witches. What about the Womanhood Club? Huh, they just got themselves barred for a start. I look up at the clock. Seven-thirty. It's then that I remember about Rainey.

Back in the room, Angel is awake. She's just chilling, chilling and staring. I peep over the edge of the tank and she goes crazy. She starts to shake her head from side to side with her mouth open, hands clenched, turning red with rage and squeaking.

'Sorry, OK. I had to go for toast,' I tell her, scooping her up. I rummage in my handbag with one hand, rocking Angel with the other arm as she ramps up the decibels. Talk about demanding. I get on the bed trying to get her to feed, but she's so desperate she can't latch on properly and I have to shove my boob at her and she gets squirted in the eye. When I look up, Lucy is here.

She peers around the door with a manic expression, eyes wide and mouth open.

'Look at you two!'

'Am I glad to see you.'

'Oh my God, she's tiny!'

I look down at Angel, who is happily guzzling and making loud swallowing noises.

'She didn't feel tiny on her way out.'

'Was it awful? You all right?'

'I have to sit on this doughnut cushion for the rest of my life. The less said about it, the better.'

'Viv, we'll never speak of it again.' She hugs me. I'm engulfed with cold fresh air and Chanel No. 5.

'Look at her! She's opening her eyes to see her auntie Lucy. Viv, did you know she's cross-eyed?'

'She's trying to focus. I already asked the midwife about that.'

'Well, look, I just wanted to pop in on my way to work. I can't stay, but I got you these.' She holds up some gorgeous jersey cotton pyjamas. 'And these.' She holds up a bottle of tequila and a tub of chocolate mini rolls. 'And for my little goddaughter, I got her very first miniskirt!' She holds up a tiny tube of leopard print attached to pink ruffle-bum leggings.

'That is truly hideous!' I laugh.

She hugs me goodbye, and whispers hot and urgent in my ear, 'I'm pregnant!'

'Really?'

She makes the manic face again, nodding. 'Early days.' She puts her crossed fingers to her lips.

'Congratulations,' I say, as she breaks for the door.

'I'll visit later, soon. I'll call you. Love you. Bye!' And then she's gone.

I wait a while after the door swishes closed for the ripples of energy to subside along with her perfume. Oh, thank God she's pregnant! I'm not going to tell her about birth. I'm going to do one of those knowing smiles when she asks. I sit for a moment thinking about Lucy and everything she's been through and our friendship and what she thinks of my mother, and then I pick up the phone and call Rainey. No answer. She'll be on the way to the doctor's by now, wondering why I haven't arranged to meet her, or sitting in the waiting room worried sick. I call the doctor's surgery. I explain the situation and ask for them to leave a message for Rainey telling her that I'm in hospital, that she has a brand-new grand-daughter, and could she call me.

'Was the appointment with Dr Savage? I don't have anyone by the name of Summers booked in,' says the efficient female voice. I imagine a receptionist with a headset and mouthpiece.

'Maybe it was a different doctor. She has an appoint-ment at eight o'clock.'

'No, there's nothing. I don't have a Rainey or a Lorraine Summers booked in today with any doctor. Sorry about that.'

'How about tomorrow? I might have got the wrong day.'

'No, she's not showing up.'

'Could she have cancelled?'

'I'd be able to see that on the system.'

'But would you have her down if she'd tried to make an appointment?'

'Oh yes, she'd be on the system, but she's not showing up anywhere. Sorry.'

'Oh. Well. OK. Thanks, anyway.'

I end the call. So where is she? What are the possible scenarios here? She bottled out of going? She's left London? She doesn't even have a second lump? I dismiss that last thought: no one would lie about a thing like that. I search for reasons, with hope and despair wrangling in my heart.

I call Rainey again. No answer.

I write a text. I tell her about Angel, the details, where to find me in the hospital.

I tell her how I'm allowed to go home tomorrow, so I could see her, and how I can't believe I'm someone's mother. How I want her to meet Angel, and I'd like a photo of them together. I'm surprised when she answers almost straight away.

Vivienne, Dr Savage tells me the second lump in my breast is almost definitely cancer and this means my future doesn't look good. I have some thinking to do. I'll probably leave this week and see a specialist abroad, and I have a lot of things to organise. Congrats on the baby. R

I sit staring at her message, wondering what the hell to make of that.

40

Songs for Your Baby

Bob Dylan – Forever Young
White Stripes – We're Going to Be Friends
Adele – Make You Feel My Love
The Beatles – Here Comes the Sun
Louis Armstrong – We Have All the Time in the World
Guru Shabad Singh – Ajai Alai
Kris Kristofferson – From Here to Forever
Indigo Girls – Power of Two
Lauryn Hill – Can't Take My Eyes off You

'Hello, hello, hello,' booms a voice as the door opens. Damon walks in, his face momentarily obscured by a pink foil 'new baby' balloon. He bats it away, revealing the full shock of his grinning jack-o'-lantern head. Christie and Michael follow behind.

'Hey, everyone's here,' I say croakily. I was napping, dreaming in snatches, mostly of Rainey. She lied about seeing Dr Savage. I don't know if she has cancer. I only know she hasn't been to see my doctor. Why did she lie? She's leaving. And if she leaves, she's won again. Max was right: I am still scared of her going, but it's more than that – she's withholding the warmth and interest I'd hoped for, and here I am again, even now, worrying about her with this knot of anger and sadness lodged in my throat. And she isn't interested in even seeing her granddaughter. Of course she isn't. Why would she be? Why did I ever think she would be? She wasn't interested in her own daughter. It's all been an act, everything smoke and mirrors to get what she wants. I feel cheated, bereft and lost all over again, and cross with myself for caring.

I sit up and adjust the doughnut cushion. Damon and Mike stand by the wall, while Christie comes forward and kisses the air near my ear. She's sporting a Scooby Doo look, wearing a calf-length skirt, 1970s-style boots, a polo neck with a pendant, and her fake glasses.

'Aww, congratulations, Viv,' she says. Then, pulling back, 'Oh my God, Viv, you look terrible. You've aged, like, loads. How was it? No, don't tell me – I might faint.'

'Yeah, it smarts a bit.'

'Oh, there she is!' she says, pointing to Angel.

'That's her.' I smile over at the cot where she's sleeping. I wait for them to coo over her, but they keep looking at me. 'I named her Angel. What do you think?'

'Angel! Get here, Angel,' Michael feigns a cockney accent and sniggers.

'Hi, Michael,' I say, and he steps forward to kiss

me. I get a lungful of patchouli and notice a huge purple love bite just above his collarbone. 'Things going well with Marion?'

'Wild times,' he says. 'Off the scale.' He peers into the cot. 'She's so tiny. Aren't you tiny, girl? You're just a tiny, tiny little girl,' he croons in a high-pitched baby voice.

Christie and I exchange a look, and Damon peers over Michael's shoulder. *Do not open your eyes at this moment, Angel.*

'Tiny, tiny, tiny, tiny, and yet one day you'll be hanging around the bus stop with the rest of those teenage glue addicts, soaking your tampons in vodka, won't you? Yes, you will!'

'Well, that's reassuring,' I say.

'Uncle Mikey's got you a present! Yes, he has.'

'She's asleep, Michael,' I say.

'Oh, I'll give it to you, then,' he says, handing me a wrapped-up box. 'It's a space hopper. I love them, don't you? It's for when she's bigger.'

'Very thoughtful. I like those "grow into it" presents. I was thinking of getting her an Oyster card, myself,' I say.

'Well, if you don't want it . . .'

'No, I do! It's really kind of you, Michael. Thank you,' I laugh.

Damon steps up. 'I got something for her, Viv, but I couldn't bring it here. I just brought a photo.' He hands me a Polaroid of two goldfish. 'The white one is Dodi, and the orange one is Di,' he says, his eye rolling excitedly. 'They've got their own tank. The gravel and treasure chest are included.'

'Wow, Damon, I don't know what to say. That's . . . quite something.' I press my lips together and smile.

The three of them then stand along the wall grinning. God, it's good to see them, those crazy guys, my team!

'So . . .'

'So now you are a mother, Vivienne,' Damon declares solemnly, 'and you shall hold your daughter's hand a short while but hold her heart for ever.' I feel my eyes swimming unexpectedly. I look at Christie and Michael. They look teary too. 'Yes, as my old mum said to me, mothers are the bows from which we glancing arrows spring forth. They are the bridge of stars leading us towards our dreams. Your daughter is a miracle of your own making. She is your immortality. May she bring you joy without end. I hope you will cherish every smile, every kiss, every tear, for this once upon a time can never come again.'

'What lovely words, Damon,' I say, trying to stop my face crumpling into sobs. 'You love your old mum, don't you?'

'She passed away, Viv, ten years back, but that don't mean I don't love her. I talk to her every day.'

Now we're all sobbing, raising our faces to the ceiling tiles, fanning ourselves, wiping our teary eyes.

'What, are you some kind of lunatic poet Damon?' asks Michael, his voice breaking.

I can't stop crying. It's like a dam has burst. My body is wracked with sobs and snot drips. Is this what's known as post-traumatic sobbing?

'Aw, now you've really upset Viv,' wails Christie, hugging me, holding me in an awkward position that requires me to lean forward uncomfortably from the waist.

'Oh, apologies, Vivienne,' says Damon.

'No, it's just . . . !' I sing, my face contorting and my shoulders heaving. I can't speak.

'Well, this is awkward,' says Michael. 'You've really hit a nerve with your tear-jerker prose!'

'I'm all right. I'm all right,' I say, gathering myself up and wiping my wet cheeks. 'Beautiful words, Damon. Thank you.' I take a few shuddering breaths.

'Well, here – I got a present for Angel.' Christie hands over a beautiful duck-egg-blue paper bag with a bright yellow string handle. I reach inside and there wrapped in tissue paper is a lion's-mane hat. When Angel is wearing the hat, it will look like she has a lion's mane. That or a weird ginger 'fro.

'Now that is seriously cute,' I say. 'Thanks so much, Christie.' Why does something as terrible as this even exist?

'All the model mums have these hats for their babies. You can get a bear, a zebra or a penguin,' she giggles.

Model mums? Perhaps it's not too bad. Angel will need a hat. She can wear that hat everywhere she goes – as soon as she can support her own head.

The Dream Team stay a little while. Damon manages to rustle up tea and biscuits, and we talk about work. I tell them I hope to be back to work in a few weeks with Angel in tow.

Then I gradually start to feel jittery in case Angel wakes up and demands to be fed – I don't want to breastfeed in front of my colleagues. How do women do it so discreetly? I have to get my whole boob out and Angel looks as if she's trying to swallow a Zeppelin. Luckily Max makes an appearance then, all wild hair and overflowing carrier bags. It looks like he's brought all the clothes we own. I notice a pair of stripy tights hanging out of a bag that I haven't worn for ten years and was keeping in case of a fancy-dress witch moment. I introduce him and I can tell he's both amazed and shocked by my co-workers. He keeps glancing around nervously and saying, 'Great!' a lot.

Finally they leave and I get to have a long hot shower and a change of clothes. I get back into bed in the lovely pyjamas Lucy brought. Max has dressed Angel in a back-to-front polka-dot sleepsuit and an 'I love Daddy' pointy knotted hat, and is dancing with her snuggled into his shoulder.

'She is handsome. She is pretty. She is the belle of Belfast City,' he croons. 'I'm madly in love,' he says, looking up with a big simple-boy smile, 'and I think she just shat in my hand and puked down me back at the same time.'

'Oh, she has.' I tuck into a Jaffa Cake while he changes her nappy.

'Oh dear, oh no, what have you done?' Max asks in a baby voice as he unfastens Angel's nappy. 'Holy Mother of God, it's everywhere. Viv, she's shat up her neck!' He reaches for the wipes. 'These are going to be useless. We'll need a fire hose for you, my girl,' he tells Angel. 'So small and yet so shitty,' he marvels.

'Don't say that to her!'

'Ah, she knows I'm joking,' he laughs.

He cleans Angel up and hands her back to me to feed her. She falls asleep almost immediately and we settle her back into her little cot. Then I tell Max about Rainey and her lump and the non-existent doctor's appointment. I show him Rainey's text message about cancer.

'They don't diagnose cancer that quickly, do they?' I ask. 'Before, she had all kinds of tests.'

'Before?'

'Before, yes, when I said she was poorly at Christmas, she had a lump in her breast.'

'Yeah, right.'

'She did. I felt it, anyway. Then she had all these tests, and now she's found another.'

'They don't diagnose cancer if you don't even go to the doctor's. She hasn't got another lump, Viv,' he says, disgusted.

'She might have a second lump but be too scared to go to the doctor . . .'

'Then why would she lie and say she has cancer?'

'I don't know.' I shake my head. 'Anyway, she's gone.'

'Remember Fat Rob at university? He did this – said he had cancer just to get attention. That's what she wants, Viv – she feels the control over you slipping so she just made this up.'

'But why would she leave?'

'She hasn't left. She's waiting to see if you come running.' Max is pacing now, palming his beard. 'Unbelievable.'

'You think she made it all up?'

'Come on, Viv, of course she did!' He spins round, and seeing my stricken face, he calms down and sits beside me on the bed. 'She wants to control you. Some people are just like that.'

'Not anymore,' I say, and my eyelids feel heavy. 'I'm tired, Max. I've never felt so tired,' I say, and close my eyes.

41

@Vivsummers Time to Let You Go #Mamagoodbye

That afternoon Max goes to register the birth.

I lie exhausted. I try to sleep again, but my mind is racing, flying, rummaging through the events of the last twenty-four hours. Everything strikes me more intensely than before. I'm vulnerable, wobbly, freshly peeled. What are we doing with a baby? Neither of us is qualified. We never took any tests, and we don't know how to put her nappy on. Not only that, I'm suddenly acutely aware of my own mortality. I mean, how many years of my natural life can I expect? How many years will we know each other? What will happen to Angel if I spontaneously combust and am just a lower leg in a slipper?

Then strange and terrible fears loom like hosts of demons. What if I threw her downstairs by accident thinking she was a pile of washing? What about scalding water, drain water, open water, frozen water? Traffic, tramps, trapped fingers? Germs, gerbils, mad dogs, wild hogs? Burst balloons, beads? Matches, ditches, witches, switches? I sit up, certain of my own incompetence. It's a cruel, cruel world to be born into, especially if you're depending on me – I really know what that's like and it's pretty hairy.

And then there's Rainey. Once again I have to accept she doesn't care about me. I've spent more time getting to know her in the past few months than ever before, with the result being I don't know her at all. After everything that's happened, she still doesn't care; she lies and manipulates and pretends, and she always will. I understand now that's just who she is; that's all there is. What's more, I'll probably never see her again. I'll just have to grow up and move on now that I'm somebody's mummy.

There's a tentative tap at the door. I look to the little square of glass and my heart thuds as I see the dark hair with the red streak.

She immediately dominates the room, the rose and musk scent and the colourful waves of scarves, the jangle of her jewellery. I'm still transfixed. She stands a little away from the bed, watching me with eyes of dark juice; she looks into my soul and something in her expression retreats from all of my hope and love.

'Hello, Vivienne,' she says softly.

I feel a single tear fall onto my face. 'Hello,' I say, suddenly tired of all this emotion.

She walks two steps across to the cot, looks at Angel and smiles.

'Huh, she looks just like you did.'

'You leaving, then?'

She looks sideways, her head cocked sympathetically, and she nods just once. I sniff and look away.

'I have to find the best medical care I can. Probably in the US.'

'Dr Savage diagnosed terminal cancer, did he?'

'He alluded to it,' she says, still gazing into the cot.

'No scans or anything?'

'None needed. He could tell, I think, after last time.' She smiles sadly. 'I mean, I don't want to go. I could get treatment here, but now that you're back with . . . with Max, I'd just be in the way, wouldn't I?'

I study her closely. Fascinating how she can lie like this.

'If you need me, though, I could stick around to look after you – you know, in case Max leaves when the going gets tough?'

'I'm moving in with him. We can't afford the flat.'

'That's not what I asked.' She frowns.

'What did you ask?'

'Do you want me to stay?'

'I wouldn't want to stop the US trip for cancer treatment.'

'I'd get treatment here. Dr Savage said they'd start straight away.'

I really want to confront her, tell her I know Dr Savage didn't diagnose anything because she never saw him, ask her if she thinks I'm totally stupid, but then Max appears, quietly walking into the room with a worried face, expecting a fight. He stands next to the bed and takes my hand, so it's us against Rainey. She looks at me intently, waiting for me to ask her to stay. I should confront her now. Do it now. But really, what's the point? I'm tired, I don't want a fight, and she'll only spin more lies until I'm choked and confused with them like a fly in a web.

'Why did you come?'

'To see you, to see my granddaughter.'

'No, I mean why did you come to London? Why did you find me?'

She opens her mouth to speak but I interrupt, 'Tell me the truth.'

'Ah the truth . . . I had nothing better to do and I was curious. I don't suppose I thought you'd take everything so seriously,' she shrugs.

'When I was seven,' I begin, hearing my own voice bright with hurt and anger, 'I thought I'd die if I couldn't see your face anymore. I remember how you left. You didn't even say goodbye.' I watch her. She drops her head, licks her lips. 'And I suffered. I really felt so worthless. The whole time I was growing up, I felt I was searching for something that I was unworthy of, and I thought there was nothing I could do about that. But there is something.'

She looks up into my face with those flecked eyes and I look deep into them.

'I can let you go and I can make sure that my daughter never feels that way.'

She shakes her head.

'So Rainey, no, I don't want you to stay. I'm letting you go and I forgive you.'

'I wasn't . . . I'm not cut out for it.'

'I know. I see that.'

'You are a nice person, Vivienne, in spite of me.'

'I know.'

And you are a manipulative liar with your pants on fire.

We look at each other for a moment.

'Goodbye, Mum,' I say for the very first time, and as I smile, my eyes fill with tears for that seven-year-old me, the one who wanted a mummy. Time to let her go too.

'Bye,' she says, and makes for the door, where she hesitates. 'See you around, hey?'

'Yeah.'

The door closes. I turn my head away. I listen to the buzz of the air conditioner, the tiny in-out breaths of my little baby. I squeeze Max's hand.

'Not if I see you first,' I mutter.

'OK?'

I nod. He flashes a smile full of love and affection. 'Let's go home.'

42

Happy Endings

A poem for Angel by Vivienne Summers

Pretty little Angel
Welcome to the world
We love you already tiny girl
We promise to protect you, we'll make it fun
May you have lots of trips around the sun

'That doesn't even scan.'

'I don't care Max, I was moved to write something.'

'Will you be wanting to get her foot prints done in clay? Shall we listen to "Isn't She Lovely?"'

'Open the door and put it on!'

'O-kay. We're home!' Max calls as he opens our door, throwing in the bags. Dave tiptoes to greet us, curling around our legs. Max squats down with baby Angel in her papoose tied to his great frame.

'Dave, this is Angel. Angel, this is Dave,' Max introduces them. Angel blinks once at the cat and screams her head off. Max gets to his feet and walks bouncily around the living room, murmuring, 'Don't you like the puddy cat? Aw, he's OK. He's a funny puddy cat. He wants to be your friend.'

Dave wears his usual 'fuck you' expression and wanders off to stare at his bowl.

'She's hungry, I think,' I shout above the wailing. 'But I'm just going to get changed, then I'll take her.'

I go to our bedroom. It's our bedroom again: Rainey is gone. I feel calm, awake and aware, like I've come round from anaesthetic, snapped out of hypnosis, shaken off a spell. I'm home with Max, and, I have to keep reminding myself, we have a baby! Each time I think of it, I feel a fresh jolt of excitement and terror. I slump on the bed and let out a huge sigh. We are starting a whole new chapter, Max and I, and it's going to be a happy one. I notice a vase of pink roses on the bedside table.

I get out of my maternity jeans and accidentally look left to the mirror, seeing the wreckage of my belly, the skin hanging like a deflated football. I turn away – I'll deal with that later: a few sit-ups, power-walking with the Bugaboo. Hold on, where is the Bugaboo?

I pull on the expensive pyjamas that Lucy bought. Seriously nice. The top has these cool flaps and press studs so you can breastfeed discreetly, although it looks very wrong with the flaps down and no baby. I go to the bathroom. Angel has moved up an octave with the screaming. Beside the sink is a jug of stunning white freesias. The Bugaboo isn't in the hallway either.

I go through to the living room, where Max is bobbing about and struggling to dock his iPod into the speakers. On the coffee table there are three jam jars packed with roses and anemones.

'I'll just get some water and I'll take her,' I say, nipping into the kitchen, where there's a cut-off water bottle full of daffodils. I run the tap and find a glass. Next door I hear the intro of 'Three Little Birds' playing – that tune again. When I go back into the living room, Angel is quiet. She's blinking and listening.

'She likes this one,' whispers Max, rocking backwards and forwards.

I put the glass down and go to them. I kiss him and then I kiss her. She turns her face to me with her tiny wet mouth on my nose. Then we dance, the three of us, all around the living room with Angel sandwiched in the middle.

'You put flowers in every room, didn't you?' I say.

'I bet your Harold Pinter didn't buy out all the flowers from Tesco Metro, did he?'

'No.'

'That's not all,' he says, and he produces a home-made card, a photo of his grinning face next to Angel, who's staring blankly from beneath her 'I love Daddy' hat. I open it and there in Max's scrawled capital letters in blue biro, it says:

WE ARE YOUR HAPPY ENDING.

And standing in that room at that moment, listening to that song with my loves, I'm so happy I almost feel guilty.

'You are my happy ending,' I say as the song ends. There's one second of silence while Angel turns from snuffley to loudly furious. I take her from Max, feeling the buttons of her tiny spine, which we made, holding her miniature feet, feeling her heart beating like a little bird's. Then I look up at Max, picturing him the first time we met in our university halls of residence. 'Nice legs. Shame about the face,' were his first words to me. He was scruffy and skinny and funny, and now I've just had his baby, this old friend, this smiling guy I've known half my life, my best love, Max Kelly, and his daughter, Angel. My little family.

'No, no. He said a happy ending! Happy!' I shout above the rhythmic screaming, trying to undo press studs in these complicated bloody pyjamas, feed Angel, and balance on my doughnut cushion at the same time.

I look at her slate-grey eyes, the sweep of lashes, her round soft cheek, and I wonder what she'd look like dressed as a bee. Hell, it's very clear that I have no idea how to be a mummy. None of it makes any sense at all. I'll just start by loving her and cuddling her a lot, and then I'll get by with the kind of seat-of-your-pants reasoning I'm known for. I'll research online. Maybe start a blog called 'The Clueless Mother'. What I know about parenting could be written on a postage stamp. It's all to do with patience and kindness and playfulness, I think. I can do that. I look at Max as he tries to untangle himself from the baby carrier.

'Jesus, what kind of crazy bastard designed this?' he shouts, stepping out of the arm loops.

'You just have to unclip it, you fool.'

He holds it in the air like Houdini. 'I've a fuck of a lot to learn,' he says. 'I'll get the champagne.'

I look at Angel. She's struggling to keep her eyes open. I hear the pop of the champagne cork from the kitchen and a cheer from Max. 'Are you and Daddy my happy ending, baby?' I say to her in the sudden quiet of the room. I stroke the wisp of dark hair at the back of her neck. She's asleep. I kiss her ear. 'My happy beginning more like.'

Epilogue

12 March 10:47

From: raineysummers360@hotmail.com
To: viviennesummers@dreamteam.co.uk
Subject: Good news!

Dear Vivienne,

I just wanted to let you know that the second lump turned out to be benign, so huge relief. I'm now looking at life anew, after staring death down. Why me? Why was I saved? I'm travelling again, Vivienne, and I know I'll find truth.

Also, in case you're wondering, I had to return that very expensive buggy I bought for you; I needed the money in case of the US treatment and now to fund my trip. I know you'll understand. You are a good person, no matter what anyone says.

Best for now,

R

Vivienne Summers Baby Angel Evelyn Kelly was born at 11 p.m. on Tuesday 5 March weighing 6 pounds.

Baby doing well, Mummy still walking funny, Daddy delirious.

Sunday at 6.20 p.m.

Lucy Bond Well done, Max and Viv – she's gorgeous! I'm going to be the best godmother ever.

Sunday at 6.25 p.m.

Damon Spyrou May she bring joy to your life in ways previously unimagined, Vivienne.

Yesterday at 12.45 p.m.

Mike Clarke Vivienne, pet lamb, I'm not being funny, but in that second shot your baby looks like she has foreseen the Apocalypse and that massive cat next to her is plotting the downfall of humanity. Angel, tiny girl, I'll teach you to space hopper out of there.

Yesterday at 12.50 p.m.

Christie Thompson Awww, I know I said I'm never ever doing the baby thing because it wrecks your body and your life, but she is so cute! #secondthoughts

Yesterday at 12.55 p.m.

Vivienne Summers Christie, I know, and she's powerless, so I can dress her up as anything I like. I already ordered a butterfly costume, it has a matching antennae head-band. Michael, she was filling her nappy, and the cat is her bodyguard. Lucy, you are already the best fairy godmother. I'm so tired and overexcited about being a mummy. #bestthingintheworld

Yesterday 1.07 p.m.

Eve Summers I'll ring you tonight to hear all about it, but huge congratulations, darling! She looks so tiny and perfect and beautiful. I'm so glad she arrived safely. Clever girl, Viv, and welcome to the world, baby Angel. We just can't wait for a cuddle. Reg and I are returning to England next month. Of course, when I heard from Max that you were in labour, I wanted to cut the trip short and get straight back to you, but you wouldn't believe who just turned up in India and is staying with us here at the house since she has nowhere else to go! Rainey has broken the heart of a powerful Colombian drug baron and now he's hunting her down? Did she tell you this? She needs to lie low for a while. #likelystory! #bloodyinconvenient

Yesterday 3.10 p.m.

Acknowledgements

Thank you to my agent Madeleine Milburn, and to everyone at Hodder, especially my editor Francesca Best. Thanks to Harriet Bourton for your invaluable encouragement.

I would like to thank the midwives of Kingston Hospital; Laura, Katie and the student who was attending her first water birth who had never heard swearing like it. I hope your hand is okay now. Thanks to everyone who worked at the wonderful Jubilee Birth Centre, Cottingham.

Sorry to my little beauties for not being around much all the months I was writing this, but think of all the lemonade, cake and chocolate éclairs on tap at Nana and Grandpa's. I'd never let you have that stuff because I'm the one who has to explain to the dentist. Thanks Mum and Dad, for everything.

Thank you Steve, for making me write and for putting the lids back on things in every respect.

Find out where Viv and Max's story began, in the first refreshingly honest, achingly funny read by

Emma Garcia
NEVER GOOGLE HEARTBREAK

When her fiancé Rob breaks off their engagement for the third time, Viv does what any girl would do – she Googles heartbreak.

Confronted by tales of misery, she decides to set up her own self-help website for the broken-hearted. But as Viv passes through the three essential stages of grief (denial, vodka, disastrous haircut), she becomes determined that it's not too late to try and get Rob back.

When things get out of hand after a drunken declaration of love at an extremely inappropriate moment, Viv's scruffy, tequila-swilling best friend Max is there to pick up the pieces. Viv starts to realise that maybe the real thing has been under her nose all this time, and now – one ex and a massive error of judgement later – she has to face the question:

What's the craziest thing you'll do for love?

Out now in paperback and ebook – read on for a taster

HODDER

I

Case Studies

'That morning I remember he was very keen to have sex.
Afterwards I went to work as normal. At about half nine he
sent a text: "I'm moving out." That's all it said. When I got
home, he'd gone. It was the secrecy that really got me, how
he'd arranged everything behind my back.

He took all the cutlery. After two years of living together, he
left me without so much as a spoon to stir my tea.'

Debbie, 28, Glamorgan

It's Monday evening at Posh Lucy's, Battersea. We've
been scouring the internet for more break-up stories
for the website.

'There was a girl I used to work with,' I say.

'Hmm?' replies Lucy, without looking up.

'And she caught her fiancé in bed with their
eighteen-year-old neighbour.'

'Nasty.'

'She used to go round to his place after that and
hang about outside. Like, every night.'

'Why?'

'So she could see him.'

'Isn't that stalking?'

'And she left little anonymous notes . . . loads of them, Sellotaped to his door.'

'Poor, sad woman.'

'That must take dedication. Imagine that – every night.' I consider going to Rob's and doing something similar, but he lives on a very busy street and I know all the neighbours because I lived there myself for five years.

I pick up the phone just to check a text hasn't come in.

'Ring him,' says Lucy.

'I can't ring him. As I've already explained to you, I'm waiting for him to ring me.'

'So you were about to marry him and now you can't even talk to him?'

'I can't ring him after I moved out, can I? What would I say? "Hi there. Have you missed me yet? Shall I come back? Want to get married?"'

'What if he doesn't ring you?'

'He will. It's about time now. He's had the first week for it to sink in, the second week to enjoy his freedom, go to the gym, watch the rugby and all that, and another week to realise he's lost without me. He'll be calling anytime now. It's textbook stuff.' I glare at her. Making her accept this theory is extremely important.

'OK.' Lucy shrugs and drains her glass. I finished

mine ten minutes ago. I suddenly wish I had a cigarette; it's been quite an intense evening with all these dumped stories. It makes me so glad I haven't been dumped.

Lucy collects up the glasses. 'Want another?' She walks with perfect posture to the kitchen. I consider the gleaming surfaces and unblemished white carpet of Lucy's flat. I read somewhere that the state of a woman's house is linked to her state of mind. If that's true, then Lucy must be mentally extremely healthy. Lucy's always been sorted, though. At university she interior-designed her dorm room. She had a colour scheme, a new colour television, taffeta curtains and scented candles. In my room next door I had a new washbag and thought myself swish. I nearly died when she knocked and introduced herself, with her perfect accent and her 'Fancy a G and T?' I was amazed at how nothing ever fazed her. I called her 'Posh Lucy' and she started introducing herself like that at the Freshers' Ball, as though it were some sort of title: 'Hi, I'm Posh Lucy and this is my little friend Vivienne.'

Anyway, she's done well for herself and she deserves it. She works very hard, so she says. I think of my own place. I haven't actually finished unpacking yet, but I know, even when I have, it's going to be depressing. You know why? Because it's a *single girl's* flat. Nothing against single girls, mind; it's just that I'm not one of them. I might have moved out, but I'm still a fiancée. I'm 'in a relationship'. I rub the skin of my wedding ring finger. It feels naked without the engagement ring.

God, I feel miserable.

A whole month without Rob. I mean, I know we're on a break, but I didn't realise it would be like this. This is a complete cut-off . . . like death.

I put my feet up on the coffee table next to a neatly stacked pile of glossy magazines. My eye falls on the cover girl with her hair blowing back and her caramel lips. 'Women who have it all,' it says across her chest. I flick through to the article. The woman with it all has high heels and an expensive-looking hairdo; there she is in her office, holding up a pen with authority. Next she's lounging in satin pyjamas with a tray of croissants, and she probably hasn't eaten a croissant since the early 1980s. There she is crouching on her private beach cuddling three gorgeous kids (although, hold on, is one of them cross-eyed?).

She really actually has it all. Beautiful home, CEO of a blue-chip company, happily married, and she still finds time to bake. She's not the kind who sits around waiting for ex-fiancés to call. I start to fill in the little quiz at the bottom.

Are You a 'Have It All' Girl?

Age: Thirty-two – and, as we know, age, like dress size, is just a number.

Relationship: On a break.

How would you describe your relationship on a scale of one to five, five being totally perfect? N/A.

How would you describe your career on a scale of one to five, five being completely fulfilling? Also N/A – what I do for a living isn't really my 'career'.

How would you rate your friendships with the key people in your life? Hmm, key people . . . Lucy and Max, I suppose. My oldest friends. I tick 'good', then change it to 'excellent' in case Lucy sees it.

What you have to do is add up your scores and find the description to fit yourself. The upshot of mine is that I should work out my priorities and set 'life goals'. Of course! Life goals are what I need.

Well, obviously I don't define myself according to whether I'm in a relationship or not, but I have to be honest here and say it's Rob: getting married to Rob, having Rob's children . . . but I suppose I should have 'Get a career' as a life goal too. I'm not a total loser and I've always thought it would be good to become a buyer for Barnes and Worth, the department store chain where I work, before going off on maternity leave.

I'm a product manager in ladies' gifting, and as

such I spend my daylight hours putting together 'gift options' so people can buy conveniently for their maiden aunts and mothers-in-law.

Summer rain bubble bath with body lotion set (you get a free toiletries bag covered with raindrops), pop-up brollies, nailcare sets, massage mitts, soft leather gloves, quilted make-up bags, animal-shaped key rings with built-in torches, seasonal headgear, grow-your-own herb kits, mini luxury jam-taster collections. You know the sort of thing.

I glance at the silent phone. It's Rob's birthday this month. Should I call and wish him happy birthday? When do you stop remembering your boyfriend's birthday? I must research this; it's exactly the kind of thing the website should tell you.

Last year I organised a surprise trip to Rome for his birthday. It was very romantic, except he said not to do a surprise trip again because he felt 'hood-winked'. But I mustn't reminisce about the good times – gritty reality is what I need. Get things into perspective. I pick up one of Lucy's broadsheets.

'Leading doctor says women putting off motherhood are risking infertility.'

I examine the picture of a woman in a suit sadly holding some knitted booties up to her face, with the caption 'Fertility falls off a cliff in mid-thirties.' Oh, now I feel very bad. I stare at the booties woman who's left it too late. She looks like me. Why do they print stuff like this? Why, when women aged thirty-something might be reading? What are we meant to do – run out into the street, find any man who can stand up unaided, and get up the duff before the pretty fertility balloon floats away, pulling up its ladder for ever? I throw the newspaper on the floor.

Anyway, I'm not mid-thirties yet. I have years before the cliff thing happens, and by then I'll be back with Rob.

Lucy returns with champagne – real champagne, mind, not sparkling wine. She can afford it: she has some big swanky job in a big swanky office in Berkeley Square. It's funny, really – I know the details of her sex life but not so much about how she earns a living. She once sat me down to explain. It was, 'Stocks, shares, market, bull, bear, risk-assessment trading, blah.' She's quite important, I think. I slurp up the winking bubbles.

'I was thinking,' I say, 'we could have a kind of dating page on the site where people are reviewed by their exes – you know, like on Amazon where books get reviewed? You can see what other people think before you buy. It might be fun.'

'Except all your exes think you're devil spawn.'

'Not all . . . do they?'

'You turned Ginger Rog gay, remember?'

'You can't turn someone gay, Lucy. It's not like a cult.'

'That guy from the RAC, then. The one you slept with after he fixed your Mini. He said you ruined his life.'

I stare at her. 'You know, you should be an agony aunt with that knack for straight talking.'

'Hmm, yeah . . . "Ask Lucy". I like it,' she says dreamily.

I pick up the phone and turn it off and on again in case there's a fault.

'Why don't you just call Rob? I don't know what you're scared of.'

'I'm not scared of anything.'

'Just do it, then. Put yourself, and me, out of your misery.'

'OK, I will.' What I really do not want to do is call Rob. I haven't spoken to him since I moved out. I'm sure the rules of 'on a break' state that I'm the one who left and so he should be the one to ring. I mean, you can't leave someone and then be ringing them up morning, noon and night. Lucy is glaring. Maybe I could just pretend to call him . . .

'And don't do that pretend phone conversation thing where you just say, "Uh-huh," a lot,' she says.

I scroll down to his number and press 'call'. I show her the terrifying display – 'Dialling Rob' – and put the phone to my ear, staring her straight in the eye. Scared indeed – ha! It rings. My heart's jumping like a gerbil in a box.

'Rob Waters speaking.'

I hang up and throw the phone like it's hot.

'Nice one,' says Lucy.

The phone rings. We both look over to where it landed. I scrabble to get it.

'It's him,' I say.

'No shit,' she says, making her eyes unattractively wide.

I jab the button.

'Vivienne Summers speaking.'

'Hi, it's Rob . . . Did you just call?' The sound of his lovely voice makes me ache.

'No, I don't think so,' I say airily.

'Your number came up.'

'All right, all right . . . I did call, but it was a mistake.'

'Oh. So. How are you, Viv? Are you OK?'

'Fine. Very, um, healthy and busy, you know . . . How are you?'

'Great.' There's a pause and I hear plates being cleared.

'Are you eating?' I say.

'Are you going on Saturday?' he says at the same time.

'Saturday? Saturday, er . . .' Yes, good! Pretend not to know it's Jane and Hugo's wedding. Pretend not to care that this Saturday was one of the dates we'd considered for our big day.

'Hugo's wedding?' he says.

'Oh yeah. I'll be there.'

'Me too. Should be a good do.' He's pretending not to care either, but I can tell by his voice he's looking forward to seeing me. We'll be in the same room. I'll make sure I look completely gorgeous. I think seeing me is what he's needed; he'll beg me to take him back.

A month apart will have been nothing. We'll sit by a crackling fire and laugh about it one day.

'Actually, I was going to call you about Saturday,' he says.

'Really?' He's going to ask me to go with him. I'll say no, of course; I don't want to seem keen.

'Yeah, I just wanted to let you know I'll be with someone . . . erm, a guest.'

I feel something snag in my throat. 'A guest? Oh. Who?' I say in a strangely high voice.

'A friend of mine.'

'A girl . . . friend?'

'Yeah.' The apology in his voice stabs me through the heart.

It takes a second for me to breathe again.

'What kind of girlfriend?'

'What do you mean, what kind?'

'Is she a friend who's a girl, or is she your girlfriend, like, you know . . . a girl who's sleeping with you?' Lucy is making cutting movements at her throat with her hand. I turn away.

'Uh . . . what does it matter?'

'Well, I don't know, does *she* matter? Where did you meet her? *When* did you meet her? Jesus, Rob, I've only been gone a month!'

'Look, Viv, don't get upset—'

'Upset? Who's upset? Not me!'

'I can't really talk now. I just wanted to let you know I'll be there with someone.'

'Me too. I'm bringing someone – not a girlfriend, obviously. No, no. So . . . I'm glad you mentioned it. I was just about to say, you know, to be prepared. Don't know how you'll feel, seeing me with someone else . . .'

'Good. Well, that's great, then – see you Saturday.'

'See you then!' I must hang up before he does. I jab 'end call'.

'Bye, Viv,' I hear him say as I collapse.